AFTER DEATH

AFTER DEATH

DEAN KOONTZ

THOMAS & MERCER

Text copyright © 2023 by The Koontz Living Trust

Published by Thomas & Mercer, Seattle

www.apub.com

Amazon, the Amazon logo, and Thomas & Mercer are trademarks of Amazon.com, Inc., or its affiliates.

ISBN-13: 9781662500466 (hardcover)
ISBN-13: 9781662513060 (paperback)
ISBN-13: 9781662500473 (digital)

Cover design by Damon Freeman

Interior illustrations by Edward Bettison

Cover image: ©pixelparticle / Shutterstock; ©LightField Studios / Shutterstock; ©Andrei Cosma / ArcAngel

Printed in the United States of America

First edition

To David and Robin Gaulke,
with admiration and affection.

Stand fast therefore in liberty . . . and be not

entangled again with the yoke of bondage.

—*Paul of Tarsus*

ONE: MICHAEL IN MOTION

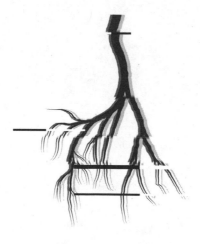

A LITTLE NIGHT WORK

The stars are extinguished, and the drowned moon floats just under the surface of a translucent lake of clouds.

Rats breed in the crowns of the phoenix palms, flea-tormented trespassers that mostly keep to their high nests and are seldom seen in this illustrious community where the masters of art and industry live sequestered on guarded estates, in denial of vermin.

At 3:10 in the morning, as Michael Mace moves briskly through an elegant residential neighborhood, a plump long-tailed rat freezes in its descent of a palm bole, oil-drop eyes filmed with a yellowish reflection of the streetlamp light. He is no threat to the creature, but it decides otherwise and retreats at speed into the cascade of fronds from which it had ventured.

Less than ten miles to the south, streets that were once as stately as this one are now dangerous to rat and man alike. The filthy sidewalks and parks are impassable in places, obstructed by ramshackle encampments of the addicts and mentally ill who give an undeserved bad name to the smaller number of sober, sane, genuinely homeless people whose needs authorities ignore. Those farther precincts crawl with feral cats that know where to find rodents, cockroaches, and other delectables in abundance.

By contrast, this monied community has no tolerance for such dreary bacchanals. The city council recently added officers to the police department in response to a sharp increase in crime, which spills across borders from adjacent jurisdictions where those in the ruling class see themselves as admirably tolerant and enlightened.

A Dodge Charger, the choice of police in this city, turns the corner half a block away. Shadows expand and arc and then contract as headlights sweep the avenue, which once carried frequent traffic at any hour. Now the lanes are deserted. The sidewalks accommodate but one pedestrian.

Illuminated, Michael neither seeks the cover of shadows nor breaks his stride. He has an urgent task ahead of him, one that might remain urgent for as long as he walks the Earth.

Past midnight, a man alone on foot is inevitably a subject of interest to law enforcement in a city as encrusted with wealth as this one. Yet the lightbar on the roof of the patrol car remains dark. The vehicle gains speed as it approaches him.

Perhaps the man behind the wheel is distracted and sleepy as he nears the end of his shift. Or maybe he has received a call to go to the immediate assistance of a fellow officer. In the light of the car's computer terminal and digital citation printer, as he flashes past, the driver seems like an apparition, less fact than form, his face a pale oval, spectral and without features.

Two blocks later, Michael arrives in a commercial district. The engine noise of unseen trucks and other vehicles arises, perversely reflected through the ranks of tall buildings, so that it seems to issue from mysterious machinery deep underground.

Here lampposts stand unlit. The city obtains its electricity from a regional power company that, in this time of shortages, has restricted usage by both the implementation of penalties and high prices. In the interest of suppressing burglaries and home-invasion robberies, outdoor lighting is largely reserved for residential neighborhoods. In these storied streets of restaurants and high-end shops offering luxury goods, businesses that once glittered from dusk to dawn are now dark after closing time.

A plague of smash-and-grab robberies has been largely cured by installing display windows and doors of bulletproof glass backed up by hidden stainless-steel shutters that slam down with pneumatic force if the glass begins to give way under attack. The shutters thwart even vehicles used as battering rams. While still on the sidewalk, potential customers are scanned for weapons—guns, knives, hammers, whatever—even as they approach the doors, which can instantly lock if a threat is detected. Regular, valued shoppers and clients are unaware that they are identified by facial-recognition programs and thus are admitted, spared from the indignity of having to explain themselves if they are carrying firearms for self-defense. Because of these precautions, the shops with the priciest merchandise can maintain an illusion of timeless glamour and riskless privilege.

A surprisingly clean brick-paved alleyway offers doors to rear entrances and merchandise-receiving rooms that are as secure as the doors to munitions bunkers and presented with simple elegance rarely found in the backstreets of commercial districts. Even the dumpsters are in good repair, freshly painted, and discreet.

In gloom that the veiled moon little relieves, preferring light but well adapted to darkness, Michael proceeds to a five-story brick building on the right. A man-size door and a double-wide garage roll-up are matte black and bear no street number or business name.

There is an electronic lock he must release and a security-system circuit he must sustain while he steps into a dimly lighted vestibule and quietly closes the door. He is so new to this life and his abilities that he still amazes himself.

The law firm of Woodbine, Kravitz, Benedetto, and Spackman owns this building, occupies all five aboveground floors, and employs sixty-one people. To Michael's left is a door that leads to two floors of subterranean parking.

He pushes through a swinging door directly in front of him and follows a ground-floor hallway that leads past rooms of records and the offices of certain members of the legal-support staff. At the end of the hallway, he passes through another swinging door.

The wealth and power of the firm are implied by the cavernous amount of unproductive space dedicated to the lobby, which at this late hour is revealed only by soft, indirect lighting. Black granite floors. Honey-toned quarter-cut anigre paneling. A domed, scalloped ceiling leafed in white gold. Millions of dollars' worth of large, dramatic—and, in Michael's opinion, tedious—paintings by Jackson Pollock present snarls of meaningless color that distract from the lustrous elegance of the piano-finish paneling.

Two elevators feature stainless-steel doors with a subdued Art Deco design. For security reasons, these lifts can be accessed only by entering five digits in a keypad. Each person who works here has a unique pass code. During business hours, clients and guests are escorted into the elevators by one of two receptionists. Although lacking a code, Michael can obtain that of anyone who works here and use an elevator if he wishes, but even if the pneumatic-rail system is quiet, the sound might alert those he's come here to see.

An emergency stairwell is required in the event of fire. One is detailed in the blueprints that are on file with the city's building department and readily accessible to him. The stairs are concealed behind paneling on which hangs a large vertical-format Pollock work that convincingly depicts and celebrates the mental chaos of extreme alcoholism. A concealed pressure latch in the frame of the painting releases the lock, and the hidden door swings out.

The switchback stairs are concrete, not metal, and each tread is cushioned with ribbed rubber to minimize the danger of a slip-and-fall lawsuit. The regularly spaced LED wall sconces operate around the clock, seven days a week.

At the fifth-floor landing, Michael listens to his own breath drawn and expelled, which is such a soft sound that what he hears might be entirely internal, the rhythmic billow and abatement of his lungs. To an observer, his stillness could suggest that he is a dead man standing, but he isn't dead anymore.

From this side, the door is not concealed, and the electronic lock is released with a simple lever handle. He steps into a room paneled in anigre. The floor is shimmering white quartzite laid in six-by-four-foot slabs instead of cheaper tiles. The receptionist's desk is a marvel of brushed stainless steel formed into curves, as if it is molten and flowing, with a celadon quartzite top. Eight comfortable chairs are available to accommodate those visitors who will be made to wait long enough to establish that they are of less importance than the man whose counsel they have come here to seek.

Currently, illumination is provided by only a pair of alabaster sconces that flank a door on the far side of the room.

To the left, beyond a wall of glass etched with a cityscape, a conference room waits in shadow—twenty empty chairs around a long table. To the right, windows look out on streets impoverished of light and rich with threat.

Michael steps around the desk and goes to the ensconced door. It opens into the office of Carter Woodbine, founder of Woodbine, Kravitz, Benedetto, and Spackman.

Ordinarily, Woodbine schedules appointments only between ten o'clock in the morning and four in the afternoon. On this occasion, however, he isn't meeting with ordinary clients, and even the great man will bestir himself before dawn when the matter requiring his attention is sufficiently rewarding.

Like the public spaces in this building, Woodbine's office is an exacting and fastidious marriage of high drama and good taste. The desk is an uncharacteristically large work by Ruhlmann, circa 1932. The lamp upon it is not from Office Depot, but shines forth from the long-ago studios of Louis Comfort Tiffany; the dragon-fly motif is a rare specimen executed largely in gold glass with vivid blue insects and no doubt appeals to Woodbine because it suggests mystery and power, the two cloaks in which he's wrapped himself throughout his career.

Although the attorney owns a fifteen-thousand-square-foot residence on two acres, a half-hour's drive from his office, he maintains an apartment here on the fifth floor. In addition to a living room, dining room, chef's kitchen, bedroom, bath, and gym, there is a concealed panic room that can withstand any assault that might be made against it. His third wife, forty-year-old Vanessa, twenty-two years his junior, lives with him in the mansion, but she has no access to his apartment, which she assumes—or pretends to assume—is of modest size and used solely when he's so overwhelmed by the demands of the law that he can't spare the time even for a short commute. This allows Woodbine to have a parallel life of quiet but intense debauchery at odds with his public image.

The apartment entrance is concealed in the office paneling, behind a large and excruciatingly pretentious cubist painting that might be by Picasso or Braque—or by a barber who cut their hair. The lock responds to a signal when an electronic key is held to a blue triangle that symbolizes something in the painting; a code reader behind the canvas confirms the signal and releases the lock.

Michael neither has a key nor needs one to finesse the code reader. The door opens, and he enters a small foyer, proceeding from there into the living room.

The apartment security system tracks all occupants by their heat signatures and pinpoints them on a floor plan displayed on a large screen in the panic room. In a crisis, sheltering behind steel plate and concrete, Woodbine would be aware of where each invader could be found, and he would be able to coordinate with a police SWAT team, by phone, to facilitate their efforts to locate the culprits and secure the premises.

Michael is now represented by a blinking red dot on that panic-room display, where at the moment there is no one to see it. Three other signifiers are also blinking.

Although Michael would prefer to be an ordinary man, he is unique by any standard, and no return to a normal life is possible for him. He proceeds.

The three men are gathered at the kitchen island on which packets of hundred-dollar bills are stacked high. The thickness of the packets suggests each contains ten thousand dollars. Together, the ordered piles must amount to at least three or four million. Tall and handsome and white-haired, Carter Woodbine is dressed in a midnight-blue silk robe over matching pajamas. His associates, Rudy Santana and Delman Harris, are fresh from the street, their duffel bag emptied of cash.

They are confident that the building's security system cannot be breached without triggering an alarm, just as they are certain that no one can know about this meeting.

When Michael steps into the room, the three men's astonishment is so great as to preclude an immediate reaction. Their heads turn in perfect synchronization, their expressions as ghastly as if he's someone they murdered and is now risen from the grave, though in fact he is a total stranger to them.

Harris is the first to shrug out of the mesmeric moment. He draws a Heckler & Koch .45 from a shoulder holster under his gray leather sport coat. Rudy Santana's thigh-length black denim jacket hangs open, and he retrieves a pistol from a hip sheath.

Because Michael has no weapon in hand and enters smiling and appears so self-assured as to be mentally deficient, the thugs are uncertain—hard-eyed and tight-lipped, but at the same time puzzled and wondering if drawing their guns will prove foolish.

Michael says, "I'm unarmed and alone. I prefer to avoid hurting anyone. I just need money. Give me half a million, and you keep the rest."

A KITCHEN CONVERSATION

If the definition of *murder* requires that the accused must have
squeezed the trigger or thrust the knife or swung the machete, then
of the three men gathered around the kitchen island, Rudy Santana
is by far the most prodigious perpetrator of homicide among them.
If the meaning of *murder* is expanded to include anyone who
finances illegal enterprises that by their nature involve vicious business rivalries and lethal violence, the laurels go to Carter Woodbine.
For thirty years, the attorney has provided the seed money for new
gangs that splinter from traditional criminal organizations, and he
has used his political influence to spare his associates prosecution.
He lobbies to keep the southern border of the United States open
for the transport of narcotics and to facilitate the human trafficking
that ensures a supply of indentured young women for brothels and
the tenderest of children for men who yearn to have them.

Even with all the sources of information available to Michael,
he isn't able to attribute a scrupulously exact number of murders
to either man. Besides, the total increases without surcease—by
the month in Santana's case, by the week for Woodbine.

The accomplishments of Delman Harris are more easily assessed.
Michael is pretty sure that Mr. Harris has committed between seven
and ten murders, a fraction of the deaths that can be blamed on
either Woodbine or Santana. Perhaps the mere sprinkle of corpses
he has left in his wake embarrasses him, leaves him feeling inferior to
these other men, which might explain why he, rather than Santana,
not only draws his gun but rashly points it at Michael, stiff-armed,
finger on the trigger, and demands, "Who the fuck are you?"

"I'm nobody."

Woodbine quietly disagrees. "You're somebody."

"I'm not any kind of cop," Michael assures them.

"He don't look like nobody's homeboy," Santana says.

"Shit," says Harris, "he looks trick."

"Pussy," Santana agrees.

"You walked right in," Woodbine says.

Michael shrugs. "You should complain to your security company."

"Fucker won't walk right out," Harris promises.

Santana looks puzzled. "Say what? Security company?"

"Stall it. Cut the roo-rah," Woodbine tells them, resorting to their vernacular. "Rudy, find out if he's righteous when he says he's alone."

Rudy Santana gives Michael the red eye. He's furious but in control of himself. He leaves the kitchen, on the hunt.

Harris is jumpy. He wants Michael to look down the barrel of his pistol and think about it. His gun hand twitches a little. His breathing is too fast and shallow.

Woodbine is calm, and he's not faking it. He stands with his hands in the pockets of his robe, studying his uninvited guest. He doesn't look concerned. Because nothing truly bad has ever happened to him, he assumes that nothing ever will. The world that is being remade by the greatest concentration of power in history is becoming a world that breeds narcissists with delusions of immortality, the like of which humanity has never seen and is not likely to survive.

Santana's absence makes Harris nervous, as if he thinks his partner might not come back. "You dumb prick, comin' in here, sayin' peel me off half a mil. How much snow you put up your nose?"

"Wait for Rudy," Woodbine says.

Three minutes pass in silence. Santana returns. "Everything is everything. Apartment and office clear. Elevators locked. If this shithead came with others, they won't be hangin' out downstairs, waitin' for an invitation."

"Pat him down," Woodbine says.

Santana warns Michael, "Give me a reason."

"I didn't come here to hurt anyone," Michael reminds him, and he submits to Santana's quick but thorough search for a weapon.

"Clean," Santana tells Woodbine. "And no ID."

Having remained just inside the door, Michael now moves to the island. "Mr. Harris, I'd be more relaxed if you would lower the gun. Your tremor makes me nervous."

"What'll be more nervous makin'," Harris says, "is a forty-five full metal jacket point-blank in your face."

Woodbine motions for Harris to lower the weapon and says to Michael, "This conversation is between you and me."

"Seems best."

"Who are you?"

"I said."

"Nobody."

"That's right."

"I can ink your hands and have your prints run."

"Won't do you any good."

"I'm serious. I can get a report from the FBI in an hour. No one but my contact there will know I asked for it or that it was ever sent to me."

"I know you can do that. There's a lot of rot in the system, and you have a nose for rot. But nobody has my prints."

"You've got a past."

"Erased."

"Not possible."

"Not for you maybe."

"There will be photographs and files you missed."

"None."

"We can hold you here while we search."

"Only if you kill me."

"Why wouldn't we do that?"

"I won't let you."

Harris mutters a curse, and Santana makes a noise of derision.

Woodbine appears more amused than concerned. He is a supremely confident guy. "What're you angling for?"

"I already said."

"Half a million dollars."

"Glad to see Alzheimer's hasn't gotten you."

"Why would I give you half a million?"

"You don't have a choice."

"To keep you from hurting me."

"Exactly."

"Do you realize how you sound?"

"Insane?"

"Totally."

"Just put my money in the duffel bag and keep the rest."

"*Your* money?"

"I wouldn't be here if I didn't really need it."

Santana and Harris are restless. They want to commit a little violence to settle their nerves.

When Woodbine takes his hands out of the pockets of his robe, they are neither work-worn nor marked by age spots. His nails are manicured and finished with a clear polish.

"How did you learn the truth?" he asks.

"About you? I'm a research wizard."

"I'm discreet. I take every precaution."

"May I explain with a metaphor? Let's say the internet is a dense jungle of information, with trillions of clues to billions of secrets. Each of you leaves a trail whether you try to cover your tracks or not. I'm right out of Kipling."

"Rudyard Kipling."

"So you learned something at Harvard. See, I know the internet jungle better than Mowgli knows the real one. To my eye, you left a trail as wide as a herd of elephants."

"Drop the metaphor. Give me an example."

Indicating Santana and Harris, Michael says, "You use burner phones with these two feebs and others."

"I go through a couple hundred disposables a year. I destroy them all. And I don't buy them myself."

"I know. Mr. Santana's uncle Ignacio, the priest, buys them for him, and Santana gives your share to you."

Santana is incensed. "My uncle is a holy man of God. Don't screw with Tio Ignacio, you piece of shit."

Quieting Santana with a gesture, Woodbine asks Michael, "How could you know this?"

"You use your limited-function burner phones when you talk to one another. But you use your smartphones for text messaging."

"Our texts are encrypted. Profoundly encrypted."

"Yeah. I know. The best encryption in the world, developed in Moscow, used by the Russian prime minister. Even the CIA hasn't broken it."

"But you have?"

"Let's say I built a back door into the computer system of the Russian equivalent of the CIA and planted a rootkit so I can come and go undetected."

"Rootkit?"

"Hacker talk. That's not really how I work. I'm not a hacker, but I wanted to put it in terms you might understand."

"So somehow you tap our phones and read through the encryption of our text messages. That's how you knew we'd be here now."

Michael shrugs. "So sue me."

"You want me to believe you've left incriminating evidence with some friend of yours, and if you don't come back, he'll turn it over to the authorities, like in the movies."

"No, not at all. What good would that do me, considering how you can buy politicians, judges, honchos in the attorney general's office, and key journalists?"

Woodbine stares at him for a long beat. At last he says, "You fascinate me."

"Thank you. But that's not my life's purpose." He pulls the empty duffel bag in front of him and begins to scoop packets of hundred-dollar bills into it.

Seeking guidance, Santana says, "Carter, what the hell?"

Harris's smartphone is in an interior pocket of his sport coat, and Santana's smartphone is in the left back pocket of his jeans, and Woodbine's smartphone is in a pocket of his robe. Although none of those devices is set on vibrate, they begin to shake three times more violently than ever before. Simultaneously, an eerie keening issues from the phones at three times the volume they previously produced, a ululant shrillness suggesting the angry shriek of an ungodly monstrous insect. The batteries instantly overheat. The three men are so startled that they fall into momentary confusion. Santana cries out—"What, what, what?"—and Harris curses, and Woodbine steps out of his slippers as he staggers back from the island, and they claw at themselves to get rid of whatever threat has manifested in their clothing. In the first three seconds, as Rudy Santana plucks the phone from his back pocket, scorching his fingers—"Shit, shit, shit!"—Michael punches his face, breaking his nose, and Santana falls, and Michael stomps on the wrist of the gun hand, and Santana's fingers spasm open, allowing Michael to stoop and take the pistol by the barrel. In the following three seconds, Michael pivots to Harris, who has put his .45 on the island and is frantically shrugging out of his coat, which has begun to smoke, and Michael clubs him with the butt of Santana's pistol, just hard enough to put him out for a few minutes.

Carter Woodbine presses his back against the refrigerator, sucking the thumb and forefinger of his right hand, which blistered when he retrieved his hot smartphone from a pocket and threw it across the room. In the throes of his reaction, he has shrugged his left arm out of the sleeve, so the open robe hangs from his right shoulder. Standing barefoot in his disheveled jammies, he looks no more impressive than a large child who's been caught on a forbidden post-midnight raid of the cookie jar.

The smoking phones have fallen silent.

After dropping Santana's pistol in the duffel bag, holding Harris's .45 in his right hand, Michael says, "Don't test me."

Removing his wet thumb and forefinger from his mouth, Woodbine says, "I'm not stupid."

"Lacking evidence, I'll take your word for it."

On the floor, cradling his injured wrist in his good hand, blood bubbling in the deformed cartilage of his nostrils, Santana breathes through his mouth, spitting out curses between inhalations.

Michael scoops bundles of cash into the duffel bag with his left hand.

"How did you do that?" Woodbine asks.

"Do what?"

"You know what—with the phones."

"Trade secret."

"You think you're cute."

"My mother thought so, but I never could see it."

"I'll find you."

"Knock yourself out."

"You're dead."

"Been there, done that, didn't care for it." He has taken maybe 10 percent of the cash on the kitchen island. The bag is heavy. "I should set the rest on fire, knowing how you got it and what worse you'll do with it."

At the prospect of losing it all, Woodbine decides respectful silence is the best response.

As he zippers the bag shut, Michael says, "What is it with people like you?"

Repressed rage forces Woodbine to speak through clenched teeth. "What people would that be?"

"Those who had every advantage but went bad."

"There isn't bad or good."

"Then what is there?"

"Opportunities. You take them or you don't."

"What name do they give that philosophy at Harvard?"

"Nihilism. It works. Looks like you live by it, too."

"I only take from nihilists. Doesn't make me one."

"So you feel virtuous."

"No. It just makes me a different kind of thief."

Michael backs out of the kitchen with the .45 in his right hand and the duffel bag depending from his left.

In consideration of the Heckler & Koch, Carter Woodbine is slow to follow. He'll probably try to use a landline to make a call. It won't work.

Michael steps out of the apartment foyer into Woodbine's public office and closes the door that is hidden by the cubist painting. It bears the signature of Picasso. He studies the work for a minute, twice as long as is fruitful.

He crosses the room and is about to step into the reception lounge when he hears Woodbine struggling with the Picasso door. The electronic lock is frozen and will remain that way until Michael decides to allow it to function, perhaps in an hour or two.

He follows the hidden stairs to the ground-floor lobby, takes the hallway to the rear of the building, and passes through a door into the upper level of the two-floor garage reserved for employees and clients, where he switches on the lights. The attorney's white Bentley sedan is parked in the most convenient of the spaces. A glass-walled office is provided for a valet who is on duty during business hours for the sole purpose of bringing the vehicles of the law firm's four partners to and from the front entrance, so that they do not need to bother themselves with negotiating the alleyway. This cubicle is protected by an electronic lock that is integrated with the building's security system. Michael releases it without triggering an alarm, enters, locates the Bentley's key where it hangs from a pegboard, and closes the door behind him.

Often he likes to walk. People who move through their days at high speed, always boxed in a vehicle, do not see the intricate details of either the natural world or the world that humanity has built for itself. The less they see, the less they understand, and the more likely they are to live in a bubble of unreality.

On this occasion, however, he has many miles to cover and a promise he hopes to keep before dawn.

TEN DAYS EARLIER:
BEAUTIFICATION RESEARCH

The food in the cafeteria is less tasty than army K rations, but at least the ambience is better than the crumbling and cratered streets of some butt-of-the-world city where the meal would likely be interrupted by a firefight. Considering that this facility is a public-sector–private-sector partnership between the Internal Security Agency and two technology firms, each valued at more than a trillion dollars, it's unfortunate that the food service is provided by the government rather than by the human resources division of one of the tech companies, which would have a better understanding of nutrition and flavor. Employees have no choice other than to eat lunch here, because before leaving the premises, they must undergo a seventy-five-minute decontamination that no one wants to endure twice in one day. Lunch boxes from home are forbidden for reasons known only to the bureaucrats who devised the protocols and who labor in a warren three thousand miles away, where no one can make contact with them.

Michael sits at a corner table with his best friend, Shelby Shrewsberry, who may be the only immunologist in the United States who is also a specialist in cerebrovascular function and the blood-brain barrier, six feet five, two hundred thirty pounds, and African American. Shelby, a genius, earned his first medical degree when he was twenty-two, but Michael possesses just slightly higher than average intelligence. Shelby plays the piano, violin, and saxophone. Michael has mastered the harmonica. Shelby has the face of a movie star—Michael not so much. They have been best friends for thirty-eight years, since they were six and their families were neighbors in a lower-middle-class community where, for different reasons, Michael and Shelby were viewed as nerds by most other kids.

Shelby, the senior biological scientist on this endeavor, has authority equal to that of Dr. Simon Bistoury, who serves as the reigning technology expert. Bistoury is a true believer in what they are doing here at the deceptively and absurdly named Beautification Research Project. Shelby, however, is profoundly skeptical about the wisdom and morality of this work, a point of view he has concealed in order to be in a position to go public and blow up the entire scheme if that becomes necessary. If he does so, he will be risking financial ruin and imprisonment, as will Michael, who was brought into this undertaking by Shelby to serve as chief of its security team. In this age when the fruits of corruption and the pursuit of power at all costs seem to motivate too many in the highest echelons of society, Shelby and Michael are no less outsiders than they were as kids; most of those in the current ruling elite would dismiss them as nerds if only they knew what principles guide them.

They never discuss their status as potential whistleblowers; at the moment, here in the cafeteria, they are discussing Shelby's romantic longing for a woman, Nina, whom he's met just three times and has not yet asked for a date. He encountered this jewel in her capacity as the accountant handling payroll and taxes for his cousin Carl, who owns three laundromats. Shelby was charmed not merely by her looks, but also by her intelligence, wit, and industriousness.

"So," Michael says, "instead of asking her on a date, you hire her as your accountant. I'm not sure if that's smoother than it is dumb, or dumber than it is smooth, or not smooth at all."

Shelby has an unconscious habit of rolling his eyes as an acknowledgment of his mistakes and shortcomings. "Yeah, well, I've never handled rejection well. I curl up and suck my thumb."

"You're tall, dark, handsome, successful, amusing, and reputed to be smart. No woman is going to reject you."

"I had plenty of rejections before I met and married Tanya."

"Back then you were just tall, dark, handsome, amusing, and reputed to be smart. You weren't successful yet."

"I was *too* tall, broad as a truck, big hands like a strangler for hire, with a tendency to glower. I'm still all those things."

"Just smile, and your face lights up, cute as a kitten."

Shelby's eyes roll in their sockets as if he's one of those novelty dolls with counterweighted eyeballs. "That's just it. When I'm around Nina, I'm so worried about making a good impression that I forget to smile. I'm so nervous and earnest, I look scary."

Pushing aside his plate of half-finished creamed beef on whole-wheat toast with carrots and red-beet slaw, Michael shakes his head. "It's a mystery how you produced two children with Tanya."

"Tanya wasn't just beautiful. She was uncannily insightful. Ten minutes after we met, she knew me better than I knew myself."

"Maybe this Nina also knows you better than you think she does, knows just what a prince among men you are."

Shelby swallows a forkful of beet slaw, and his face puckers. He washes the slaw down with iced tea, and his face puckers again. "Don't you think that's more luck than any man should expect—to meet two women who totally get who he is in his heart?"

After pretending to think about that, Michael says, "Are there really stranglers for hire?"

"Given our ever-darkening world, why wouldn't there be?"

"Do they use their bare hands or a wire garrote?"

"Hands, wire, rope, scarves, rubber tubing—they have to switch it up, otherwise the job would get boring. Another thing is the age difference. I'm forty-four, and Nina is thirty."

"Humbert Humbert salivates over Lolita. I'm making a civilian arrest, you pervert."

"Maybe it's funny to you, but it's a serious consideration. When Nina's sixty-five, I'll be seventy-nine."

"Yeah, you're right. And when she's a hundred and ten, you'll be a hundred and twenty-four. Be careful, or your eyes will roll right out of your head."

Shelby sips more iced tea. "I think the people who make this stuff also make the brew you drink before a colonoscopy."

"You know what *I* think? Although it's been eight years since cancer took Tanya, you feel that getting serious about Nina is like cheating on Tanya."

"No, no, it's nothing like that."

"Betraying her."

"You can't betray someone who has passed away."

"Dishonoring her memory."

Shelby sighs. "You're relentless. You'd have made a great prosecutor during the Spanish Inquisition."

"Your kids are grown, and you miss having them in the house."

"What does that have to do with anything?"

"You live alone. You're not the kind of guy who can live alone. Right now, you're a lonely, forlorn, miserable stylite who could be happy if you'd allow yourself to reach out to Nina."

"'Stylite.' Been reading more than your usual comic books?"

"You said her son is special."

Shelby's scowl softens into a sweet expression. "John. He's a good kid. He's the kind of kid who's the hope of the world."

"So if Nina will date you, and if she's sufficiently lacking in judgment to fall in love with you, and if then she's foolish enough to marry you, you'll have not only a wife but a little family, a new adopted son to mentor and inspire and make as neurotic as you are."

Shelby sighs. "That's a dream worth having, isn't it?"

"So turn it from a dream into a reality."

"I think maybe I will."

"Don't think. Just do it. None of us knows how long we've got, pal. Next week we could be gone. Fate favors no one, especially not a too-tall, truck-wide, glowering, potential strangler like you."

Looking past Michael, toward the entrance to the cafeteria, Shelby mutters, "What's our S-O-B doing here?"

That would be Dr. Simon O. Bistoury, the co-director of the project, technology expert and primary pain in the ass. Ninety-nine percent of the time, he has his lunch sent up to his office. On the rare occasion when he shows up here, it's not for food but for the chance to kvetch to someone, anyone, about whatever has his shorts in a knot at the moment. Simon Bistoury is not a happy man.

Michael taps Shelby's lunch tray. "Hurry up and finish."

"I want dessert. I won't forgo dessert even if it means having to listen to Simon. Dessert is the only thing worth eating here."

"He's probably pissed off because he's heard about some major success with the killer robot dogs."

Although Bistoury believes in the work they're doing, he thinks they'll need five more years to have success. The position he really wants is that of the project director at a facility north of San Diego, where many billions are being spent to create a four-legged AI robot soldier with significant firepower, based on the skeletal structure and highly flexible spine of a dog. They don't look like dogs. They look like something from Hell; no one will want to pet them. However, Bistoury is convinced they can be designed, produced, and battle ready a lot sooner than any breakthrough is likely to occur here at Beautification Research. Dr. Bistoury is a scientist, but he's more about success than science. Success and glory.

"Damn," Shelby says, "he got coffee, and he's coming this way."

Michael sighs. "Didn't I just tell you that none of us knows how long we've got?"

Simon Bistoury arrives and stands glowering down at them. "The bastards down at Encinitas have knocked it out of the park."

"I don't follow baseball," says Shelby.

"They got their dog-form bots. Limited AI autonomy or remote-controlled, capable of integrated action in the autonomous mode."

Michael says, "I have a friend whose dog can hold three tennis balls in his mouth at the same time."

"Their budget's twice as large as ours. What're we supposed to do with a lousy two billion a year?"

THE BLUE HOUSE

Even at this hour, when real-world devils have just recently gone to sleep and only honest working folks are preparing for the blessing of labor, Michael can't curb Carter Woodbine's Bentley in front of Nina Dozier's house. To do so will make her a subject of even greater interest to the gangbangers who currently harass her.

He parks the sedan in the lot of a dentist's office where the greater disorder of her neighborhood meets the lesser disorder of another community. En route, he'd stopped to take a hundred thousand dollars from the half million and had secreted those ten packets in the spare-tire well of the car's trunk. Now he slips the straps of the duffel over his right shoulder, his hand within the open top of the bag, holding Santana's pistol in a relaxed grip, and he sets out to walk eight blocks.

Although this is a crime-racked area, he doesn't think trouble is inevitable or even likely. For all its dangers, this is not an outpost of Hell. Nevertheless, there is no safe neighborhood these days, and any homeboy with an active imagination might be as interested in a duffel bag as in the flash of a solid-gold Rolex.

This is a residential district where precious illumination is allowed in a time of shortages; however, the lampposts are old and insufficiently bright, and the milky globes atop a number of them have been shot out or broken with stones. The street trees are nearly as old as the city and have not been properly maintained in decades; through the intricate thatchery of branches, the veiled glow of the westering moon is reduced to a stippling of gray light on the otherwise dark sidewalk.

When any vehicle approaching from behind him slows down, he tenses in expectation that it will stop, that a confrontation might occur. They all motor eastward, toward a thin, ashen radiance along the eastern rim of the world that is rising as though the lost continent of Atlantis is slowly surfacing in the sea of night.

The houses are mostly bungalows, stucco or clapboard, on small lots. Some are maintained with pride. An equal number are crumbling toward condemnation, the lawns long neglected. Perhaps 10 percent are abandoned. This is Vig territory, a gang as dangerous as the Bloods or the Crips, their name shortened from *vigorous*, to imply that they have drive, force, and strength.

Nina Dozier's stucco bungalow is in good repair, colorless in these last minutes of darkness but, in daylight, pale blue with white trim. Two small bedrooms. One bath. A living room that also serves as a home office. An eat-in kitchen. Maybe seven hundred square feet in all. The house had belonged to her mom and dad. She inherited it, along with a mortgage, when they were run down and killed in a crosswalk as they were coming home from a local market with bags of groceries.

The hit-and-run driver, later caught, was a methamphetamine freak with a long rap sheet, recently released on bail after being charged with carjacking. He was driving a stolen Lincoln Aviator that he totaled later that day, without injury to himself.

Because Nina's son will be sleeping at this hour, Michael goes around the bungalow to the back, as they arranged. She is sitting at the kitchen table with a cup of coffee, slim and fresh-faced, one of those women who seems too small to withstand the storms of this world but who walks through them all unbent, a mahogany Madonna.

He taps softly on one of the four panes in the top half of the door, and she looks up. In spite of the proofs that he provided to her, she is clearly astonished that he has shown up as promised. Her surprise isn't accompanied with relief; she is accustomed to people and fate disappointing her just when her expectations are highest.

She disengages the two deadbolts and opens the door. Michael steps into this humble home in which lives the hope of the world.

A BRIDGE OVER TROUBLED WATER

Nina fills a heavy, white china mug with coffee for Michael, refreshes her own, and sits across the table from him. She needs the caffeine, for she has slept not at all this night. In fact, since he first approached her the day before yesterday, she's been in a state of anticipation that has made it difficult to concentrate on her work or on anything else.

At thirty, after putting herself through college, she is in her sixth year of business as a certified public accountant. Her clients own small businesses in the neighborhood. She keeps their books, prepares their taxes, and makes sure they are in compliance with state laws regarding employees. None of them is getting rich, and neither is she, but she counts it an accomplishment, almost a triumph, that she can support herself, provide for her son, and grow her savings such that she might be able eventually to give the boy a chance for a better life than she has shaped for herself. In this hard and darkening world, she is proud of what she has achieved—and grateful that she is wiser than she once was, that she doesn't need to depend on anyone.

When she was sixteen, she made a profound error of judgment. His name was Aleem Sutter. He was a charmer, charismatic, a liar who could make a young girl believe he was true to the bone. He knocked her up and then walked away. Everyone said she shouldn't carry the baby to term, but she did. She hoped that when Aleem learned he had a son, he would help support him. Didn't happen. However, almost from the day the baby was born, though he should have been a burden, he was a joy. Never fussy, always smiling, curious and inquisitive from the start, quick to learn, John became quicker year by year. He is thirteen, good-hearted and reliable and truthful—everything that his father was not and still is not. As any mother should, Nina believes that her boy is special, though she never imagined that a stranger would one day knock on her door to tell her that Shelby Shrewsberry thought a boy like John could be the hope of the world, a stranger who would amaze her with his uncanny powers. But along came Michael. For thirteen years, Nina has lived for her child, now with more love and hope than ever—though there are risks, dangers.

The abilities that Michael has demonstrated seem magical, but Nina understands that his gifts were born from a strange confluence of science and wild luck. The odds that such a wondrous thing would flower from horror and tragedy are beyond calculation. She thinks of it as a miracle, but Michael does not. He insists he is no messiah, no anointed redeemer, nothing more than a guy who was in the wrong place at the wrong time when, in the midst of catastrophe, one thing went right. He recognizes the corrupting nature of power and the need for humility to avoid becoming one more monster aligned with those who would consign most of humanity to bondage.

From the duffel bag on the floor beside his chair, he withdraws a wad of hundred-dollar bills fastened with a rubber band and puts it on the table. "As I promised. This is one of forty."

Although she believes in him, she hesitates to touch what he offers. Because John is sleeping in a front room, she speaks softly, and so does Michael. "Where did you get all this?"

"I took it away from some bad men."

"How bad?"

"Drugs and human trafficking."

"Dirty money," she says.

"The uses they would put it to would've only made it dirtier. You'll use it well. You'll make it clean again."

"So much."

"I might need a year or more to understand how best to use this crazy power, before I dare to do what needs to be done. During that time, for Shelby, I want to know you and John are all right. He was my best friend. I owe him. There's nothing else I can do for him."

He wants her to sell this house and move somewhere that drive-by shootings are rare, where gangbangers don't rule the streets. Where she and John can't be found, where they'll be safe.

A month ago, Aleem Sutter came back into her life. He's now the boss dog of the Vigs in this county. Having a gang-age son who's living straight is embarrassing to him and suggests to his homeboys that he bends to the will of a woman. He's sniffing around the edges of their lives, wary of Nina, but he's rapidly growing bolder.

"I give up my accounting, how do I say I earned this money?"

"Stop using a credit card. When you pay cash, your wealth becomes invisible."

"Some things can only be paid by check or such."

"Each month, deposit what cash you need in your account."

"The IRS, they'll smell out the discrepancy sooner or later."

"You won't have to deal with the IRS anymore."

"That's a nice dream."

"I've set it up so the IRS's computerized records will show you paying quarterly and filing annually, but you won't ever pay again."

"What do I say when they audit me?"

"I've set it up so they never will."

31

"You set it up."

"You saw what I can do."

"Yeah, okay, but . . . sweet Jesus."

"I've coded your IRS file with an automatic audit reject."

"How does that work?"

"A few hundred people in government are so powerful they've exempted themselves from audits. I tucked you among them."

"How do they get away with that?"

"It's a tight-held secret. Besides, people who tell them they can't do something—those people meet with grave misfortune."

"Corruption everywhere."

"We're playing their game only to bring them to justice."

She stares into her mug. Reflected in the dark brew, her eyes swell and shrink freakishly with the movement of the liquid, as if some force that speaks only through symbol and suggestion is warning her that what she is doing will deform her vision and her soul.

Michael says, "Aleem has seen a lawyer."

"What do you mean?"

"The GPS record for his Cadillac Escalade is accessible to me. Yesterday, Aleem parked for forty-seven minutes at the building occupied by Bucklin and Aimes, a law firm that vigorously defends gangbangers like them. He's got another appointment there today."

"This has something to do with me?"

"Mr. Bucklin enters notes about meetings on his laptop. In this case, I don't respect attorney-client privilege. I snooped. Aleem was there to discuss what paternal rights he has regarding John."

Nina's heart quickens. "Rights? None. He has no rights. What dime did he ever give me? What birthday did he bring John a present? None. He's never as much as spoken to the boy."

"It's not that simple. The law doesn't always go from *A* to *B* in a straight line. In fact, it's usually a long and twisted route."

Her mouth is dry. She wets it with coffee. The rim of the mug briefly rattles against her teeth.

She says, "When John goes to private school, I drive him to and from Saint Anthony's, keep him close. But it isn't right to make him a prisoner. He goes out to play ball with friends, goes anywhere, I worry Aleem will take him. But I didn't think about lawyers."

"In the end, I doubt Aleem will be patient enough to use the law. You're right to worry he'll snatch John."

"I'm up and down and up ever since you first came here."

"If he did go to court, you know how long the law will take to settle the situation in your favor?"

"Too long. And if Aleem grabs John, he'll deny it. Aleem will hide him away, pretend he knows nothing."

"And you? What happens to you?"

She meets his eyes. She sees kindness in them. Or it's what she wants to see. Since the death of her mom and dad, there has been too little kindness in her life.

"Aleem won't give me a chance to get John back. He'll make it so I'm said to be an addict when they find me stone dead of an overdose. I know I've got to get away from him, but . . ."

Michael's voice softens to a sympathetic whisper. "It's hard to leave a life that's working."

"It *was* working. I don't know about now."

"I understand more than you think I do, Nina. You're thinking Aleem wants your boy, and I want your boy, and is it one and the same thing."

"Is it?"

"He wants to make the boy into a gangbanger. I want to see him reach his full potential. And I want him always with you."

"It's so Twilight Zone. It's a big damn thing to do this."

"Huge," he agrees.

"But I keep going back to how you told me the truth about where the money comes from. You didn't make it clean and neat."

"I never lie. Not since I died. Before sometimes, not since."

"Are you my bridge? My bridge over troubled water?"

"I will be if you'll let me."

"Because of Shelby Shrewsberry."

"Yes. And because of your son."

"I wish Shelby had told me how he felt. He seemed like . . . like such a good man."

"He was the closest I've known to a saint. Not just my best friend . . . maybe my only one."

"Good men haven't often crossed my path."

"Take this new path. Maybe that'll make all the difference."

THE BOY

The sky is overcast and the morning light bleak, but following Nina's decision, the kitchen is filled with a spirit of quiet hope, as though what has begun here is the sanctification of a world gone wrong, which might in fact be the case if Michael's intentions can be fulfilled.

She puts the duffel bag full of money in the pantry and gives him an opaque plastic bag with a drawstring closure, which she uses for groceries. He stashes the two guns in the sack, less concerned about keeping one in hand now that his eight-block walk will be in daylight.

"I could drive you," she says.

"Thank you, but I'd rather walk." Walking, he can more easily be in two places at the same time.

"I'll list the house with a broker today, sell it furnished. Notify my clients I'm closing up shop, shoot all their data back to them. Not much to pack 'cept clothes and memories. We can be out of here in maybe four days."

"Sooner is better. What'll you do if something goes wrong and you need help?"

"I'll do exactly what you told me."

"I just want to hear you say it."

"I keep my company website open. If I need you, I post a notice says, 'The ninth hour.' But how often will you check?"

"I'll know the moment it's posted."

"Oh. Yeah. I still can't get my head around that."

"Some days, neither can I."

The swinging door creaks open. The barefoot boy steps in from the hall and stands there in his rumpled pajamas, knuckling grains of lingering sleep from his eyes. He comes fully awake at the sight of Michael. "You're him."

On his first visit to this house, Michael had come under the guise of a potential new client seeking Nina's accounting services. John had been attending classes at Saint Anthony's.

"Pleased to meet you, John."

"Mom told me about you, but not everything."

"She's been waiting to see if I'd keep a promise I made. I believe now she'll tell you the rest."

John is good-looking, with large brandy-brown eyes that seem to be lit from within. Michael cannot read minds or discern the quality of anyone's character with a divining rod, but judging by what Nina has said and what the teachers at Saint Anthony's School have written in their student reports, he believes this is a smart and steady kid, a fine man in the making. John's posture, the inclination of his head, his quiet voice, and a hesitant manner suggest a healthy vulnerability that will inoculate him against the psychotic degree of self-esteem that shapes other boys into gangsters like Aleem.

He reminds Michael of Shelby.

"You're younger than I thought," John says.

By one calculation, Michael is forty-four, but in another sense, he is only four days old. To the boy, he says, "And I suspect you're older than your years."

Nina confirms, "He's that, all right," and the boy ducks his head, shying away from the praise.

"It won't be easy leaving your friends."

"What friends?" the boy asks.

"I know you have them."

"You mean school friends."

"A hard thing for most kids."

"School friends aren't forever. Everyone grows up and moves on. That's how it is."

Impressed, Michael says, "I know you'll help your mother through this."

If John is ever capable of looking at his mother without his intense love being apparent, this is not one of those moments. He clearly adores her. "We're always all right."

"Always," she says.

"Stay home from school," Michael advises.

"I'm not afraid," the boy says.

"It's not about being afraid. It's about being smart."

His mother says, "You can help me pack, sweetheart."

"So we're going."

"If we really hustle," she says, "we can be out of here tomorrow afternoon."

"To where?"

"Wherever we want. We have resources."

"The sooner the better," Michael reminds her.

He smiles at John, and the boy responds to the smile with a sober expression that says he has been aware of the stakes for most of his life.

THE ARM OF THE STATE

The declared purpose of the sprawling Internal Security Agency is to seek, discover, monitor, and eliminate every threat to the nation that might arise within its borders, and the ISA actually does some of that. As the agency has evolved, however, its primary purposes are to guarantee the perpetuation of the labyrinthine and unelected bureaucracy that in truth runs the country, ensure the prerogatives of the ruling class, and to monitor that only the right kind of people are gorging themselves at the public trough. With the tens of billions of dollars in its annual budget, the ISA is a vast wasp's nest that can dispatch swarms of agents to every real, fabricated, and imagined crisis.

Among those busy hornets of the law, Durand Calaphas is unique. While some other agents might be dedicated to the job, Calaphas is *obsessed* with it. He has no wife, no children, no significant other. His mother and father are living, but he finds them too tedious to be worth his attention. His IQ is 178, well above the number that would qualify him as a genius. James Bond is licensed to kill, but considering the importance of the cases assigned to Calaphas, he is not merely licensed but pretty much *required* to kill on a frequent basis. He has no compunctions about killing, whether it is justified or not. The ease with which he commits lethal violence has given him the highest case-closure record in the organization. Consequently, while other operatives work in pairs and larger units, Calaphas's desire to work alone is honored, much to the relief of the numerous other agents who would be afraid to partner with him.

Six days after the catastrophe north of the city, Calaphas is camped in the office of the late Simon Bistoury, co-director of a facility where fifty-four perished and one has gone missing. He has spent the past six hours drinking bottles of green tea sweetened with honey while reviewing high-definition security video on a fifty-five-inch LED screen. He has become fixated on forty-six seconds of video captured by cameras in the makeshift morgue that was established in this building in the wake of the disaster.

Ostensibly, this facility was a private enterprise, the research division of a beauty-products company tasked with developing formulas for moisturizing creams, wrinkle eliminators, exfoliants, makeup, lipstick, and other products. In fact, it was a top-secret project co-financed by the federal government and two high-tech firms whose names are more familiar to Americans than are the names of their senators.

The microorganisms being developed here were neither viruses nor bacteria, but a hybrid of nanomachines and archaea—the former made by human scientists, the latter by Nature. Until 1978, archaea were thought to be bacteria, but they are quite different; bacteria are ester-based organisms, while archaea are ether based and the more stable of the two. Because neither nanomachines nor archaea can cause infections, no one foresaw a need to conduct this research in a level-four isolation lab under the strictest of protocols, but at least the building was constructed to maintain a hermetical seal that is 99.65 percent effective. When the lungs and then the bloodstreams of the staff were invaded by the latest version of the hybrid microbe, these men and women weren't infected in the classic sense of the word, but they perished in minutes.

One of the dead—no one yet knows who—proved sufficiently courageous and perspicacious to trigger a lockdown before anyone could flee and bring this mysterious contagion to the outside world. Every possible exit is covered with multiple cameras, none of which recorded the departure of an escapee.

Nevertheless, of the fifty-five who were on duty, one man is missing, as if he turned to mist. All evidence suggests that he perished with everyone else. Yet his corpse is not among the dead.

Three hours after the event, when a remote inspection of the premises through its security cameras showed no living survivors, ISA specialists had taken advantage of the facility's hermetical seal, pumping the building full of a series of gases that destroyed all microorganisms and corroded all man-made nanoparticles. The sterilization and phagocytic cleansing were deemed complete after six hours, whereupon agents entered the building wearing inflatable-plastic suits and airtight helmets, breathing oxygen from bottles strapped to their backs. For six hours, they tested surfaces in all labs and other rooms for evidence that lethal organisms had survived the purging gases. Then, sixteen hours after the initial alarm, the building was flooded with purified air and aggressively vented to be sure that no pockets of gas remained in the structure; this required two hours. No longer specially suited up, agents spent the next eight hours exhaustively photographing all the dead in situ and moving the bodies into a large chamber that had been the cafeteria but that had been converted into a temporary morgue where rows of folding tables served as catafalques. Portable chillers kept the temperature between thirty-four and thirty-six degrees. End day one.

By the late afternoon of day two, the ISA had identified four military coroners who qualified for security clearances regarding the most sensitive matters, and who also had no reservations about signing nondisclosure agreements so stringent that they would be financially ruined and imprisoned for violating them.

Those four were brought to the site, where the largest laboratory had been converted into four fully equipped autopsy stations. For four days, these highly experienced forensic pathologists have been bringing their skills to bear on the fifty-four corpses chilling in the former cafeteria.

Now, in the project-director's suite, Durand Calaphas sits in a comfortable Herman Miller office chair that he has rolled to within three feet of the enormous wall-mounted screen. He uses the Crestron control to study those forty-six seconds of enigmatic video over and over again, sometimes selecting quadrants of the image to enlarge to full screen, sometimes watching the sequence in the format in which it was filmed.

On the screen, the time display certifies that this video was shot forty hours after the deadly event. Four days ago. By then, the forensic pathologists had been brought here. At that time, they had been in a nearby lab equipped with autopsy stations, being briefed before going to work.

The scene is the cafeteria that's been converted into a morgue. Three banks of ceiling lights are operated independently. So as not to tax the portable chillers by adding heat, only one bank of lights is on, the smallest of the three, over the long serving station with its empty food wells. The rest of the room is dimly limned but not dark. Maybe it's some flaw in the camera lens that makes the scene appear to be underwater, the quality of light reminiscent of that issuing from an illuminated aquarium that hasn't been kept as clean as it should be. Although still wearing the clothes in which they died, the victims lie beneath sheets, on fifty-five tables. No one is in attendance of the dead.

The first inexplicable development occurs on a table in the middle row of five. The camera that records the moment is mounted on the ceiling, one of three in the room. The shape beneath the shroud is alike to all the shapes on fifty-four other tables. Suddenly the sheet rises, as if the corpse beneath it has attempted to sit up. The white cotton cerement slides away, onto the floor, revealing—nothing. It's as if the resurrectee vanished in the act of rising. If the sheet hadn't clearly been covering something, Calaphas might believe a draft and gravity conspired to mimic a ghostly presence. But the sheet hadn't been lying flat on an empty table; a body had been under it.

The second inexplicable development occurs ten seconds later, at a table just a few steps from the first. Apparently, impossibly, under its own power, a sheet draws back from the face and torso of a victim, a woman in her forties who stares with sightless eyes. Her mouth is open in a silent cry. After three seconds, the shroud flows into place, again covering her. It's as if an invisible man wanted to confirm the nature of the place in which he found himself and, having done so, respectfully covered the deceased.

The third inexplicable development begins thirty-seven seconds after the first, when the door to the room eases inward, admitting a narrow blade of light from the corridor. No one enters. After three seconds, the door opens wider. The hallway appears deserted. Perhaps the door wasn't tightly closed and has swung open of its own weight. No. Now it swings shut and remains closed. Durand Calaphas is not a superstitious man, the furthest thing from it, but it seems to him that a specter opened the door, peered out to be sure no one was in the corridor, and then quickly exited the makeshift morgue.

As one who believes this world has no great moment or meaning, that the Earth is little more than a killing ground to be enjoyed by those who have a taste for blood sport, he is not convinced to revisit his philosophy by these ghostly occurrences. Intrigued, he replays the forty-six seconds to exhaustion, straining for an explanation—until he sees a fourth thing that he has repeatedly overlooked.

Because of the poor lighting and maybe because this particular camera produces video of a lesser quality than the others, he needs to review the evidence often before he notices three moments in the sequence when faint, pale plumes manifest out of nothing and quickly dissipate. For a few minutes, they mystify him, but just as he is prepared to attribute these manifestations to glitches in the stream of digital video, he remembers that the morgue is chilled to between thirty-four and thirty-six degrees. The plumes must be exhalations of the resurrectee, who somehow remains unseen by the camera.

Ghosts do not respire. Neither can there be such a thing as an invisible man.

Calaphas's phone rings. The call is from Hugo Schummer, one of the agents securing research files and overseeing the pathologists who are performing the autopsies. All fifty-four cadavers have been identified. The one project-staff member on the duty roster not yet accounted for is the head of security, Michael Mace.

TAKING A BREATHER

The clouds thicken into a gray plain that in places folds into narrow tectonic valleys where gathered blackness gradually acquires a power that will crack the sky and loose a deluge. In Michael's current mood, as his thoughts circle around Shelby Shrewsberry and the untimely end that befell that good man, he wonders if the current signs of Armageddon will soon bring the world to the real thing. He also wonders if he can delay the descent of that ultimate darkness with his gift. Perhaps, instead, he might unwittingly be the agent of the final great war and the subsequent Apocalypse.

In Carter Woodbine's Bentley, he is southbound on Pacific Coast Highway. The elegant car isn't yet on the National Crime Information Center's list of stolen vehicles. Michael has planted a data trigger in the NCIC computer system; he will be alerted when the Bentley's license-plate number appears in that registry, and he'll immediately remove it from there, and then trace backward to delete it from the files of any city, county, or state law-enforcement agency that provided it to the NCIC. No beat cop or highway patrolman will be looking for these wheels. Besides, the crooked attorney is unlikely to report it stolen and risk that Michael, if apprehended, will explain where he got the four hundred thousand in his possession.

Michael is likewise able to replace Woodbine's name with his own in the Department of Motor Vehicles' records, assigning ownership of the car to himself, should he care to do so. If his purpose were theft, he'd clean up the chain of title by invading the records of the automobile dealership from which the Bentley was purchased and replacing Woodbine's name with his own as the buyer; whereafter, it would be necessary to penetrate the files of the bank through which the attorney issued payment to the dealership and erase evidence of the transaction. All that effort would require a few minutes, but it would be a waste of time. Soon Michael won't be living under his own name, but rather under a long series of false identities crafted with such attention to detail that they can't be disproven. He has borrowed the Bentley only for a day or two.

To the right of the highway, empty parking lots lay in service of a wide, deserted beach. The sand slopes but two or three degrees to a sea that takes its color from the sky, as always it does, ash-gray now and with no grace of foam on the chop. A wind has come out of the north to whirl fine sand and paper litter into pale robed and hooded ghosts that haunt the day like the spirits of monks sworn to some strange faith, weaving southward on a fitful pilgrimage.

Michael continues to Newport Beach, cruising along the fabled yacht harbor, past water-view restaurants on the right, with luxury-car dealerships and boatyards on the left. Farther south, in that neighborhood of Newport known as Corona del Mar, a bustling place of busy shops, he turns right off the coast highway into a village of tree-lined streets, where quaint single-story homes have mostly been replaced by large houses in an architectural potpourri.

Ocean Boulevard follows a bluff high above a public beach. On the inland side of the street, multimillion-dollar residences crowd one another on narrow lots. Seaward, a grassy park is punctuated here and there with driveways to houses that are pinned to the bluff with steelwork and concrete pillars. It is to one of these that Michael pilots the Bentley, with no need to consult the sedan's navigation system.

The home is ultramodern, not impressive from the street, toward which it presents only a dark slate roof, a sleek wall clad in slabs of white quartzite, heavily tinted windows, and three garage doors of brushed stainless steel. Having intruded into the computerized records of a company that facilitates the booking of private homes for vacationers all over the world, Michael knows that the owners of this place, Frederico and Jessica Columbia, are currently enjoying someone else's spacious apartment in Paris for the next month. The family from Paris, at the moment vacationing in Brazil, will arrive to occupy this house in six days. In five days, a housekeeping service will prepare the premises in advance of the French guests. For four days, the place offers Michael a refuge.

He parks in the driveway and walks to the front door and pulls open the drop lid on the large, decorative mailbox. Frederico and Jessica put a three-week stop on mail delivery, while they are out of the country. Michael has gone online to rescind that order, and mail should be delivered starting today. At the moment, the box is empty.

Although he's sure that no one is in residence, he rings the bell and waits and rings it again.

The deadbolt is automated. Michael lacks an electronic key, but there is also a keypad that can be used by relatives or house-keepers or property managers, to each of whom a personal code is issued. The codes are programmed in the house's security-system computer, which is always online and accessible by Vigilant Eagle, the alarm company that services the home. Having gone swimming deep in the data sea of Vigilant Eagle's computer, Michael knows those codes. He inputs the five digits assigned to the property management firm, which unlocks the door and simultaneously turns off the burglar alarm.

The residence has four stories that shelve down the face of the bluff. Michael enters a stunning twenty-foot-square foyer featuring a black-granite floor and blue-glass ceiling. The space is paneled in stainless steel into which has been etched a 360-degree forest scene with ghostly deer among the silvery trees, illuminated so cunningly that the source of the light can't be directly seen.

This highest level is also occupied by an indoor swimming pool that lies beyond a hidden door to the left and the garages that can be reached through a hallway accessible beyond another hidden door to the right. Directly ahead, elevator doors and a stair-head door are integrated into the dreamlike forest scene.

He proceeds to the garage, where he has parked in front of the first space. Lacking a remote control, he needs to come here and raise the door with the wall switch. He drives the Bentley inside and lowers the segmented door and returns to the foyer and takes the elevator down to the next level.

The top floor of the house sits on solid land, but the floor under it is pinned to the face of the bluff, which gives its main rooms a panoramic view of the Pacific Ocean. The elevator and spiral stairs open to an alcove off the living room. In addition, this level offers a dining room and a chef's kitchen to the left; to the right are a library, two powder baths, and a generously pro-portioned guest suite.

The remaining bluff-side floors below contain the master suite, three other family suites, a fully equipped gym, and a ten-seat home theater.

Here on the main floor, the bleached-sycamore library, white and modern, includes a bar with a colorful backlit art-glass wall.

An under-the-counter refrigerator contains a selection of beers and cheeses. One wine cooler holds chardonnays and pinot grigios and champagnes, while the other is reserved for superb cabernet sauvignons. In various cabinets of the bar, he finds a selection of nibbles—canned nuts, pretzels, crackers of several kinds—as well as glassware, flatware, plates, and a variety of cloth napkins.

He opens a can of almonds. Another of macadamia nuts. Prepares a plate of cheeses surrounded by crackers. After putting the food on a table beside an armchair that faces the view, he opens a bottle of Caymus cabernet. He pours a few ounces into Riedel stemware, returns to the chair, puts the bottle on the table beside the cheese, and sits with the wineglass in both hands, close to his nose, enjoying the aroma before taking a sip. "To Shelby, who will not be forgotten or go unavenged," he says, with the intention of getting pleasantly drunk.

He doesn't know if he can get drunk anymore, since rising from the table in the makeshift morgue, but damn if he isn't determined to give it a try.

Over the past four busy days, sleep has eluded him. He doesn't appear to need it any longer, as though the hours that he spent in death—or something like it—have provided all the sleep he'll need henceforth.

He wonders why, of fifty-five victims, only he came back to life. He suspects that something unique in his genome provided him with protection. However, with the forces surely arrayed against him, the why of his resurrection is not his primary concern.

TWO: THE HOLLOW MEN

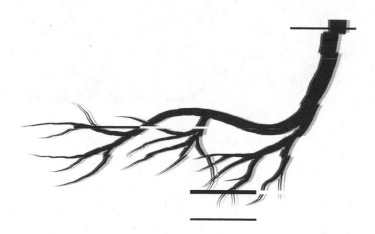

MICHAEL MULTITASKS

The wind flows swift out of the north, and the sky swoons low and pregnant, with rain soon to break. The sea is a gray mystery in which the varied population of that world, in the billions, swims its plains and valleys, crawls its lightless floors and the slopes of its submerged mountains, unseen and indifferent to the land-born who build great cities and the weapons to destroy them.

In his armchair, facing the big library windows, Michael savors the austere vista and the cabernet sauvignon and the cheeses, as he tracks the items he hopes to receive in the mail this afternoon.

Four days earlier, twenty minutes after he had slipped out of Beautification Research, he had been sitting on a bench in a park six blocks from that facility, adapting with surprising speed to his reanimation and to the strange power that came with it. He could not go home again. He dared not. He had no money, no phone, only the clothes he wore. However, because of what he'd become, anything he would ever need could be obtained with minimal risk and effort.

Six hours after he rose from the cafeteria table where he'd been placed to await autopsy, he'd taken refuge in a house in the flats of Beverly Hills. The owners, Roger and Mary Pullman, were vacationing in Austria, having swapped homes with an Austrian couple, Heinz and Erika Gurlitzer; the details of their arrangement were easily accessed in the records of the company that provided this service. After their first week in California, the Gurlitzers had moved on to another handsome residence owned by the Pullmans, this one overlooking the Pebble Beach golf course and the ocean north of Carmel. Michael found Roger Pullman's clothes to be a good fit, and the refrigerator was well stocked.

His first day in Roger and Mary's house, he'd gone exploring far and wide across the internet and deep into numerous computer systems, including several that were the most secure in the world. Being prudent, he first identified his next refuge—the house slung on the bluff in Corona del Mar where now he enjoyed wine and cheese—and surfed the web and the Dark Web for a source of funds that he might take for himself without legal or moral consequences, which is how he turned up the nasty truth about Carter Woodbine, attorney and financier of drug trafficking.

Also on that first day of his new life, he had gone spelunking in the gloomy caverns of the California DMV's poorly designed and antiquated system. Within twenty minutes, he understood the process by which a driver's license was created, and he acquired the names of the private-sector companies with which the state contracted to produce and mail them. He was able to transfer the photo on his existing license to the blank template on which all licenses were formatted, entered a name he invented, and inputted his own height, weight, eye color, and hair color. He decided to make himself four years younger than he actually was—Why not?—and chose July fourth for his birthday. For an address, he supplied that of the Corona del Mar house that he would next occupy. When all the required data was entered, after he claimed the status of a new resident of the state, the system automatically assigned him a driver's license number. Then he repeated the process two more times, using different names.

A license application might ordinarily take a month or even six weeks to be processed through the unoiled Rube Goldberg machinery of the improbably vast and infernal bureaucracy before the precious, laminated card with its tamperproof holographic details arrived from the DMV. However, Michael had found it easy to flow the cards that he created to the top of the manufacturing-and-issuing system, and then to sluice them neatly into the proper channel for priority mailing. They should arrive here today—three proofs of identity that will withstand the most intense scrutiny if he needs to use them.

He watches the first of the wind-driven rain slant in from the north, skeins of glistening beads that unravel past the bluff-side house without wetting the glass, which is protected by the roof of the exterior deck. He sips the cabernet and simultaneously peruses the data archives of the local post office's address scanner, in which he discovers that nine pieces of mail, bearing this street number, were sorted during the night and are now aboard the delivery truck that serves the neighborhood. At the same time, he's able to admire a squadron of pelicans gliding south in formation, on their way to shelter from the storm.

Having immediate and unrestricted access to every corner of the digital universe, without need of a desktop computer or laptop, with neither a tablet nor a smartphone nor other device, Michael feels a little like he felt as a boy in early adolescence, when sometimes he experienced exhilarating dreams in which he could fly effortlessly, like the gliding pelicans.

CHASING A GHOST

Sudden torrents beat on the triple-pane, hermetically sealed windows of the late Simon Bistoury's office. Wind-driven rain that falls without thunder or pyrotechnics, in a particular quality of sullen daylight, in an intense volume, can summon a precious memory and fill Durand Calaphas with yearning. This is not a sentimental feeling, not in the least maudlin or melancholy. It's a sharper variety of nostalgia, a keen longing to relive a moment of triumph, combined with a fervent hope that he'll one day experience something as profoundly satisfying as that best moment of his past. He swivels the office chair to watch the silver rain that slices through the gray morning. Although his current task requires urgent attention, he allows himself two or three minutes to imagine that he is four years in the past, on an assignment that led him to an unexpected enemy of the state. The handsome Nantucket-style shingled house on the harbor. The French windows full of soft light, a promise of warmth in the cold rain. The wife glimpsed in the kitchen, busy with baking. The puddled patio furnished with teak chairs and tables. The dock, the gangway, the slip, the fifty-six-foot coastal cruiser snugged in the single berth. Light in the below-deck portals. The drumming rain masks what small noises he makes while boarding the boat and descending the spiral companionway. Gifford is at work in the galley, preparing to use a metal cleaner on the stainless-steel sink. He looks up, surprised, and says, "Felicia didn't say you were coming." A short conversation ensues. However, Durand has not paid this visit to hear Gifford's excuses or his confession. He zippers open his raincoat as if to take it off, draws a somnifacient-dart gun, and scores a direct hit in Gifford's neck. The man collapses, unconscious. Calaphas drags him into the vessel's only stateroom, which is furnished with built-in cabinets, a bed, and one armchair. He hoists Gifford into the chair. A gun safe is fixed to a rail of the bed frame; the number code to open it is Gifford's birthday. Calaphas retrieves the pistol, puts the barrel in Gifford's mouth, and blows out the back of his skull. He positions the gun on the man's lap. The ISA will make sure that the coming investigation will be cursory. In that moment, Calaphas knows he is a giant among men. He has the courage and the fortitude to do anything required of him, absolutely anything; he's destined for greatness. In this age when most people have such soft spines that it's a wonder they are able to stand erect, it is a rare individual who can, at the call of duty and without remorse, kill his brother.

The memory is not sweet. He is not the kind of man who could *delight* in such a memory. He isn't a sociopath. He is merely dutiful and realistic about the future that lies inevitable before him. This will soon no longer be a world where family, friends, and faith are foremost. That world is fading fast. The fate of humanity depends on severely limiting our loyalty only to the system that sustains us and to the determined visionaries who sustain the system. Calaphas can't *delight* in such a memory, but he can take deep satisfaction from the fact that killing Gifford proves that his commitment to the New Truth is complete and that he won't become a reactionary who seeks even a moment's solace in the old, imperfect past.

He swivels his chair away from the window and returns his attention to the computer.

Every employee record at Beautification Research includes a photograph—except one. The first screen page of the file for the director of security, Michael Mace—no middle name—features white space where the photo should be. No problem. The DMV has a photo.

Among the information contained in the file is Mace's driver's license number. Durand Calaphas, being a senior ISA agent, has full and easy access to every government computer system on the federal, state, and local level without the need to seek a court order or so much as file a freedom-of-information request. When defending the nation from internal threats, he will never be impeded by the Bill of Rights. He is aware that some say the ISA itself is the greatest internal threat to the United States; of course, those who say such things are the suspects the agency is most intensely surveilling. Now, using Simon Bistoury's office computer to invade the California Department of Motor Vehicles' computer via a back door, he inputs the license number from the employee file—and is disturbed when the words INCORRECT NUMBER PLEASE REENTER appear on the screen. Calaphas consults Mace's file and repeats the entry, with the same result.

When he enters the name Michael Mace, he scores twice. Each man has a middle name. Michael David Mace is eighty-four years old. Michael Morley Mace, thirty-two, is a little person, four feet two inches tall. Calaphas is looking for a forty-four-year-old man who is six feet tall.

To be hired for this project, Mace had to receive the highest level of security clearance from the Department of Defense. No one at the DOD is aware that the ISA has planted a rootkit in their system, allowing senior agents to prowl through the records of all the services without being detected, but of course the military and Congress are among the institutions that must be most closely watched for evidence of seditious intentions. The file on Michael Mace no longer exists in the DOD's system.

When the Defense Intelligence Agency had conducted a deep investigation of Michael Mace for his security clearance, the ISA, FBI, CIA, NSA, and Homeland Security would all have become aware of that and would have undertaken their own exhaustive inquiries into his past. They should all have photographs of him.

Calaphas needs another seventy-five minutes to discover that none of those organizations any longer maintains a file on Mace. Evidently, someone has zapped them all.

OUT OF THE STORM

Such a deluge could ensure that this isn't a drought year in California. The storm is a good thing, received with gratitude, but Nina Dozier always worries her way through the lightest drizzle, frequently checking the ceiling, room by room, for the first sign of wet plasterboard. The roof is old, and when it begins to fail, a few patches won't fix it. Even on a little house like hers, a new roof can be expensive. On this occasion, however, she isn't fretting about leaks and water damage. Being in possession of four hundred thousand dollars with which to start a new life, she can regard the storm the same way people in Beverly Hills see it—as just a change in the weather.

Because she and John visited Disneyland for three days to celebrate his tenth birthday, he has had a suitcase for three years. Not all of his things are going to fit in the one bag, so she has assembled two of the banker boxes that she uses to store business records. After she gets him started packing, she steps out of his bedroom and follows the short hallway into the living room, on her way to the kitchen.

From an armchair, his Common Projects sneakers propped on the footstool, Aleem Sutter says, "Girl, you're still seriously fresh."

She halts, rocking slightly on her heels, as if she's walked into a glass door.

He says, "Time don't work on you. How is it you look cherry as you ever did?"

Nina says nothing. She's thinking about the pistol clipped to the bed frame in her room.

"Wasn't you I come here about, but now I seen you up close, damn if I don't got that old feelin'."

"Go away."

"Nowhere better to go." He swings his feet off the ottoman but remains in the armchair, relaxed and insolent. "Back when, wasn't nothin' you liked better than a ride on the Aleem machine. My taste runs to high-school skirt, but you want to ride again, it don't cost you even a quarter."

"You're a disgusting pig."

His soft laugh is warm, but his eyes belie the pretense of amusement. "You always had some fire in you."

"This is my house."

"A shitty little place to raise a kid."

"I told you to get out."

"You said 'go away.' Ask a lawyer, he'll explain 'imprecise is just advice. To get a conviction, use the right diction.' I learned me a lot of law since back when you was makin' my baby."

"Get the fuck out, Aleem."

He rises from the chair and stretches extravagantly, arms extended as if he's nailed to a cross, rolling his head to loosen his neck muscles. After a yawn, he says, "What you just done there is you undermined your status as a victim. Every word you say, you got to think to yourself how sayin' it might be like pissin' on your precious status as a victim. A pretty girl talks dirty, a man might think she comin' on to him, so what he does don't count as crime."

"I'm calling the police."

His voice is laced with mockery. "Why would you do that 'stead of you just break up with me? We got somethin' beautiful, how you know my needs and I know yours, how we satisfy each other, our old flame burnin' bright again. But, hey, if you go hormonal on me, you say hit the road, I got so much respect for you, baby, I'll leave, no argument. R-E-S-P-E-C-T."

The house is warm, but Nina is cold in flesh and bone. Cold but steady. She won't give him the pleasure of seeing her tremble. "Your crazy talk doesn't scare me."

He feigns puzzlement. "Crazy? Nothin' crazy about love, baby. It makes the world go round."

When he steps past the footstool, she does not back away. Any sign of weakness will encourage him.

As he retrieves something from a pocket of his jacket—an Our Legacy jacket that costs God knows what—he says, "And nothin' proves our love more than this."

A key. It's how he got in here.

"Where'd you get that?"

"Where I get it? You don't remember?"

"Don't say I gave it to you."

"You know me, sugar. I only say what's true."

"Don't say it's from me."

"You want it back?"

"I want it. There's no 'back' involved."

"You want the other one, too?"

She says nothing.

"Remember? You give me a second, case maybe I lost this one."

"You can't have him."

"Him? A key don't have no him or her about it."

"Damn you."

"And here I thought you was a church lady."

"Put both keys on the table there."

"You want the third? The fourth?" He takes a step toward her, then another. They are five feet apart. He returns the key to his jacket pocket. "Got me a homeboy used to work for a locksmith. You want, he can come change out the locks, make you feel safe."

John steps out of the hallway, into the living room. He has retrieved the pistol from his mother's bedroom. He holds it in both hands, aimed at the floor.

Aleem says, "You gonna pop a cap, boy?"

John looks to his mother.

She tells him to put the gun down, but he doesn't.

"You know what it means—pop a cap?" Aleem asks.

John says, "No."

"It means shoot someone. You gonna shoot someone, boy?"

"Leave him out of this, Aleem."

"Can't leave him out of a thing that's all about him."

She says, "John, go to your room."

Favoring her with a cobra smile, Aleem adopts a sweet tone at odds with his words. "Sugar, much as I love you, sometimes you're a dumb cunt. This'll go down nicer iffen you keep your mouth shut when I'm talkin' to my son. Can you do that, sweet thing?"

She has sheltered John, kept him from all influences of the street. He's a good kid, but short on hard experience. He's not imprudent, certainly not rash, but there's no telling what he might do if Aleem strikes her. He might interpret a slap to the face as prelude to homicidal violence. Even if he only wounds Aleem, what happens to him then? Not juvenile detention. But something. He'll be taken by child-welfare authorities for psychological evaluation, be separated from her for days, maybe longer, maybe a lot longer. Bad things sometimes happen to kids when they're in the custody of the state. She feels as if she's on a wire, above an abyss.

To John, Aleem says, "They teach you nothin' but ignorant shit at that Saint Anthony School?"

The boy stares at the gun in his hands.

"You pull a piece on a guy, be ready to use it, 'cause he's gonna pull his on you, 'less he's your father."

From the moment that Aleem first spoke to her, Nina has not heard the rain beating on the roof. For her, the house has been submerged in the stillness of some horrific potentiality. Suddenly she once more apprehends the drumming cataracts, a sound that fills her with dread, as if a grievous and unstoppable fate is rumbling toward them on tracks from which it can't be derailed.

Aleem says, "Do them priests teach you it's righteous to pop your own father, a good way you get to Heaven, see Jesus?"

John is fixated on the gun that he holds.

"Only future matters, boy, is here in this one world. You seen your future, Johnny?" Aleem waits, and John doesn't respond, and Aleem says, "What kind of altar boy don't got the courtesy to answer his own daddy? Tell me now—you seen your future?"

"No."

"Well, I seen it clear. You drink Jesus poison at school, get womanized here in this shithole house, then the rest of your life, you be jammed and jacked up by every guy with balls, till you can't take it no more, till you go on the pipe, maybe one you're freebasin' coke with, maybe one comes at the business end of a fuckin' twelve-gauge, suckin' buckshot to get outta your nowhere life. You hear me?"

"Yes."

"You believe me?"

After a hesitation, John says, "I don't know."

"You don't know."

"I don't."

"You better think about it. Think real hard. Better get down for yours like I got down for mine. I'm holdin' down this whole county, boy, holdin' it down tight. I got the power to smooth you into the set, get you up on it, make you a Vig. By the time you're sixteen, you be rollin' high, makin' bank big-time."

John raises his head and looks at his mother. He's embarrassed for himself, for her.

"Look at me, boy."

John looks at him.

"Don't be no pussy. Don't be no trick. Tell me you won't."

"All right."

"Tell me. Say it. Come on, boy, let me hear it."

"I won't be a pussy."

"Say it all."

"I won't be a trick."

"You know what a trick is?"

"I guess so."

"A trick is a phony and a sissy."

John chews on his lower lip.

"No son of mine gonna sit down to piss or get on his knees for anyone."

"Enough," Nina says.

The face Aleem turns on her isn't his, but instead the face of something that lies curled eternally at the bottom of the pit of the world, waiting for its hour to devour. Such fury, such malevolence, such thirst for power, such an appetite for violence have never before so keenly whetted his stare and clarified in his features. "You want to keep your teeth, then shut your damn mouth." He means it. He will badly hurt her.

John issues a thin sound of pure torment. Although the pistol is still pointed at the floor, it swings back and forth like the pendulum in a grandfather clock, as if counting seconds toward a moment never to be forgotten or redeemed.

To the boy, Aleem says, "You my own blood. I can't but love my own blood. You know how much I love you?"

John continues to make that grievous noise.

"I love you so much, I won't never let no Christer or no Oprah wannabe take the starch outta you, turn you into a pussy lawn boy or head-duckin' wage slave. I'll kill you 'fore I see you brought down from a full man to some pathetic crawlin' thing that shames me 'fore the world. Thirteen is old enough to make your name, be where it's at, makin' the rules 'stead of livin' by the man's rules, do a bitch whenever you want one. I'm gettin' a sweet place ready for you. I'm settin' it up nice and tight. So you better get yourself ready."

John says nothing.

"You get yourself ready, boy. You hear me?"

"Yes."

"You hear me?"

"Yeah. It's good."

"What is?"

"Getting out of this place."

"It's a shithole, ain't it?"

"Boring," says John. "Nothing exciting ever happens here."

"And nothin' never will," Aleem assures him. "Not here."

"I heard about you."

"That's all bullshit."

"I don't mean what she said. What I mean is, I heard about you on the street. You are somebody."

"More than just somebody, son. You'll see. Time comes, you'll be somebody. You won't be John Dozier no more. John Sutter. If you want, we'll spin up a new first name, somethin' true street, a name everyone'll know and someday bow to."

John turns a defiant look on his mother. She's afraid that he's going to overplay it. She prays that he won't say anything further, not another word. Sensing deception, his father could decide to take him now.

Triumphant, Aleem turns to Nina, regarding her with the icy contempt he has for all women. "You known this day was comin'. He was only ever yours till he was old enough to be mine."

Her response is little more than a fierce whisper. "I hate you."

"That's good. Hate gives you somethin' to hold on to, keeps you from fallin' apart. Never was true love makes the world go round. Hate makes the world go round. Just remember which of us, you or me, is the better hater. Now I know the boy's mind, I'll pave his way into the set, get my crew used to the idea, be ready for him in a few days. Don't even think you can take him and run. There's nowhere I can't find you. No law's gonna help you. It's the law lets me be what I am. There's no real law no more. And after you been found, what'll you do with your life? Won't be no one wants to hire themselves a blind accountant."

"He wouldn't go with me, anyway," she lies. "There's too much of you in him. I've spent thirteen years trying to counsel it out of him, but it's in his blood."

Aleem leaves as he came, by the front door. He uses his key and then rattles the doorknob to be sure the deadbolt is engaged, making the point that he has locked them up in every sense of the word.

CONVENIENT RUINS

Alone in an agency sedan, Durand Calaphas maneuvers through flooded intersections, around tree branches broken off as if by the hand of some enraged giant and cast down on the pavement, contesting with incompetent motorists who are unaccustomed to driving in heavy wind-harried rain or who are compromised by whatever drugs have clouded their minds. He passes through suburbs with romantic names that once fired the American imagination with images of lush palm trees and sunshine and girls like those tanned beauties in the songs sung by the Beach Boys. All changed. Even the heaviest rains can't wash away the shabbiness. Past boarded-up shops. Past a metastasized encampment of addicts who have cast themselves out of civilization and onto its crumbling ramparts.

Four miles short of his destination, he slows almost to a stop, intrigued by a long-haired and bearded derelict costumed in clothes as ragged and filthy as the tattered ravelings of an ancient mummy's cerements. The man lies on his back, on the sidewalk, unaware of the storm or embracing it as his preferred way to bathe—or dead.

It is the last of these possibilities that induces Calaphas to pull to a stop at the curb for a closer look. These days, people who once died discreetly are found in parks and other public places, having succumbed to overdoses or violence. His father, Ivor, is a mortician who owns three successful funeral homes, above the largest of which the old man still lives with Durand's mother. During his childhood and adolescence, Durand had much experience of cadavers, whom Ivor referred to as "our quiet and respected guests." Durand has been fascinated—if not obsessed—with the dead since he was at least seven years old, when at a quarter to midnight on Halloween, alone with a corpse in the cold-holding chamber adjacent to the embalming room in the basement of the funeral home, an eighty-five-year-old man, felled earlier that evening by a stroke, spoke to him.

The vagrant on the sidewalk abruptly sits up and surveys the rain-swept day with bewilderment, as if his most recent memory is of going to bed in a suite at a four-star hotel. Calaphas at once loses interest in the man and pulls away into traffic.

The late—and apparently resurrected—Michael Mace lives in a town less corrupted than others in the orbit of the city. It's one of those places referred to as a "bedroom community," a term meant to define it as a bland, soulless snoozerville by those who think all action, spirit, and wisdom concentrates only in big cities. In fact, it is attractive, reasonably well preserved, with tree-lined streets, and it seems to be governed by those with the courage to defend their way of life against those who insist on change for the sake of change.

The sedan's navigation system brings Calaphas to an address in mid block, where it looks as if a cognizant tornado with specific intentions touched down to catastrophic effect. However handsome Mace's residence might have been, it's now a waste mound of rubbled masonry and collapsed blackened structure, the contents reduced to wrack and ashes.

Calaphas gets out of the car, locks it, pulls up the hood of his raincoat, and follows the front walkway, shattered window glass crunching underfoot. The fire must have been intense. Everything burnable has been reduced to dross that the rain compounded into a carbonaceous mud. Metal pipes had half melted into bearded serpents and other fantastical forms.

In spite of the ferocity of the blaze, the neighboring homes stand untouched. Although the lots are wide in this suburb, the failure of the fire to have any smallest effect beyond the property lines is curious.

Treading cautiously, Calaphas circles the ruins, studying the scene from multiple angles. Outdoor furniture is tumbled across the back flagstone patio—six chairs, two sun loungers, small tables—the metal frames intact, the scattered cushions badly scorched and soot stained. The swimming pool is a swamp. After he has come 360 degrees to the front walkway, he is convinced that, even with a skilled team of forensic excavators, he won't find what he most wanted when he came here, which is a photograph of Michael Mace.

LEANING TOGETHER,
HEADPIECES FILLED WITH STRAW

Because maybe Nina knows he drives a black Cadillac Escalade, Aleem is traveling in a white Lexus SUV driven by his homey, Kuba Franklin. Earlier, Kuba parked two blocks from Nina's shit-can house, and Aleem walked to her place.

Now that Aleem is back in the Lexus, riding shotgun, Kuba takes them into Nina's block and parks across the street, at a distance but within sight of the house, so they have a clear line on whatever might go down. He lets the engine run to keep the heater on, but he switches off the windshield wipers, so as not to be too obvious.

"You drippin' all over my upholstery," Kuba says.

"Fuckin' weather app said won't be no rain till four o'clock. I ruin this jacket, I oughta sue their ass."

"What makes *me* wanna jack up somebody is my health app."

"You got a health app?"

"Too much data, man. Too much naggin'. Says eat this, next thing says iffen you eat it, you get cancer."

"You got a health app?"

"Sends me an alert, says it can track my menstrual cycle, predict when's my next period. They think I'm goin' trans or what?"

"You confuse 'em, spellin' Cuba with a *K*, like a girl might. What's the point, gangbangers like us havin' a health app?"

"Come sixty-five, I want my brain and balls workin' good."

"Sixty-five?"

"I wanna enjoy retirement."

"How old are you, homey? Twenty-eight, twenty-nine?"

"Twenty-seven."

"Only way you get as far as fifty is Jesus pullin' a miracle for you."

"I believe in positive thinkin'."

"You do, huh?"

"I do."

"So a carload of Crips or Bloods, gunned up for a ride, pulls up next to us, outta nowhere."

"This is too deep into Vig ground."

"Nowhere's too deep. They got themselves a full-auto breakdown loaded with slugs in a big-dick magazine."

"You gotta worst case it to make your point."

"They hose us through your window. How does positive thinkin' make a difference?"

"It's better than negative thinkin'."

"It is, huh?"

"Damn right."

"How's it better?"

"You worry about a thing, you're callin' it to you."

"That your philosophy?"

"A piece of it, yeah."

"So now I'm gonna worry about a good-lookin' bitch knockin' on this window to give me the sweetest piece of head I ever got. Hope this don't take too long 'fore it happens."

Kuba laughs.

Aleem says, "You see the error of your philosophy."

"No way. I'm laughin' in spite of myself. It don't mean you're Socrates."

"Don't matter how long you live, homey. Matters that you get what you want when you want it. Matters that you jack them up 'stead of they jack you up. Matters that no one never wants to die enough to disrespect you."

They sit for a moment without speaking, cocooned in the roar of the downpour, which to Aleem is the sound and the promise of power, matching the quieter but persistent roar within him, the power within him to enforce his will with violence and be known as a war god of the streets.

Kuba says, "What Miss Nina do when you told her how it's gonna be?"

"What's she gonna do 'sides what she did? She hangs her head, says 'yes, sir.' She knows better than back talkin' me."

"But you don't trust her."

"Ever known a piece of tail you could trust?"

"Not even my mother."

"There you go."

"How long we in this?"

"If I spooked her bad, she'll split after dark. If not, she'll hang here a day, maybe two, get her business done."

"You sure she put the house for sale?"

"Clarise, the ugly bitch sells dirt in this hood, she knew she didn't tell me, her little shop better have fire insurance."

"Maybe we just snatch the kid now."

"And the brother who needs more convincin'? What about him?"

"We just do it, then Antoine he'll come along."

"Or won't. Not a chance worth riskin'. Antoine got ambition."

"Who don't?" Kuba says.

"Antoine got it big-time. For now."

"For now?"

"Not so much come day after tomorrow."

Kuba thinks about that. "Antoine gonna be enlightened?"

"A sudden education."

Kuba spends time thinking about it and then says, "Somebody might have a chance to move up come day after tomorrow."

"You got somebody in mind?"

"I might."

Aleem smiles. "You ready to make a recommendation, I'll value it highly. Most highly."

The afternoon slowly darkles, and rain falls in such volume as to float an ark large enough to spare all the species of the world from extinction.

A VIRTUAL JOURNEY

Aware that the GPS in the post-office vehicle indicates that it is in front of the house, Michael puts aside his wineglass and takes the elevator up one floor and crosses the foyer, where the etched-steel forest is forever without weather, where the still and silent deer gaze perpetually in witness of those who come and go. He steps outside into the rain just as the mail truck pulls away from the curb. He takes nine envelopes from the box beside the front door, returns to the house, leaves six envelopes on the foyer floor, and descends to the library with three pieces of mail, all from the Department of Motor Vehicles. The licenses, each with his photo but featuring a different name, should get him through the coming year.

However, he'll soon be the most wanted fugitive in history. As those hunting for him become more aware of his capabilities, they'll adopt strategies and tactics that force him to change identities as frequently as a chameleon changes colors as it scurries across the vibrant palette of a tropical forest.

Having drunk two generous servings of cabernet, he concludes that changes to his metabolic process have rendered him immune to the inebriating effect of alcohol—which is a disappointment—though he does feel somewhat relaxed. With a wine as good as Caymus, he's happy to drink it for the flavor alone, and he pours a third glass.

In the armchair, Michael stares at the Pacific, where earlier Catalina had loomed in the distance and container ships had wallowed at anchor in the long lineup for the port of Long Beach. At the moment, all is formless—rushing rain, billowing mist, the ocean a gray amorphia of swells and swales and flung spume.

He is at all times linked to the internet by electromagnetic waves produced and managed by his own strangely altered physiology. Without need of a computer, he can for the most part reach into any website or digitized archives with which he is familiar, pore through its content, and access whatever information he needs in seconds, while remaining entirely aware of—and active in—the real world. In addition, if he plants a data trigger in a system, he'll be instantly notified when the event that he has anticipated in fact occurs; the alert will come in the form of a brief text message he created with the trigger, appearing as neon-blue letters in his mind's eye, as though he's a clairvoyant receiving a vision.

Sometimes, when he is seeking to assemble and understand a complex chain of information, or when he knows what to seek but not quite where to seek it, he must enter the funhouse maze that mirrors this world in infinite fractal passageways, which is the internet and all linked computer systems, *plunge* into it rather than merely *reach* into it. In such a case, for the duration of his explorations, he loses all conscious awareness of the real place in which he exists.

He closes his eyes and prepares to enter the wonders of that alternate world built of ones and zeros, which can seem as fluid and chaotic as any moment of any storm. He has learned that negotiating its megacomplexity of channels is easier if he visualizes himself proceeding in a form of transport—such as a car quickening through a multilayered labyrinth of highways or a sleek cigarette boat speeding through a planet of endless Venetian canals. This time, he imagines himself behind the wheel of a self-driving Tesla, speeding toward the destination that he speaks aloud to its AI driver. His body remains relaxed in the armchair as the Tesla rockets him from the real to the virtual. Although he knows that his body reposes in the library, he can no longer see the room; he can neither hear nor see the storm-tossed ocean beyond the windows.

Because total immersion in an abstract world of coded data ferried on electromagnetic waves would confound the senses and be so disorienting that rampant panic might rapidly spiral into madness, the archaea-nano hybrid particles that have invaded Michael's brain provide him with the ability to instantaneously translate that data into images that match the form of transportation that he has imagined. In this case, it's a driverless Tesla on a highway system as fantastical as one that might be created if Christopher Nolan and George Lucas had collaborated on a science-fiction film based on an idea by Jorge Luis Borges. As he perceives them, the lanes are a wild ravelment snaking through a vast darkness, lighted by off-ramp signs glowing an eerie green. He flashes through underpasses, races upside down through barrel loops, takes corkscrew feeder lanes that drop him vertically through uncounted horizontal layers of freeways, and descends an exit ramp under the sign BEAUTIFICATION RESEARCH. Without any consequence of impact, he passes through a wall of the virtual version of the building in which he died, and he comes to a stop.

The information that he's taken this mental voyage to discover appears herewith on the windshield of the Tesla, as if displayed on a computer screen. From the archived video provided by a multitude of high-definition security cameras, he reviews the activities of investigators who entered the facility after its decontamination. Some wear black jackets emblazoned with bold, white letters— ISA. Of the multitude of ISA agents swarming the building, one seems to be an outlier, never associating more than briefly with the others as he tours the premises. He spends time alone in Shelby

Shrewsberry's office and then proceeds to camp out in the office of Dr. Simon Bistoury. His head is shaved, his features bold, his profile like that on an ancient Roman coin.

From within the imaginary Tesla, through the medium of his avatar, Michael now watches archived video of Bistoury's office in which the ISA agent watches *earlier* archived video of the cafeteria that had been converted into a temporary morgue. He rewinds and watches the video of the agent as the agent repeatedly rewinds and watches a sequence in the morgue. Resurrected Michael sees the agent discover the moment when the sheet over dead Michael rises and then slides to the floor.

◆ ◆ ◆

Michael had awakened from death an hour before he rose from the posture of a corpse. For a few minutes, aware that he was himself but also more than he had been before, he lay there processing the impossible. He dared not move until he understood his condition. Initially, his heart had not been beating; neither had he been breathing. As he listened to the mortal stillness of his body, a double fear came over him—horror that darkness would take him again and forever, as well as dread of the future that might lie ahead of him and beyond all human knowing. If total terror had seized him, he would have thrust up from his makeshift catafalque at once. However, he knew much about the work being done at Beautification Research and understood that, even as dangerous as it was, good might come from it as easily as evil. He realized that the marriage of living archaea and nanobotics had succeeded in some way that neither the scientists on the bio team nor those on the tech team anticipated. The stasis from which his mind had first ascended now relinquished its hold on his body; three minutes after regaining consciousness, he had felt his heart resume beating, and he had breathed.

For fifty-seven minutes more, he'd remained motionless, in a wonder of self-discovery, reaching out into the world beyond this world, the coded world that is born of this world but is not patent or tangible, the world of the internet and the cloud and all that is virtual, a shadow of reality and yet with the power to shape the truth of which it is only a dark reflection. Soon he realized that he was no longer merely a user of the internet and all sites and systems linked by it, but also that he could be of it, not just as a fish is of the medium in which it swims, but rather as water itself is of the river. He had no need of a computer to plunge into the currents of data. In that chilly morgue, lying under a sheet, he had reviewed the security video and other archives of the facility to learn how the staff of Beautification Research became infected and to witness how rapidly they perished. He saw himself fall dead. He suspected he might be unique, the only one among the deceased to pull a Lazarus. If that proved to be the case, the government and the technology companies partnered in this enterprise would consider him to be a miraculously transformed lab rat that must be studied further, as a possible whistleblower who could expose them to public outrage and congressional investigation, as a likely litigant who might drain their bank accounts, and as a threat to their power by virtue of his own. One thing they would not consider him: a human being like them, with inalienable God-given rights and a heritage of freedom.

As he had at last risen from the cafeteria table and the sheet had slid off him, he had reached into the video stream flowing from the camera and replaced the pixels that composed his image. Second by second, as he made his way out of the room and then the building, he erased the visual record of his escape. He'd known that eventually they would discover that *he had gone missing. He only hoped to gain time to better understand the power that had been given to him and how best to use it.*

He could have bought more time by erasing all video from all cameras; in the first few hours following his resurrection, he had not always been thinking clearly. Nevertheless, he perceived value in letting them gradually discover what he had become. With time to consider his astonishing capabilities, they would grow increasingly fearful and separate into factions, each with a different view of how to find and capture him. A fugitive is safest when the posse that's after him is frightened and filled with division.

◆ ◆ ◆

Now, in Michael's strange new life, his avatar sits in the front seat of the metaverse Tesla, where archived video from earlier this very day plays on the windshield, showing the nameless agent repeatedly viewing morgue video recorded four days ago.

Michael gives voice to a new destination, the computer system of the Internal Security Agency, and in an instant he is rocketing through the fantastical maze of highways, as if he is a boy at play in a life-size slot-car setup of infinite complexity. In seconds, the imaginary Tesla penetrates the highly guarded ISA data center that, in the real world, is located in Utah. In those archives, Michael seeks and quickly finds the order dispatching a team of agents to Beautification Research after the catastrophe that occurred there. One by one, he flips through the agents' files, each of which includes a photo as well as a name, until he finds the man with proud Roman features, who is as noble-looking as Julius Caesar but whose eyes suggest a Nero who sets fires for pleasure and delights in the suffering of others. Durand Calaphas.

FIRE MARSHAL

Durand Calaphas is indifferent to most people. Their lives hold no interest for him. In his estimation, their beliefs are generally foolish, and their passions are tedious. They have no destiny except to work, pay taxes, consume, and die—all while, preferably, making little trouble. In a world shaped to a more intelligent plan, there would be fewer of their kind, which is a basic doctrine of the New Truth. He calls them "Extras" because they are to him like the actor wannabes who people the crowd scenes of movies, given no dialogue and lacking the talent to be granted any.

Calaphas does his part to correct the problem of that excess population. The only people he has more than a passing interest in are those whom he is authorized to liquidate. Unlike the Extras, people who earn termination are figures of at least some substance, if only because they have done something to earn a death sentence and therefore make themselves part of Calaphas's destiny, which is one of greatness.

Occasionally, he encounters someone who isn't on his kill list but to whom he is not indifferent, to whom he takes an immediate and intense dislike. Nolan Freeman, the fire marshal for this county, is one of those.

The first thing Calaphas sees when he enters Freeman's office, on the top floor of a three-story firehouse, is a memorial wall of firefighters who died on duty in this jurisdiction. Each is pictured on a small plaque that is fixed to a larger display with room for additions; under the photo is his or her name, length of service, and date of death. At the top of this honor roll, in the center of its width, the phrase AMERICAN HEROES is written in fancy script. Surmounting it all is a flag fixed flat to the wall. Calaphas hates the idea of heroes, which he believes is merely a tool with which the gullible are manipulated into doing all the dirty, dangerous work of society for meager wages, forfeiting their meaningless lives in a lost cause. He despises the flag and America, which will soon be washed away by the New Truth. He interprets the memorial wall as the work of either a fool who believes in duty, sacrifice, justice, freedom, and the sacred value of life, or a phony whose every word and action is calculated to burnish his image in the eyes of his superiors.

Given the uncompromising principles by which Calaphas lives, he finds it difficult to smile at Nolan Freeman and shake his hand. He would prefer to kill the sonofabitch and cut off his genitals and nail them to the memorial wall. However, he's seeking information related to Michael Mace that might prove essential to understanding that fugitive and finding him; he must play the role of a dedicated public servant who believes in all the delusions that men like the fire marshal cherish or purport to cherish.

Behind his desk, Freeman sits at attention, spine straight and shoulders back and chin raised, as if perpetually proud of having risen from the firehouse ranks to his current title—or as if he has hemorrhoids. "The case screams arson, yet I can't prove it. There was something very strange about that house fire. It might help me to better analyze the evidence if I knew more about Michael Mace—why he is, as you say, on the run and wanted."

In the visitor's chair, Calaphas amuses himself by mimicking Freeman's posture, as a subtle way of disrespecting the man while presenting himself as an earnest fellow member of the establishment.

"I'd like nothing better than to assist you, Marshal Freeman, but I can only say that Mace is a terrorist wanted in the deaths of more than fifty patriotic Americans. Everything else is classified, a matter of national security."

When Calaphas mentions fifty victims, the fleshy features of the marshal's broad, dark face tighten in indignation. No doubt he sees himself as one whose anger is always righteous, the impersonal and unselfish displeasure at unworthy acts, which never needs to be regretted and for which no repentance is required. Gifford, Durand's late brother, had been likewise certain that he lacked the capacity for resentment and vindictiveness.

"The fuel load of that house," Freeman says, "should have made for a slower-spreading fire than what happened."

"Fuel load?"

"That's the weight of all burnable matter in the structure plus burnable contents, multiplied by the BTUs that each type of material can produce. A pound of wood, depending on the species of the tree it's from, gives you eight thousand to nine thousand BTUs per pound, oily pine more than oak. Plastic puts out twice as much as wood. Then there's the heat-release rate, how fast a particular material burns, measured in BTUs per second. The faster and hotter the fuel burns, the quicker a fire spreads. This one didn't have a phase in which it smoldered. It stormed through that house from ignition—the free-burning phase—to the flashover phase in record time."

"Gasoline, kerosene?" Calaphas asks.

"We couldn't find a trace of any liquid accelerant. The burn was nearly as complete as it gets, but even so there would still be evidence of an accelerant if one was used. There's always evidence. One of the strange things here was the extreme conductivity."

"Conductivity?"

"Conductivity. When they burn, some things retain a lot of their heat, while other substances spread the heat fast to nearby materials. Paper, most of your fabrics, carpets, mattress stuffing—they're highly conductive. Air itself is highly conductive. Most fires spread by convection, superheated air circulating through the structure."

This is more detail than Calaphas thinks he needs. Freeman is showing off, relishing this opportunity to prove that someone like him can rise from nothing to this expertise. Nevertheless, Calaphas leans forward as if fascinated. "Air? But air doesn't burn."

"Ohhhh, but it does, Agent Calaphas. You must understand, air is rich with oxygen. All flame is burning gases. When any material combusts, it oxidizes, producing flammable gas. The more air that is circulating in a house, the faster the place burns. Fire *seeks* air. That's why flames burn upward."

Freeman is smug about his superior education, as though the nature of fire is by far the most important knowledge in the world. Calaphas is in particular offended by the word *"ohhhh,"* which seems to have been drawn out and delivered with a note of mockery, and by the words *"you must understand,"* which he suspects carry the same meaning as if Freeman had said *you ignorant fool.* His antipathy toward the marshal has become so intense that he will kill the bastard just as a matter of principle, not here and now, but in a week or a month, when the Michael Mace matter has been resolved and there is time to plan and execute a richly satisfying end to the wizard of fire.

"In this blaze," Freeman continues, "the house was actively ventilated immediately prior to ignition."

It galls Calaphas that the marshal pauses to wait for his student to request further enlightenment. Repressing his hostility, he says, "I'm sorry. What is 'actively ventilated'?"

"The Mace house had four exterior doors. Three on the ground floor—one at the front, one at the rear, and another on the east side. The fourth was in the master bedroom and opened to a balcony above the back patio. Immediately prior to ignition, those four doors were unlocked and thrown open simultaneously."

"How can you know simultaneously?"

The marshal adopts a sage expression and nods as if accepting praise for the thoroughness of his investigation. "According to the background we've been able to put together, Mr. Mace is a longtime security expert. His house featured electronic locks that could be monitored from his smartphone, engaged and disengaged as he wished. According to his housekeeper, he preferred not to entrust anyone with a key, though she had her own code to open the front door. The security company he founded nineteen years ago, which he sold but in which he still holds an interest, monitored and archived all system activity at that house. Their records show the doors were opened remotely and simultaneously one minute before fire broke out."

"You said the doors were 'thrown open.'"

"They were burglarproof, with concealed pneumatic hinges that allowed them to be operated remotely, closed against an intruder or opened to police if someone somehow gained entrance and barricaded himself in there."

"'Remotely.' So Mace wasn't in the house for any of this."

"Evidently not."

"Then how did the fire start? Who started it?"

"Evidence indicates three primary ignition points. Fireplaces. One in the master bedroom upstairs. Two downstairs, living room and family room. All featured ceramic logs, natural gas, and electronic starters. The valve regulating the flow of gas to the house failed to restrict the pressure to a safe level, and once the fireplaces ignited, the flow appears to have increased in a measured but rapid manner until flames would have been *gushing* out of those three fireboxes, across the floors and up the walls."

"How could the valve fail?"

Freeman raises his eyebrows. "When you arrest Mr. Mace, we'd like to have a chance to ask him that and a few other questions."

"The house—wasn't it large enough to require fire sprinklers?"

"Yes, but the sprinkler system didn't function. We believe the standpipe responded to a maintenance command and drained itself—and all the smaller pipes—of water."

"Shortly before the fire?"

"Nothing I can prove in court."

Calaphas becomes aware of the roaring of the rain on the roof, a sound that for a time entirely faded from his awareness. He looks toward a window, beyond which the world appears to be deliquescing, as if he might walk outside into the melt of this civilization—or simulation—into a gray nullity that provides no material with which to craft the simplest item. In childhood, until he was fifteen, he had experienced nights when, unable to sleep, he was overcome by the perception that the darkness beyond the windows was a void, that he was—and always had been—the only real person in the drama of his life, that all the rest of it had been a product of his imagination, which now began to fail him. On those occasions, perception at times hardened into conviction, and he lay trapped in a paralytic panic, until exhaustion overcame him and the deeper darkness outside flooded into the dark bedroom and poured into his eyes and spiraled him into the refuge of blind, dreamless sleep. However, the belief that you're the only real person on Earth is a condition called solipsism, and he has come to understand that his situation is not so bleak as that. His situation is more amazing than that, and his destiny is magnificent.

"Are you all right?" Freeman asks.

Calaphas turns his attention from the rainy day. "Excuse me?"

Freeman looks at the window and then at Calaphas again. "You've gone as pale as a ghost."

After taking a moment to collect himself, Calaphas says, "It almost seems as if Michael Mace performed a remote-control high-tech torching of his own home."

"Yes, doesn't it? But why? Given his background as a security expert, he would know that he'd come under suspicion. Considering the circumstances, whatever insurance company issued a policy on that house would take extreme measures to avoid paying up."

"He's on the run from the law," Calaphas says. "There's no way he could collect the insurance anyway. Mace started the fire to destroy evidence."

"If that was his intention," Freeman says, "he did a damn fine job of it."

With window shades closed and lamplight low and rain rumbling, the small house feels like a claustrophobic bombproof warren beneath a city under attack. Nina and John hurry on their appointed tasks with heads thrust forward and shoulders bent as though worried that the ceiling might collapse on them.

She can imagine only one reason why Aleem didn't take the boy with him. To commit a kidnapping, even of his own son, he needs the approval of someone above him or equal to him on the ladder of gang authority. He could receive that dispensation tonight. Chafing at any restraint, which is his nature, he might decide to snatch the boy without gaining consent.

The law offers Nina no assistance. The police are underfunded and demoralized. Key figures in the government are patrons of the gangs and get their cut of the drug trade.

Her pistol was once her father's. It came with a belt holster. Her dad had no concealed-carry permit, but sometimes he carried the gun anyway. Because criminals respect no legitimate authority, the law often restricts only the law-abiding, who are expected to go defenseless in the name of social order. She fits the holster on her belt and slips the pistol into it.

When the luggage is loaded into her well-used Ford Explorer, after she and John put on rain jackets, she takes the duffel bag from the pantry and puts it on the kitchen table. She withdraws four packets of hundred-dollar bills, forty thousand dollars, and pushes two of them toward John.

"Twenty thousand each. It's our desperation money in case something happens to the duffel bag or it gets taken away from us."

"Forty thousand."

"My son the math whiz."

"That's a lot."

"Not when we have to build a whole new life."

He pulls a single hundred out of one packet and examines it with something like wonder. "It's real."

"I gave up counterfeiting."

"How much is in the bag?" he asks.

"Another three hundred sixty thousand."

"You serious?"

"When am I not?"

"Where'd you get it?"

"I've been saving pocket change."

"From how many people's pockets?"

"It was a gift," she says.

"Who gives anyone four hundred thousand?"

"You better thank God somebody did. Your jacket has zippered pockets. Tuck those two bundles away, keep them dry."

He puts the loose bill in an exterior pocket. "It's like a lucky penny. A lucky penny except ten thousand times over." He slips the bundled bills into inner pockets. "It was that Michael guy."

"Well, Aleem didn't suddenly get a conscience."

"Why's that guy giving you so much?"

Pocketing her two wads of cash, she says, "You remember Shelby Shrewsberry?"

"The really big guy, your client."

"Michael's doing this for him."

"What's Shrewsberry got to do with it?"

"Michael can explain it better than I can."

"When?"

"When the time comes. Carry the bag for me."

John picks up the duffel and follows her into the garage. "Is Michael rich?"

"He's better than rich. He's a miracle. Put the bag in front of your seat, prop your feet on it. We need to keep it where we can get at it quick."

In the Explorer, as Nina puts up the garage door with a remote, the boy says, "We left lights on in the house. I'll go back."

Although Nina is always penny-wise, she says, "Stay put. We're out of here. Lights look better if Aleem's homeys cruise by."

She drives out of the garage and puts the door down and turns left into the street. In a get-down gangsta mood, the wind brags loudly, shatters rain against the windshield, tumbles an empty trash can along the street. Filthy water rolls along gutters and shears up from the tires as the Explorer cuts across a flooded intersection.

John says, "He's white."

"Who is?"

"This Michael guy."

"You have a problem with white?"

"No."

"You better not. We don't do color."

"I know we don't."

"You better know."

"I'm just wondering."

"Tell me."

"Well, you know."

"Yeah, honey, I know."

"I need to say it?"

"Say it to own it."

"Are you and him . . . ?"

"No. He's cute. He's smart. Maybe it could be, him and me, once I had enough time to study him. But that isn't what this is."

"I'm just trying to understand."

"Me too. It's crazy but it's real. Until he has a chance to explain it to you, just think of him as maybe like Moses."

"Moses Gompers across the street?"

"No. Not Moses the pothead. Moses. It's like Michael has seen the bush that burns without burning. He's come down from the mountain with a power in him and a way to set a wrong world right."

"You're kind of scaring me," John says.

"Well, I'm kind of scared myself."

"You don't scare. You've never been before."

"Not that you knew."

Heading south for the freeway, she turns right. A white SUV had appeared behind her seconds after she'd driven out of the garage. It remains on her tail. Maybe it's a problem. Maybe not.

"Honey, get my phone out of my purse and switch it on. Be ready to make a call when I tell you."

"Who're we going to call?"

"Michael. He's the closest we have to Ghostbusters."

FOR THE RECORD

Now that I can see the vague shape of the future, which is more than most people ever see, and now that I know the man who means to track me down and kill me, I've come to the conclusion that I must spend my idle moments recording some essentials and archiving them in the cloud, in a place that only others like me could discover— should there ever be any others like me. Perhaps they might learn from my mistakes if I get myself murdered.

Absolute knowledge is absolute power. Following my infection, apparent death, and resurrection, everything that can be known is mine to discover with little effort. Data flows into me in megabytes per minute, is absorbed, is understood. They say that absolute power corrupts absolutely. I don't consider myself incorruptible, but I believe that I have been somewhat inoculated against the desire for power and the inclination to abuse it, inoculated by virtue of the narrow and always crumbling path I had to follow along the cliff of child-hood, which is a story for a later recording. I do not desire power; events have conferred it on me. I believe that by the way I intend to use this power, I'll bring about a better world; however, I'm aware that I, like any human being, am capable of wandering into delusions and, in the name of justice or equity or myriad other noble purposes, become a monster who leads multitudes into a slough of misery. I can only hope that being aware of that risk will help me avert it.

Generously fund a hundred psychologists to study Agent Durand Calaphas, and they will provide a hundred shelf-feet of reports that explain him as a product of his parents' faults and inadequacies, or as an innocent soul driven to crime and violence by the injustices of an iniquitous society, or as the spawn of historical forces as vaguely defined as they are impossible to address in retrospect. The Internal

Security Agency, the records of which I have pored through, would dismiss those hundreds of reports as claptrap and consign them to a shredder. They have identified him as a "manageable sociopath," which they consider a gift of Nature. The best science we have indicates that sociopaths are equally distributed among all races, all ethnic groups, and all economic classes, perhaps constituting as much as 10 percent of the population. Because of their ability to pass for normal, the agency considers them a priceless resource, and it is pleased to have Calaphas because his "utter lack of conscience and his pleasure in the application of extreme force" make him a valuable asset. Those who run the ISA are hard men and hard women. Ambitious and dedicated to their ideology, they believe that the means justify the ends, that evil actions sanctioned in the service of their agenda aren't only defensible but also courageous. Their top-secret case files reveal their world as a dark wonderland of self-righteous deception, cruelty, violence, and atrocities committed as casually as Onan seeded the soil of Judea.

Dr. Gifford Calaphas, older brother of Durand, was a prominent and much admired virologist whose research was in part funded by the National Institutes of Health. Judging by all evidence, I believe he was a good and honest man. He came into possession of proof that a high official of the NIH had over the years taken tens of millions in kickbacks from numerous scientists that received the institute's grants. He brought this information to the FBI, from whence it was leaked to a senator who was the brother-in-law of the NIH official and who shared the kickbacks. The senator was an ardent protector of the Internal Security Agency, assuring it ever-greater funding. When Durand Calaphas was informed that Gifford was a traitor and national security threat, only the most superficial—and faked—evidence was provided, but the assassin needed nothing more.

If I end up dead again, this time permanently, and if by then another like me somehow arises to follow in my footsteps, that other will be you who is reading this. You might understand, as I do, that evil is real and that the viciousness of your enemy has no limits, but if you have any doubt, dwell for a while on Durand Calaphas and the people who sent him after Gifford, and then absorb their other case files. You must never be like them, but you must always try to think like them to avoid underestimating the depths of wickedness to which they're capable of descending.

VOICES AS MEANINGLESS
AS WIND IN DRY GRASS

Above the storm, the sun is sliding away from this half of the planet. Here in the tempest, all the paycheck pussies are on their way to happy hour for a few glasses of whatever might smooth the wrinkles out of their minds. The freeway pilgrims who can't afford several cocktails are crawling home to their nothing houses to say a prayer before they eat the beans and rice their god provides, their workday done, and nothing for them now but to stream a movie and get ready to kiss the boss's ass again tomorrow.

For Aleem Sutter, his average workday is three hours long, at most four, thirty minutes here and fifteen there, ragging the swing men to stay true to their promises to supply the goods, making sure the mules don't forget how bad they'll be jacked up if the weight of a shipment goes down even an ounce during transport, jamming dealers to meet their quotas, keeping the homeboys motivated with snaps, lots of Benjamins. Aleem doesn't need to work a full forty because he has so many worker bees laboring for him. Right now, two blocks from his current position, four once-hot quiffs, now too old and skanked out to sell their booty even to cougar lovers, are spending eight hours capping up bulk barbiturates and parceling them into fifty-cent bags, tax-free cash work to augment the government checks they've been receiving illegally since they turned fifty.

When he isn't working, like now, Aleem is usually chilling out with his homeys or doing some tail, or what he calls "adventuring," which is looking to get into some kind of trouble just to see if he still has the brains and balls to get out of it. Right now, riding shotgun in Kuba's Lexus SUV, he's tending to some domestic business, making sure his rights as a father are respected, following Nina's Explorer, trying to decide if the treacherous bitch is just going out for a quart of milk or making a run for it.

Kuba says, "I hate this shit."

"What shit?"

"This weather."

"We got a drought."

"Not tonight we don't."

"Gotta have rain, brother."

"We already got us an ocean."

"Can't drink ocean water."

"Damn surfers pissin' in it."

"It's the salt," says Aleem.

"I put salt on everythin'."

"Drink salt water, your gut blows up."

"Blows up, huh?"

"Blows up."

"You the man, Aleem."

"Got that right."

"You the man, I respect you, but shit."

"Say what?"

"Salt don't explode."

"Eat a box of Morton's, see what happens."

"Salt ain't a brick of C-4."

"So see what happens."

"Aleem, where you get these ideas?"

"You ever gone to school, Kuba?"

"I gone seven years 'fore I offed that teacher."

"I forgot about that."

"Had to drop out, change my name, join the gang."

"Best thing you ever done."

"I'm up on it," Kuba agrees.

"You was what—thirteen?"

"Twelve. Teacher always talkin' his big ideas."

"Some of 'em they got more ideas than brains."

"He kept jammin' me about my future, had this big idea who I could be."

"Who you could be?"

"If I wasn't the me I was."

"Who'd he have in mind?"

"In mind for what?"

"Who'd he think you could be?"

"Some bow-tied pressed-pants university jerk-off never does nothin' but books."

"What kinda future is that?"

"No kind. Hey, man, your lady is makin' moves."

Aleem leans forward, squinting through the rain-smeared windshield, between the whisking wipers. "She's juicin' it."

"And she keeps changin' lanes, tuckin' herself out of sight. Maybe she's made us."

"Give her space. Let the bitch think she's done a ghost."

He looks down at his smartphone, where the tracking-app display reduces Nina, John, and the Explorer to a blinking signifier. Four days earlier, when the kid was at school and Nina was getting her hair done at a parlor two blocks from home, Aleem went to her place and used his key and planted a GPS device of his own in her Ford.

"It's killer four-five tech, not some double-deuce junk brand. Nowhere she goes we can't find her. She's pickin' up speed now."

Kuba says, "I can't see her no more."

Frowning at the display, Aleem says, "She won't be goin' to Cheesecake Factory to grab dinner. Bitch is breakin' for somewhere."

"Takin' your boy like she never needed you to make him. What's wrong with a woman like her?"

"She was a child, her folks spoiled her. She's too big on herself," Aleem diagnoses. "No gratitude."

"What happens the GPS app goes down?"

"It won't go down."

"What happens she ditches the Explorer?"

"You're supposed to be all positive thinkin'."

"I can be positive and stay real."

"She don't got enough snaps to throw around on new wheels."

"She's an accountant, man. She been makin' bank. Accountants they got suitcases full of Benjamins."

Aleem doesn't think that's true, though maybe it could be. The possibility that Nina has the money to switch vehicles is troubling. Fortunately, Aleem is forward thinking, always preparing measures that will help him cope with unexpected developments. Three of his ace kools, the best backup boys with whom he's tightest, have his tracking app on their smartphones and are able to shadow the add-on GPS in Nina's SUV. Each also has a disposable phone, as does Aleem, and now he uses his burner to call them one by one and get them on the case. Each of the three is partnered with his main man. Maybe Nina can shake off one tail, but she can't shake off four vehicles and eight homeys. However, they have to move fast, before she gets too far ahead, parks the Explorer, sets out on foot, and finds a new set of wheels.

Putting aside his burner, staring at the screen of his iPhone, Aleem says, "I shoulda known better what I was gettin' into with her. The bitch was always trouble."

Kuba nods, sucks air through his teeth, and says, "All of 'em are, sooner or later. Least she's hot."

"Even hotter back when. That's how they get you."

"Iffen they're hot," Kuba says, "it's fly fishin'. She's the hook hidden in pretty feathers, we're the fish got no chance."

"You talkin' wisdom now," Aleem says. "Fly fishin'. We got no more chance than a junkie he wants to quit but goes right on loadin' his kit with China white. I been long addicted."

Not for the first time, Kuba misunderstands. "Addicted? Shit you are. I never seen you do a line or even take a toke."

"Addicted to pussy," Aleem clarifies. "My name is Aleem, and I'm a pussyholic."

"Man loses his judgment in the presence of it," Kuba agrees.

Aleem sighs. "Loses all common sense. Iffen you don't have it, you can't sleep, can't eat, can't do business with a clear head. So you do her, she's never been so satisfied, callin' you baby, callin' you Superman. Then thirteen years later, she's dissin' you, runnin' away with your child, knockin' your whole life off the rails, playin' you for a fool."

The subject vexes Kuba. "It's a tragedy is what it is."

"It's more than a tragedy."

"A tragedy and a crime."

Aleem says, "It's all that. Worse, it's an affront."

"The front of what?"

"An affront. An insult, man. Spittin' in my face."

"A woman so much as talks smack at a man, he got to teach her regret. Spittin' in your face got to have consequences."

"Pains me how she must be breakin' my boy's spirit."

"She has her way," Kuba says, "he'll be dancin' ballet and wearin' makeup."

"That won't never happen."

"You take him from her, she won't just stop. Not her."

Aleem is silent, staring at the blinking signifier, while Kuba pilots them through the thrashing rain. After a minute or two, he says, "Okay, here's how it is. Our crew gets her blocked, the bitch got nowhere she can go. Hakeem and Carlisle they take the boy to my crib, settle him down. Other four homeys get back to their business. You and me, we make damn sure Nina can't get her hook in no one never again."

"What's Antoine gonna say?"

"Antoine he ain't relevant no more. We don't tell Antoine. I keep the boy out of sight. Day after tomorrow, it won't matter what Antoine wants. He won't be givin' orders to no one, nowhere, about nothin' no more."

Kuba likes the plan so much, he's nodding like a bobblehead doll. When he stops nodding, he says, "How you see it goin' down with Nina?"

"How *you* see it?" Aleem asks.

"I don't mean no affront."

"You my brother, Kuba. Talk free."

"I mean, she was your woman."

"She's nothin' to me now. 'Cept a pain in the ass."

"I'm thinkin' it's a wasted opportunity iffen it's a quick trey eight in the head."

"What opportunity?"

"She weren't your woman once, I woulda been on her long ago."

"You want to tear off a piece 'fore we pop her?"

"Sure would be somethin' to remember in my old age."

Aleem is aware of Kuba's preference for heavy action. Whenever some fresh who's being pimped gets out of line to an extent that she can't be rehabilitated for the market, Kuba sets aside a full day to break her down so much that nobody wants to look at her again, let alone touch her. Aleem has never been present for one of those sessions, but he's seen the aftermath. He is intrigued. Nina has been such a threat to his reputation and so smug in her churchified ways that she deserves whatever she gets.

"I wouldn't mind storin' up a memory myself," Aleem says.

Kuba has such a sweet smile that few people could ever imagine what lies behind it.

"Let's catch up with her again," Aleem says.

Kuba accelerates into the wind, the rain, the night, and the promise of a passion for which there is no Valentine's Day card.

IN THE TWILIGHT KINGDOM

At a corner table with a panoramic view of the elegant room, Durand Calaphas orders a four-hundred-dollar bottle of wine, which he might or might not finish. He is in no hurry. Later, he will have the filet mignon, which lists on the menu for seventy-six dollars, side dishes additional, and will probably cost eighty-two in another month. His job comes with such a generous expense account that no purchase of his has ever been questioned, and his credit card, issued by the agency, has no charge limit as far as he is aware. This is the bold new age of Modern Monetary Theory, which holds that excess has no consequence because the government can tax the economy into prosperity and the treasury is bottomless, or something like that.

The restaurant is around the corner from the street of streets, in this neighborhood where millionaires and billionaires have for decades come to shop for outrageously priced merchandise, which is where they will continue shopping as long as there is both vanity and social order. The former is never in danger of being exhausted, but the latter seems less certain in a country where many of those in the higher echelons of power seem to yearn for anarchy in the style of Batman's nemesis, the Joker, for anarchy and the brute authoritarianism that will follow. Calaphas heartily approves of this managed descent from democracy to anarchy to soft tyranny.

The tablecloths are of fine cotton so meticulously processed and tailored that they drape like heavy silk, with the soft curves that remind him of thick, powdery snow that has sifted down in the utter absence of wind. The lighting is soft, the shadows sculpted and strategic, the candle glow glittering off polished glassware, stainless-steel flatware, architectural elements leafed in white gold, and the jewelry of dazzling women who believe that ostentation is a virtue.

Calaphas is savoring his first glass of wine and contemplating the appetizers listed on the menu when Julian Grantworth appears and takes a chair at the table, uninvited. Julian is the deputy director of the ISA, currently on this coast because of the catastrophe at Beautification Research. Fortysomething, tall, as lean as a greyhound, with blue eyes and a social-register nose and otherwise the pinched features of one who suffers from chronic constipation, he's a fortunate son of the Philadelphia Main Line, the product of prep schools and Princeton. If he doesn't travel to London twice a year and spend two days with a team of tailors on Savile Row, then those tailors come to him each spring and autumn.

Although Julian is Calaphas's superior, he's always deferential because he's afraid of his underling. "I'm sorry to interrupt you at your dinner, Durand, but I'm afraid there's been a wrinkle in the case."

"Wrinkle," Calaphas says, doing his best to pronounce the word in a way that expresses subtle amusement and subtler contempt that will keep Grantworth off balance. The power of Calaphas, a one-man department within the ISA, is a result of his willingness to perform the dirtiest of dirty work while making no effort to protect himself from the legal consequences of his actions. He knows they monitor his phone and internet activities, assess everything he does, to determine if he's salting away evidence that might implicate them, which he is not. None of the others in the ISA would risk their freedom and privileges with such nonchalance. Some call him—as Julian Grantworth has done, but never to his face—a *monstre sans souci*, a monster without cares. Calaphas is not only invaluable to the agency, but he has also acquired the status of a foundational myth, as if he were fundamental to the founding of the ISA and will always be the soul of that lethal machine. Lesser men regard him with something like superstitious awe, which is some insurance against anyone attempting to displace him. "What's the wrinkle?"

At the moment, the nearer tables are not occupied. Grantworth waves off the approaching waiter and speaks quietly. "There was this incident at three thirty this morning." He consults his wristwatch, probably for no purpose other than to be sure that Calaphas sees it's a vintage Rolex Daytona worth maybe two hundred thousand. "Fourteen and a half hours ago. Just a couple blocks from here."

"What incident?"

"One of our friends outside the agency, a man who believes in the New Truth and has connections of enormous value to us, was robbed of half a million in cash."

"What—he uses a wheelbarrow for a wallet?"

"He's an attorney, but he's more than that."

"Cocaine or fentanyl?"

"Let's just say he represents various Central American and Chinese interests."

"Let's just say."

"He's in his office with two associates—"

"At three thirty in the morning."

"He's an overachiever. The building is a fortress—electronic locks, concealed doors with steel cores, high-end security system, a secret apartment. The thief waltzes through all that."

"One guy?"

"He's not even armed."

"Three of them, one of him—and he isn't dead?"

"It's best you hear the rest from our friend. Carter Woodbine." Grantworth slides the attorney's card across the table. "Woodbine is pissed, and he's calling on his relationship with us to find this thief."

"As if we're his personal police force?"

"Like I said, he's a valuable asset to us."

"Your asset, not mine. I don't owe him anything."

"Woodbine and those he's aligned with keep the drugs coming across the border in the volume we need. Mass addiction is a key to the social change that the ISA was formed to foment. The chaos and violence caused by a vigorous drug subculture, the dropouts who become mental and unemployable—all of that helps pave the way for the New Truth." Grantworth taps the business card that Calaphas hasn't picked up. "He'll be able to see you in his office at nine o'clock this evening, assuming that works for you."

"Put someone else on it. What I'm already chasing is bigger than this Woodbine can ever hope to be."

Grantworth's smile is as thin as a line scored by a knife in a block of white Cheddar. "It's connected to your assignment. One of Woodbine's associates who was present when the robbery went down is a man named Rudy Santana. Six years ago, he spent three days in a courtroom, as a spectator, giving moral support to the defendant who was an associate of his."

"Everyone has associates these days. More like he was giving the defendant the red eye to be sure he didn't rat out his homeys."

Grantworth shrugs. "Anyhow, Santana says the man who took the half million was a witness in that case six years ago, a security expert who was testifying for the prosecution. He couldn't remember the name. We've gone through court records and discovered it was Michael Mace. That was before he sold his company, before Shelby Shrewsberry hired him at Beautification Research."

After rolling some wine around his mouth, Calaphas says, "This attorney have any security video of Mace?"

"No. He's a ghost, as at the lab in the valley. But Santana has a photo from the time of the trial. He's printed it out for you. And Woodbine has something else he wants to discuss with you, something he's not keen to share with just everyone, not even with me."

"You know what happened at that lab. Happened to Mace?"

"We have a pretty good idea."

Calaphas figures "pretty good idea" means that the highly educated dimwits at the executive level have it half figured out at best. He says, "Tech wizards have been enthusiastically predicting it for maybe thirty years, but they didn't think it through far enough—what it would be like, what power and abilities would come with it. Now, thanks to archaea, it's happening."

Archaea, a microbial life-form once thought to be bacteria, is capable of horizontal gene transfer, carrying genetic material from one individual into another, from one species to another. In nature, this is a random process, perhaps serving evolution, but perhaps of little effect. At Beautification Research, scientists had undertaken experiments to determine if archaea could be adapted to transport intricate nanomachines into human cells with the hope of combining the knowledge and skills of the human brain with the greater data-storage capacity, processing speed, and fluid knowledge-sharing of computers. The billionaire tech cultists believe this is inevitable and will lead to a vastly improved human race millions of times more intelligent. They call this revolution the "Singularity." They dare to believe they'll live long enough for technology to advance to the point where they can transcend their biological limitations and become immortal cyborgs. It's fallen to Calaphas to clean up after the scientists whom the tech royalty and the government funded.

He says, "As an elite class, they want to be the first to benefit from the Singularity. A society of godlike overlords."

"That is an ungenerous assessment of their motives," Grantworth protests. "They see themselves as benefactors of all humanity."

Calaphas smiles. "How humble of them." He pauses to enjoy more wine. "When the transforming event occurred, it was the result of an accident. Fifty-four killed, only one . . . elevated. Michael Mace *is* the Singularity, the entirety of it. You realize that?"

Grantworth appears profoundly uncomfortable. "Some speculation has begun to that effect."

"The irony," Calaphas says, "is that we don't know what makes him so special. Why him and not the other fifty-four? A breakthrough has occurred, but we don't know why—and it can't be replicated."

"It can be replicated," Grantworth disagrees. "If we can find Mace and study him."

The cabernet has a superb bouquet, which Calaphas enjoys as he stares at the deputy director over the rim of the wineglass.

At last, intimidated by that stare, Grantworth says, "What?"

"Apprehending this man is about as likely as finding and arresting Bigfoot."

"If you don't feel you're up to the task—"

Calaphas puts his wine down and interrupts, succinctly describing what he believes are just a few of the extraordinary abilities that the lab accident has conferred on Michael Mace.

By the time that Calaphas finishes speaking and picks up his wineglass, Julian Grantworth has not just paled; he has gone gray. "No one man should ever have such power."

Calaphas raises his glass as though in a toast. "Ah, a sudden enlightenment. Better late than never."

Pushing his chair back from the table, Grantworth says, "I must confer with the director immediately."

"You go confer. Form a committee of experts. They can devise a strategy. That's always effective."

Grantworth hates his underling almost as much as he fears him. Getting to his feet, he looks as if he is marshalling the nerve to upbraid Calaphas for his insolence or even remove him from the case—but he isn't able to summon enough courage to act. His expanding chest deflates, even as the swollen artery in his left temple pulses more rapidly, more visibly. He issues only a statement that is in fact a question: "You're staying on the case."

"After I've had dinner."

"Woodbine and Santana at nine o'clock."

"Wouldn't miss it. One thing."

"What?"

The other tables in this quadrant of the restaurant are still vacant, but Calaphas lowers his voice to a stage whisper. "It'll be next to impossible to apprehend Mace and hard to find him. But if I can find him, I can kill him."

"The director might have other ideas."

"He's a man of big ideas."

"Take no executive action until you receive instructions."

"'Executive action.' How you thrive on euphemisms."

Grantworth chews on his lower lip, contemplating a forceful response, but again he lacks the fortitude to do what he knows he should. He is no doubt thinking about his second wife, the stunning Giselle, whose great beauty makes him the envy of other men, and of his first wife, Martha, whose looks were as common as her husband's and who died in a tragic accident that not only freed Julian but also enriched him with an inheritance of thirty-two million dollars. Calaphas and Grantworth both know to whom he owes his good fortune, though they have never discussed the matter; Calaphas is willing to speak the truth about what happened to Martha, but her widower dares not raise the subject.

Grantworth lifts his chin, and his nostrils flare like those of a show horse entering a dressage competition, and he looks down at Calaphas with what he imagines is withering contempt. "Woodbine and Santana at nine o'clock." He turns and makes his way through the restaurant. He is tall, slim, with the ramrod posture of a guard at Buckingham Palace, his exquisitely tailored suit the summation of him. He thinks he's good at the game, but he doesn't understand the rules of the simulation in which they exist.

TRIGGER

In the library of the ocean-view Corona del Mar house, all the books are as white as the bleached sycamore shelves on which they are ordered. The spines feature no titles, no authors' names, no publishers' logos. Michael examines several and discovers that the original jackets were replaced by thick but flexible white vellum trimmed to fit each volume precisely. Thrillers by Janet Evanovich and David Baldacci, novels by John Irving and Don DeLillo, romances by Nora Roberts, and nonfiction tomes on a variety of topics are shelved with no regard to subject or genre. They seem to have been bought by the pound from a used-book dealer, not to be read, but to represent the concept of a book. Shape without form. Shade without color. This is the *idea* of a library as it might be in the virtual world of a shooter game where the avatars are too busy killing and being killed to have any time to read, where the only purpose of a library is to serve as the scene of yet another violent encounter during which the all-white decor will be vividly splattered with gore.

Among the data triggers that Michael has planted in systems connected to the internet, one is at the ISA. It notifies him any time his name and that of Durand Calaphas appear within two hundred characters of each other in written reports or within thirty seconds of each other in recorded statements or conversations. As now. Blue neon flows through his mind's eye, providing a location in the ISA archives. Standing with book in hand, he mentally ravels the blue light toward him, as if he is reeling in a fish. He opens archived audio of a conversation between Calaphas and Julian Grantworth, the deputy director of the ISA, conducted mere minutes earlier and just now transmitted by Grantworth to his one superior at the agency. If others had been present in the library, they could not have heard what Michael hears.

"I'm sorry to interrupt you at your dinner, Durand, but I'm afraid there's been a wrinkle in the case."

"Wrinkle. What's the wrinkle?"

"There was an incident at three thirty this morning . . ."

Michael returns the white-jacketed biography to the shelf. In the end, all books are white books, those that are wise and those that are foolish, white jackets and white pages. The world reads but does not long remember, and what truth people find in books they most often dismiss as irrelevant. Humankind, the poet said, cannot bear very much reality. Delusions are preferred, delusions and the comfort of a virtual reality.

"Woodbine is pissed, and he's calling on his relationship with us to find this thief."

"As if we're his personal police force."

"Like I said, he's a valuable asset to us."

Michael steps to a window. The storm and the surging sea speak of one truth, which isn't invented by men or women, which can't be rendered obsolete by the so-called New Truths that enfever them. The metaverse isn't a universe, only a vague and distorted shadow—a cartoon—of the majesty of space-time. Even in their most intricate design, virtual realities—whether those that men and women invent for themselves or those conjured by tech wizards—always will be voids into which troubled souls empty themselves.

"Anyhow, Santana says the man who took the half million was a witness in that case six years ago, a security expert who was testifying for the prosecution . . . Michael Mace."

Men and women of a certain class, a self-congratulatory elite who have much learning of what is currently thought important and little understanding of their own human nature, dream of immortality through quick self-evolution into cyborg form, instant access to all knowledge without the effort of study, godlike power. This is yet another void, just the latest version of the fantasy of absolute authority that has wrecked so many civilizations over the millennia. Michael is the embodiment of the Singularity, but he intends not to use his power as the dreamers dream of using theirs. Instead, he wants to live long enough to bring the world back to reality before it descends irretrievably into delusion.

"This attorney have any security video of Mace?"

"No. He's a ghost, as at the lab in the valley. But Santana has a photo from the time of the trial."

Rudy Santana has a photograph. Maybe it was originally on his phone, where Michael could have found and deleted it. But Santana has now printed it.

Michael scrubbed every photo of himself from every website, from every file and device connected to the internet. He burned links to his past when he incinerated his house and everything in it. As a security consultant, he has long followed his advice to wealthy clients and has been camera shy, although a few hard copies of photos surely exist. However, he has imagined that the ISA, even with its vast resources, will need weeks to find an image suitable to assist them in a nationwide search.

Weeks would give him time to squirrel away somewhere and prepare to do what he feels destined to do. Now, depending on the quality of Santana's snapshot, Michael might have only a day or two before the ISA is able to share his image with thousands of agents by the old-fashioned expedient of wanted sheets and posters printed with obsolete technology and then distributed by hand.

A realization pivots him from the window. Now that they have so unexpectedly, fortuitously connected him to Carter Woodbine, they must know that he fled Beverly Hills in the attorney's Bentley. They are able to monitor its unique GPS signal and swiftly track it to its current location, the garage on the top floor of this residence. In fact, they should already be blocking off the street, surrounding the house.

Having died once, Michael has no doubt that he can die again. Although he was reanimated, the next death will be final because it will be so violent that it will put him beyond all possibility of resurrection. His enemies will see to that. He is the Singularity, but the merging of man and machine does not provide immortality; a machine reduced to radioactive melt and scattered scraps of metal cannot be repaired.

From his previous invasion of ISA's computer system, Michael has imprinted in memory everything in Durand Calaphas's agency file, including his iPhone number. As he leaves the library, navigates the living room, and takes the stairs to the top floor, he also goes online, into a bottomless sea of microwaves carrying data. Because he already knows the number and GPS signal of Calaphas's phone, he instantly finds the agent in a Beverly Hills restaurant. He quickly enters that phone, speeds through the list of contacts, and locates the number for Grantworth. By the time he reaches the foyer, he is in the deputy director's phone, where he accesses CONTACTS and grabs the number for the ISA director, Katherine Ormond-Wattley.

Crossing the foyer into the hall that leads to the garage, he mentally enters Ormond-Wattley's phone as she's in the middle of an encrypted discussion with the president's national security adviser, Pierce Leyton. Michael hears what Katherine Ormond-Wattley says and also hears what *she* hears after Leyton's encrypted transmissions are translated into normal English, or into English that's as normal as Leyton is able to speak it. They're talking about a cable-network prime-time host whom they would like to destroy professionally if they could do so without seeming to be behind whatever lie about him they might concoct and document with manufactured evidence.

As Michael enters the garage and turns on the lights, he drops through the contacts on Director Kathy's phone and finds Carter Woodbine's number. He slides into the agency's audio archives and listens to the attorney's initial conversation with the director.

He had taken the half million from Woodbine shortly after three o'clock in the morning, but the attorney hadn't placed his call to Ormond-Wattley until 1:35 in the afternoon, approximately ten hours later. Strange. On the phone call, Woodbine seeks the assistance of the ISA, not only to recover the money but also to find Michael and determine how the five-story fortress that houses the law offices of Woodbine, Kravitz, Benedetto, and Spackman was penetrated. Stranger still, during the conversation, he never mentions that his Bentley has been stolen, which he must have known hours earlier.

The attorney wants them to find Michael and the money, wants them to grill the thief until all secrets are spilled, but he doesn't want them looking for the Bentley.

Michael walks around to the back of the sedan. The name of the Bentley dealership and the city in which it's located are on the complimentary license-plate frame.

He settles in the front passenger seat and pulls the door shut. He pops open the glove box, sorts through the contents, and extracts an envelope containing the validated registration card issued by the DMV.

This is one of those occasions when he is seeking a complex chain of information and doesn't know exactly where to find all he needs. He must go exploring. Instead of conjuring a self-driving Tesla in his mind's eye, he imagines the Bentley is able to navigate the microwave connections and data flows of the internet symbolized by labyrinthine layers of superhighways, streets, and alleyways. He doesn't need to start the engine or put on the seat belt, for neither the car nor he will leave this property. The garage fades. Michael accelerates into the virtual reality of the World Wide Web. In a few seconds, the sedan takes an exit ramp and comes to a halt inside the computer of the car dealership, figuratively speaking.

Michael summons Woodbine's file from the customer records, and it appears on the windshield as though on a screen. Over the past sixteen years, the attorney has purchased two Rolls-Royces and three Bentleys from this dealership. He paid cash for the third Bentley fourteen months earlier. He didn't take delivery himself, but had the car shipped directly to a high-end customizer, Classic Wheels, in Oxnard, California.

A Bentley is not a car that anyone would chop, channel, sparkle out with cool details, and convert into a street rod. Besides, this most recent of Woodbine's Bentleys looks as it did on the showroom floor.

Seconds later, Michael is in the computer of Classic Wheels, in Oxnard. The data display on the windshield isn't as slick as that of the Rolls-and-Bentley dealership, but he finds what he needs.

In every vehicle with a GPS navigation system, the transponder that communicates with the satellites issues a unique signal. That signal is the car's—and therefore the owner's—ID, which is known to the DMV. Law-enforcement agencies may seek to obtain your car's navigational ID to review the archived history of its travels or to track you relentlessly in real time. State and local police mostly take the trouble of obtaining a court order, though there have been cases in which certain federal agencies have in recent years been of the mindset that the protections of the Constitution do not apply to everyone. Carter Woodbine has had the Bentley's navigation system reworked so that he can leave it functional for convenience when he is out and about on honest business or can, by flipping a switch, kill the transponder and eliminate satellite tracking of the vehicle. At the moment, it is off the grid and can't be tracked.

Another alteration involves the clever restructuring of the rear passenger compartment and the trunk. Michael studies the work order and mechanical drawings until he's certain he understands the changes that have been made.

Because they materially affect the operation of the car and might raise safety issues, these are changes that are required by law to be reported to the DMV. This is the responsibility of the owner, not of the customizer. From Classic Wheels in Oxnard, Michael takes a quick spin to the DMV computer in Sacramento and consults the records there, using the seventeen letters and numbers of the vehicle's validated registration card, confirming that Woodbine failed to comply with that requirement.

The Bentley has been altered to serve as the attorney's getaway car if he needs one. Considering his connections to the country's power structure, it seems unlikely that he will ever be on the run from the law, but his preparation for every eventuality is why he's prospered in a dangerous business.

The virtual, eerily lighted highways swooping through infinite darkness now fade, and the reality of the garage coalesces around

Michael. He returns the Bentley's registration to the glove box and gets out of the car and goes around to the driver's side. He settles behind the wheel and starts the engine.

He powers down the window in his door, powers down the window in the front passenger door, raises the lid on the console box, powers up the window in the passenger's door, powers up the window in the driver's door, and shuts the lid on the console box, with no delay between each action. As he learned from the records of Classic Wheels, this six-step combination activates the customized feature in the rear passenger compartment; the motorized bench portion of the back seat recedes into the trunk with a soft purr.

Michael gets out of the sedan and opens the rear door. The backrest remains in place, but where the richly upholstered bench had been, there is now revealed a secret six-inch-deep compartment that runs nearly the width of the vehicle and measures about eighteen inches front to back. This contains an AR-15 rifle with four spare magazines and plastic-wrapped packets of hundred-dollar bills. He isn't prepared to count this sky-is-falling stash, but it's no less than two million dollars.

Carter Woodbine is certain to have offshore accounts totaling tens of millions, secreted in tax havens that have no extradition treaties with the United States. However, if catastrophe strikes and his political connections collapse, he could suddenly go from being a treasured friend of the high and mighty to a pariah. In that case, he will need this pot of money to get out of the country, slip deep into Central—or even South—America, buy overnight citizenship under a new name in some hellhole dictatorship, and then charter a suitable jet to convey him to a mountainous principality or an island nation where at least a significant part of his wealth is safely stored.

Michael has taken from Woodbine not just five hundred thousand dollars, but perhaps as much as three million when the value of the Bentley and its cache are added to the haul. In service to the furious attorney, exceedingly dangerous men, perhaps numerous and hoping to receive a generous reward, will be on the lookout for this car across Southern California. Nevertheless, at least for the time being, no police or federal agents will be seeking it.

He returns to the house, to the library, to the wine and cheese and crackers, to the striking view of the storm that is comforting in its textured and bracing reality. In spite of the superhuman abilities that have been bestowed on him, he remains unaware that within the hour he will be swept from his refuge into desperate circumstances.

THREE: BURY THE LIVING

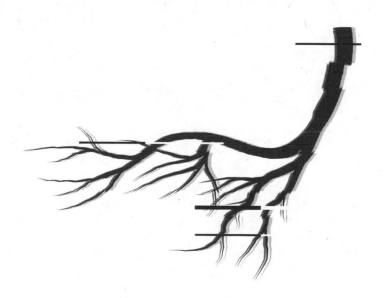

EDEN

Following the three-lane blacktop, Nina knows what the rain and the night conceal. Grassy hills rise in the east, and beyond the hills lies the lesser desert, and beyond the first desert waits the true and more barren desert. To the west is woven a webwork of small cities and suburbs that crowd the shores of the sea, far from LA but bustling with commerce and compulsion, with ecstasy and horror, grace and cruelty, where most people are time ridden and wearier than they might know.

This broad and fertile valley lies between those two worlds, a quiet refuge. She came here once before, eight years earlier, when John was five years old and her parents were a year away from their encounter with a hit-and-run driver. The four of them enjoyed a rare family vacation, three days at a mom-and-pop motel with a swimming pool. The town at the south end of the valley, to which she and John are at the moment headed, is a picturesque mix of Victorian and Spanish architecture, with numerous art galleries and craft shops, in part a farm community—apple orchards, nut orchards—and in part a low-key tourist destination because of the local history and two popular annual festivals.

Her dad had called it Eden. Compared to the hood where Nina was raised, it's as close to Eden as anywhere she has seen. Sometimes she daydreams of retiring here. How much better it would be to start a new life in this valley not in thirty years, but now.

As the road curves, the headlights sweep through the orchards. The producing groves are farther south. At this northern end of the valley, broad fields of trees have died in recent years and not yet been cut down, a consequence of foolish state water policies that have also destroyed tens of thousands of acres of once productive farmland in the Central Valley. At the moment, there is abundant rain, but California is a place of periodic droughts that require wise preparations. Illuminated by the sweeping beams, the leafless trees bristle with withered branches that, in the wind, jitter like agitated arachnidan colonies in a dream infested with tarantulas.

This is early-to-bed country, where those who work hard for a living rise before dawn. This ugly weather further discourages travel. The rearview mirror reveals dark, empty lanes. Hours have passed since Nina had reason to suspect a tail. Now headlights appear behind her, at the height of what might be a pickup perched on oversize tires. She imagines some teenager and his date hurrying to meet the be-home-by hour that was set by her parents.

However, when she rounds a curve, the straightaway ahead is blocked by a pair of angled SUVs, big Lincoln Aviators. As she takes her foot off the accelerator, the vehicle behind her proves to be two. They approach fast, side by side.

Having seen the double pursuit in the passenger-side mirror, John leans forward, squinting through the windshield at the hulking Aviators. "They aren't cops."

"No," she agrees, desperately scanning the ground to the left and right as their speed falls.

"Aleem?" John says. "Aleem all the way out here?"

All the way out here because they mean to take the boy. All the way out here because they mean to finish her.

"They tagged us," she says.

Although Aleem and his crew can't have known her destination, they must be pleased that she has led them to hundreds of acres of abandoned apple orchards, in the isolation of hard rain and fierce wind, an ideal place for a boy to be snatched into a life of crime and violence, for a woman to be murdered and buried where her body won't be found for years, if ever.

"The phone," she says, and John plucks it out of a cup holder to do what they previously discussed. "Upload the post."

The depth of the drainage ditch alongside the highway can't be gauged with water racing through it, but it's maybe three feet wide. The land slopes up about four feet from the ditch to the orchard at an ascendable angle, but if the ditch isn't just a foot deep, if it is as much as three feet, the Ford's undercarriage might get hung up when the front wheels drop. The Explorer has four-wheel drive, made for rough overland travel, but she's driven it only on paved roads. She doesn't know the full range of its abilities and limitations.

They are coasting toward the blockade, with two vehicles fast approaching behind them. White light floods through the liftgate window, filling the Ford as though a supernatural visitation has come upon them.

Ahead, the filthy surging water vanishes into a culvert over which an access road to the dead orchard offers an exit from the closing trap, though not a certain escape. Nina brakes. The tires stutter on the slick pavement, and she pulls the wheel hard to the right, and the Ford leans into the turn so that she holds her breath and thinks, *Please.*

Then they are off the highway, heading west. The barren apple trees stand in tight regimental order, preventing her from driving between any two of them; however, the alleys separating one row of trees from another were made wide enough for harvesters to pass in their machines and trucks. Years with little rain and much hard sun have cured the land into hardpan that the current torrents haven't softened much. Pools have formed, dark mirrors across which the headlight beams skip, and repeatedly the Explorer raises wings of water that flare out into the orchard.

"Posted," John declares. Uplit by the glow of the iPhone, his face is a séance apparition. "But what does it mean—'the ninth hour.'"

"It's code, a call for help that won't look like that to anyone other than Michael."

"But what can he do when he's . . . wherever he is?"

The alleys to the left and right are suddenly flushed with light that silhouettes the gaunt trees and alchemizes the lead-gray rain to silver, as the squadron of SUVs enters the orchard, racing to cut off Nina from most of her options.

THE HAUNTED ORCHARD

Kuba follows Nina, gaining on her, while the homeys in the other SUVs flank her in parallel alleys. He says, "What's this fuckin' place, all these creepy trees?"

"Some kinda orchard," Aleem says.

"I don't see no fruit."

"It's a dead orchard."

"What's the point?"

"What point?"

"Point of a dead orchard?"

"No point to it. Trees just died."

"Why they don't cut 'em down?"

"Probably costs too much," Aleem theorizes.

"Shitload of firewood here."

"Can't sell rotten termite wood. They'll cut 'em down when they got somethin' better they wanna do with the land."

Most of the alleys between the tight rows of trees run east-west, but it turns out that every so often there's one that goes north-south. Suddenly the Explorer's brake lights flash red, and Nina whips the vehicle to the left, heading south.

Surprised, Kuba overshoots the intersection. He slams on the brakes and shifts into reverse. The tires spin, sloughing up gouts of mud. They head south in the bitch's wake. Now, instead of walls of leafless wood flanking them, there are row ends separated by wide east-west harvesting alleys.

"Creepy damn trees," Kuba says.

"So come back on your own time, cut 'em down."

"What they grow here?"

"How'd I know? Peaches, apples, cantaloupes."

"Cantaloupes don't grow on no trees."

"What then? They grow on tables in the market?"

Kuba says, "They grow on vines."

"Like giant bunches of grapes, huh?"

"I seen 'em once."

"You was high. What you seen was in that movie, space-alien seed pods, they grow imitation people in 'em. Homey, get on the bitch 'fore she's gone."

"I'm closin'. I'm on her." Kuba glances at the rearview mirror. "Shit. What we got now is we got a five-car caravan."

Aleem checks the side mirror and sees that the three other SUVs in the squadron have turned into this same southbound alley.

"They don't get parallel real quick," Kuba says, "she can go anywhere."

Even as he speaks, the three trailing vehicles peel off into intersecting alleys, two eastbound and one westbound, the drivers urgently looking for other north-south passages on which they can get parallel to the Explorer.

"It's a maze," Aleem says.

Kuba says, "It's a graveyard. Like wood tombstones. Spooks me."

"Nothin' dead here but trees."

"They say trees got spirits."

"What spirits?"

"Like souls."

"Who says?"

"Some people."

Aleem says dismissively, "Tricks who sniff an elbow of flake every day."

"No, smart people. On this podcast."

"You got a health app, now you listen to podcasts?"

"Just the one podcast."

"When you goin' to college, get a degree, put on a suit, be a hornologist, teach everyone about trees?"

"The word ain't 'hornologist.'"

"So what might the word be, professor?"

"All I'm sayin' is if trees got souls, this place is totally fuckin' haunted."

"You don't know the word. Forget souls. Just kick it up and ram the bitch."

"You feel the shimmy? Turf's turnin' slick as ice. I kick this humper up any more, she'll spin out."

"Kick her up," Aleem insists. "It can't fly, it shouldn't be called 'Aviator.'"

Kuba's concern proves to be a premonition of sorts. Ahead, the Explorer fishtails right, left, right, tree shadows leaping like spirits trying to escape the dead wood in which they have long been imprisoned. The rear passenger-side bumper clips a tree trunk.

"Ram the bitch!" Aleem shouts. "Ram her, RAM HER!"

The dinner hour is well past and the evening maturing. Michael is checking out the contents of the freezer compartments in the two large Sub-Zero refrigerators, in need of something more than cheese and crackers, when the words THE NINTH HOUR, in blue neon, stream into his mind's eye.

He closes the freezer drawer and turns to the kitchen island and places his hands palms down on the granite top, which is cool and hard and real. He enters the Verizon telecommunications network as easily as opening a door, translates Nina's smartphone number into binary code, projects it into the system, and John answers on the first ring, all in seven seconds.

John and his mother are in serious trouble, but the boy is calm. "Four SUVs are after us. I don't know how many gang-bangers, like a whole army. We're in San Diego County—"

"I know," Michael says, for he has entered the navigation app on Nina's phone. The map display that appears in his mind shows their blinking signifier to be two hundred yards from the nearest paved route, a state highway, and moving fast. He switches on their speakerphone feature, so Nina can hear him. "I know where you are, but why have you gone off-road?"

"Roadblock," John says. "We split into this orchard. A huge, freakin' dead orchard. Just sideswiped a tree, but we're okay."

Nina says, "We must be tagged. They're all around us, trying to cut us off."

"Stay cool," Michael advises.

He summons a second display that glows in his mind's eye softly beside the first, this one from the international GPS monitoring system, framing the same plot of land through which

Nina is racing. Fortunately, it's very lonely territory; there aren't a confusing multitude of blinking signifiers, only thirteen. Her vehicle—actually her iPhone—emits only one; the Explorer is too old to have a navigation system. Each of the other SUVs issues three signals. In every case, one ID number on the display is that of the vehicle, and the other two represent smartphones carried by the occupants.

Aleem has marshalled seven of his homeboys to help him snatch John and do God knows what to Nina. More likely than not, mother and son will both end up dead, because the boy won't be taken easily or let them harm Nina without going to her defense.

"Aleem and seven others," he tells them. "Keep moving while I deal with this. Keep moving, or you're finished."

The United States government—and most others in this age that is sliding toward universal tyranny—has instituted a clandestine vehicle-control project that, like everything else, is no secret to Michael Mace since his resurrection. Years earlier, when it was recognized that the technology would soon exist to equip all new cars and trucks with a kill switch that could disable the engine via a microwave-carried command linked to the vehicle's GPS identifier, defenders of liberty protested vigorously. All politicians wishing to appear righteous swore that this outrage would never be committed as long as they drew breath. Some remain unaware that it's been done through the auspices of the Environmental Protection Agency, while others are aware and comforted by the knowledge. This power of "mobility restriction" has not been—and will not be—revealed for any ordinary law-enforcement purpose, such as foiling a carjacking or bank robbery or to stop a child abductor in flight with his prey. It must remain secret, so that should the country ever experience a serious insurrection, those in rebellion will be surprised and disempowered when the wheels they rely on will turn no more.

In this instance, in the case of Aleem Sutter and his crew, Michael has no compunctions about violating the right they have assumed they possess, the right to kidnap and murder as they choose.

GOING TO SEE THE WIZARD

Durand Calaphas leaves his agency sedan in the restaurant lot to be retrieved later. With the hood of his raincoat providing anonymity, he walks to his meeting. The rear entrance of Woodbine, Kravitz, Benedetto, and Spackman, attorneys and eager financiers of death by heroin and fentanyl, is two blocks away, but he travels five blocks to get there, to prevent traffic cams at intersections capturing an image of a man walking directly from the restaurant to the law offices. The roll-up door is raised, as he was told it would be. Inside, a lean man in black jeans and a black denim jacket worn over a red T-shirt stands beyond the reach of the in-blown rain. As Calaphas arrives, this agitated specimen expresses his impatience with obscenities. His nose is bandaged, bruises extending under his eyes. "Where the hell's your car? No one said you'd walk in."

"I had dinner nearby. This kind of weather invigorates me."

"You was supposed to be here at nine o'clock."

"Isn't it nine?" Calaphas asks.

"You're twenty-five minutes late."

"Really? That much?"

"You didn't call or nothin'."

"Like I said, I was at dinner."

"You don't have no watch?"

"A quite good one," Calaphas says, pulling his coat sleeve up to reveal a gold Rolex. "It was my brother's. His widow wanted me to have it, to remember him by."

The man answers that with a hard stare, as if he has killed people for less than being late for an appointment. "You kept us waitin'."

"After dessert and coffee, I had a good port. You know how it is with port—you want to savor it. You don't just slug it down."

Exasperated, the man repeats, "You kept us waitin'."

"And who might you be?"

"Santana. Woodbine's bein' pissed off in his apartment. Harris, too. They been here since eight thirty."

"Then why are we chatting and making them wait even longer?"

After considering Calaphas in silence for a moment, Santana says, "Somethin' wrong with you?"

"How do you mean?"

"How do I mean?"

"If you're asking if I'm ill, the answer is no. If you're asking if I've had too much to drink, I haven't. But maybe you're implying something else."

After another silence, Santana says, "I see you now."

"Do you?"

"Real clear."

"Because I could always administer a vision test."

As Santana goes to a control box mounted on the wall and puts down the big roll-up, Durand considers a glass-walled cubicle with a sign above its door that reads VALET. Against the back wall of that space is a pegboard on which only a few electronic keys hang. As an experienced player, he often notices things that seem mundane but that eventually prove to be essential to a winning strategy.

Santana opens an interior door, and Calaphas follows him into a vestibule.

"Leave your raincoat. Don't go drippin' all over the place."

As they proceed along a hallway toward the lobby at the front of the building, Santana speaks a name and says, "Know who that is?"

"He's a United States senator."

Santana mentions another name.

Calaphas says, "Investment fund boss. Oversees trillions."

The third name is Katherine Ormond-Wattley, the director of the ISA, to whom Calaphas answers if he answers to anyone. "Them three," Santana says, "is so tight with Woodbine they're Siamese twins."

"Four twins."

"You get what I'm sayin'?"

"With some effort."

"Get it outta your head how Woodbine's just some mouth-piece you can keep waitin' while you have port. I don't work for no pocket-change pussy. The man is on the ladder, not just on it, high up."

"Good for him. Good for you. Look, I'm sorry. It's been a long day, that's all."

Although of a style different from that of seventeenth-century France, the lobby rivals the Hall of Mirrors in the palace at Versailles as an effort to impress on commoners that he who resides here has pockets deeper than the sea.

The elevator is accessed with a code that Santana enters in a keypad. The cab rises in silence, so smoothly that they don't seem to be moving.

"Respect gotta be paid," Santana says.

"I won't embarrass you," Calaphas assures him.

This will be a far more interesting meeting than Calaphas has expected. That understanding comes to him not as a premonition; it has become his considered *intention* to make it interesting.

VIEWPOINTS

Sometimes, Aleem is too enthusiastic for his own good. He knows this. He is profoundly self-aware. He is a get-it-done guy who has no patience for the hindrances of the world. The worst hindrances are people, and he has killed more of them than he should have. He doesn't regret excessive murder or think it is immoral. Nothing is immoral unless you believe it is, and even if you believe something is immoral, you're wrong. That's Aleem Sutter's philosophy. When he admits to having killed more people than he should have, he's only acknowledging that sometimes offing a treacherous buttface isn't worth the risk involved. If he better managed his enthusiasm, he would on some occasions do nothing more than cripple the dude for life or, if the hindrance loves his mother, Aleem would be better advised to just disfigure the bitch and *threaten* to waste her to keep her little mama's boy in line. The ecstasy, the overpowering exaltation, of shooting an adversary in the face or spilling his guts on his shoes can, if Aleem's not careful, spin quickly into a frenzy, such delirious excitement that he might make a big mistake. He knows that he must guard against healthy enthusiasm deteriorating into frenzy. He is more self-aware than anyone he has ever known.

At the moment, as he urges Kuba to ram the Explorer, he knows that his anger at Nina has swollen into rage and that rage can sour enthusiasm into the most violent and least wise of intentions. But what he feels is not his fault. She's making him this way. She takes the boy and runs, and then she doesn't just give up at the roadblock like she ought to, and now she's forcing them to chase her through this zombie forest. It's as if, right in front of his homeys, she keeps telling him that she's going to cut his pecker off, or as if she thinks she has essentially already cut it off, humiliating him.

She makes the situation even worse by handling the Explorer as if she went to some Hollywood school for stunt driving and graduated at the top of her class. Except for clipping the right rear fender on a tree trunk, she's pumping that four-wheel so expertly that Kuba not only is failing to catch up with her, he's beginning to fall farther behind.

"Don't let this happen," Aleem warns.

"Everythin' is everything', boss."

Everything *isn't* all right, and the fact that Kuba calls him "boss" is proof that the ass-kisser knows it.

"You want a piece of that quiff," Aleem says, "better catch her soon. Longer it takes, more likely I'll break her neck 'fore you can strip her down for action."

"I'm up for that," Kuba says.

"Up for that? Up for what?"

"Do what you need, then so will I, just so she's still warm."

"Man, you're spookier than dead trees."

Grinning, Kuba admits, "I got my ways."

◆ ◆ ◆

In the passenger seat, John sits at attention, the phone a rectangle of light in his hands. "What's Michael doing?"

"Saving us."

"How can you be so sure?"

"You'll see."

"Nothing's happening."

"Only been a minute since he answered our post."

"'The ninth hour.'"

"Is it ever."

The vast orchard seems to span a burnt-out world, the black and haggard trees with their tortuous rickrack of branches standing to monument the death of humanity in a last war of all against all, the gangbangers' SUVs like robotic scourges prowling the aftermath to eradicate remaining survivors. Nina has never been so terrified as she is now. These barren but ordered woods evoke horrors as diverse as scenes in a James Cameron movie and Golgotha falling into midday darkness. Yet in peril, as also in loss and grief, she sees, as she always does, moments of strange beauty. Sweeping light silvers the water streaming down black bark. The air is briefly but richly diamonded with wind-tossed raindrops. For a moment, the twigwork of backlit branches seems to form logograms that float in the air with mystical meaning, like comforting messages in some language that she has known in a previous life and will know again in a life to follow this one. Some might say that it's a fault—but she thinks it is a gift—to perceive beauty and the hope that it represents in even the ugliest moments of life.

Nothing is more desperate, with more potential for horror, than being pursued by Aleem and seven of his cold-eyed barbarians swanked out in their ornamental gold, each with two knives and more lethal surgeries to his credit than a death-camp doctor. If they take John, they will bring to bear their formidable powers of persuasion and intimidation as well as all the temptations of the flesh to turn him, warp him, corrupt him. He'll resist. He is a good kid. But he is only a kid. And even if he resists to the point where they lose patience with him, he'll end up in an unmarked grave. Such deranged men mock virtue, but in fact they fear it and won't long tolerate its presence among them. As a gang boss, Aleem can't afford for his legions to reach the conclusion that from his seed has sprung a young man of integrity and rectitude. Earlier this very day, he had said, *I'll kill you 'fore I see you brought down from a full man to some pathetic crawlin' thing that shames me 'fore the world.* That had not just been roo-rah. He meant it. Likewise, she entertains no illusions about her own fate if they catch her; as many of them as want will pull a train on her, and when they're finished, they'll kill her hard and jam her, naked, in a deep hole.

She's never owned another vehicle and has put a hundred forty thousand miles on the Explorer, so it's almost like an extension of her body as she takes evasive action through the maze of apple wood, waiting for Michael to work a miracle. In spite of the Explorer's age, she has less concern that the vehicle will fail her than that the orchard will surprise her when a dead tree pulls its rotting roots out of the saturated soil and crashes onto her. Moments ago, she swerved around a fallen tree that half blocked an intersection. She has driven over several wind-shorn branches that clattered against the undercarriage, but they were rotten or already badly fractured, and they did no damage. Her luck is not likely to hold.

A rattling arises at the back of the Explorer, on the starboard side. Maybe the damaged fender is coming loose.

She doesn't dare cut her speed. The bad boys in their glamour wheels have found other north-south alleys. Accelerating recklessly, they are pulling parallel to her once more.

Whatever Michael is able to do, Nina must escape the orchard. In spite of the ordered rows, this is unpredictable terrain that will throw her a hard surprise sooner than later.

Furthermore, she needs to get far enough ahead of her pursuers to have a few minutes to search the vehicle for the transponder they have planted on it. If she can't find it quickly, she and John will have to continue from there on foot.

The rattling noise escalates into a violent knocking.

◆ ◆ ◆

Kuba has his philosophy—think positive, don't draw something bad to you by worrying about it—which Aleem dismisses with a term he once heard in a movie when he was streaming because he couldn't sleep. *Magical thinking.* Reviews said the flick was hilarious, but it was about as funny as hemorrhoids. In it, one fool actor accused another fool of "magical thinking," which Aleem immediately knew was a true, important concept. Most people he's known engage in magical thinking to one degree or another; they are convinced that believing a thing is true in fact makes it true. He has many uses for people who go through life inventing their own truth; once you know what fantasy they live in, they are easy to motivate and manipulate.

Aleem's philosophy is simply what the street has taught him: Shit is what it is, and people are what they are, and a lot of them can be bought off with money or guilt or fear. That's how he keeps himself and his homeys out of jail—for the most part—even when their collection of rap sheets have to be maintained in ring binders. If a politician or a district attorney wants to believe you're a victim of the system, you play the victim and manufacture convincing evidence against your accuser or the cop who arrested you; if the magical thinkers want to believe you're an advocate against injustice, you talk the talk and donate money or hours of your personal time to the true-believing community-activist groups. On the other hand, if they have spines of butter and want to believe you're all-powerful and too dangerous to confront, you reinforce their assessment by taking a page from *The Godfather* and putting severed horses' heads in their beds. It's never actually a horse's head or a bed. Sometimes your family pet is chopped and put in your refrigerator, or your beloved sister spends an unexpected evening with a large man who devotes eight hours to the quiet and patient explanation of what her life will be like when she's blind and para-plegic, or your neighbor's house burns down with the family in it and at their funeral a mourner you don't know takes a moment to tell you how terribly sad he will be if anything like that happens to you and your children.

Now, because Aleem is not into magical thinking, because he is about being real and meeting every challenge boldly and *getting what he wants*, he draws his Heckler & Koch Mark 23, which weighs more than two and a half pounds, has a ten-round maga-zine, and is loaded with full-metal-jacket .45s, the kind of serious gun that says you don't have it just to plink rats at the city landfill.

"Damn it, Kuba, I don't care about no shimmy, slick-as-ice spinout. Catch the bitch. Ram her *now* or you got consequences."

"Consequences?"

"What'd I say?"

Kuba's forehead suddenly has a shine. "Jesus, Aleem."

"Don't Jesus me."

"All right."

"Don't Jesus me!"

"I get it. I got it."

"Ram the bitch!"

"Doin' it," Kuba says as he accelerates.

"Stop her *now*."

Even if a dude is your homey and your ace kool, he needs to be afraid of you deep down, needs to know that your fuse is always lit and short. Sometimes, you have to get your Joe Pesci on, be like that hothead he played in *Goodfellas*. Otherwise, even your main man can wonder if the crown will fit him better than it fits you. Like everyone, Aleem needs friends, but he never forgets that a best friend is potentially his worst enemy. It is a display of weakness, not a full moon, that can cause your homey to go werewolf on you.

Kuba is standing on it, and the Aviator is surging forward. All the leaves and fruit and bark that the orchard has shed in its long dying—a rotting sludge and the fungus that feeds on it—sloshes against the undercarriage and spews out from beneath the tires. The bow of the vehicle falls and rises, and the chassis shudders, and the back end tries to fishtail, but sweating Kuba holds tight to the twisting wheel. They are coming up fast on the vintage Explorer, which has a smaller engine and can't outrun the Lincoln, coming up fast and faster. Aleem feels his face flush with excitement, as he imagines the Explorer brought to a halt and jammed against a tree, imagines yanking open the driver's door and dragging Nina out from behind the wheel and throwing her down in the muck. When the boy sees that, he'll know who owns this family, who has the *power* and always will.

They're seconds short of ramming the Ford when the Aviator's engine fails. The Lincoln doesn't sputter or cough, just cuts out. The Ford pulls away. The Lincoln loses momentum in the swampish mud and forest mast, quickly coming to a halt.

"What's this shit?" Aleem demands.

Pushing the starter, Kuba says, "Wasn't me."

"Get it going."

"It's dead."

"Like shit. Try again."

"Dead. It's dead. Put that away."

"Put what?"

"That cannon in your hand. I didn't do nothin'."

"We got lights, wipers."

"Battery's not dead."

"No shit."

"Just the engine. I didn't do it."

The taillights of the Explorer are dwindling into the storm.

Aleem turns to peer through the passenger window. In parallel alleys, three sets of headlights are screened by dead trees and driving rain, but all remain visible enough for Aleem to discern that they're stationary. Only the Explorer is still on the move.

Kuba sees the situation, too. "How they do this?"

"Who?"

"Gotta be cops."

"What cops? You see cops?"

"We're screwed if it's cops."

"There's no cops."

"There's somethin' for damn sure."

Aleem looks out the windshield just as the Explorer goes dark. The beams don't fade into the night; they suddenly blink out. The Explorer is near the limit of visibility in the storm, a small gray mass barely recognizable as an SUV, no longer receding. "She been stopped, too."

Kuba says, "She don't even have lights."

Aleem holsters his pistol. "Let's go."

"It's dead."

"We ain't." Aleem puts up the hood of his jacket and opens his door.

◆　◆　◆

The Aviator that's gaining on Nina suddenly falls behind, as do the SUVs flanking her in other north-south alleys. They seem to have come to a sudden stop.

"Michael," she says, and a small laugh of relief escapes John.

The respite from terror is brief. Something happens related to the impact with the tree, which had seemed of little importance. The rattle becomes a louder knocking. The knocking erupts into a three-note tolling like an iron bell. The Explorer shudders violently. The instrument panel brightens with an array of warning lights, some of which Nina has never seen before, and the fuel gauge falls to zero. The Explorer rolls to a stop, the engine dead.

She switches off the headlights. She hopes they are far enough from Aleem and the others so that it might appear as if they have driven out of sight. She can't rely on that. "We're on foot from here," she says, taking the phone from John. "Bring the duffel."

"What about our suitcases, the stuff in back?"

"Leave it all. Just bring the Tac Light in the glove box, but don't switch it on."

As she opens the door and rain shatters over her, Michael's voice comes from the phone. "Why have you stopped moving?"

"Breakdown," she says. "Hit a tree, ruptured the gas tank. I don't know what else. We gotta run for it."

"Turn your phone off and get somewhere safe. Save the battery. I'll track you by it. Be there maybe in as little as two hours."

She turns off the phone and pulls up her hood and gets out into the howling night and closes the door and looks toward the distant Aviator. It's only an SUV, a fancy kind of truck mostly obscured by its headlights and the storm, but it looks mysterious, as though it was made on a far world by unknowable creatures and has come from beyond the moon and down through the night to this orchard for a purpose too strange to be fathomed by human reason.

At the front of the Ford, she meets John—"Stay close"—and leads him out of the southbound alley and west through darkness, splashing across saturated ground that sucks at their inadequate shoes. She isn't blind, but the colorless landscape is black and grainy shades of gray, like a CT scan, and her sense of vision is reduced to something like computed tomography that requires the training of a radiologist to accurately and easily read the way ahead. The trees are shapes without form, but they are a shade darker than the sky and thus define the harvesting alley, although the treacherous footing prevents her from hurrying as fast as she would like. She doesn't dare use the Tac Light and reveal their location. She doesn't want to move among the trees until her eyes become somewhat dark-adapted, when she will be better able to discern and avoid low-hanging limbs and the snares of fallen apple wood that could trip them or gouge them with the ragged spears of broken branches.

They have gone fifty or sixty yards when her fear suddenly ripens into dread, which she takes to mean that intuition is warning her of an imminent, lethal encounter. She stops and halts John and looks north, surveying the cloistered night from west to east. The lights of four vehicles were previously visible, filtered through the trees, but now all is darkness. The headlamps have been doused. Aleem and his seven homeys haven't gone away. They're coming for her and John, and though they're as hampered by the darkness as she is, they have eight times more guns than she has and God knows how many knives. More important than weapons, they have an unshakable confidence born of the overweening self-esteem that sociopathic gangbangers all seem to share, and they will never stop any more than wolves, electrified by the scent of prey, will relent in the hunt.

Since John issued from her and she first saw his sweet face, Nina has wanted nothing more than the freedom to make something of herself and support her child, the freedom to raise him to be wiser than she had sometimes been and to be a blessing to others. But in this world where the powerful too often fail to see the humanity in those weaker than themselves and seek to rule by fear, freedom is fragile, sustained only by sacrifice and fierce determination.

She has unconsciously pressed her right hand to the waist of her jacket, under which she can feel the pistol nestled in the belt scabbard. She doesn't want to be forced to use the gun, but if she must, she will. The men seeking her are not the kind to whom you can turn the other cheek without exciting in them the desire to answer your submission with a bullet in the head.

Although her eyes are not fully acclimated to the dark, she leads John into the row of wind-clattered and graceless trees along the south flank of the alley. Past that rampart of dead wood, they come to another east-west harvesters' passage and hurry across it, into more trees, as if they know where safety lies, though they do not.

THE PAIN OF LIVING AND
THE DRUG OF DREAMS

When Calaphas and Santana arrive in the fifth-floor apartment, Carter Woodbine and Delman Harris are facing each other across the kitchen island, silent and solemn, as if that granite slab is an altar on which someone will be sacrificed at midnight if not sooner. The attorney is dressed in Dior Homme—black suit, white shirt, striped tie—at a cost of maybe six thousand dollars, projecting the image of a reliable traditionalist. Harris's zippered Hermès jacket in a bold abstract pattern of green and gray and black costs nearly as much as a Toyota; he wears it over a black T-shirt, with black slacks by Berluti and Converse sneakers, four or five colorful Montecarlo silver-and-alutex bracelets on his right wrist, a Cartier Drive watch on his left. He is obviously convinced that he's above the law, considering that any cop who's ever worked the narcotics division would, on sight, ID him as a major player in the drug trade. These two look as if they attired themselves out of the same issue of *GQ*, neither of them having noticed the pages that most appealed to the other. They are united by their beverage, Macallan Scotch served neat, and by the offense they have taken at Calaphas's lack of punctuality, which they express not with words, but with tight lips and stares as sharp as ice picks.

Calaphas offers no apology for his tardiness. He doesn't even acknowledge it. He's got his own agenda, as he always does. "You have a picture of Mace?"

Printed on glossy photographic paper, it lies facedown on the island. Without a word, Woodbine turns it over. Calaphas doesn't find anything impressive about Michael Mace's appearance. The guy looks like a TV game-show host whose smile and pleasant banter with contestants help the lonely, the unemployed, and the homebound get through the pain of living.

"Julian Grantworth might already have told you that we're after this man. The photo will help."

Woodbine says, "What did Mace do that has you on his trail?"

"I'm not at liberty to say."

"I'm not an average citizen, Mr. Calaphas."

"Yes, I am aware of that."

"Your agency and I have mutual interests."

"But this," Calaphas says, "is a matter of national security."

Woodbine nods and considers his Scotch without bringing it to his lips. "National security. So let's speak in private."

"It'll still be national security in another room."

"Come with me," Woodbine insists.

Calaphas remembers what Grantworth said at the restaurant. *Woodbine has something else he wants to discuss with you, something he's not keen to share with just everyone, not even with me.*

Leaving Santana and Harris without a target for their bitter incensement, Calaphas follows the attorney through the glamorously furnished apartment to the gym. The room measures perhaps twenty feet by twenty feet. It contains no exercise equipment.

"It used to be lined with circuit-training machines," Woodbine says, "but I'm of an age when all that bores me. I had it removed."

The exercise equipment has been replaced by one item, a chaise longue upholstered in a fabric with a leopard-skin pattern.

As Calaphas ponders the furniture, Woodbine feels the need to explain. "It's a meditation room now."

The walls are paneled in floor-to-ceiling mirrors, as is the door by which they entered. If a window exists, it's been concealed by a mirror. One reflection repeats another, making a multitude of this two-man meeting, and the ceiling reflects everything below it.

Although curious about the nature of the attorney's meditation sessions, Calaphas restrains himself from asking, because he doesn't wish to have his excellent dinner turn sour in his stomach.

Woodbine says, "This Mace character, the crazy things he can do—I realize that's a national security matter. You can't tell me, and I don't want to know. However, I have a mutual opportunity to discuss with you."

They lock eyes.

Woodbine must see something that he needs to see, because he continues. "For some of us, there's going to be more opportunity in the new America than you ever dreamed."

"That's why I'm aboard for it."

"You're aware that your agency and I are business partners."

"It was suggested, yes."

"It's a lucrative business, enough profits to go around, plus the agency and I share certain ideological goals."

"The New Truth," says Calaphas.

"If you did a bit of business with me, it would be no different from your director, Katherine Ormond-Wattley, or deputy director doing business with me, which they do. It's all in the family."

After a silence in which he seems to be reflecting on a series of profound personal losses, Calaphas says, "The agency is the only family I have now."

The attorney conjures a courtroom expression of sympathy. "I'm sorry to hear that."

Calaphas shrugs. "It suits me."

The attorney places a hand over his mouth as though deciding whether he dares to say what he wishes to say, and he gazes at the mirrored ceiling, where he looks down on his upturned face, an uncertain soul who is his own and only god. He decides to proceed. "I didn't tell Grantworth, but Mace drove away in my Bentley."

"Some car."

"I want it back."

"Why didn't you tell Grantworth?"

"I had the Bentley customized."

"I assume you didn't just add tail fins."

"I can switch off the transponder when I'm not using the navigation system."

"So you can't be tracked. That's not illegal. Not yet."

"The customizer also built in a secret compartment. Not for drugs. It contains an unregistered AR-15 and three million in cash."

"Run-for-it money," Calaphas surmises.

"I'm not likely to need it, but I sleep better knowing it's packed and ready. I'd rather the ISA doesn't know I made such . . . preparations. It looks like the agency doesn't have my full trust, and that's not really the case."

They consider each other indirectly. Woodbine turns his head to his right, and Calaphas turns his head to *his* right, which is the attorney's left, so that they are looking at opposite mirrored walls in which their reflections curve away to infinity.

"So what's this opportunity you mentioned?"

"If you find the Bentley, you can take the three million for yourself and bring the car to me, and we're square."

They face each other again, and Calaphas says, "You must really love that car."

"It's not the car."

"I didn't imagine it was."

"It's the rifle, the AR-15."

"You made some use of it."

"One incident. Four dead."

"You're an *activist* attorney," Calaphas says approvingly. "Once the gun had a history, why didn't you get rid of it?"

"I meant to, as soon as I had a replacement." His mouth curls into a snarl. "Then along comes fucking Michael Mace."

The attorney is a well-practiced liar, but Calaphas is a living polygraph. The details about the customized Bentley are true, and the three million dollars is true, but the claim that four were killed with the gun is a lie. The snarl isn't an expression that comes naturally to a man who has spent his life looking earnest and magisterial in courtrooms. The use of the F-word, when such language isn't his style, is a calculated emphasis meant to sell his anger and his story. He wants the Bentley more than the three million, and the reason he wants it has nothing to do with the vehicle or rifle.

Calaphas says, "Three million is more than the right number. But if the navigation-system transponder is turned off, how am I supposed to find your car?"

"The three million is mostly in hundreds, but some is in three-inch-thick bricks of twenties. One of those bricks is hollowed out to accommodate a transponder."

"It reports to your iPhone."

"Yes. But maybe it's gone dead. Or maybe there's a limit to its transmission radius, and Mace was out of range before we realized he took the Bentley. He somehow controlled the security system here, kept us locked in and blocked our phones for hours after he left."

"Then what good is the transponder to me?"

"I imagine that's a problem that you—with all the agency's technology to draw on—can find a way to solve. It's beyond me, though surely not beyond you. Though you must be . . . discreet. This is between you and me. No third party."

Calaphas furrows his brow and gazes at the floor, as though puzzling through the twists of some Gordian knot. "How do you explain Mace not showing up on your security video?"

"Somehow he must have taken control of the system, froze the cameras and walked right past them."

"What does your security company say?"

"They said it's impossible, so they're gone."

Calaphas looks up from the floor. "Gone?"

"How could I trust them? I threw them out and told them to shut down service instanter. Katherine recommended another company."

"Katherine Ormond-Wattley?"

"Yes. A company with ties to the ISA, a military contractor with better tech than the firm I used. They'll install tomorrow."

"You don't have security now?"

"No video, no alarms, but no one can get through our electronic locks."

"Michael Mace did."

"I don't think Mace is coming back," Woodbine says. "I wish he would, so we could have a shot at him."

Calaphas doesn't need to get by the electronic locks. He's already inside.

Looking past the attorney, he considers the opposing-mirrors trick of endless reflections. An infinite Durand Calaphas is a true expression of his destiny, but the truth of Woodbine's prospects is not what the mirrors appear to predict.

"Listen, do we or don't we?" the attorney asks.

"Do we what?"

"Have a deal."

"Absolutely. And you won't be sorry you trusted me. But there's this thing about Rudy Santana. He felt I was disrespecting you by being late. He did something stupid to impress me."

Woodbine's expression is wonderfully textured—a mild, doleful chagrin—and could be mistaken for sincere by the most perceptive of jurors. "I need men who can interface between me and the animals on the street who keep the merchandise flowing. Santana and Harris aren't perfect, but they're the best I've found."

"I understand. But I think you should know Santana mentioned three names to prove how high you are on the ladder." As Calaphas repeats those names, the lawyer's eyebrows arch. "For your own good, Mr. Woodbine, you might have a word with Santana about discretion."

"I will," Woodbine declares. "I'll speak with him as soon as you're on your way."

"Meanwhile, that transponder links to your smartphone."

"To one of them. One I reserve strictly for that purpose."

"I'll need it."

"It's on the counter in the kitchen," the attorney says, moving away, past the leopard-patterned chaise, the multiplied reflections of which offer infinite accommodations where one can lie for the focused contemplation of God knows what.

The former gym and current meditation room is thronged with replicates of Calaphas and Woodbine moving toward the exit from myriad directions, folding into and out of the room's corners with great flexibility, seen retreating from the door even as they are approaching it. If these kaleidoscopic images can be disorienting, Calaphas is not confused as he follows Woodbine, for his attention is concentrated on the action he must take. At the same time, the regimented chaos of attorney and assailant in all their iterations makes it difficult for the target to recognize peril is imminent. Calaphas draws the small aerosol can of chloroform from a pocket and says, "Oh, one thing I forgot," and Woodbine turns, and Calaphas sprays his host in the face. All the Woodbines around the room—whatever their size, whether coming or going—collapse to the floor.

The esteemed partner of Kravitz, Benedetto, and Spackman—who are elsewhere engaged in criminal enterprises—is not dead, only unconscious on the meditation room floor. For the time being, that is how his assailant wants him.

When Calaphas enters the kitchen, Rudy Santana and Harris are drinking Scotch and watching a TV that has risen out of the island on a motorized lift. They're entranced by the cleavage of an actress and are engaged in a spirited discussion about whether her splendid breasts are larger than those of another actress they admire and would like to jump. They are for a moment oblivious of Calaphas.

No one's life is a smooth ride from the womb to the grave. The poor and the rich, the wise and the foolish, the smart and the dumb, the beautiful and the ugly all suffer on occasion as they journey through the world. Physical pain, mental anguish, worry and failure, loneliness and sorrow are visited on everyone, even if not in equal distribution. Calaphas has arrived at the conclusion that we endure the pain of living by taking refuge in dreams. We dream of striking it rich, of falling in love with—and being loved by—an ideal mate, of being acclaimed for what talent we might possess, of jumping the bones of an actress with epic cleavage. In

Calaphas's opinion, these dreams are drugs as surely as are marijuana and cocaine and heroin, and all but one of them can be the death of you if you don't indulge it in moderation. The only such dream certain to bring you genuine pleasure and spare you the suffering that people can cause you is the dream of exercising absolute power over others, but only if you *act on the dream.*

As Santana and Harris belatedly look away from the cleavage on which the camera lingers, glasses of Macallan Scotch in their right hands, Calaphas acts on his dream. He puts one metal-jacketed round point-blank in Santana's face, another in Harris's throat, and he steps around the corner of the island and looks down where they have fallen in sprays of blood and brains and spilled Scotch. Rudy is dead, the architecture of his face remodeled beyond anything Picasso might have imagined. A rasping noise escapes Harris along with blood that spurts between the fingers of the hand that he has clamped to his throat. Calaphas says, "The Hermès jacket is high fashion, but being fashionable is a particularly shallow dream," and drills him with another round.

A LITTLE NIGHT MUSIC

Aleem doesn't do bad weather. Snow is cocaine, which he sells, but the real stuff has no appeal for him. Ski gear makes every dude who wears it look like he belongs in an advertisement for stupid pills. To learn the slopes, you've got to fall down and make a fool of yourself a few hundred times, and Aleem has too much self-respect for that. The only men who slop around in the rain are those who have no choice, because either they're job slaves who have to work when it's wet or they're under some woman's thumb, running errands that she won't do unless the sun is shining and birds are singing, or they're mental cases who sooner or later are going to drown like turkeys do, just standing in the rain with their mouths open. To Aleem's way of thinking, when shit is falling out of the sky, the only right places to be are a pool hall, a backroom poker game, a casino with cocktail waitresses who have cleavage worth looking at when the cards aren't, or in bed with a couple of fresh ladies. Bad things happen to people in bad weather. They slip and fall and end up in a wheelchair, or they take a hit of lightning, or they catch pneumonia and spend weeks coughing up blood or whatever people do when they have pneumonia, because Mother Nature is a mean bitch. Yet here he is out in the storm, slogging through mud, his shoes already ruined, everything he's wearing destined for a dumpster. And why? Because fourteen years ago, Nina Dozier wanted him so bad that she tricked him into doing her until she could have his baby, and now she wants the boy for her own, as if she made the kid herself, just carved him out of wood and brought him to life like Pinocchio. Aleem is soaked, cold, miserable. He is so pissed at Nina that he's lost all interest in doing her with Kuba; he just wants to kill her hard but slow, if they can get her someplace dry. He is so angry that he can't imagine any development that would crank up his rage even further—which is when he and Kuba become human jukeboxes.

His iPhone is safe and dry in a zippered inside pocket of his jacket when music explodes from it at a far greater volume than he has ever before heard the device produce. He is so startled that he stumbles and slips and nearly falls in the mud, and Kuba cries out as if a cold and ghostly hand has grabbed his scrotum. The music is so loud that the phone is vibrating in Aleem's pocket and quickly growing warm. They're stalking Nina, listening for any sound of her and the boy that might carry through the whistling wind and drumming rain, while she's for sure listening for any sound *they* make, and if this is happening to him and Kuba, it's probably also happening to their six homeys. He's now furious, the way he gets when only blood will calm him, not just because some trickster techie is screwing with them, but because the music is, of all things, "Macarena," by Los Del Río, freakin' *dance music*, maybe the lon-gest-running song ever on the charts, nothing hard and street about it, six steps down from the Bee Gees. It's not bad enough that the music is announcing their position, but it's also *embarrassing*.

Aleem zippers open his jacket and reaches inside and zippers open the pocket and extracts the phone and tries to switch it off, but he can't. The phone won't shut down, and it won't let him get out of the music app. And there's this lame video, pure punk cheese, of idiots in Spanish costumes dancing and grinning, thrashing around a ballroom as if they ought to be foaming at the mouth. He fingers the volume slide, and it moves down, but the music continues to boom into the night.

Kuba is shouting obscenities, agitating his phone as if Los Del Río can be dispensed from it like salt from a shaker. Frustrated, he throws it down in the mud and raises one foot, but he can't bring himself to stomp on it, maybe because it's not a cheap burner, but probably also because his contacts include the numbers of ten or twenty fresh ladies, none of which he has committed to memory. Plus he's got photos on there of some of his best moments, selfies of the part of him that he's most proud of, taken just as it achieved liftoff, treasured mementos that he's loath to lose.

There's no way to save the phones, but it's a mistake to break them. By way of example, Aleem throws his down next to Kuba's and turns and shambles away into the wind and rain, toward that section of the orchard where Nina and the kid are most likely to be found. Maybe she'll assume their position is still defined by "Macarena," while in fact they're coming at her from a different direction.

After a moment, Kuba catches up with him, hunched and hooded. "You see this comin'?"

"See what?"

"All this weird shit."

"What—I'm Nostradamus?"

"How she do that?"

"The phones wasn't Nina. Neither was the Aviator."

"How you know?"

"She's an accountant is all she is, not some genius hacker."

Aleem shivers. His shirt is wet. He forgot to close his jacket after he got the phone out. He zips it up.

Raising his voice to compete with the wind, Kuba says, "So it's the boy?"

"The boy don't have gear for a trick like that."

"How you know?"

"Nobody has gear for that."

"Somebody does. You see that video? Man, it *sucked*."

"Could make a man go deaf and blind," Aleem agrees.

They are far enough away from their phones to hear "Macarena" playing elsewhere in the orchard.

"Mockin' us," Kuba says. "We find who, I'll give him a livin' autopsy."

Aleem says, "Nina's got to know who."

"Man, that music eats your soul," Kuba says.

"Could be worse."

"How?"

"Could be Abba."

"Shit, it could be 'Dancin' Queen.'"

"Didn't I just say?"

EN ROUTE

Southbound at high speed in the Bentley, slaloming lane to lane through traffic that is fast-moving yet slower than he can tolerate, Michael Mace is muttering in frustration at the discrepancy between the astonishing mental powers of his life as a resurrectee and the very human physical limitations to which he remains subjected. When he wishes, he is able to perceive the billions of electromagnetic waves—carrier waves—of data that flow through the intricate webs of wires and glass fibers civilization has spun, that also course through the air from transmitter to transmitter, to receivers beyond counting, passing through buildings and people and trees without any effect, television programs and Zoom conferences that are invisible while in transit, streamed music and cell-phone conversations that cannot be heard until translated from digital code into audible tones. Every river of data will wash him quickly to a computer or a network of computers, most of which are sluiceways that will spill him into the internet. He can be in New York in a few seconds, in Washington or Paris or Beijing, or in a surveillance satellite in orbit above Earth. All the secrets that the world so jealously keeps are not hidden from him. However, to help Nina and John in that damn orchard, he needs to be there in the flesh.

He wonders if that is true, if he could have—should have—done more from a distance than use the government's secret kill switch to disable the engines of the four SUVs, more than turn the bad boys' smartphones into Macarena locators that revealed them to Nina and prevented them from coordinating their search for her. A smartphone is a handheld computer. Hackable. If he can tap Spotify to stream whatever music he wants to their phones, amp up the volume of the speakers, and magnify the vibrator function, perhaps there is some way to feed a charge to a phone's lithium battery that will rapidly overload it and cause it not merely to grow very hot but to explode, injuring whoever is carrying it. If that might be the case, he lacks the genius to see how it can be done.

Those who have long predicted the Singularity have imagined that the physical integration of man and machine will lead to all manner of amazing powers, as well as to a radical enhancement of the human intellect, making human beings hundreds or thousands—or even millions—of times smarter than they currently are. The expectation of amazing powers seems to a limited extent confirmed, but Michael can testify that the übergenius theory is less science than wishful thinking, comic-book thinking. He's still processing events with the same slightly better than average brain that has gotten him through forty-four years of life and a day or so of death.

Perhaps his reflexes are better, even markedly better than they were when he was twenty, because in spite of the rain and the road condition, he's finessing the Bentley through traffic that's for the most part doing between sixty and seventy miles an hour, while he stays between eighty and a hundred. He doesn't need the navigation system that Woodbine left switched off. He knows where he's going, having entered Nina's phone and confirmed the location of her GPS signal.

He isn't expecting a highway patrol car to be parked along the shoulder, radar cone exposed to the rain. On a night when there will be three times as many accidents as usual because of the weather, the police avoid further distracting motorists by declining to give chase to the most egregious scofflaws among them. Indeed, it's not a radar trap that puts him at risk. After racing around an eighteen-wheeler at ninety miles an hour, he sweeps past a

CHP black-and-white, a Dodge Charger, that's cruising twenty yards ahead of the big truck. Cutting speed now is pointless. He's already barreling away from the patrol car, already clocked, when the lightbar on its roof brightens and its siren sounds.

He isn't constantly aware of the infinitude of electromagnetic-wave streams that carry data around and through him, doesn't see, hear, smell, taste, or feel them in the usual sense. The powerful nanotechnology that was conveyed into every cell of his brain and body by the archaea provides him with a sixth sense that's difficult to comprehend in human terms. His sixth sense is like a second self. That cybernetic persona, his shadow self, is continuously alert to all frequencies, capable of identifying the systems using them for transmission and instantly "reading" the content. The billions of cells that constitute Michael also compose the most sophisticated transmitter and receiver of data in the world. He contains billions of conventional tuning capacitors paralleled by small variable capacitors, which allows his shadow self to scan the entire spectrum of frequencies and fine-tune to precisely the one he desires at any moment. He is not actively aware of this shadow self until he seeks its service. Then he needs only to *think* what data stream he wishes to enter, at which point he can see-hear-understand what information it carries. More important, however, is his capacity to control that data stream and insert instructions into it. That is his primitive understanding of how Michael and Shadow Michael work, which in fact he can no more explain than a five-year-old piano prodigy can explain how, after hearing a sonata by Mozart only once, he's able to play the piece impeccably and with passion beyond his years.

Although Michael needs merely to *think* what he wants from his shadow self, he usually speaks the request, for a lifetime habit of vocalizing can't be broken in a few days. Just as Amazon's Alexa can often translate a slightly inaccurate search request and provide the information needed, so Shadow Michael knows what Michael wants even when his request isn't a precise description of the subject. After returning to life and ghosting out of Beautification Research, during his days in the Beverly Hills house of Roger Pullman, whose clothes he still wears, his understanding of his strange power had rapidly evolved because it was part of the function of the nanotech shadow self to instruct him with tutorials that unspooled like vivid daydreams.

Now, fleeing with the cruiser in pursuit, he says, "Insert me into California Highway Patrol's system of in-car computer terminals and digital citation printers. The nearest mobile unit."

He retains an awareness of the highway ahead of him, as well as a keen recognition of the challenges of the traffic and weather, but another scene appears in the upper right-hand quadrant of his range of vision, rather like a screen in screen on a TV. The inset image is provided by the camera in the computer of the pursuing patrol car. He can see half of the driver's face—a square jaw, a nose broken more than once, one eye set deep under a formidable brow.

The officer finishes speaking into the microphone of the police radio, and a dispatcher begins to answer him, but Michael shuts down that avenue of communication. He has control of the patrol car's computer and equipment associated with it. He douses the flashing lightbar on the roof. Kills the siren. He switches on the outside speaker by which the officer can blast instructions at motorists, cranks it up to the max, pulls a Sirius radio signal out of the air, and feeds "Proud Mary" by Creedence Clearwater Revival through the system at such thunderous volume that he can hear it in the Bentley. The black-and-white loses speed and falls back from him. From the computer, he can slide into the car's basic electronics, so he pops the trunk-lid release and shuts off the headlights. He turns the heater and fan to the highest setting, giving the patrolman some Mojave Desert in the middle of the downpour that has overwhelmed the windshield wipers, which have been shut off and locked.

In the upper right-hand quadrant of his vision, Michael sees the frantic officer, who's virtually blinded without headlights and wipers, guiding his disabled vehicle to a stop on the shoulder of the freeway. The cop will have a cell phone to call for assistance, but in this weather and under the circumstances, he probably didn't get a chance to read the Bentley's license-plate number. And before Michael exited the squad car, he erased the video recorded by its bow and stern cameras. If the plates are reported to the National Crime Information Center, Michael will receive a blue-neon warning in his mind's eye and either delete the listing or change some of the numbers around to confound the authorities.

Rain falls, darkness deepens, and Michael races south toward an interstate exit, a lonely state highway, a quiet valley, and a dead orchard, where Nina and her son need the kind of help he can provide only with the AR-15. Earlier he retrieved it from the compartment under the back seat. It's now wedged barrel up between the passenger seat and the dashboard. One extended magazine with twenty rounds has been inserted in the rifle. The three spares lay on the seat. As a security specialist and licensed bodyguard, he is trained in the use of various firearms, including this one. But he's never shot anyone. He's never *killed* anyone. He is highly skilled with the AR-15, and he knows full well that Aleem and his crew are killers who give nothing to the world but misery and grief. But he has never killed anyone.

BEING PREPARED

The chaise longue is low to the floor, which facilitates the transfer of the unconscious attorney onto it, where he lies faceup in the center of the former gym as well as in countless reflections of reflections, like an army of sleeping clones. His arms trail off the furniture, hands resting palms up on the floor. His wrists are secured to the legs of the chaise with long, plastic zip ties. He is murmuring, muttering, a few minutes from regaining consciousness.

Calaphas is never without his Springfield Armory .45 Tactical Response Pistol, a second pistol that can't be traced to him, an aerosol can of chloroform provided by the agency, and a combat knife with a spring blade. He also always carries four zip ties; during his lifetime, the world has become a place where such convenient instruments of restraint are ever more frequently essential to the conduct of business.

Since childhood, Durand Calaphas has believed in being prepared for unexpected opportunities. He was thirteen when he began to carry a knife, a simple switchblade. A week past his fifteenth birthday, he put it to interesting use. For the month of July, he was staying with his grandmother, Jane Jones, in rural Ohio. Jane was a twinkly-eyed white-haired cookie-baking pie-making apron-wearing cliché whose unvarying and tedious daily routine confirmed what Calaphas sometimes believed back then—that he was the only real person in the world and that everyone else was a product of his imagination. His grandmother lived in a Victorian house with much ornamental millwork, a grandfather clock swinging its pendulum in the front hall, the arms and headrests of furniture protected by antimacassars that she crocheted, and sweet aphorisms rendered in needlepoint framed on the walls. The house backed up to a woods where Calaphas, during one of his explorations, encountered a sixteen-year-old boy, Bill Smith, who possessed no more depth than a walk-on character in a thinly written TV show, just like Grandma Jane. Bill wore chunky hiking shoes, kneesocks, khaki shorts with patch pockets, a sweat-stained white T-shirt, braces to straighten his teeth, and horn-rimmed glasses with tortoiseshell frames. He carried a book about mushrooms, with full-color illustrations of a hundred seventy common varieties. He said he was going to be a mycologist, a biologist specializing in fungi. He wasn't merely interested in mushrooms; he was *fascinated* by them. He thought Calaphas must also be obsessed with mushrooms, as if no other reason existed to be in the woods. Calaphas followed the wannabe mycologist around for more than an hour, expecting this prince of nerdhood to become semitransparent and thereby prove that he was a dreamed presence in a dreamed world, imagined into the scene to keep Calaphas entertained. When Bill found a colony of cortinarius alboviolaceus, an edible variety that he declared delicious, he began to harvest them into a plastic bag, which was when Calaphas got the idea to test Fungus Bill's reality by harvesting *him*. Although he was a year younger than the amateur mycologist, Calaphas was by far the stronger of the two. He drew his switchblade and fell on the startled boy, cut his throat with one furious slash and then drove the blade between ribs, into the nerd's heart. He sat beside the corpse for a while, waiting to see if it would fade away, but it didn't.

This was when he began to reconsider his belief that he was the only real person in the world. If Bill Smith was real, then so might be whoever found his body and the police who would investigate the murder. A fifteen-year-old boy like Durand would not be the first suspect in such a case. Nevertheless, he took steps to ensure that he was unlikely to fall under suspicion at all. He pulled off Bill Smith's khaki shorts and underwear, cut away the primary evidence that the nerd was male, took the severed package deeper into the woods, and dropped it through a vacancy in a rock formation, into the inaccessible cave below. Now the authorities would be searching for some adult pervert with a macabre collection of genitalia in his home freezer or in jars of formaldehyde. A fresh-faced boy visiting from Colorado would excite no interest. Having come into the forest bare-chested, in sneakers and cut-off jeans, he needed to deal with the blood he'd gotten on himself. A stream cut through the trees and fed a swimming hole in its passing. Calaphas bathed in those cool mossy-smelling waters, and sat in a meadow until the sun dried his hair and clothes. In spite of the blow to his philosophy of life that these events had delivered, when he returned to the Victorian house, his grandmother still seemed to be a thinly imagined figure in a lame TV drama.

All these years later, the most recent Bill—Carter Woodbine, Esquire—groans and opens his eyes and rolls his head from side to side on the chaise. His chloroform-abused nose issues a clear, watery discharge. He tries to move, but his zip-tied hands prevent him from sitting up.

Standing over the chaise, Calaphas waits until his captive is awake and giving voice to his outrage in a flood of invective. He focuses Woodbine's attention by knocking on the man's forehead as though on a door. "Is anyone at home?"

The frivolous nature of this insolence at last alarms the self-assured attorney, and his contorted expression of indignation fades out as fear fades in. He has never before been at a loss for words either as a servant of the law in a courtroom or as a caring patron providing capital and connections to visionary entrepreneurs in the dark-market pharmaceuticals industry. However, when Woodbine looks into Calaphas's eyes, he sees something there that silences him and from which he is powerless to look away.

"I have your iPhone. I need the pass code," Calaphas says.

In fact, he might not need the use of Woodbine's phone because he can probably find the Bentley by other means than locating the AirTag signal. Being a prudent man, he always likes to have a backup plan in case the sure thing turns out not to be so sure, after all.

Instead of providing a pass code, the attorney says, "Santana?"

"Dead."

"Harris?"

"Dead."

"If I give you the code?"

Calaphas has the pleasure of saying, "Dead."

"Then why should I cooperate?"

They both know the answer. In this otherwise deserted fortress, with its state-of-the-art soundproofing and triple-pane windows retrofitted with a quarter-inch bullet-resistant laminate, the sounds of the world beyond don't intrude. No volume of screaming arising within these rooms can be sufficient to gain the attention of anyone beyond its walls.

Calaphas says simply, "Do you relish pain to the extent that you would like me to spend the night in the application of it?"

Instead of replying to that question, Woodbine provides the pass code to his phone. When he has answered a few other questions and senses that this brief interrogation has come to an end, his eyes are swimming with what might be bleak and bitter sorrow. The only witness to any weakness he reveals is the man who will murder him, but the attorney bites back any plea for mercy he might be desperate to express. Whatever arrogance had been instilled in him at Harvard Law, he didn't acquire machismo there. His years of associating with the likes of Santana and Harris have evidently evoked in him the idea that the proper response to impending and inescapable death is austere fortitude, even if he has to fake it. He says only, "I'd like to understand."

"Understand what?"

"You're ISA."

"They pay me, yes."

"You believe in the New Truth."

"As I interpret it." Calaphas reaches under his suit coat and draws a gun from the belt scabbard on his left hip, the weapon with which he shot the men now entering rigor mortis in the kitchen.

The attorney turns his head to the right and gazes at the receding multitude of reclining Carter Woodbines in the mirrored wall. Perhaps he is considering that infinity of selves and is *reconsidering* his scorn for those who believe in an immortal soul and life eternal. Addressing the reflections of Calaphas, he says, "Well, then we're allies."

Calaphas corrects him. "There are no allies in this game."

"I already offered you the three million."

Allowing himself a sigh, Calaphas says, "It's not about the money, though of course I'll be glad to have it."

"Not about money? Then what's it about?"

"The score. It's about the score."

Turning his head to face his executioner directly, Woodbine appears to feel imposed upon, as though it's unfair that, oppressed by dread and despair, he should have to make room in his emotional wheelhouse also for the form of anxiety that is called perplexity. "Score? We met less than half an hour ago. What have I ever done to you? What score do you have to settle with me?"

"That's not what I mean by 'score,'" Calaphas says, and shoots his puzzled captive in the face.

He holsters the pistol and draws a pair of gloves from a coat pocket and sheaths his hands. These are not fine leather that might excite someone who thrills to a certain fetish. Ninety-two percent cotton, 8 percent spandex, they are for wiping surfaces Calaphas touched and for preventing the further laying down of fingerprints. Because he touched little in this apartment, he needs less than two minutes to complete the task.

Confident that the building is unguarded on this night between one security company and another, the cameras blinded and the video recorders shut off and the alarms without voice, Calaphas leaves the apartment and passes through the deceased attorney's office. In the receptionist's office, he enters the numbers in the elevator keypad that he watched Santana enter earlier. He rides down to the ground floor and follows the hallway from the lobby to the back vestibule. In the garage, he proceeds to the valet's cubicle, where a spare key to the stolen Bentley hangs on a pegboard; he pockets it. He returns to the vestibule, where his raincoat hangs. He slips into it, pulls up the hood, and steps into the night through the back door.

Although some other businesses have exterior security cameras and traffic cams observe many—but not all—intersections, he knows how to spot them, how accurately to gauge their field of vision, and how to avoid most of them. By a circuitous route, cloaked and hooded and with his face averted, crossing streets mid block to avoid the intersections, making use of narrow service ways between buildings, where there are no doors and therefore no cameras, he returns to the parking lot by the restaurant, where he left his sedan.

No one in the ISA expects a report of his meeting with Carter Woodbine until at least tomorrow morning. If Calaphas is right about what, in addition to three million dollars, is stowed in the secret compartment of the Bentley that the attorney wanted so badly, if he can locate the transponder in the hollowed-out bundle of currency—and he can, he will, in mere minutes—then he will find and kill Michael Mace long before morning. Dead once, the fugitive can be made dead again, permanently this time. Whatever Mace might have become, regardless of the gifts the Singularity has granted him, he isn't immortal, for if he were, he wouldn't be on the run for his life. When Mace is dead again, which he will be before dawn, the murders of Woodbine, Santana, and Harris can be pinned on him. That done, Calaphas will have won the prize of all prizes.

He has no doubt that this is the highest level of play and that his cumulative score, racked up over the years, will soon make him the master of the game. All the signs are here to be read. A great treasure almost within his reach. Hidden with the treasure, a secret something—the magic key, the Ark of the Covenant, the crystal of infinite power, the one ring that controls them all, whatever—the possession of which is the entire point of the game. And guarding the key or ark or ring is Mace, with powers that will defeat all but the most clever and determined player. Which is Durand Calaphas. All the signs are here to be read. This world is real in its way, but it's a *virtual* reality, a simulation, created by beings of a higher order. The world is a game. Those who live in this construct are as alive as Calaphas is, not imaginary as he once believed, and for one of them there is a game to be won and a prize.

Behind the wheel of his car, he pulls back his hood and starts the engine. He activates the navigation system, which has features that are exclusive to the Internal Security Agency. A list of the previously entered addresses appears on the screen. Ignoring those, he enters SAFE HOUSES / LOS ANGELES COUNTY. A new list of eight locations is provided, three preceded by asterisks, which indicates they are currently in use, either sheltering fugitives from the law, whom the agency wishes to protect, or serving as secret interrogation centers where agents are sweating information out of enemies of the state. He makes a selection, declines vocal guidance, presses start, and initial directions appear in white letters on the windshield.

Warning himself not to become overconfident and to respect the cunning of those who designed this challenge, he drives out of the parking lot, into the night and the rain and the city, toward the hope of triumph, toward an escape from the game, toward a new life in which the played becomes a player in a higher—and true—reality beyond this one.

THE RED-EYED SCAVENGERS
ARE CREEPING

Henceforth forever appleless, the orchard trees stand in solemn order like monoliths that once had a potent meaning. Now, tortured by time and disease and bad water policy, they offer the one message about life no one wants to hear, their branches skeletal, trunks cracked like ancient stone cenotaphs, dead roots rotting into significant soil.

Nina and John splash along a harvester's alley where four rusting farm machines of indeterminable purpose loom large, canted on split tires or broken axles, evidently abandoned because they were worn out and no longer possessed any resale value. In the gloom and rain and mantling mist, the machines are eerily suggestive of Jurassic-period life-forms. Mother and son hurry past them, cross the alley, pass between withered trees in yet another row, and come at last into a clearing where geometric slabs of darkness imprint barnlike buildings on the darker fabric of the night, some two stories and others three. This is the complex where, back in the day, freshly picked apples were brought by the hundreds of thousands to be washed, polished, packaged, and either shipped or otherwise processed.

Nina imagines that on a night with moonlight, these weathered clapboard walls, standing on concrete-block foundations, softly glow silvery gray and have a certain melancholy beauty. Now they are black and sinister.

The structures are not so forbidding that she can forsake them for the wilderness of deadwood that is her only other option. The map on her phone can direct her to the highway that bisects the valley, but at this hour and in this weather, traffic in this rural area is minimal. She is less likely to encounter a helpful motorist than to fall into the hands of Aleem's homeys, at least two of which will surely have made their way out of the orchard to patrol the road on foot.

Unfortunately, she fled home without her phone's charging cord. The battery is down to 26 percent, and she must preserve it in order for Michael to find her by the GPS signal. She can check the phone briefly to discover true west, and follow a harvesters' alley to its end, where the fertile flats give way to rugged, rising land. Beyond those wild slopes and ravines, within a mile or two, perhaps three, lie busy multitudes in a chain of towns nearer the coast. Even here in the orchard, however, the ground is treacherous; already, both she and John have stumbled and fallen more than once. Two points of mild pain afflict her, one in her left knee, the other in her left ankle. Nothing is broken, but nothing is as it should be. In the brush-covered hills beyond the orchard, sustaining a fractured ankle or leg would be a serious risk even if she weren't already limping. Besides, they need to stay somewhere that Michael can more easily come to their assistance.

"Here," she says.

John agrees. "Yeah, but where here?"

They move among the buildings, none of which is the same scale or style as any other, suggesting that construction occurred over several decades, as the orchard grew to require ever more servicing, with an immense crop that had to be processed in a timely manner. A few bear huge block letters on the gable walls, above the great doors, and although the white paint is badly faded, the words can still be read, seeming to identify different processing strategies: One building declares CIDER & JUICE, and the largest announces WHOLE FRUIT; here is SPECIAL ACCOUNTS, and there is SPECIALTY PRODUCTS. The smallest is labeled OFFICES, and the second largest, lacking block letters, might once have been a long garage in which company vehicles and farm equipment were stored.

Their pursuers are unlikely to decide to devote a precious hour or more to these rambling buildings. For one thing, in the dark and under the cover of the storm, Nina and John could conceivably move from one building to another in a prolonged cat-and-mouse game. More to the point, Aleem knows that she never hides from anything, that she always pushes forward. Because he isn't aware that she's been hurt and slowed by a limp, he will most likely assume that she's quickening south, toward the help that lies beyond the orchard, in the first homes on the outskirts of the valley's only substantial town.

Nina favors the largest structure because its immensity seems to provide more hiding places if a search of this crumbling complex occurs. She leads John to the maw once shuttered by a great door, and inside. Big roll-ups are missing from all the buildings, perhaps salvaged in bankruptcy. As the boy stifles two sneezes in one hand and blows his nose in a Kleenex, Nina switches on her Tac Light, shields the beam with a cupped hand, and probes the darkness. She finds an uneven concrete floor that, on a dry night, might reveal their footprints in a thick layer of dust and debris. However, with the roof leaking and floor drains not functional, water rises to the thresholds of the missing doors, an inch deep in most places.

Turning, she sweeps the cowled beam across the ground behind them. The muddy surface, thatched with a mat of dead wild grass, retains impressions of their passing only briefly before the wet broom of the storm erases all evidence.

She leads John into the foul-smelling ankle-deep water of the packing plant. The night is cool, but the pool through which she moves is colder, eliciting a shudder both physical and mental. She halts, wondering if this place offers the refuge that they need.

The Tac Light reveals a cavernous structure longer than a football field, perhaps a hundred feet wide. Support columns rise about thirty feet to the ceiling. The processing machinery is long gone. Along the right-hand wall are what might have been a series of offices and storage rooms.

Nina turns to look back through the space where the great door once hung. This isn't an accounting problem that can be solved by finding an error of addition or subtraction. She has no mathematics by which to calculate and compare the risks of the two courses of action open to her. She looks at John, who clutches the duffel bag, his rain-wet face glistening. She almost asks what he thinks—this building or the night—but she doesn't want to frighten him further by expressing her doubt.

"This is best," he says, as if he can read her thoughts. Maybe to some extent he can. Their love for each other binds them not only heart to heart, but also mind to mind. "With your ankle, this is best, Mom."

The only windows are thirty feet above the work floor, near the ceiling. Little light can rise to those panes, which are occluded by grime and the diligent work of generations of spiders. Nevertheless, she dims the Tac beam with two fingers across the big lens.

She wants to tell her boy everything's all right, they'll come safely through this night, but she never lies to him. In her mind's eye, she can see Aleem and his homeys, those rats with their faces concretized by the lust for power and hatred that is the essence of them, challenging her with that hard stare they call "the red eye," which demands submission and threatens murder. There is no safe place tonight. She kisses John's brow and leads him through the foul-smelling water in this walled lagoon, toward the rooms along the right-hand wall.

SAFE HOUSE

This particular property in the ISA portfolio is a safe mansion rather than a safe house, on an acre of land behind a gated estate wall, in a gated community of multimillion-dollar residences. The architecture is Tuscan, as the community's design committee imagines that to be, though they seem to have in mind a different Italy from the one in Europe. It has seven bedrooms, ten baths, a home theater, as well as indoor and outdoor swimming pools, among other amenities.

Calaphas puts down the window of his sedan and gets his hand wet as he enters his nine-digit agent-ID number in the keypad. The handsome gate rolls open as he puts up the window. He follows the driveway to the portico at the front entrance.

Several dangerous people of interest to the agency have been interrogated in this residence for days or even weeks at a time, without being charged with crimes and without the interference of attorneys. They generally are brought here in a state of sedation, in the trunk of a car, and are kept in a windowless basement room. Once vital information has been extracted from them and their guilt has been confirmed, they are processed by a PowerPak cremation system that reduces them to ashes and bits of stubborn bone, humble remains that are more easily disposed of than awkward corpses.

The primary purpose of the place, however, is to temporarily house people—often entire families—from other countries, people who serve the New Truth movement and whom the agency wants in the United States without informing immigration officials about the backgrounds of these individuals. Here, they are assigned new names, given life histories to memorize, supplied with documents to support their new identities, and put on the agency payroll. In a few cases, they are provided with the services of a superb plastic surgeon.

Leaving his sedan in the protection of the portico, Calaphas climbs four steps and enters his nine-digit agent ID in a keypad by the front door. The electronic lock disengages a trio of deadbolts, and the door swings open, and he steps inside.

The safe house is overseen by Bob and Joy Klink, who have an apartment here. Having been made aware of his arrival when he passed through the front gate, they are waiting to greet him in the foyer. They know Calaphas, but Bob examines his agency ID anyway, and Joy requires him to submit to a retinal scan with a handheld device.

"Buzz us if you need anything," says Bob, and they depart.

Calaphas proceeds to an office for visiting agents. He needs a workstation programmed to provide, with minimal keystrokes, access to all computer systems in which the ISA installed undetectable rootkits. That is every system of significance in federal, state, and local government, as well as those in the private sector.

He withdraws Woodbine's smartphone from a jacket pocket and switches it on and enters the pass code. He activates the link to the transponder that the attorney planted with his run-for-it money, and a map of the current vicinity appears on the screen, but nothing further occurs. Maybe the transponder is dead.

As he puts his iPhone on the desk to prepare it, he realizes that Mace, with his extraordinary abilities, might have learned the name of the agent assigned to find him. If he has Calaphas's phone number, he'll be able to track its transponder. Using the intercom, Calaphas buzzes Bob Klink to request a new iPhone from the safe-house supply, specifying that it must not be registered to him.

Bob is remarkably efficient. He produces the phone in five minutes, along with a refreshing bottle of Calaphas's favorite ale.

"I also must have a car from your motor pool, one with a disabled navigation system, so it can't be tracked. You'll need to keep my agency car here until I return for it."

Using the computer, Calaphas enters a Department of Defense satellite system that can track any registered transponder, and he inputs the number he got from Woodbine. In a minute, the screen fills with a map. A blinking red dot puts the vehicle—and Michael Mace—in south Orange County, speeding toward San Diego County, as if he's heading for Mexico. The transponder is active, after all; the glitch was with the app linking it to Woodbine's phone or with the phone itself. Even as Calaphas watches, the Bentley exits the interstate and proceeds inland on a state highway, which isn't what Mace would do if his destination was the border.

The DOD system can continuously track a few thousand vehicles simultaneously. Calaphas instructs it to stay on the Bentley and to link with his new agency iPhone until further notice. The map on the computer now appears on the smaller screen of that phone, the red signifier blinking. He backs out of the Department of Defense system and shuts off the computer. He pockets both his new phone and Carter Woodbine's, which he'll plant on Mace's corpse.

In the basement, the safe-house armory lies behind a steel door. Access is granted when he enters his agency ID number in the keypad. The forty-foot-square room is a wonderland of weaponry. He selects a prepacked carrying case that contains an AR-15 and four loaded magazines with twenty rounds each, all snugged in a formed-foam lining for rattle-free transport. A pair of state-of-the-art night-vision glasses might prove useful, as might a police lock-release device. Although he avoids negative thinking, he takes a lunchbox-size medical kit that contains prescription painkillers, antibiotics, antinausea medicine, wound-site coagulants to slow bleeding, and other items that might be useful in a time of stress.

His replacement car is waiting in the portico. It's dark gray rather than black, but otherwise identical to his previous vehicle. He puts his requisitions on the floor in back. Behind the wheel, he starts the engine. He props his phone in a cup holder, so that he can see the screen with the map and the blinking signifier. The game is on, the end game in sight.

WE ARE ENCOMPASSED WITH SNAKES

Aleem and Kuba have no flashlight, but they have confidence in their superior animal instincts, in their predatory skills. They are men among men, testosterone-powered walking versions of the seventy-ton Marine M1A1 battle tank, like in that cool movie, shelling the shit out of any dumb bastard or bitch who gets in their way, always plowing forward, always taking ground. The night doesn't scare them. Neither does the storm. The trick is to keep moving south, toward the end of the orchard, toward the hick town, which is Nina's only hope of help. At any moment, she and the boy are going to come into view, slogging along, neither of them with the stamina to outrun their pursuers.

Although all the wood here is dead, the orchard reminds Aleem of the jungle in El Salvador, which was the last time he was among so many trees. He is well traveled. He's been to El Salvador twice, Colombia once, and even to Venezuela. There was a time when a gang boss rarely went farther from the hood than half a tank of gas could take him. Leave your turf too long, and some fool would take it for his own, so then you'd have to wrench it back at some cost in blood and money. These days, however, a man in Aleem's position has to be not just a warrior but also a diplomat. Now that certain politicians and bureaucrats find it profitable to open the country to more drug traffic, gangs from Central America are operating everywhere from the suburbs to the heartland. Those machete boys are crazy violent, but even they recognize it's bad business to conduct open warfare in pointless turf battles. It's a big country and, for the foreseeable future, still rich enough to support huge numbers of hardworking criminals. To negotiate mutually beneficial turf boundaries in major cities, some cool specimens in the State Department, on their own hook, from time to time fly leaders like Aleem south to lands of higher humidity, more snakes, and truly incredible numbers of large insects, to establish trust and a sense of community with others in his line of work.

Usually those conferences take place in urban settings. But on one memorable occasion, the boss of bosses with whom Aleem spent two days in discussions, Pepe Blanco, had a luxurious horse ranch on a two-hundred-acre grassy plateau surrounded by jungle. The days were filled with negotiations, but the long evenings were given to lavish banquets awash in the finest wines, attended by the most beautiful young girls that Pepe's scouts had found and brought to the ranch after buying them from their families or killing those parents who were too virtuous for such bargaining. On the second night, as part of the entertainment, Pepe and his inner circle took Aleem and the man from the State Department off the plateau and into the jungle, to a clearing where three activists, notorious for their resistance to a government run by gangsters, had been brought for what Pepe called "their penance." A young priest. A university professor and novelist of some renown. A woman physician whose work with the poor included proselytizing against illegal drugs and the men who sold them. Each of the penitents was bound to a different tree along the perimeter of the clearing. Tall, fragrant torches produced little smoke, but their aromatic fumes effectively repelled flying insects. Across the ground and from the palm fronds, palpitant light billowed like discarded silk veils. Tables draped in white linen trimmed in arabesques of lace held an appealing variety of tapas, fresh fruit, and cheeses. Dom Pérignon was chilled in chests of ice and served in elegant Lalique flutes. Three holes, each about six feet deep, had been dug with a backhoe. And now six husky men with shovels stood ready to fill them. The physician, bound hand and foot, was thrown into a grave;

she cursed her executioners as moist soil was spaded onto her by the industrious workmen, and then she began to cry out the names of her children as she disappeared beneath the raw earth. Pepe and his guests were much amused, although the man from the State Department, T. Denby Danford, expressed concern. He fretted that such cruelty was unnecessary when a bullet to the back of the head would provide the same result as being buried alive. When even Denby realized that his distaste for this soiree was causing offense to the celebrants and souring their mood to such an extent that a fourth grave might be dug, he kept his opinion to himself, turned on the charm, and took refuge in more champagne. Soon, not even muffled cries came from the physician's grave. As the workmen finished filling it and tamping down the soil, a classical guitarist and a bongoist provided festive music until the time came to bury the professor who was also a popular novelist. Interred with copies of his books, he screamed defiant accusations, using words that puzzled Aleem and most of those present. Finally the fool's mouth filled with dirt and he was unable to find air to breathe, whereupon the musicians returned to their instruments in high spirits. The young priest proved to be by far the partiers' favorite. He evoked the most laughter as he resorted to the Lord's Prayer while the busy shovelers worked up a sweat, especially when he spoke the words that Christ had spoken as the nails pierced Him: "Father, forgive them, for they know not what they do." It was an evening to remember, a celebration of the values that brought them together, a bonding revel. Aleem was exhilarated, filled with pride to be Pepe's brother from another mother, filled with hope for the future, brimming with ambition. When they returned to the grand house on the grassy plateau, he was offered a girl of sixteen, Margareta, for the night. He told Pepe that two days in this place had tempered him, as steel is tempered to make a better sword; he was such a hard man now, he might damage one lover beyond repair; therefore, in consideration of Margareta's health, it would be better if a second girl were also provided so that neither would be ruined forever in the process of satisfying him. This tongue-in-cheek braggadocio delighted Pepe. Seventeen-year-old Selena was sent to Aleem's room with Margareta. He used them well and long and with no respect, but when at last they left him before dawn, he remained sleepless in the recognition that the most stimulating and thrilling moments of the night had not involved those lubricious girls, but instead the three people lying six feet under the jungle floor without benefit of coffins.

Now, in this orchard of dead trees, where "Macarena" no longer echoes, soaked to the skin for the lack of rain gear, his mud-caked shoes heavier by the minute, with four decommissioned vehicles to be somehow repaired and started and driven away, with as many as eight discarded phones to be retrieved, Aleem has reached the end of his patience. He no longer wants to rape Nina in company with Kuba, and he no longer wants to watch Kuba take her apart over several hours. His fury at her for putting him in this position burns in his mind with such intensity that it will consume him if he doesn't soon make her pay, burns as hot as the wrath of Pepe Blanco, which drove that righteous, proud man to deal as he had with the physician, novelist, and priest. Neither putting a bullet in Nina's head nor stabbing her a hundred times will be sufficient to repair the damage she has done to Aleem's pride. Nothing short of burying her alive will satisfy him.

Her *and* the boy. John has been witness to his mother's total lack of respect for his father and to Aleem's humiliation at the stubborn woman's hands. After so many years in Nina's company, the kid has for sure been infected with her pigheadedness. Bringing him into the gang, trying to reform the little Christer-schooled brat and instruct him in the hard truth of life as it can be found every day on the street, would be like Caesar adopting Judas before Judas stabs him in the back. Or whoever it was who stabbed Caesar, if it was Caesar who was stabbed and not the guy who fiddled while Rome burned, or maybe Paris. On Aleem's favorite TV show, this hard-ass gang boss has an eighteen-year-old son who's even more ruthless than his old man, but loyal, totally loyal. Aleem now sees that, in this case, life isn't going to be like TV. John is a bent nail, bent so bad by his mother that he can't ever be hammered straight enough to be of any use. Besides, the kid is on a baseball team. In Aleem's opinion, baseball is a pussy sport no less than polo or volleyball. Real men are into football and basketball. Life is too short to take a kid to see baseball or to watch him pitch a game. And John takes piano lessons, which isn't an instrument Aleem can approve. When he thinks piano, Aleem thinks Liberace, a dead dude his grandmother collects on vinyl, and he thinks Elton John. He doesn't want his homeys getting the idea that the boy walks on the far side of the street. Fatherhood isn't how TV paints it. Aleem fell for that TV-dad shit because he has a sentimental streak. A sentimental streak can get you killed. Put the bitch and the brat in a hole, fill it in, tamp it down, and then life can get back to normal.

Ahead and to the east, a sudden brightness is born in the dark. The beam paints detail on the featureless dark shape of Kuba before it shifts to Aleem's face. As the light quickly slides down his body to pool at Aleem's feet, Hakeem Makuda says, "We thought maybe you was them," and he approaches with his main man, Carlisle Sharkey.

"Where you get a flashlight?" Aleem asks.

"We keep one in the Aviator just in case," Carlisle says.

Hakeem's worst character fault is a cockeyed sense of humor, revealed when he says, "A man can't never be sure he won't wind up in a dead orchard at night in a storm, his wheels broke down, and a bitch to find."

"Happens often, do it?" Kuba asks, humoring Hakeem.

"Often enough so I don't go nowheres without my bitch-finder, Carlisle. If he the last man on Earth and one woman left somewheres in France, Carlisle he'd smell her exact location."

"And I'd know what to do with her," Carlisle assures them.

Another light swells out of the trees to the west, and then yet another, as Jason James and his main man, Speedo Hickam, arrive to make it a quorum.

Orlando Fiske and Masud Ayoob have most likely returned to the highway to patrol the perimeter of the orchard.

"Everyone got damn flashlights," Kuba says.

It's obvious that, in addition to having flashlights, everyone is wearing hooded raincoats except for Kuba and Aleem.

Before anyone can comment on that, Aleem places the blame for his condition where it belongs. "Didn't 'spect to be humpin' around in the rain, huntin' the bitch. We figured she'd be screwed at the roadblock."

"She weren't," says Hakeem.

"No shit."

Carlisle, who has no discernible sense of humor, says, "Wish I really could smell out the bitch, Aleem, but that's just Hakeem bein' stupid."

Speedo Hickam says, "What the hell happened to our wheels, all gone dead at the same time?"

"We don't know," Kuba says.

"Carlisle favors a supernatural explanation," says Hakeem.

"I said *un*natural," Carlisle corrects. "That don't mean ghosts and shit. I ain't that kind of fool."

"What you sayin' then?" Kuba asks. "Space aliens?"

"What I'm sayin' is we don't know what's goin' down here, we shouldn't walk blind into it."

"So just bone out, run away scared? You not talkin' like a Vig now. That's Blood talk, Crab talk."

Crab is what they sometimes call a Crip, and Carlisle is offended. "Don't be jammin' me, Kuba. I ain't no more scared of nothin' than a tiger pisses himself he sees his shadow."

Hakeem says, "That's some tangle of words, bro. You got a translation?"

"Don't talk like a basehead. You know what I said," Carlisle replies, avoiding the admission that he lacks a translation.

Speedo Hickam changes the subject. "What about them barns or packin' plants, or whatever they are?"

"What packin' plants?" Aleem asks.

"Past the next row of trees. Lot of rat holes there where she might've gone to ground."

Aleem shakes his head. "Nina ain't the type for no rat hole. She'll keep movin'."

"Yeah, well," says Jason James, "say she keeps movin'."

"I just said it."

"Then we got a whole world to search," Jason continues. "That true or is it true? So say the bitch goes to ground, then it's just them buildings. You see the math?"

"You got a point," says Kuba.

"Reason I sleep so well at night," Hakeem says, "is 'cause we got Jason, how his lightning mind can calculate a thing."

"Vegas won't let me play blackjack no more," Jason reveals.

"Yeah, all right," Aleem says. "Show me them packin' plants."

The cold water exacerbates the pain in Nina's strained ankle, preventing her from putting her full weight on her left foot. She leans against a wall while John hurries ahead with the Tac Light, roiling the water and the sodden flotsam in it, opening doors and inspecting the spaces beyond, softly calling back to her to report what he finds.

Of the seven rooms along the right-hand wall of the packing plant, two are small lavatories. The other five are larger, each about thirty feet wide and nearly as deep. Two must have been offices, because they have windows that look out on the vast work floor. The other three were probably storage rooms.

Two storerooms are empty, but when John opens the door to the third, he stage-whispers, "Here, Mom, look at this."

When she steps through the door, she discovers a chamber half filled with trash stacked haphazardly in one corner. Broken ladders. Fifteen or twenty moldering wooden crates. Rusting five-gallon metal drums. Plastic containers that resemble large laundry baskets. A wheelbarrow with a bent brace and missing wheel. An office chair from the torn seat of which rises a white cobra of foam padding. Large panels of plywood, a scattering of empty burlap bags, opaque plastic sheeting spooling off a four-foot-long cardboard tube.

"We can hide under this stuff, hide behind it," John says. "I can move things around, make a space for us."

"The whole mess will shift and fall down around you."

"No, Mom, I can see how to do it," he insists. "We'll ease in behind it, sit with our backs to the wall. They open the door, see nothing but trash, and they go away. They go away."

"There's no time."

"Three minutes is all I need," he says, propping the Tac Light on an overturned bucket and setting to work. "Maybe four. I see how to do it."

"Hurry," she says as she steps out of the room. At opposite ends of the building, each of the gable walls is open to the night where the big roll-ups once were. She pulls the door shut behind her, blocking the spillover from the Tac Light, and though darkness folds her into its cloak, she feels exposed.

WHAT LIFE HAVE YOU IF YOU HAVE NOT
LIFE TOGETHER?

Michael remembers the late Shelby Shrewsberry riffing on how, from the human perspective, storms seem chaotic, though they are not because they are the inevitable result of nature's meteorological laws. The ineluctable influence of temperature on the speed of airflow and the speed of airflow on temperature. The balance between pressure and gravitational force. Friction between the wind and the earth. The intricate action of waves and tides in the atmosphere. The condition of the atmosphere-ocean interface. All of that and much more form a mechanism so complex that we can perceive many of its moving parts and how they interact without ever being able to predict with certitude what weather this machine might produce tomorrow, and even less what it will provide next month. *When the sun is in an active phase,* Shelby said, *the Earth warms, and when the sun is in a phase of very low activity, all life on Earth is driven toward the equator to endure the long centuries of an ice age. The sun is the one and only master of the climate, and though its thermonuclear reactions seem chaotic, they are no more so than the weather on Earth that they affect. The truth is, Michael, the only genuinely chaotic thing in the universe is humanity.*

So it seems as Michael quickens along the interstate, for the heavy traffic moves faster than the weather warrants, as if not only he but also everyone on wheels this night is hurrying somewhere to save a life. Although they lack Michael's enhanced reflexes, the drivers often follow a mere car length or two behind one another and change lanes without signaling. They jockey recklessly for position, as if nothing is more important than arriving at their destinations ten seconds faster than they might otherwise get there if they drove with any recognition of their mortality.

He finds himself mourning Shelby, not for the first time since being resurrected, but more poignantly than before. The big guy was a light in life as surely as the sun. In spite of being the same age as Michael, for thirty-eight years he had filled the role of a big brother. Shelby's remarkable intelligence ensured he was an outsider from an early age; by middle school, when he became tall and strong, his peaceable nature and humility provided another reason for most kids to ridicule him. In the school they attended and in the streets of their neighborhood, physical power was more honored than wisdom or accomplishment. Any guy as big as Shelby was expected to use his size to intimidate and get his way in all things. Brute strength combined with a determination to dominate was much admired. Shelby's gentleness invited mockery to which he responded with a smile or a joke. In the small minds of his tormentors, his response confirmed that he was what they mocked him for being—feeb, wimp, coward, loser—even though Shelby frequently broke up fights when a smaller kid was targeted by a bigger one or by a group. On those occasions, he chastised the instigators of the violence and said something that was true but which nevertheless led them to mock him further: *What life have you if you have not life together?*

In childhood and adolescence, Michael had been an outsider for reasons different from those that condemned Shelby to that status. His mother, Beth, had been known throughout the neighborhood as a mental case. Some adults called her "Batty Beth," but to most kids, she was Bugshit Beth or worse. She earned the names. Because she didn't engage in physical violence—only the emotional kind, with her son as primary target—she wasn't committed to a psychiatric ward, therefore never diagnosed. Maybe she had not always been a colorful eccentric, but Michael had never known her otherwise. She married at just seventeen. Her husband, Lionel—Michael's father—was seven years older, a city employee in the street department. Shortly before Michael's first birthday, Lionel was killed when the brakes failed on a flusher, a water-carrying street-cleaning truck, and he was crushed against a building wall. Because the flusher proved to be poorly maintained and obvious negligence was involved, the city avoided a courtroom by promptly authorizing a settlement, part in cash and the rest in the form of an annuity that would pay Beth a monthly sum for the rest of her life. Over the years, she complained that her attorney sold her out and took an under-the-table payment in return for accepting far less than was warranted. Maybe that was the case, maybe not. One thing for sure is true: Michael never heard her say that she loved Lionel or that she missed him. When Beth was in her best mood, she called her son "Mickey" or "Mickey Mouse" or "Mouse." On those days when her grip on reality unraveled further and her spirits darkened, she either didn't speak to him or called him "boything" or various obscenities.

That unstable environment, with the heavy burden of humiliation attending it, inspired his interest in the security industry, which to him was all about safety and stability, preventing irrational people from ruining the lives of the rational. Deadbolts, electronic locks, perimeter alarms, motion detectors, bullet-resistant glass, panic rooms, the strategies and tactics of bodyguards: He wanted to know everything he could learn about how to make life safer for others and, in the process, for himself as well. Later than should have been the case, as recently as a year ago, he came to understand that eighteen years of life with his mother had also inspired in him a fear that committing to marriage might trap him in a domestic situation alike to what he had escaped when he was eighteen. There were women in his life, some whom he loved, but when a relationship became too promising, he eased away from it.

Now, as he exits the freeway for a state road, motoring into sparse traffic and away from suburban lights, the night becomes immense. The wind and rain seem to be sweeping everything off the curve of the Earth, into a void. Those long-ago words Shelby spoke come to him again, with greater power than ever. *What life have you if you have not life together?* Those were not, Shelby said, his own words, but were those of a poet who more than half a century earlier foresaw the evolving isolation that an ever-more mechanized society would impose on those who existed within its coils and circuits. *What life have you if you have not life together?*

Michael has become the long-heralded Singularity, much less of a mutant than those who desire such a transformation hope to become themselves, but a mutant nonetheless. The insertion of nanowork into every cell of his body, into his genome, has in some ways made him more gifted than all other human beings. At the same time, he's at risk of becoming so different from other men and women that he will have no life in community with them. The internet and the millions of computers associated with it, the virtual reality that therein exists and that will become more vivid in the years ahead, is not a reality at all, and to live in such a fabrication is to be buried alive without the release of death. Desperate and empty and confused people might choose such an existence. Such a choice will lead not to Shangri-la, but to a vortex of madness. Avatars do not make a community; they are shadows of people, not people. Mile by mile, Michael more fully understands the truth of the future that could overtake him, and he is chilled to his core. Nina needs him, and John needs him. Michael needs them even more than they need him. His commitment to them must be complete, at the risk of a second and permanent death, if he is to have a hope of a life in true community with others.

FOUR: THE STILL POINT

HORSEMEN

Bearing no light, Aleem and Kuba and Hakeem and Carlisle and Jason and Speedo are born out of the dead trees like a final fall of spoiled fruit.

Before them, buildings slab the clearing, darker than the night and without detail, large but giving the impression of greater size than they possess, magnified by their mystery.

Aleem is reminded of a cool video game in which the ultimate sequence is set in a ruined castle where the Princess of Time lies bespelled in a secret redoubt, during the last hours of the world. She alone has the power to turn back the clock to an age of peace and plenty. As a player, you can choose to be Prince Endymion, in which case your goal is to find the princess and wake her so that she can live in the world to save it. Or you can be one of the Four Horsemen of the Apocalypse—Pestilence, War, Famine, or Death—who are seeking the princess to murder her and complete the destruction of the world. Because the weapons given to Pestilence and Famine take longer to obliterate someone, Aleem has always chosen to be either War on a red horse or Death on a pale horse. The horses look like powerful stallions, but they are really machines equipped with all kinds of kick-ass weapons. With his skill at devising strategies and tactics, with his keen reflexes, Aleem routinely runs up such a kill score of knights defending the princess that Prince Endymion is doomed, the princess remains asleep, and the world ends in a most satisfying frenzy of rats and bats and bursting bombs.

Here, no princess awaits him. Just maybe one uppity bitch who needs to be brought to her knees, apologize, plead for her life, and be buried alive with the boy she's turned into a hopeless pussy. As satisfying as burying her alive would be, Aleem knows that he might have to forego that pleasure because of the need to deal with the SUVs. Although Kuba has hoped to use Nina for a while, he'll have to be satisfied to wet his combat knife in mother and son and fantasize the sex later.

So much to think about. So it is when you're the king wolf in the pack, everyone relying on you. If the vehicles won't start, then wipe them down to eliminate fingerprints. When the smartphones are retrieved, if at least one is functioning, Aleem will call someone to drive here and take the crew home. Otherwise, Jason can hustle into town and find a public phone. Come morning, report the vehicles stolen, blame a rival gang. If the eight of them were never here, they don't need to explain Nina's Explorer. Anyhow, no one but Aleem's homeys know John is his son. Once Nina was knocked up and Aleem didn't want to deal with that, she was ashamed to have fallen for his sweet rush, a gangster like him, and she told no one who the father was. If an eager homicide dick or a green and high-minded prosecutor smells something, Aleem has a friend who is also a friend of the district attorney; the DA is a reasonable man who knows the value of time and will not waste his or that of his office on cases that can't—or shouldn't be—proven.

As the six men stand in the rain, looking at the complex of buildings, Jason Jones reveals that he has been thinking about the situation just as Aleem has been. "Say we find her."

"Say," Aleem encourages him.

"We come to teach her a lesson, take the boy, make him into a righteous brother. That it?"

"She can't be taught," Aleem says.

Kuba reminds them of a key fact of life. "A bitch can diss a man only so much, then he can't say he's a man no more iffen he still takes any shit from her."

"That be truer than true," Carlisle agrees.

Jason says, "So we pop her and take the boy?"

"We kill 'em both," Aleem says.

For a long moment, the only sounds are the rain falling and the wind blowing and the skeleton trees creaking their dead joints.

Speedo breaks the silence. "You a hard man, Aleem."

"That news to you?"

"I always known," Speedo says. "Just not how hard."

"You better know how hard."

"I got it now."

"He ain't my son no more. It's too late for him to be. She made him over into a trick poodle."

"It's a tragedy," Kuba says.

Jason is concerned about the logistics. "So we pop a couple caps, then what we do with two stiffs?"

"We get my Aviator runnin'," says Hakeem, "we could tie 'em to the roof rack."

Carlisle disapproves of levity in this situation. "Whoever you tryin' to be, Hakeem, you for sure ain't no Kevin Hart or Dave Chappelle."

"Can't leave two stone-dead here with our wheels," Jason says.

"We call Modeen and Lincoln to come get us," Aleem says. "They bring plastic sheets and tape, wrap her and him, take 'em with us. We set our dead wheels on fire, say the Crips or MS-13 stole them. Why they drove here and burned them—who knows?"

Speedo wants to prove he really gets—and approves of—how hard Aleem is. "Back home, call Hector Salazar, bring the meat to him."

Hector—of Salazar Marine Services—owns two substantial boats. He has a taste for taking risks of all kinds, a talent for evading authorities, and no moral compunctions whatsoever.

"Hector he takes the bodies out to sea," Speedo continues, "chops 'em into chum, feeds the sharks."

"Sounds like a plan," Jason says.

"Only thing," Kuba says, "nobody's gonna pop no caps, 'cause then we gotta throw away a gun has a bad history and maybe gotta wrap up loose brains and skull pieces. A knife don't have no history like a gun. And done right, it's neater."

"It ain't just a plan," Hakeem declares, "it's an episode of *The Sopranos*."

"Three teams," Aleem says, "two men to a building, till we searched 'em all. Remember the bitch has herself a piece, a trey eight, and she knows how to use it."

Jason and Speedo each has a flashlight, so Aleem takes one for him and Kuba.

They move away from the trees, toward the buildings, one man short of being the Magnificent Seven, like in that old Western Aleem has watched several times. Even though they're only six, they have an important advantage the seven didn't possess, which is that they aren't to any extent whatsoever restrained by a foolish sense of community values, by honor, by pity—or by anything, really.

The chance of finding Nina and John in one of these buildings is low, and the likelihood that the plan Aleem cooked up to deal with the four SUVs will work is even lower. However, this world doesn't reward second-guessers. You can change direction if a fork in the path appears and has promise, but you can't back up and rethink, because in this business, to both your enemies and your homeys, that looks like retreat. Retreat is seen as weakness, and the weak die young, which they deserve to do. The only thing that Aleem despises is weakness. Once you commit to an operation, you have to drive forward hard, never doubting, never relenting. If the result isn't what you hoped, even if it's a disaster, you can learn from it *after it's done.* Anyhow, no mistake he can make is so bad that it can't be erased with enough violence and cash. With a shitload of money, he can buy his way out of most trouble, and when money isn't enough, he can kill his way out, which is why he has the respect of his homeboys and not just of his homeboys, but also the respect of all those who are gangsters disguised as pillars of their communities, as friends of the working man and woman. You can't win a war if you don't drive forward hard and harder even when fighting seems hopeless. And to Aleem Sutter, life is war.

THE ONLY WISDOM WE CAN HOPE
TO ACQUIRE

To Nina's right, pressed against her, felt but unseen, John sits in two inches of cold water, deep in the rat hole, under the artfully rearranged trash, his back to the wall. He has wrapped his arms around the duffel bag that rests on his lap, less to safeguard the money than to anchor himself against the nervous spasming of muscles that might rattle the rubbish heap around them.

The Tac Light is switched off, propped across Nina's thighs. She grips the pistol in both hands, though she can't imagine how she can effectively use it. The gun has a ten-round magazine. She's not a bad shot, but she can't take out eight men who are heavily gunned up. To her left is the opening to their hiding place, concealed by a splintering and delaminating sheet of fungus-riddled plywood over which is draped a long, rumpled length of filth-encrusted, opaque plastic like the cast-off ectoplasm of some ghost that has finally ceased to haunt this world.

She feels swallowed up and helpless, the room as dark as the belly of a whale. The air reeks of many forms of foul matter and the putrefaction of perhaps a rat or two. She's shivering and can feel John shivering against her. She hesitates to caution him about his rapid, anxious breathing. He's smart and brave, and when he hears someone in the building, when the door opens to this room, he will fall silent and still.

Some moments, she can hardly believe that she has come to this, fugitive and cornered with her child. But those moments slide into others when it seems that she could have expected nothing else but what was befallen her. For a long while, she holds terror at bay by remembering what previous darkness she has endured and what truths have sustained her.

Her seduction by Aleem, when she was sixteen, was not one sorry misstep by a girl who otherwise followed a safe and sensible path. She had begun to rebel against her parents when she was thirteen. Her father and mother, both gainfully employed, worked hard and lived frugally, paid their taxes, went to church, drank little, and were satisfied with simple pleasures like television, library books, and board games. They lived without complaint and by the rules, but to what avail? Money was a constant worry. Their only assets were a twenty-year-old Ford and a tiny blue house in a neighborhood where no one dwelt by choice. In the fever of adolescence, Nina came to see them as kindhearted fools whose contentment with their lot was in fact surrender to the meanness of the world. She saw others who were not so weak, who refused to accept what was ladled out to them, who went after what they wanted by whatever means necessary. They drove flashy cars and wore the latest styles, both men and women, some of them only a few years older than she was. She knew what they did, what they dealt in, and she knew it was wrong. But if poverty was the reward for doing right and success was the reward for doing wrong, then Earth had become so grievously distorted in its turning that no one possessed the power to restore it to its intended shape. In her daydreams, she became one of the fast crowd. And in her daily life, she indulged in petty rebellions—using language her parents would have found shocking if they'd heard it, taking a few tokes of a girlfriend's joint, leaving home buttoned to the neck but showing cleavage when she got to school. All these years later, she can't remember how all those little insubordinations abruptly became a revolution against the future that she saw her parents crafting for her, but it seemed to happen in a moment, and the moment's name was *Aleem.*

Her moral fiber had stretched with elastic ease, but it had not broken, and it snapped back into proper form when at last she came to understand the cruelty inherent in the life that the fast crowd lived. Aleem's reaction to her pregnancy was cold, uncaring. *Marry you? Only pussy-whipped feebs get married. Any fool gets married, he's puttin' some pump like you above his homeys. That don't go down good. Not good at all. I got no time for daddyhood, sugar. Aleem Sutter, he's on his way up. Ain't nobody gonna hold me down. That thing in you, it just a tumor, that all it is to me. Your problem. Douche it out, use a coat hanger, whatever you got to do, just don't come round to me no more. We done, you hear? The way you cling, a man got a future can't be dragged down by that. Push this on me, I'll knock you out sure as I knocked you up. Never was no baby born from a bitch nine months dead. You hear me? You want a future of your own, then it be your little pig, not mine.*

Even though Nina was sixteen and foolish, she understood the irony of where her hunger for the fast life had led her: into deep mortification and into the shelter of her parents' arms, into their small but stable home, where in time she came to understand that they weren't the losers she'd imagined them to be. They were wise enough to know that the limited extent of their education and the nature of their skills, with hard work, would provide them with a refuge from turbulence, wise enough to know that this was a great blessing in an ever-turbulent world. Simple pleasures are no less pleasurable than costlier pursuits. Pleasure is all in the heart, a matter of delight rather than dollars. A faithful dog can provide more joyful moments than a yacht. It's only envy, a sickness of the mind, that causes disdain of simple things and greatly overvalues extravagance. In her parents' loving care, in time and with some effort, Nina arrived at the one virtue essential to peace of mind—humility. We can work hard to better our lives, but the world is not ours to rule or to shape other than it was first shapen. Her mother said there was no wisdom greater than humility, and her father said it was the only wisdom we can acquire that allows us to progress successfully and happily in life.

Now, eight years after losing her parents, she misses them no less than she did back in the day. She is not given to the conceit that her mother and father look after her even now that they are no longer of this life. She needs no ministering ghosts. She would not call them back from their higher place to this lower world even if she knew how. Yet she feels—or needs to feel—that she and John are not in this squalid place alone, that there is mercy in the matrix of the world and that they will be shielded by an act of grace until the gangbangers leave and Michael arrives. As the minutes mount into half an hour, as the second hand on the radiant dial of her watch sweeps her and John into an unknowable future, the pervasive smell of death has so suffused her that it has also become a taste on her tongue.

HERE IN DEATH'S DREAM KINGDOM

The smaller building that bears the large white word OFFICES seems as if it will be the easiest to search, but once Aleem and Kuba get inside, they discover a warren of rooms on two floors. The place is a sieve, two or three inches of water throughout the lower floor. Debris floats on the rank and slimy tide—empty beer cans, foil bags once filled with potato chips or corn chips, pale condoms ballooning like jellyfish or slithering like translucent snakes.

"Must be where country kids sneak away to party," Kuba says.

Grimacing as the beam of the Tac Light plays across the draff and garbage, Aleem says, "Might better take a sample of this, send it to your health app, see what you contaminated with."

"All these offices. Who knew apples was big business?"

"Since Adam," says Aleem.

"What Adam that?"

"Don't be ignorant. Adam and Eve."

"Adam I know, he with Simone."

"Weren't no Simone then, only Eve."

"Simone she got a nice ass."

Having cautiously checked out the ground-floor offices, as Aleem leads Kuba up the stairs, he says, "You got an iPhone, homey."

"Back in the mud somewheres."

"I mean—you know their symbol?"

"What symbol?"

"Their company symbol. Apple's symbol."

"Ain't it an apple?"

"Apple with a bite out. It's a symbol of knowledge."

"An apple someone took a bite, I don't want it. That ain't a symbol of knowledge, that a symbol of garbage."

"I'm talkin' the first apple off the tree of knowledge."

"Tree of knowledge? Eat an apple and it's like you gone to college, now you can be a dentist? You the man, Aleem. I respect you, but shit. This here's another weird idea, bro, like your explodin' salt."

They proceed a few steps into the upstairs hall, something crunching underfoot, before Aleem stops and slowly brooms the light from baseboard to baseboard. All is dry here. The stain is worn off the tongue-in-grove hardwood, and the planks are cupped. Hundreds of dead beetles lay in regiments like a vast defeated army under a thin shroud of gray dust. No one could pass this way without leaving a trail of disturbed dust and scattered bugs.

Leading the way down the stairs to the swamp, Aleem says, "I know you heard of the Bible."

"Heard about the 'cyclopedia, too. So what?"

"An apple off the tree of knowledge, it's a Bible story."

"Since when you read the Bible?"

"Never done. But when I was little, Grandma Verna she told me some Bible stories."

"Your same Grandma Verna she runs upper-class whores on the Westside?"

"Who has two Grandma Vernas?" Aleem says as he steps into the dismal waters on the ground floor.

"That mean old woman, got them implant teeth could crack a walnut, wears more diamonds than Tiffany ever sold, why she poundin' a Bible?"

"She don't pound it. She just finds it entertainin'. Like Goliath the giant."

"The seven-foot wrestler, tattoo of a snake comin' out his belly button."

"I'm talkin' the first Goliath. Check it out, man. He was ten feet tall."

As they slosh through the party debris where once commerce was conducted and busy workers supported families by supplying something real and nourishing, Kuba says, "This Goliath, he live in a castle between the tree of knowledge and the tree of salt?"

Speedo Hickam is waiting for them just outside the front door. In his long black raincoat and hood, he reminds Aleem of a nun, too soft to endure hard weather like a man. "We found somethin'."

"What somethin'?"

"You gotta see. Over at Whole Fruit."

As the three head toward the largest building in the complex, Kuba says, "Another thing, with all respect, nobody ever been ten feet tall."

Aleem says, "Speedo, you know about Goliath?"

"He a wrestler, bites the heads off baby chicks?"

"That's him," Kuba confirms.

"Ain't real chicks," Speedo says. "They's marshmallow chicks like them at Easter."

"Real as real can be," Kuba insists.

"You want to think so, that's cool with me," Speedo says.

"Grandma Verna she say the way it happened, this shrimp David figures he can jack up Goliath, bring him down. Goliath he picks up little Davey, loads him in a fuckin' big slingshot, and splatters him all over the side of the temple."

"What temple?" Speedo asks.

"Don't matter what temple. Important thing is David been taught a moral lesson."

At Whole Fruit, Jason, Hakeem, and Carlisle are waiting just outside the big opening that once was filled by a roll-up door. When Jason directs his light at what they found beyond the threshold, Kuba declares, "No tooth fairy left it. Bitch is here somewhere."

Aleem can almost feel her head in his hands, his thumbs pressing through the warm jelly of her eyes.

The darkness is so thick that it seems to have substance. Nina feels it pressing on her, coiling in her ears. The air is oily with this darkness, as though it leaves a residue in her lungs when she exhales.

Now and then, she thinks she hears voices, ordered packets of sound different from the wind howl and rain chatter that is muffled by the walls of the packing plant. These moments of suspected human presence do not seem to issue from within this building. They're as brief as they are faint, like voices from some nameless Beyond that you might expect to hear at a séance. Time passes without the storeroom door being thrown open.

John is afflicted with allergies, and the environment here challenges his determination to be silent. The poor kid stifles a sneeze and minutes later another, perhaps clamping his hands over his face or pinching his nose—God forbid that it happens if one of Aleem's homeys *does* step into the room—and both times he whispers, "Sorry," and she whispers, "It's okay."

Maybe ten minutes pass, and he makes a furtive sound, which must have been his hand digging in a coat pocket, because then he blows his nose discreetly. Following a silence without an apology, he reveals a problem in a voice so soft that she strains to hear him.

"Oh no. It's gone."

She whispers, "What?"

He barely breathes his reply: "The lucky hundred."

For a moment, his words don't compute for her, but then she remembers. In the kitchen. Before they fled their home. He pulled one bill from a bundle, examining it with wonder. *It's real.* He tucked the banded hundreds into interior pockets of his jacket, but he folded the loose hundred into an exterior pocket. *It's like a lucky penny ten thousand times over.* Maybe the same pocket where he had kept folded Kleenex. Now it must be in the water around them.

"Forget it," she whispers. "We have so much more."

After a freighted silence, he says, "Maybe I didn't lose it here."

He'd first blown his nose when they stepped into the building, just inside the threshold.

"The wind will have carried it away," she assures him.

"Maybe not."

"The wind will have taken it," she insists.

THE BITTER BITE

He takes the turn at considerable speed, the heavy Bentley pressing to the pavement as though it possesses a gravity greater than that attendant to all other things on Earth. In the sudden turning, its bright beams slap across the trunks and lower branches of the leafless grove ranked on the elevated land. The trees twitch as if physically struck and shuddered by the light, and then fall away into darkness as the headlamps align with the slick blacktop straightaway on which glittering raindrops dance like spilled diamonds.

Michael's shadow self lives in the nanotech that webs every cell in his body, and those skeins are woven into the spectrum of data-bearing electromagnetic waves that is the worldwide web of the internet and all the computers connected to it. As the car slows with the barren orchard on both sides, a stylized and luminous compass appears in the upper-right quadrant of his vision. This signal seeker leads him not by indicating magnetic north, but by pointing toward the transponder in Nina's smartphone.

He pulls onto the shoulder of the road and puts the sedan in park and switches off the lights and wipers. He shrugs into the thigh-length Helly Hansen rain jacket that belonged to someone at the house in which he'd meant to spend a few days, a respite upended by the mad-dog gangbanger, Aleem. Zippered pockets accommodate the three spare magazines for the rifle as well as a box cutter that he found in a desk drawer in the Corona del Mar residence. He pulls up the hood and secures it under his chin with the Velcro strap. When he checks the mirrors, the road behind him, to the north, is dark and at the moment untraveled. He kills the engine, retrieves the AR-15, and gets out into the storm.

The door is open, and he is behind it. When he looks over the top to be sure no traffic is coming from the south, he sees someone approaching, forty or fifty feet away. The guy is tall, wearing a full-length black raincoat with a deep hood concealing his face. He's a medieval figure, like a mendicant monk on a pilgrimage to ancient Rome, who has crossed half a world and a thousand years from one step to the next. He isn't on the shoulder of the highway, but he walks in the middle of the southbound lane. He calls out, "Need help there, mister? She break down on you?"

It isn't his shadow self's high-tech analytic capability that warns Michael of danger. It is the profound intuition with which he was born, an unshakable recognition of evil. This stranger is not a generous Samaritan venturing into foul weather and darkness with the hope of doing a kindness for someone. Nevertheless, Michael isn't capable of opening fire on the man without being certain of his intentions. Besides, the crack of the rifle will carry far even through the cry of wind and sizzle of rain, announcing his presence to others of Nina's pursuers sooner than is ideal. He raises his voice above the storm, and by his words he asserts both that he knows what's happening here and that he has been called to assist. "I'm looking for Aleem."

The apparition halts twenty feet away. Still no face can be discerned in the hood, not even the slightest trace of eyeshine. "What's an Aleem?"

There's no curiosity in the question, as ought to be the case if this is an average citizen, but only a cold note of challenge, which pretty much identifies the man as one of the gangster's crew.

As he responds, Michael reaches back into the car, feels for the added kill switch on the steering column, finds it, and flicks it, activating the GPS and navigation system. "I was told Aleem needs transportation. Here I am."

"Told how?"

"He phoned Brett Bucklin, and Brett phoned me. I live in the area. You know Brett Bucklin, Aleem's attorney?"

"How Aleem phone you?"

The longer Michael stands behind the open car door, the more it appears he's using it for protection, and the less it seems that he is who he claims to be. He can't go forth with the AR-15 in hand and assume the response will be judicious. The stranger hasn't seen the rifle and might take it as a threat no matter how casually it's carried. Michael props the weapon against the open door, butt plate on the pavement, and steps into the southbound lane. "No, he didn't phone me, he phoned Brett Bucklin, his attorney in the city."

"All our phones went to shit."

"Evidently not Aleem's."

"Wind is shoutin' you down, man."

Michael raises his voice. "Aleem's phone didn't go to shit."

Rain blows under Michael's hood, and he blinks it out of his eyes. The gangbanger might be holding something in his right hand. Michael can't quite be sure. The darkness and weather are aids to deception.

"So you sayin' Aleem called Bucklin."

"That's right."

"Then Bucklin he phones you."

"Like I said. Can we get this done? This weather sucks."

"You here for transportation, take us where?"

"Wherever you all need to go."

"Say what?"

Michael raises his voice again. "Wherever you want to go."

"Eight plus you in one car."

Michael tries to let the wind outspeak him without making it obvious that he's doing so. "An associate of mine is on his way in an Escalade. He'll be here in a few minutes."

"Louder, man. Who will what?"

"I can't outshout the damn storm," Michael says and moves toward the man. They're only five or six steps apart. "My name's Easton Ellis. Who're you?"

"Masud. Why Aleem call a lawyer 'stead of another homey?"

"None of your homeys live here in Shitkicker Valley," Michael says, going online as he speaks, entering the navigation service's system, sliding down the transponder signal into the Bentley, taking over its electronic controls.

The car alarm shrieks and the headlights flash, startling Masud, who brings up the pistol in his hand, aiming at the sedan. He might not be one of Aleem's more intellectual thugs, but he'll only need three seconds to realize that if someone in the Bentley poses a threat, then so does the man who was driving it.

Michael needs less than two seconds to thumb the razor lock on the box cutter concealed in his right hand and slash the wrist that Masud exposes when the raincoat sleeve slides back from his extended gun arm. A thin razor cut is instant hot-wire pain, worse than a knife slash, a shock to the system. The pistol clatters to the blacktop.

As the car goes dark and silent, Michael body-slams the wounded man. Masud goes down in a billow and rustle of raincoat, rapping the back of his head hard on the pavement, and Michael falls atop him, pinning him to the road. The dreaded moment is upon him, the mortal task he has the training to fulfill but for which the necessity has never before arisen and certainly never the desire. At a distance of mere inches, he at last sees the face within the cowl, a countenance as human featured as his own, eyes briefly clouded by concussion. Masud is a monster, one of eight who must not reach Nina and John before Michael can spirit mother and son away. Cruelty, brutality, and murder are essential to these men's business model, and there's no way to thwart them but the hard way. He plucks Masud's dropped pistol from the pavement, grips it by the barrel, raises it above his head. Masud's eyes clarify, and Michael hesitates, and Masud's frozen features distort with hatred. Michael hammers the butt of the pistol into a sudden snarl and glare of homicidal fury, hammers it again and again and yet again, until the struggling man goes slack under him.

The highway is little traveled at this hour, in this weather, but there has been no Armageddon that made the world a graveyard. Someone is likely to come along at any moment.

Michael gets to his feet and tosses the gun into the drainage channel, where it vanishes under the rush of muddy water. He grips the dead man by the ankles and drags him off the blacktop, onto the shoulder of the highway, and rolls him into the same ditch. Although the current is swift and the runoff is deep enough to cover Masud, the corpse is not borne away. Animated by trapped air, a portion of the black raincoat swells above the turbulent surface of the runoff, shuddering and strange, as though a vengeful spirit strains to free itself from the body in which it can no longer enjoy life.

Badly shaken by what he's done, Michael looks at the tortured shapes of the apple trees, which stand in cryptic testament to the history of humanity. He remembers Nina telling him this valley is as near to Eden as anywhere she's ever seen; that was when the orchard was productive. Knowledge is transformative and elevating, but it isn't a reliably sweet fruit. They say that, from the first Eden, innocents came naked into the outer dark with the bitter knowledge of lost immortality and a grim recognition of a new life measured in meager years that quicken to the grave; worse, they soon learned that although they must submit to death, they could also subject others to it on as little as a whim, and for some that became a pleasure. Michael takes no pleasure in it, and he hopes that he won't have to kill anyone else. His duty to Nina and John, however, will require him to do what must be done. Killing and murder are different things, and killing evil men to prevent them from murdering others is not wicked work. Just the same, he'd rather not be burdened by such memories as the sound of flesh splitting and facial bones shattering under the hammering butt of a pistol.

He returns to the Bentley and retrieves the AR-15 and closes the driver's door. He hurries south, looking for an entrance to the orchard that bridges the flooded drainage ditch.

One end of the sodden hundred-dollar bill floats in the rippled surface of the packing-house flood, and the other end is pasted to the concrete threshold over which the murky water laps and recedes. The wise, sad eyes of Benjamin Franklin gaze up into the light with which Jason reveals this evidence, which is more than a clue but less than proof that Nina and the boy might be sheltering in this place. The bill is neither filthy nor half rotted away, but clean and whole, as though it must have been dropped here minutes earlier.

Soaked and chilled and muddied, denied the comfort of the SUV and the convenience of a phone, mocked with "Macarena," foiled and humiliated by a woman who seems to have the power of a true witch, Aleem is in a homicidal mood. His fury is so great that he dares not show it. A man of his position can't afford for his crew to see him ruled by emotion. At all times, he must be perceived as in iron control of himself, dispassionate and obdurate in his pursuit of his goals. An excessively emotional man—even if the emotion is furious anger expressed with vicious cruelty—is thought to be a weak man, one who will be relentlessly plotted against by his underlings. When he finds Nina, he'll kill her quickly, lest the delight of seeing her torn by pain becomes too much to contain. To compensate for abstaining from the pleasure of torturing her, he'll destroy her spirit. He'll cast her into despair by shooting John twice in the face, in front of her, before blowing her brains out, thus killing her twice, and he will do so with apparent indifference.

Puzzled by Aleem's silence and his continued focus on the hundred-dollar bill, Jason says, "You with me here?"

"Speedo," Aleem says. "Go back and find your phone, see does it work now. It don't, then hike into town, call Modeen and Lincoln."

Speedo is a tough little bastard, but he's the smallest among the crew, the least useful in this action. Besides, of them all, he's the one who can most easily pass for a church boy whose only gang is God and all His angels. Girls think he's sweet and funny. Old ladies look at him and figure he spends his time delivering meals to shut-ins. Most men seem to view him as an earnest young hustler who probably delivers newspapers before school, mows lawns in the late afternoon, and works at the car wash on Saturdays.

"Remember," Aleem says, "they bring plastic drop cloths and strappin' tape, so we can wrap two burritos for Hector Salazar."

Speedo is amused. "Give Hector some takeout for his afternoon at sea. I'm on my way, bro."

Through all of that, the wet currency at their feet has held Aleem rapt, so that Jason says, "We goin' in?"

"Gimme a minute," Aleem says. "I'm thinkin' out a strategy."

That's a lie. The events in the orchard have left the first-ever hairline crack in Aleem's self-confidence. The hundred-dollar bill seems to be an omen, like the painting of the wolf in *The Portent*, which should have been a movie with sequels, except they killed off the entire cast and left nowhere to go with the story. After he saw that flick, he wondered if there might be truth in the concept of karma, if maybe the shit you did to others would sooner or later be done to you. The thought had bothered him for a day, maybe two, before he got over it. But now the hundred-dollar bill has brought back memories and spooked him.

When Aleem was seventeen, eighteen, the gang was led by Tatum Krait, whom nobody ever called Tatum, whom everyone called Mamba or sometimes Doctor Mamba, everyone but his father, Walter Krait, who despised him and called him Tumtum. Then a real mamba bit Walter, who died. After the results of the autopsy were revealed, the medical examiner declared the cause of death a rattlesnake bite because, for one thing, mambas weren't native to Southern California and, for another thing, he understood that was what he needed to declare to ensure that nothing terrible would happen to his eleven-year-old daughter. Mamba saw Aleem as a young man of promise and groomed him for a leadership position, first by secretly assigning him the job as the axe in the human resources department. Sometimes a swing man gets greedy and too often steps on a shipment, cutting it too hard with baby laxative, until it's bunk. Or an authorized dealer finds his own source and underreports sales. Or a mule is seen on a pier, pretending to fish side by side with a known DEA agent. Termination must ensue. So young Aleem cultivates an image as a party animal and get-along guy. No one he asks to a one-on-one meeting suspects where it will lead. When they are alone, he opens a bottle of whatever he knows his target prefers and pours and says he is speaking for Mamba, who wants to express his gratitude for work well done. With a second round, sometimes a third, Aleem is laying on the praise, swapping stories, sharing some laughs. When the mood is high, he produces three plastic-wrapped bricks of Benjamins, the thank-you from Mamba, thirty thousand. The doomed know full well what they've done, but they believe they've gotten away with it, always bask in the praise, and take the bonus with delight, Ben Franklin regarding them with his wise and sad eyes from every bundle of cash. On the way out of the room,

Aleem puts his arm around his guest, telling him how valued he is, which is when he slams the stiletto between two ribs and into the heart. It's part of his job, by himself, to get the body into a van, which he can do because he's strong and has the right equipment, including a hydraulic hand truck. He drives the van to the funeral home with which Mamba maintains an arrangement. A cremation occurs. In the three years he's the axe, he resolves seven such problems and begins his ascendancy.

Now, after the inexplicable events in the orchard, in his weary and disheveled condition, the hundred-dollar bill in this unlikely place conjures from his memory the axe work that he performed with such satisfaction in his late teens and stirs in him something akin to superstition. In movies in the genre of *The Portent*, this vast and lonely acreage of dead trees and abandoned buildings is a place where a deformed psychopath wearing a leather mask is as unstoppable as any robot terminator.

Aleem reminds himself that he doesn't believe in omens or in karma. In the manner of an old dog, he shakes himself to cast off the stupefaction that has overcome him. He raises his eyes from the money and regards his homeys. Gathered before him, they are familiar yet mysterious in some way he can't explain. "Hakeem, Carlisle, go round the far end, block that big open door. You're in position, signal with a flashlight. Jason, Kuba, and me—we come in from this end, clear the place. Nina shows with her trey eight, don't take no shit. Try just to cap the bitch's knees. Leave the face shot for me. I done earned it."

WHIRLED IN A VORTEX

Michael is guided by the stylized compass glowing in the upper right-hand corner of his field of vision, in a manner similar to the way that battle data is projected onto the windshield of a fighter jet. He hurries through phalanxes of death-smitten trees that stand like faceless totems of some race long extinct. The ground is muddy here where grass has failed, sucking at his shoes as if the earth itself is sentient and malevolent and wishes to pull him deep underground and entomb him among the rotting roots that once conveyed sustenance to the countless limbs of the orchard.

As he passes between two haggard trees and into yet another harvesting alley, he nearly collides with a fast-moving figure so poorly revealed in the rain-slashed gloom that it might be either a man or a woman, perhaps a boy, although too tall to be John or Nina. The individual startles, nearly falls on the slippery mat of dead grass, regains balance, and issues a name and query in a voice male and unfamiliar—"Orlando?" Whoever this might be, he's no innocent happening through the apple grove on this night of all nights. He's one of Aleem's crew, an experienced murderer. Even as the stranger speaks, Michael reverses his grip on the AR-15 and closes the last step between them and chops the butt of the rifle at the other's head. The contact is solid, and the man collapses.

Michael drops to his knees on the stranger's chest, hears a subtle crack and a plosive exhalation, but still the man has the power to buck and twist, to reach out with both hands, trying to find his attacker's face. Turning his head to the side to protect his eyes, Michael holds the rifle by barrel and stock, employing it as a crushing tool, pressing down with all his weight and strength on the throat. He is gripped by an awful, primitive desperation that is born not from fear for his life but from an intrinsic regret that he has been reduced to this brutality, yet he does not relent, must not relent. None but a gargling sound escapes the stranger, and as his strength wanes, his hands flutter down onto the rifle and find Michael's hands. He does not claw for relief, but presses Michael's hands as if this encounter has resulted in an unanticipated bonding, his touch soft and supplicant, expressing a plea for mercy, though he himself has perhaps never granted the same to anyone. Michael bears down even after the limp hands slide off his, bears down with prudent respect for the deception that is so often the human way. When at last he lifts the rifle from the throat, the only response from the stranger is the rising odor of the blood and vomit that fill the mouth that shapes a silent scream.

Michael rolls off the corpse into a muddy puddle, where he lies on his back for a moment, rain beating on his face, the rifle held across his chest. The swift wind has many voices, skirling over him as though with varying opinions, at once forgiving and unforgiving, speaking of righteous necessity but also of penitence, the heady wine of violence and the sobering bread of peace, and it seems to him that there is truth in all of it.

He gets to his feet and hesitates, considering the corpse. No nearby ditch exists in which to roll the body. In the immensity of the ruined orchard, the likelihood is low that one of the dead man's companions will stumble across him. As he seemed to have been on an urgent task, however, he is sure to be missed soon. His unexplained disappearance will alert the others to the existence of a potential threat.

Shaken, in no way reassured by the outcome of his first two skirmishes, with a sense of time running out, Michael moves forward. He is guided by the virtual compass, which proves only that

Nina's phone is switched on and signaling, not that she remains alive. The wind diminishes significantly as he makes his way to the next tree line, as if the storm might be in the process of exhausting itself, but though the rain now falls in plumb skeins, it descends in no less volume than before. He passes between trees so disfigured that they seem not formed by nature, but rather assembled by some avant-garde artist working with the splintered bones of numerous species both Earthly and alien to sculpt mockeries of creation. Beyond lies open territory, a complex of buildings— and five men clustered in the pale backwash of two flashlight beams that are aimed at the ground. They are standing in front of the largest structure, at a doorless entrance above which Michael can make out the words WHOLE FRUIT in ghostly white letters against dark weatherboarding. The virtual compass glowing toward the periphery of his vision points directly at this packing plant and now changes in color from amber to red.

Nina and John must be somewhere inside that building, cornered or already captured. It's essential that Michael know which is the case. Remaining between two trees, though phoneless himself, he reaches into the telecom system with which Nina purchased service and calls her. Evidently she is holding the phone, for she answers on the first ring.

Although the five men are sixty or seventy yards away, Michael whispers, "Have they found you?"

"No," she whispers. "Where are you?"

"Looking at a building called 'Whole Fruit.'"

"My God. Thank God."

"Five of them are outside. Maybe they're about to come for you. I think I can take them, most of them. Can you stay low and hidden?"

"Not for long. We—"

He interrupts. "Stay low, low and hidden," and disconnects.

As far as he can tell, the five men are focused on Whole Fruit and on one another, none scanning the night for a threat, but he can't be sure. Although he will be a small dark form moving through the vast rural darkness, through curtains of rain, he is loath to step out from the cover of the trees. However, these men are fifty or sixty yards from him, and he needs to close the distance before opening fire. The only chance he has of taking out these five—and one other somewhere; six remaining of the eight—is to maintain the advantage of surprise until he has significantly reduced their numbers.

After killing Masud, he hoped that he would not have to kill anyone else, although he knows it to be a hope unlikely to be fulfilled. The second killing, even more intimate than the first, has weighed on him no less. It has reminded him that the true foundation of duty is not hope, because it is human to hope for the wrong thing. Duty is based on something more profound than hope, on faith that what is too wrong to endure will be made right, rectified by a system of justice that underlies all of nature, far beneath the subatomic level, a system that may right a wrong in a day or through the passage of time or outside of time. The schedule isn't ours to protest or endorse. His duty is to act with all the skill and wisdom he possesses, not with hope but with conviction.

The nearest building is directly south and about twenty-five yards from his position. Whole Fruit is maybe thirty yards farther and to the southwest, past a smaller structure that bears the word OFFICES in big block letters. He can't see the name of the building against which he intends to shelter, for the flank of it is toward him and the word or words will be emblazoned on the gable wall, as is the case with the other places.

In recognition of the treacherous footing and because even a dark figure crossing a dark landscape is more likely to draw notice if it is proceeding at a run, Michael leaves the trees and makes for the nameless building at a quick but prudent pace, bent low, fearing a cry of recognition. He reaches the structure without discovery and stands with his back against the wall, ten feet from the corner and just out of sight of the gathered men.

Ideally, he would have had time to practice with the rifle, to learn the idiosyncrasies of its operation. He has had much practice with AR-15s, but every weapon has a unique personality. Accuracy depends to some extent on an intimate knowledge of the piece with which he's working.

Even this much closer, he can't hear the men's voices above the hiss-plop-plonk-rattle of the rain in the near absence of wind. The dull tolling of his laboring heart thrusts lifeblood through tens of miles of arteries, arterioles, capillaries, venules, and veins, an astonishing construction to which the addition of the nanotech in his cells, comprising his shadow self, amounts to little more than an add-on for convenience, like outfitting a Tesla with WeatherTech floor mats.

He eases to the corner of the building and looks toward Whole Fruit. The five men remain tightly grouped, the better to receive their due justice here and now, rather than outside of time.

". . . cap the bitch's knees. Leave the face shot for me. I done earned it," Aleem concludes.

Jason, Hakeem, and Carlisle are good with that, but Kuba has an issue. "Say we take Nina without we have to shoot her."

"That her decision," Aleem says.

"Then we don't got to go directly to the face shot."

Jason says, "I think I see where you goin'."

"All the trouble the quiff give us, she got to get more payback than just a four-five in the face," Kuba says.

Carlisle, being Carlisle, says, "Iffen that hundred was hers, she probably don't got more than another one. That blue dump she live in, doin' tax work for laundromats and nail shops, she ain't got half what it takes to pay me for the shit she put us through."

"My man," says Hakeem, "only stupid Philistines think money's the only thing makes the world go round."

Impatient with his homey's geographical prejudice, Carlisle says, "What shit you talkin', Hakeem? Peeps in Philadelphia they ain't no dumber than anywhere else."

Kuba clarifies his concern. "Me and Aleem saw eye to eye on the way here, how she ain't nothin' to him no more—"

"And never was," Aleem injects, to be certain that no one here gets the idea that he would allow any woman to be more to him than a source of sexual satisfaction. "She always was just a prime pump."

"Woman like her turns a boy like John into the trick he is now," Kuba continues, "she got to be taught what wrong she done. Anyone don't want to teach her—he got somethin' wrong in his head."

Jason nods thoughtfully, flicking rain off the rim of his hood. "We talkin' about pullin' a train on her?"

"If I know Kuba," says Hakeem, "we ain't talkin' about readin' her righteous passages from the Bible."

As much as Aleem just wants Nina and her brat dead so he can stop thinking about them and get on with his life, he is wary of backing out of his promise to let Kuba not only jump her but also break her down. Kuba is his main man, and they are tight, but that doesn't mean Kuba lacks the potential to be the next Antoine. When he wants something bad enough, he leans on Aleem in a way he never should, and maybe Aleem has indulged him too often out of brotherly affection. That can better be corrected in days to come, not in this weird place with everyone jacked up by what's gone down. They need to relieve their tension and feel good about themselves again, feel powerful.

Jason says, "That building, Cider and Juice, it's dry. Okay place to party, say you got a hot piece like Nina."

"Gonna be hours 'fore Modeen and Lincoln get here, after one o'clock," Hakeem observes. "Say we don't have Nina to play with, how we gonna pass time without we do somethin' we'll wish we hadn't?"

"First," Aleem says, conceding the issue, "we gotta grab the bitch without no extra holes in her. Hakeem, Carlisle, go round the far end, block that big open door like I said. Jason, Kuba, and me—we come in from this end."

Just then, Jason's face pours out of his hood. Because the sound of the shot comes a fraction of a second after that gush of biological debris and is muffled by the rushing rain, this radical event appears supernatural, diabolical. For a fateful instant, as Jason's corporeal life seems to evaporate inside his raincoat and the roomy garment folds to the ground as though it's been cast off, Aleem and his homeys are flummoxed by bewilderment, as if Jason has proven to be a magician of astonishing power. The truth registers with them, and they pivot away from the dead man. The second and third shots punch Kuba in the back, and he pitches to the earth in front of Aleem, twitching like a cockroach that's been stepped on but not fully crushed, screaming into the puddle in which his face planted.

Aleem Sutter knows guns the way a carpenter knows a hammer, not the way a man with military training knows guns. When Aleem resorts to a firearm rather than a more intimate weapon, he kills those whom he needs to kill in deserted warehouses and abandoned factories where the bodies can rot undiscovered for years, or he surprises them in dark alleyways, or he blasts them from a moving vehicle. He never experiences firefights in which survival depends in part on the ability to quickly deduce the point from which incoming rounds originate. Although he's seen the pistol that Nina possesses, though he's searched her house in her absence and knows she doesn't—or didn't previously—own a high-powered rifle, he's seized by the conviction, unlikely as it is, that she's the shooter and is cutting them down from the cover of Whole Fruit. He crouches and hurries away from the cavernous opening in the gable wall. He turns the corner of the big building, rises to his full height, and races west along a twenty-foot-wide sward of dead grass and mud between Whole Fruit and Specialty Products, away from the killing ground, as the rifle bangs out rounds as fast as the shooter can squeeze the trigger.

A PHONE CALL

To Nina, the shots sound as if the rounds are powerful enough to penetrate walls, and the board walls of this place are probably already weakened by termites and time. In their rat hole, she and John slide down as low as they can.

After the last of the shots and shouts and screams, a silence settles but for the incessant rain. For a minute or so, the absence of shooting is worse than the clatter of it, because she worries that Michael took return fire—five against one—and that he is either dead or badly wounded.

Then her phone vibrates in her hand. She takes the call, her voice hushed. He's all right. He's not been hit.

"Four of them are down," he says, his voice as quiet as hers.

"Dead?"

"Or as good as. Plus two I got earlier."

Shaped by hard experience, Nina has become something of a church lady at heart, a homebody, a cookie baker, a tinkerer in the garden, crunching numbers for a living, not a lover of excitement, a seeker of peace and simple pleasures, who values the lives of others hardly less than she values her own. So she is surprised to feel a bloodthirsty thrill travel through her at the news that Michael, amazing Michael, has killed six. Surprised but not in the least dismayed. She's aware of the original and accurate translation of the commandment—*Thou shalt not murder*—and it is Aleem and his kind who transgress all interdicts that make civilization possible. If there are none who will stop their kind, kill their kind, then they will murder, murder, murder until no one is left to be their victims. The violent will bear it away.

"One ran," Michael says, "went around the side of Whole Fruit. The eighth man I haven't seen yet. Stay where you are till I get them."

"Or they get you."

"This isn't their turf. They don't know who I am, where I came from. Their cars, their phones, now this—they're panicked."

"They don't panic."

"They panicked all their lives. Cowards afraid they'll fail if they have to live by hard work and meet the world each on his own."

"Maybe. But they're still dangerous."

"Not so much when they aren't in a pack. Stick where you are, Nina. It won't be long, and we'll be on the road."

He terminates the call.

Nina has held the phone a little bit away from her ear, so John could hear the full conversation. He says, "I want to be like that."

"Like what?"

"Like him."

"You're already on your way."

"I don't mean the Singularity thing."

"I know what you mean, honey."

"He'd still be what he is without that. It's not what matters."

She reaches out in the darkness to touch her son's face.

"What do you think?" he asks.

"About what?"

"About him."

She says, "He's something."

"He is, isn't he?" John says, hope piquant in his voice.

Nina says nothing more. She knows the leaning of her heart, which has occurred unexpectedly during this wild day; however, there is a time to every purpose, and now isn't the time for that. If a thing isn't ready to be, then wanting it too intensely is an affront to the ordained order of the world. For thinking so, she could be accused of being superstitious, but she thinks so nonetheless. She allows herself only a silent plea: *Deliver him from evil.*

THE WINE OF VIOLENCE

Patrolling the highway on foot to prevent Nina and the kid from getting into town from the southern portion of the orchard, Orlando Fiske has felt left out of the action, if there *is* any action after the breakdown of their vehicles and the weirdness with their phones. Masud Ayoob patrols the north section, a few hundred yards away, and from time to time they confirm each other's presence by a two-fingers-in-the-mouth whistle so loud that it shrills through all the weather noise even at a distance. Orlando continues to whistle now and then, though it's been a while since Masud whistled back. This concerns him, but he doesn't know what to do about it. If he heads north to check on Masud and as a consequence Nina and the boy slip past him and find help, Aleem will kick the shit out of him. Orlando is a team player, a do-what-you're-told guy. He's not comfortable taking the initiative.

On the other hand, he's also a guy who likes action, who needs it almost like a junkie needs his junk. Orlando has a low boredom threshold. He likes gangbanging because there's always something going down, turf to protect. Skimming dealers needing an arm broken or a finger cut off. Runaway whores who have to be found and brought back and made to understand what a different future they'll have if somehow they get a splash of acid in the face. Fools who've got to have money wrung out of their veins after they borrowed at 20 percent a month. Orlando and Masud are wide-spectrum enforcers, teaching hard lessons to those associates and customers in several businesses that the gang finds most important to its bottom line.

There was a time when Orlando mourned the end of the workday and endured his hours of rest feeling forlorn and forsaken. He has never needed more than five hours' sleep a night, which leaves at least eight to fill before setting out in the company of Masud with a list of enforcements for the day. For many years, Orlando didn't know what to do with himself when he wasn't on the job. TV doesn't offer much of interest. He has no hobbies; he once decided to learn to play the guitar, but the effort so frustrated him that eventually he took a hammer to the instrument. Although the face nature formed for him had made even his mother wary of Orlando by the time he was six, and although his long-armed short-legged rough-jointed body lacks athletic grace, he has been able to get girls to fill some of the lonely hours, girls who would trade sex for drugs, but they were never choice specimens, and sometimes he got not only pleasure from them but also an infection.

His life changed three years earlier, when Alana came into it. He was thirty-four then, and Alana was twenty-five. She was fresh, as pretty as any girl he'd ever seen, sexy but not slutty—*totally mobile*, as the homeys say—meaning that she could be taken anywhere without embarrassment, not that Orlando went anywhere he couldn't also take a slut. They met through a dating service, Enchantment Now, and Orlando's face didn't frighten her off, even though it was actually his photo. Written for him by his mother, his what-matters-most-to-me statement attracted Alana two hours after being posted: *I hope to meet a woman who works hard like me, keeps no secrets, and goes to church. If you are a homebody like I am, if you drink in moderation but shun the phony party scene, if what you want most of all is to fill the lonely hours with someone who cares deeply for you, please consider me.* His mother thought—and still thinks—that he worked in a bank, verifying the details in loan applications. He felt awkward on the first date with Alana and thought it didn't go well, but the next day she called him and arranged a second date. They've been together ever since, and it's a beautiful relationship.

Alana is a fine cook, and he enjoys helping her prepare dinner in the cozy kitchen of his Craftsman-period bungalow. Many evenings, she reads novels to him, and though he has never been much of a reader, he listens with delight. The stories she chooses are always gripping and sometimes move him to tears, which he never knew he could produce until she read *Little Women*. They play board games and 500 rummy. They take long walks and talk about things that he never imagined would interest him, but they do. The sex is great, better than he's ever known, and she's never given him an infection. Alana is a ninth-grade English teacher, but she's very ambitious. Last year she was awarded California Teacher of the Year. She earned a master's degree in school administration. She intends to be an assistant principal in two more years, when she's thirty, school principal by the time she's thirty-two, superintendent of the entire district by the time she's thirty-six, and California secretary of education in her early forties. Superintendent and state secretary are the positions in which an officeholder oversees the largest sums of public funds in the education system, with so little effective oversight that tens of millions can be siphoned off with little risk of discovery. Alana intends to retire at fifty if not sooner.

It is a testament to Alana's intelligence and insight that, in spite of the what-matters-to-me-most statement that Mother wrote for Orlando and regardless of his extreme awkwardness on their first date, the dear woman discerned the truth of him: his occupation and his unquenchable need for what he calls "action." When they met, she was two years from being California Teacher of the Year. Because of her beauty and high academic standards, she had become the target of a few students, hormone-crazed fourteen-year-old boys, who had no interest in learning, carried knives, and thought the best way to prove their masculinity was to disrupt her class, torment other students, and openly make lewd suggestions to the teacher. With a keen nose for Alana's ambition and resentful that she had turned down his romantic advances, the principal provided her with no assistance and failed to punish the miscreants. With her classroom in chaos, she lost hope of grooming her best students to win the academic contests that would bring them and their teacher to the attention of the state education establishment. Without the support of the school administration, she risked acquiring a reputation as a pushover for those students inclined to say, "Piss off, bitch," rather than "Yes, ma'am." She began looking for a knightly champion. Four months later, she found Orlando through Enchantment Now.

Not long ago, this had been a country in which fourteen-year-old boys carried penknives instead of switchblades, if they carried any knife at all. Back then, they had never seen pornography other than the comparatively wholesome nudes in *Playboy*. Beer was their inebriant of choice rather than the smorgasbord of drugs currently available. Once, sociopaths among them were so few that high school shooting rampages were as rare as authentic film of Bigfoot. After decades of rapid progress, it's not that country anymore.

Some nights, Orlando steps out of his happy home to engage in a session of student counseling, although on most occasions he adds an appointment to his and Masud's daily enforcement list. Never has a fourteen-year-old boy repeated his boorish behavior in the classroom after he has been accosted by two large men who look as serious as Orlando and Masud. They shove the kid into a van, take him to an abandoned warehouse, strip him naked, zip tie him to a chair, hold a combat knife to his package, and inform him in detail how he will have to urinate for the rest of his life if he doesn't die from loss of blood. If he is fortunate enough to receive urinary diversion surgery, the flow will fill an exterior collection bag that he'll need to empty manually. Orlando always concludes the encounter by warning the clueless youth not to speak of this encounter to anyone and be nice to his English teacher, unfailingly nice and obedient, or he won't get another warning. No second chance. Next time, all his dangling parts will come off, and if ever again he is happy enough to sing, he'll be an ultra soprano.

Alana has explained to Orlando that he's not a bad man, not by comparison with so many others in this ever-darker world. Yes, his inebriant of choice is the wine of violence, but he commits violence against those who think no rules should apply to them; therefore, he maintains order in his neighborhood, when he could just as easily unleash violence on the innocent, as so many others do. She says he is a scourge, as Moses in the Bible was a scourge. Scourges provide a service without which civilization cannot exist. Each time she tells him this, she then does him until he's exhausted. He thinks she is one day going to be an amazing secretary of education.

Now, he wishes that he could be at home, listening to her read a novel, instead of patrolling this lonely highway, and he marvels that he, never having completed ninth grade, could have as his lover such a beautiful, brilliant woman. Having won the love of an angel like Alana, surely he can learn to play the guitar; he might just buy a new one.

A series of rapid rifle shots interrupts Orlando's reverie. He crouches instinctively, but the rounds aren't aimed at him. Screams cut through the night, so sharp with pain and terror that it seems flint-thin flashes of light should accompany them as they strop all things in their passage. More shots and dying screams allow him to perceive by intuition and conjecture the location of the action. He draws his SIG P245, leaps across the drainage ditch, and hurries through the rain, the dark, and the trees in their ordered but worthless plenitude.

LIFE YOU MAY EVADE,
BUT DEATH YOU SHALL NOT

Michael knows this place to be an enterprise destroyed by officials of great power and no wisdom, ruined by a lack of water and now drowned in a deluge that no effort has been made to channel into reservoirs. Nevertheless, as he sidles between Whole Fruit and Specialty Products, keeping his back to the wall of the former, the structures seem to be more meaningful than mere abandoned buildings of concrete and weatherboard and corrugated steel, like edifices in dreams that are simultaneously as ordinary as office buildings and yet as ominous as temples to gods unknown on Earth.

His eyes are fully dark-adapted. Among the quartet of dead men that he passed a moment earlier, the flashlights lying in the mud and skimming their beams across the puddled water had not to any degree diminished his night sight, for he'd squinted against their influence. Still, the deep gloom doesn't fully clarify, and he repeatedly freezes at the perception of dark figures that prove to be phantoms.

When he was a very young child, in his fourth and fifth years, he had been afraid of the dark. For some reason that made sense only to his disturbed mother, Beth, she tormented him with her insistence that his father, crushed by a city truck before Michael's first birthday, had come back from the dead. She said that Lionel, though rotting and crawling with worms, was watching their house at night, eager to grab his son, carry him back to the cemetery, and take him down into the grave, into the coffin out of which he had clawed his way. *Your father was a mean and jealous man. He doesn't want you to smell a flower when he no longer can, resents you enjoying cake when he can't taste or swallow anything anymore. If you dare go out alone after nightfall, you'll never see the sunrise again.* Perhaps the tapping at a window was a moth drawn to light, and maybe the curious noises on the porch were made by a raccoon exploring as raccoons do, and conceivably the clatter on the roof was a neighbor's cat chasing a rat, but always Mother knew that it was Lionel testing the window latch, the door lock, the possibility that the chimney might provide an entrance to the house. Too young to understand that his mother was at best mentally ill and, at worst, might enjoy tormenting and manipulating a child into nervous submission, he lived those last two preschool years in her thrall and in a quiet dread of sunset. She lent credence to her rants about the walking dead by paying a locksmith to add two deadbolts to the front door and two to the back, as well as upgrade all the window latches. Every afternoon, prior to nightfall, she took Michael with her on a ritual tour of the house, making sure every lock and latch was engaged. She drew the curtains tight shut to ensure that the envious dead man could not get a glimpse of his son that would intensify his passion for reunion. Young Michael slept with a night-light, and when he woke after midnight, the gathered shadows in this or that corner, or the dark beyond the open closet door, assumed the shape of a man at whom he stared for ten minutes, twenty, half an hour, dreading movement that would confirm his father had gained access to the house.

Nearly four decades later, having long shed his fears of the walking dead, Michael is nonetheless wary of the phantoms presented by this rainy night, because one of them might prove to have substance and a gun. When he reaches the end of the long building, he looks north, past the back gable wall of Whole Fruit, then south along the back of Specialty Products. To the west, the interminable procession of dead trees continues. That sight increasingly depresses him with its endorsement of the theory that there are people who create and build and people who can only destroy, and that the latter are winning because their task requires less thought and labor.

Aleem most likely didn't turn right and enter Whole Fruit, in front of which his dead companions lie. He doesn't know for sure that Nina and John are hidden in there or where to find them. He'll want to put distance between himself and the site of the shooting, find a refuge from which to assess the situation. He believes that he's gone from seven homeys as backup to just three, when in fact it's one. In either case, he's possessed of a gang mind, deciding tactics according to the strength of his numbers; he isn't his best in one-on-one encounters. He'll be rattled by this change in circumstances and by his inability to identify who has come to the aid of Nina and the boy. Not least of all, this environment is alien to him; his world is the city and its suburbs, and the only thing this orchard has in common with his usual territory is its decayed and decaying condition. He's accustomed to going into conflict with boldness and swagger, but here the hunt requires stealth and patience, a prospect that will surely unnerve him. Because he has always seen himself as being above others, he'll feel more confident if he literally takes the high ground, a vantage point from which he can look down—and shoot down—into the common area onto which all these buildings face, with a bird's view of the main pathways along which someone might appear in cautious search of him.

As the wind rises again, Michael moves south toward the back of Specialty Products.

◆ ◆ ◆

Along the eastern flank of the muddy common area, from north to south, stand Cider and Juice, Special Accounts, and the single-story building that served as an enormous garage for trucks and orchard machinery. Cider and Juice faces the building labeled OFFICES. The garage stands opposite Specialty Products. In the middle, Special Accounts is opposite Whole Fruit, where four dead men are sprawled in their voluminous black raincoats, which the wind billows like the membranous wings of prehistoric airborne reptiles that have fallen through time and the sky. The crisp white beams of two dropped flashlights intersect in a Greek cross of equal arms, as though in an ironic memorialization of the deceased.

From a glassless window at the end of the hallway on the second floor of Special Accounts, Aleem commands a view of the common area and of the wide passageways flanking Whole Fruit. The passageways between other buildings are beyond his monitoring. However, if the shooter is here to rescue Nina and John, and if Nina and the kid are hiding in Whole Fruit, as the hundred-dollar bill seems to indicate, then he might try to bring them out through the common area. Very likely, he won't be looking for Aleem and remaining members of the crew; these decrepit buildings can't be searched in silence or in this blinding dark, and using a light would make him an easy target.

Aleem doesn't understand who this gunslinger could be. The guy comes out of nowhere, blazing away like John Wick in those bitchin' movies. Because you can't totally trust anyone, Aleem might think one of his homeys who is not yet dead—Speedo or Masud or Orlando—is taking out the entire inner circle of the gang to give himself a clear path to the top. But Speedo's head is a pot of thin soup that is never at full boil; he's no more likely to envision himself as the leader of the pack than he is to decide to rush off to medical school to be a heart surgeon. Masud loves kittens; he always has three or four, and when they become grown cats, about two years old, he kills them and gets new kittens. A man who has a soft heart for kittens is not a man with political ambition. Orlando Fiske is a harder guy than Speedo or Masud, and he takes pleasure in jacking up people until they break. However, these past few years, with his hot schoolteacher cooking for him like Julia Child and also cooking like a porn star, Orlando is in a relationship that he never imagined a knee-buster as ugly as he is could expect. He's become domesticated, and he isn't going to risk what he has for a chance at something he never previously seemed to want. Aleem doesn't know anything about farming, whether apples or corn or soybeans, but he knows enough about cash flow to be sure that whoever owns a dead orchard can't afford a security guard to watch for trespassers; besides, no security guard is going to ruthlessly blow the crap out of people with whatever version of an ArmaLite rifle this guy is using. Then who the hell is he?

Standing, waiting, watching at the broken-out window, listening to rain on the roof ticking like a thousand clocks counting down to some dire event, Aleem scans the night. He's on the lookout for the shooter, but he repeatedly fixates on the four corpses and has to remind himself to remain alert for movement. He isn't afraid. He's concerned. He'll admit to being concerned. Who wouldn't be concerned in his position? Even the fearless

assassin, John Wick, would be concerned. Aleem has some mis-
givings about his situation, a mild apprehension that's only what
a man with a strong survival instinct would feel. He will wait here
until the dude with the semiautomatic rifle appears, and then
he'll open fire or not. Depending on the circumstances, it might
be best to lie low and wait for dawn. If Speedo and Masud and
Orlando appear shortly, in response to the rifle fire, Aleem can call
down to them and reveal that they're looking for just one man,
which he's pretty sure is the case. When his homeys set out to
find their quarry, Aleem can remain at the window and sound the
alarm to bring them running if the rifleman comes creeping into
the common area. Aleem is the equivalent of an army general,
and good generals function best from the heights, overlooking
the battlefield below, so they have a full picture of the conflict.

◆ ◆ ◆

Specialty Products is as big as Whole Fruit, but it has a second floor.
No windows here on the ground level. From outside, Michael saw
windows upstairs. The big roll-up is missing at the back, but the
gable wall at the front has no large opening. He is convinced Aleem
isn't sheltering here; he would have run farther from where he saw all
his homeboys meet their maker. Yet Michael proceeds with caution,
the AR-15 in his right hand, the buttstock pressed between his arm
and his side. The flashlight in his left hand emits a blade-thin beam
between his masking fingers, the light momentarily fanning away
the darkness to reveal the inflow of the storm in which wallows a
miscellany of colorless debris, small shapes not readily named.

To the right is a large shaft, open at one end. The gate and cab
are missing, but dangling hoist cables and roller-guide shoes and

a pile of counterweights tumbled on the floor confirm a freight elevator once occupied this space. The steel rungs of an emergency ladder are embedded in the right-hand wall, though there has to be another and easier access to the upper floor.

He turns away from the shaft and wades through the ankle-deep lakelet, sliding his feet along the concrete floor to minimize the water noise. When a hampering length coils around his left foot, he thinks *snake*, but it's only a cable from which he is able to free himself quickly. In the right front corner of the building, beyond a doorless opening, an enclosed staircase with wide treads offers him the second floor. Michael switches off the light and stands blinded, listening for anything other than his breathing and his thudding heart and the ceaseless rustling of the rain. He climbs slowly in the vertical dark, and although he should be heavy with exhaustion and dread, he feels all but weightless, like black smoke rising in a soot-lined flue, as if the new life he's had for five days, since waking from death or something like it, is evaporating from him.

Moving from tree to tree, Orlando Fiske passes along the flank of a building on his left, and then he comes to an open area around which other structures loom. Two flashlights lay bright cones across the ground. All about lie shapeless forms that might be mistaken for mounds of black-plastic trash bags if one beam didn't terminate in a face and conjure from the unblinking stare twin amber radiances with red coronas, like the animal eyeshine of a coyote eternally caught in headlight beams as it traverses a highway. The other cone reveals a beseeching hand and a gold watch encircling its wrist.

Orlando keeps moving along the screen of trees, away from the killing ground and toward a building bearing the word OFFICES above its front door. He has the SIG P245 in a two-handed grip, alert for any moving shape in the shapeless night, wondering who has taken down those four homeys and why. Nina is said to have a trey eight; but the reports he heard were too loud and sharp and rapid-fire to be from a handgun. No one in Aleem's circle of ace kools would turn on him or on each other. Orlando hears rumors about Antoine scheming for a coup, but that fool doesn't know they came two counties south in pursuit of Nina and the kid. When he's past Offices, he leaves the trees, hurries across open ground, and presses against the back wall of that building.

Studying the darkness, he waits for intuition to guide him, but his usually reliable intuition has lost its voice. Although he tries to puzzle together what he's heard and seen into a coherent picture, he can make no sense of the situation. This is the worst— knowing he needs to kill someone but having no idea whom.

Then Orlando moves just because it's his nature to feel safer in motion, always to choose action over inaction. When he arrives at the missing roll-up door at the back of the third building, he glimpses a dim radiance in that otherwise unilluminated, cavernous space. The pale emanation sweeps left to right, then right to left. The beam is so constrained as to produce no backwash, and it isn't possible to make out a figure, let alone to determine if he's friend or foe. The light is near the far end of the building, but Orlando can't deduce if the carrier has proceeded from this west entrance or has just stepped inside from the east end. The beam turns directly to the right, and holds still for a moment, fixed on something. When it switches off, Orlando drops to one knee, his left side against the frame of the big doorway, presenting as minimal a profile as possible while maintaining a shooting position, in case the light winks on again and the man with it makes his way in this direction.

◆ ◆ ◆

Michael comes off the top of the stairs and steps to one side.

Whatever chamber he's in, the air moves in cool currents and carries the scent of rain, evidently entering by certain broken windows and exiting by others. Even a night without moon and stars is less dark than a lightless enclosed space; soon he begins to discern the vague rectangles by which the night breathes through the room. As he moves toward the front of the building, the window glass that litters the floor crackles underfoot.

A rustling startles him, but before he can click on his light, a soft *who-who-whooo* defines the noise as the fluttered wings of a resident owl annoyed to have an uninvited visitor and adjusting to its roost. This nocturnal raptor will wait until the rain stops to venture into the night in search of prey, but if it becomes too disturbed, by noise or light, it might soar out a window with a cry of protest. If it's a great horned owl with a four-foot wingspan, its sudden flight will be something of a spectacle; Aleem and the one other remaining gangbanger will likely suspect that the location of the mystery gunman has been revealed.

Michael moves cautiously forward and stops a foot from a window that looks down on the common area and at three structures arrayed east of it. He's directly opposite a single-story building that might be a garage. To the left of that is Special Accounts. In the open ground between Special Accounts and Whole Fruit, four dead men sprawl around the crossed flashlight beams, like black-robed satanic priests prostrating themselves in expectation of a demonic presence soon to appear at the intersection of lights, in answer to their invocation.

If Michael's analysis of Aleem's psychology is on the mark, the creep is more likely to be on the second floor of Special Accounts than anywhere else. There he has the best view of the entire common area and can particularly monitor Whole Fruit, where he seems to be aware that Nina and John have hidden.

The gable wall features three windows on the second floor. None is any longer graced with glass. Michael stands at an angle to all three. He has the clearest view of the southernmost window and an okay line on the middle one, but the farthest offers him little or nothing. If he's been fortunate enough to deduce Aleem's response to the death of his four lieutenants, maybe luck will be with Michael a little longer, just long enough to send Aleem Sutter to Hell with the others.

The owl rustles its wings again and scratches with its talons at whatever perch it occupies.

The moist draft continues to flow out of the night and through the room. The air seems to have the faint scent of blood on it, but that odor is the product of his imagination and his irrational but entirely human sense of guilt for having killed even those who would have killed him.

As rain slants inside and patters on the floor, he shifts his attention from the nearest Special Accounts window to the middle one, and it's at the latter that at last he sees movement, a shape. Too nervous or too eager for vengeance, the man can't hold himself back at a prudent distance. Whether he's Aleem or the other bastard not yet held to account, he's one of them and must be eliminated. Then he actually leans out of the window to take a quick and better look north and south. He isn't hooded, and his identity is no longer in doubt. Aleem.

Michael brings up the rifle, sites in, and squeezes off four rapid rounds. The first is a hit, maybe only in the left shoulder, and the screaming starts after the second, but it stops abruptly with the third, which might or might not have scored. The fourth shot is wasted on the place where Aleem had been.

Disoriented by the crash of gunfire, the owl swoops around the room, feather-dusting the walls, and Michael ducks, and the bird finds the window, soaring away in search of safer shelter.

Aleem is either dead or down and in bad shape, but the eighth man is still out there. Whether the remaining thug is in a position to see what just happened or instead must rely on sound alone to determine the situation, he is likely to know from where Michael took those shots. Depending on his appetite for confrontation after all that has occurred, he might be coming. So get out now, get out fast.

Michael returns to the stairs. Switches on his light. Rolls it down the old, canted steps to illuminate the way. He quickly follows the spinning beam, left hand on the barrel handguard of the rifle, right hand on the pistol grip, finger light on the trigger. On the landing, with one foot, he sends the light rolling again, down the lower flight of steps. At the bottom, he takes one hand off the AR-15 to retrieve the light from the murky water, clicks it off, shoves it in a deep patch pocket of his jacket.

Having entered the building from the back, he leaves by the front, stepping into the common area, sweeping the rifle left and right. Nobody there. Nobody obvious. He's not crossing to Special Accounts, not going to climb to the second floor and confirm that Aleem is dead. There's no time for that, and the risk is too great to be taken. If Aleem isn't dead, he will be in minutes. He'll bleed out. There's no one to call the EMTs, no medical help near enough to save him. Michael keeps moving fast, dodging, head ducked, making as difficult a target as he knows how, heading toward Whole Fruit next door. One guy is still out there somewhere, but it's a fool's game to go looking for him on sloppy ground that doesn't preserve tracks, among these buildings that constitute a three-dimensional spider's web of traps. Let the enemy do the searching. The bastard knows where Nina and the boy have taken refuge, so he'll go there just like Michael's going there, the location of the showdown ordained, if not the outcome.

He steps around the cross-lighted quartet of dead gangbangers and moves boldly into the building, the compass in the corner of his vision now glowing blood-red. He retrieves the flashlight and holds it loosely in the hand with which he grips the forward handguard on the rifle, which isn't ideal but the only choice he has. He splashes through the shallow flood and arrives at a series of rooms on the right, at a door that makes the compass needle throb. He throws the door open. Without venturing across the threshold, he declares, "It's me, Michael."

In the influx of light, a length of opaque plastic billows. A moldering slab of plywood topples. Nina and then John crawl out from under what seems to be a solid mass of trash. The sight of mother and son stirs in Michael emotions that he doesn't fully understand, that speak of something more than the satisfaction of having done for them what Shelby would have wanted to do if he had lived.

Whatever else he is feeling and whatever it means, he will have to delay consideration of it until they are out of the orchard and on their way to a refuge where they can safely put the past behind them. In that place, he can also determine how to use his gift to unwind the coils of destruction that humankind has wound about itself during decades of progress from reason to unreason.

A TROUBLED GUEST

ON THE DARK EARTH

Curtained by the rain, shrouded by the night, cloaked likewise by a shadow of deception that is provided by the prince of this world to those who serve his violent purpose, Orlando Fiske slinks unnoticed, staying close to the wall of the packing plant, toward the common area where the dead lie. He pauses only when the shooter, rifle in hand, departs the building from which he killed Aleem and crosses the mouth of the wide passageway, crouched and quick, to the front of this same packing plant.

Orlando knows it was Aleem who was taken down only moments ago, because in the scream he could recognize his homey's voice. He is a connoisseur of screams, having heard so many in the most intimate of circumstances over almost two decades. The personality of a man and the tonal quality of his voice are not altered by sharp pain or the terror of impending death, but are in fact amplified in their unique characteristics, if one has the ear for that kind of thing.

As the mysterious gunman passes, Orlando doesn't seriously consider taking a shot at him. His SIG P245 is a reliable weapon; however, when he factors in the distance and wind and swiftness of the target, the chances of a kill are just north of nil. And his quarry has a semiautomatic rifle, a weapon with range and perhaps with an extended magazine, which allows him to answer a shot with a sleet of return fire that will be devastating.

Orlando continues along the building and comes to the corner and hesitates and then eases forward, just his head, to reconnoiter. Reflecting the crossed beams of light on the ground, raindrops craft short-lived silver rings in the puddled water. The dead have yet to be carried off by Valkyries, which he knows about because Alana has read aloud a really good story in which sexy Valkyries conveyed the bodies of slain soldiers up to Valhalla. The rifleman is nowhere to be seen. Judging by the fact that the four were gunned down here and that Aleem chose as his vantage point a window overlooking this very scene, Orlando surmises that Nina and the boy have hidden in this packing plant and that her nameless rescuer has ventured inside to bring them out.

He turns the corner, exposing himself to anyone who might be lurking anywhere in the common area, and he sidles along the gable wall toward the entrance to Whole Fruit. When he peers inside, he sees a small, shielded light receding and the suggestion of a figure maybe halfway through the building. Again, the situation suggests that taking a shot is too risky. Orlando can imagine several ways things could go wrong for him if he tries to follow the shooter into that dark and flooded structure.

As an enforcer for the gang, he has not been called upon to be imaginative in his daily labors. There are a limited number of ways to pinch, pummel, pierce, abrade, and maim an individual and still leave him or her in a condition to make right the wrong that has been done to the gang. And if it's a case in which the offense is unforgivable, then the simplest methods of resolution are the best—a bullet in the back of the head or a wire garrote cinched around the throat with grave determination. But a loving woman has expanded his mind. During the years Alana has read to him on most evenings and on rainy weekend afternoons, he has developed an appreciation for cunning characters and clever plot twists. One such twist now occurs to him, and it is irresistible.

He steps away from the gaping entrance to Whole Fruit, out of sight of the rifleman in case that individual should happen to look back, and he studies the distribution of the corpses: the angles at which they lie to one another, how legs are bent and arms are tucked or not tucked, how one hood is rucked back from an exposed head but three are not, and other fine points of Death's artful composition. They all wear the black, hooded raincoats that are gang issue, as he does. Unfortunately, he lacks the time to drag one of them away and take that place as his own.

However, when the rifleman returns with Nina and young John, he's going to shepherd them around this grisly scene as quickly as possible. He will be surveying the night for threats, yes, but he will expect any danger to be erect and in a shooting posture or on two feet and moving fast. He won't be focused on the dead, who can do him no harm. If he's not focused on them, he's not going to notice that they number five instead of four.

His mind racing but his heart beating slow and steady with the conviction that the author of a clever ruse will see it play out as planned, just like it does in novels, Orlando decides that he should not face the door to the packing plant. If by chance the rifleman glances down and sees eye movement or blinking lashes, the trick won't work. Orlando lies on his side near the late Kuba, out of the crossed flashlight beams, with his back to the building, head turned toward the north end of the common area, where he believes the three are most likely to proceed. His raincoat is zippered open to mid chest, his right hand tucked inside, the pistol held against his heart and in a firm grip. His left arm is thrown behind him with the palm up, as he imagines it might have been cast in his death throes, and the skirt of his coat is arranged just so. When they are past him, eager to flee the orchard in whatever vehicle the rifleman arrived, Orlando will sit up and shoot them from behind, at close range. All that is required of him now is a little patience.

◆　◆　◆

Replacing the magazine of the AR-15 with a spare, Michael warns them with a single whispered word, "Quiet."

Clutching the duffel bag, John follows his mother out of the storeroom where they were hidden.

Michael says, "There's one still alive."

As she's putting her gun away, Nina decides to keep it in hand and pocket her flashlight instead.

In the dim radiance of Michael's shielded beam, mother and son seem to float on the air like mere images of people who once were of this world but now linger here to haunt.

With gestures, he indicates that he will lead and Nina should follow John.

"Take this." His voice is hushed as he places the flashlight in the boy's free hand and switches it off. "Use only if I say."

Swallowed in darkness, the boy says, "Okay," with no tremor or hesitation.

"We'll pass some dead men," Michael whispers. "Just look away."

With that, he leads them toward the front of the packing plant, one hand on the pistol grip of the rifle, the other with a firm hold on the handguard at mid barrel, the buttstock against his shoulder.

◆　◆　◆

Feigning death, Orlando relishes the prospect of telling Alana about this when next he sees her. After years of listening to the tales she has read aloud, he has learned to craft the events of his day into little stories that frequently wring from his lady a gasp of surprise or a shudder of horror or a laugh of sheer delight. In this, he feels that he is giving back, returning to her some of the pleasure that she has shown him can be found in storytelling. She has taught him more than he would have imagined when they had their first date after meeting through Enchantment Now, and the most important lesson he has learned is that a successful relationship is all about giving. Who would've thought? Orlando has been especially amazed that this truth applies to sex no less than to other aspects of a relationship. Before Alana, he had given no thought to what a girl felt when he was doing it to her. He finds it funny to realize now that he had assumed girls took no pleasure in it, that they only claimed to be thrilled so they could get their money or, on those occasions when they weren't whores, to avoid maybe being hit for not stoking a man's pride with faked orgasmic cries. Some days he thinks he loves Alana, and some days he *knows* he loves her, but he no longer has a day when he doubts that he loves her.

Orlando finds himself wondering about this guy who came out of nowhere, this mysterious rifleman, wondering what his motive might be. He's for sure not some lawman, because they never come alone and because they don't shoot seven dudes in one episode without flashing a badge and telling everyone to put down their weapons. Besides, in recent years, there has been mutual respect and shared interests between the gangs and many district attorneys, between the gangs and the most clear-thinking politicians, even between the gangs and some sheriffs and police chiefs who have realized the futility of putting their lives on the line when the previously judgmental establishment has evolved to include both lawmakers and lawbreakers who recognize the wisdom of cooperation.

In a moment of sudden enlightenment, Orlando conjectures that no man alone sets himself against eight armed gangbangers for mere money, or for vengeance, or for sport, and certainly not as a matter of principle, but only for one thing—love. Before Alana, he would not have achieved this moment of illumination. Nina has a guy whom Aleem never knew about, a guy who will do anything for her, even hang himself out there in order to blow away the leader of a gang and the leader's main men. It's Romeo and Juliet all over again, Harry meets Sally, Bonnie and Clyde; it's the thing that makes the world go round, even if some guys, like Orlando, take half their life to realize what that is. Masud and Speedo are certainly dead, which is the way it has to be when Romeo has an AR-15 and burning love in his heart. Seven have died trying to thwart the love of a man for a woman. It's an epic right up there with the best novels that have a romance in them, and he can't wait to shape it into a story that will leave Alana wide-eyed.

This is a night for serial enlightenments, for now he realizes that if he shoots these three in the back and subsequently gives each the coup de grâce of a second bullet in the head, he won't be able to tell Alana about the rifleman's love for Nina, not any of it. The anecdotes with which he charms her concern the strange and sometimes amusing twists and turns of his daily enforcements. They occasionally involve a killing, but he has never wasted anyone who was a great romantic figure. Considering the disrespect and trouble that some ninth-grade boys have given Alana, she might warm to an account of his killing John, but she will freeze at the realization that he also popped the devoted and adoring rifleman and his true love, Nina. If Orlando avenges his homeys yet wants to share Alana's life as she ascends through the education establishment to positions in which she controls the dispensation of many millions of dollars, he dare not share with her the events of this night. She will inevitably wonder if he truly believes in her love for him and his for her, if whether the time might come, some currently unimaginable circumstance, when a sense of duty to his homeboys will require him to kill his own true love. Such a tragedy will never occur. As she has changed him, Orlando is now—as he'll always be—incapable of committing such a horror, but she will not be able to put out of mind the Orlando as he was before he knew her. Suspicion. Suspicion poisons relationships.

The thing is, he can't bear not sharing with Alana the stirring tale of the romantic rifleman who, in the grip of passion, killed so many that his true love might live. It will be the best story that he's ever told her, and she has a love of stories, being an English teacher and all. Abruptly, yet another revelation thrills him—that if he does *not* kill these three for whom he is lying in wait, the story he'll then tell Alana will be even better, even more stirring, and she will see that Orlando and the rifleman are of like kind, two shining knights for whom love for a woman trumps all else, even duty to their homeys.

Oh, but how completely this violates the code, the utilitarian ethics that have shaped his life in the gang. He can continue being an enforcer, and he will no doubt still enjoy the work, but if he doesn't kill these three, he will know that he hasn't always been faithful to the gangbanger creed. As he waits for them to pass by, as he hears them approaching, he lies in a misery of conflicting emotions, in a torment of conscience, not least of all in fear of being unable to explain to the new masters of the gang why he alone survived events in the orchard. He presses the gun flat against his heart. His hand grips the gun. His finger slides from trigger guard to trigger. He eases the weapon out of his raincoat. To kill or not to kill. Man, boy, woman—they pass him unawares, presenting their backs as easy targets to this fifth of four corpses. A way out of his predicament occurs to him, another revelation, and so he watches as they walk toward Cider and Juice, as they continue to the nearest row of dead apple wood, as they disappear into the night and rain.

He has not been faithful to the gangbanger creed. He has left his homeys unavenged. He can live with that.

THERE COMES A MOMENT WHEN
EVERYTHING IS STILL AND RIPENS

As they make their way through the orchard without risking the flashlight, the rain stops, but the wind sighs a while longer. The trees rattle their bare limbs like dry bones, as if they were never wetted in the downpour.

Michael leads John and Nina, who still limps slightly, across the surging torrents in the drainage ditch, where the runoff passes through a culvert. The road lies dark and untraveled, and it seems they might be the only people in the world.

The one remaining gangbanger never sets upon them. Maybe he'd been sent into town to call for help before the shooting started.

Where the body of Masud was once marked by a portion of his raincoat filled with air and ballooning above the racing water, there is now no indication of him. Perhaps the coat deflated, and he lies waiting to be revealed when the flood relents, or maybe he has been washed farther south.

The Bentley stands alongside the highway, where Michael left it, such a handsome and unlikely conveyance that it might be taken for a mirage. They are wet and muddy, but it doesn't matter what a mess they will make of the interior, for even a Bentley is just a car.

John gets into the rear compartment with the duffel bag that contains nearly four hundred thousand dollars, and he slumps on the back seat, under which lie millions more. Peering out at Michael, the boy says, "Is it over?"

"Yes. That part is over."

"Was that the worst?"

"I hope so."

The boy shrugs. "I guess we'll see."

When Michael leaves his rifle with the boy and closes the door and turns, Nina is there with him, although he thought that she had gone to the passenger side of the sedan. She puts her arms around him, her head against his chest. He embraces her, and they stand in silence. A moment has come when everything is still, when perhaps something is happening that he has not anticipated but that he is willing to accept.

THE BUSY BEE HAS NO TIME
FOR SORROW

In the rain and then in the absence of rain, in the rainless wind and then in the absence of wind, Orlando Fiske lies among the dead. He's taking time to think through his predicament. He also wants to be sure that those he failed to kill are long gone, that there is no chance he will encounter and be shot by the rifleman. As he rests in the company of the dead, an agreeable calm settles over Orlando, for no one in this moment and place is capable of deceit or violence. Nevertheless, he doesn't want to fall asleep among them.

After twenty-six minutes as measured by his digital watch, he rises from the discreetly draped carnage around him. The rifleman has no reason to linger with the woman and boy. He will have taken them away in whatever vehicle brought him here. Nevertheless, for now, Orlando keeps the pistol ready in his right hand.

With his left, he undoes the radiant cross by plucking one flashlight off the ground, leaving the other as memorial until its batteries fail. Before departing, he plays the beam across the gable walls of the six structures, imprinting the scene in his memory, so that he can craft a story for Alana that is full of vivid details.

Leaving the buildings, he heads north into the orchard. He is overcome by the strange feeling that he is walking out of a dream, that if he turns to look back, he will find only the edge of a cliff and a bottomless abyss beyond. Being read to by Alana has made him aware of metaphor and symbol; therefore, maybe the fear that the scene he remembers was never real is an expression of his amazement that he has proved to be capable of mercy in the name of love. Or maybe the cliff and abyss are a metaphor that stands for the fate that awaits him if he can't explain his survival to those who will rise to fill the vacancies in the gang leadership. This metaphor and symbol business is tricky, with numerous possible interpretations that conflict with one another. If only he had finished high school, he might not be so confused in moments like this.

The light by which he finds his way also reveals to him a body lying faceup in a harvesting alley. Mouth and eyes wide open, Speedo says nothing, sees nothing. What a night.

When he reaches the Aviator that Masud had been driving, in which Orlando had been riding shotgun, it stands where it broke down in concert with the other three SUVs. The front passenger-side door remains open, as he left it.

On the seat lies his iPhone, where he threw it in disgust as "Macarena" shrieked forth. The screen brightens. He winces, but no dance music ensues. The charge is at only 20 percent.

Whoever the rifleman had been, he was also a wizard, not like Merlin with his spells and formulas or itinerant Gandalf roaming all the lands of Middle-earth, but a tech wizard no less powerful than those wielding true magic. The story that Orlando is crafting—not the one for Alana, but the different one for Antoine—will make no mention of a rifleman wizard.

If the phone works again, perhaps so does the car, both having been released from the spell cast over them. He goes around to the driver's side and gets behind the steering wheel. The key is in the cup holder, discarded there by Masud, and when Orlando presses the ignition button, the engine at once turns over.

He checks his contacts and places a call to Antoine. It's still an hour till midnight. Antoine doesn't hit the sack until at least three in the morning. He answers with one word, "Yeah."

"You goin' to Disneyworld," Orlando says, "you gotta see me."

Antoine breathes into the phone for a few seconds and then says, "Okay, I know you."

Orlando gives him the number of a burner phone and hangs up. He retrieves the disposable from the console box. It rings little more than a minute after he turns it on, which is just long enough for Antoine to have found his own burner.

"What's up?"

"Aleem he been plannin' to whack you."

"What shit is this?"

"True shit. Day after tomorrow."

"You Aleem's man."

"Not no more. Aleem he's dead."

Antoine says nothing.

"So you don't get whacked now."

After a silence, Antoine says, "You spinnin' me."

"No spin, man."

"So how it happen, accordin' to you?"

"Aleem tries to snatch his boy from Nina. Means to smooth him into the set, get him up on it."

"That kid's a fuckin' choirboy, can't be trusted in no gang."

"Agreed," says Orlando. "So Nina and the kid run for it. But her car been tagged. Aleem gets himself a posse, chase her down."

"What posse?"

"Him and Kuba, three other SUVs, six more us homeys."

"All for that choirboy. Aleem he lost focus."

"Agreed," says Orlando. "He let personal shit take him away from business."

"I been sayin' for some time."

"So we chase the bitch to San Diego County. She hides out in this huge old dead orchard."

"Dead what?"

"Apple orchard. Like a thousand acres, I don't know, nothin' but dead trees and broke-down old buildings."

"This gettin' weird, man."

"Gets weirder. Turns out she done set a trap. We go in there, we take fire six ways, gangbangers everywhere."

"Bloods? Crips? Who we goin' to war with?"

"They was prob'ly mustachios. MS-13. Eighteenth Street Gang. Who knows? It rainin', dark, no one wearin' their colors or do-rags. Heard one shoutin' Spanish, that's all. Won't be no war iffen we don't know who."

"We don't want no war."

"Kills profits," Orlando agrees.

"Who's down 'sides Aleem?"

"Kuba, Hakeem, Carlisle, Jason, Speedo. My main man, Masud."

"Jesus. All Aleem's aces but you."

"I ain't his ace kool no more. I popped the shitface coward."

Antoine is having trouble keeping up with the narrative. "You popped who?"

"We go in, Aleem is bringin' up the rear."

"That ain't right."

"Damn right it ain't, him supposed to be the wolfman. Shootin' starts, our homeys goin' down like ducks, he turns and runs. I pull him down, we got to shoot back, but Aleem he punches my face, breaks loose, gonna run again."

"This what I always knowed about him," Antoine declares.

"I lose it, man. My homeys bein' torn up and him runnin' to save his skinny ass. So I go after him."

"What else a good man gonna do?" Antoine says.

"Nothin' else," Orlando says. "So I take him down, I'm standin' over the fucker, him dead—and I realize all the shootin' stopped. No fool left to be killed but me."

"So fast."

"Blitzkrieg, man. So I hump outta there."

"Where you now?"

"Comin' home."

"Where Nina?"

"Wherever she figures no one can find her. You know what?"

"What?"

"I don't give a shit where she gone. This Aleem's mess, not hers. Don't you think?"

"She nothin' to me," Antoine agrees. "No time to find her, jack her up, when our own roof comin' in on us. But right now it ain't my decision."

"Will be, we throw in together for the sake of Masud, Speedo, and the others. Got to close ranks now, focus. Most homeys known for a while how it ought to be you, not Aleem."

"That why you call me 'stead of someone else?"

"Exactly why."

"How long till you be here?"

"Your place—three hours. Maybe less."

"We got the night to get down how it happened."

Orlando adds, "And how it gonna be."

"Break it to the homeys before tomorrow's news."

"Way I see it," Orlando says, "everything is everything."

"Everything is everything," Antoine agrees.

"We all gonna be a better team than how we were."

"That be truer than true. One more thing."

"I'm here."

"Sorry about Masud, bro. Must be hard, your main man."

"Comes with the life," Orlando says. "We know what price we might gotta pay to be free like we are."

They terminate the call.

After taking time to review the conversation, comfortable with every exchange between him and Antoine, Orlando gets out of the Aviator, kneels beside it, takes a deep breath, and slams the right side of his face into the back door. The pain is bad enough to be reassuring, but he repeats the act. There's good blood, although no facial bones are broken. By the time he gets to Antoine's place, the bruising will be extensive. For a coward, Aleem had a hard punch.

FIVE: IN THE GAME

TILT

The blinking signifier on the screen of the iPhone, in the cup holder of the agency sedan, remains stationary mile after mile. Why Michael Mace has stopped in a rural area of San Diego County and whether he has settled there for the night, Durand Calaphas cannot know. His concern is that Mace, given the unknowable powers that the Singularity has conferred on him, might discover the compartment under the back seat and then the hollowed-out brick of twenties in which the transponder is concealed. Calaphas must find the fugitive before the man knows that an agent of the ISA is close on his tail, and put a few bullets in his altered brain before he realizes he is in imminent danger.

Calaphas is little more than half an hour from Mace's position when the rain ceases falling and the Bentley is on the move again, bearing away its millions of dollars along with the most wanted man in the game. It's annoying that Calaphas is no longer closing the distance between him and his quarry. Looking on the positive side, however, for whatever purpose Mace had stopped, it had not been because he searched the Bentley to confirm a sudden suspicion that it was carrying an active transponder.

All will be well. Calaphas is confident that all will be well. He will never be reduced to such penury that he will need to go begging to his tedious parents, Ivor and Phyllis. He will never be dragooned into serving as a director of one—or all three—of their funeral homes, condemned to the solemn and stifling atmosphere of grief-counseling rooms and coffin-sales rooms and viewing rooms, a world of thick carpets and velvet drapes hushing away all sounds that might distract from mourning. The thick fragrance of roses and other flowers had cloyed in his nostrils so that at times he felt he must be suffocating. Having grown up, with his brother Gifford, in the apartment above the largest of the three operations, every night "our quiet and respected guests" were at rest in the basement or in ground-floor chambers, already made up and dressed to star in their pre-burial coming out the following morning or being preserved prior to costuming for a command performance the day after tomorrow. Even as oppressive as that environment had been, Calaphas acknowledges, because of the place, at the age of seven, he came to understand that a great destiny awaited him.

Halloween, back in the day. After a well-rewarded evening of trick-or-treating, he falls into bed exhausted at nine o'clock. He wakes two and a half hours later, insomnolent on a lingering sugar high, still much excited by the paraphernalia of the holiday. Black cats, bats, witches on flying brooms, caped vampires, jack-o'-lanterns with candle-flame eyes, ghosts, ghouls, and monsters in infinite variety! Supernatural threats can cast a strangely romantic thrall upon a boy, especially a boy of his high intelligence and uniquely angled mind. Shortly before bed, an elderly man who died from a massive stroke had been brought from the hospital as Durand and his brother were stuffing themselves with chocolate. Gifford dared Durand to meet at midnight and descend into the basement, to the cold-holding chamber adjacent to the embalming room, to spend the witching hour with the deceased. Forbidden from venturing into that place other than in the company of their father or mother, Durand declined. Because of his refusal, he was mocked by Gifford. Now, awake at eleven thirty, he feels it necessary to prove himself by going into the basement alone.

Barefoot and in pajamas, with but a penlight and the ambient glow of the city that pales the windows, carrying a single foil-wrapped Hershey's Kiss for a special purpose, he makes his way down through the funeral home, into the basement, a realm that always seems vast to him. The cold-holding room—which Gifford sometimes calls the "meat locker" when their parents can't hear—has a white ceramic-tile floor. In fact everything therein is either white or matte-finished stainless steel. Normally, the room itself isn't as arctic as it is this night. In one wall, three refrigerated morgue drawers can accommodate quiet and respected guests. Death is busy this Halloween; two drawers contain deliveries. Because the third drawer isn't functioning properly, the temperature of the chamber itself has been set low enough to cause Durand's breath to feather from him in frosty plumes. The eighty-five-year-old man, concealed beneath a sheet, is on a gurney in the center of the room. Father and his team of technicians will set to work at 5:00 a.m., and all viewings and funerals will be conducted precisely on schedule.

This is a windowless space, and after young Durand closes the door and turns on the overhead fluorescent panels, he switches off his penlight. He is very cold and somewhat uneasy, but he is stone determined to hide the Hershey's Kiss where his father won't likely find it, so that tomorrow he can tell Gifford where it is and thus prove he has been here. He opens a cabinet door and drops to his knees and tucks the candy behind bottles of whatever, farther back than anything the embalmers and cosmeticians might need for the work that currently awaits them.

He circles the gurney on which the approximate shape of a man lies under a sheet. He hasn't seen this customer, and he wants to be able to describe the deceased to Gifford, as absolute proof that he didn't just plant the Hershey's Kiss and hastily retreat. He's seen many dead people, of course, mostly in their open coffins after they have been spruced up and dressed for Heaven. For the most part, he doesn't find cadavers scary, but instead boring. It's an unusual situation, however, this being Halloween and the body freshly dead and Durand alone with it, so that the skin on the nape of his neck crawls, and his throat feels tight.

Three times, young Durand pinches the sheet between his thumb and forefinger, intending to peel it back and reveal the face of the corpse. Again and again and again, he releases the shroud without fulfilling his intention. He grips the pull on one of the morgue drawers. But he has previously seen the two deceased who came in during the late afternoon. Describing them to Gifford will only reveal that, in spite of having come this far with the Hershey's Kiss, he lacks the courage to confront, one to one, the corpse for whom no drawer is available.

He's embarrassed by his fear. He has never before been alone with the dead here in the basement at such a late hour, only in viewing rooms on the main floor. This is somehow different. Maybe because here they are underground. That's where the dead go when they are done with life. Underground. It's their territory. Especially from midnight to dawn. Durand is trembling. His dread angers him. Other kids his age, even older kids, treat him with respect, almost with awe, all because he lives with dead people, sleeps upstairs untroubled while in the basement dead people are doing who knows what. Some kids are even a little scared of him. They're eager to hear his latest stories about living with corpses, although after an unusually weird or gruesome anecdote, he can see they regard him with some trepidation. He enjoys being respected, and being feared is even better. Just seven, he already understands that being feared is a source of power, and that people who are fearful can more often be made to do what he wants rather than what they want. Fear is for the weak. His fear *infuriates* him, and he is shamed by the rapid, frosty exhalations that plume from him. At last he flips the sheet back, revealing a deader that is, at first, no more to be feared than any other.

The head is crowned with a thin tangle of white hair, and the forehead is mostly smooth except for a purplish cut above the left eye, which he might have sustained by falling against something when the stroke hit him. There is a wound, a gap in the flesh, but no blood, maybe because someone washed it off after the old man died, as they were preparing to send him to the funeral home. He's flat on his back, facing the ceiling, but his eyes are closed. Durand likes it better when the eyes are open, allowing him to gaze into them; he never fails to win a staring contest with a corpse, regardless of how big and mean-looking it is. This one's face is as pale as chalk, wrinkled, bristling with beard stubble. His mouth is open, not wide, less than an inch, as if he intends to reveal some secret but has forgotten what he meant to say. Durand is just tall enough to look down on the gurney and see the whole face of this latest quiet and respected guest. Confident that he can adequately describe the man to Gifford, he pinches the sheet to draw it back into place—which is when the head turns toward him and the eyes open and the corpse makes a croaking noise as if a frog has taken up residence in its throat.

Durand drops the sheet and startles backward. The deader's eyes aren't empty, as have been so many eyes that he has stared into, and they fix on him. From the mouth issues a pearly vapor much fainter than the rich exhalations that steam from Durand. A word whispers from between the cracked, pale lips: "You."

Although he feels compelled to run, Durand is unable to move. The fear he despises has returned, along with shame that burns in his cheeks in spite of the deep chill in the chamber, shame at the fright that coils around his bones and cinches his joints and immobilizes him, shame at the weakness the fright represents.

The blue eyes of the respected but no longer quiet guest are so bright and hot with intention that it seems they ought to burn twin holes through Durand. The man says, "Give me."

Durand's father has shared tales of the mortician's trade from times long gone, prior to his own practice of the arcane art, when on occasion a person thought to be dead, delivered for embalming, suddenly regained consciousness, sat up, and asked for a shot of whiskey or a roast-beef sandwich, the whereabouts of his wife or the location of the nearest bathroom. As modern medicine advanced and the certainty of the patient's passage could be confirmed by cardiac monitors and electroencephalograms, such rare occurrences became rarer still and eventually unknown in the developed world.

What lies before Durand, its grizzled face turned toward him, is so extraordinary that it represents one of the worst errors by a physician in this decade—or here, as midnight nears, evil Halloween energy has conjured a dead man back to life with wicked purpose.

Although not rising from the gurney or moving other than his head, the apparition contorts his face from a beseeching expression into something less benign. His eyes narrow, and his mouth twists into a cruel snarl. "You, you, you, GIVE ME!"

Months earlier, Durand's great-aunt Pelagia suffered a massive stroke that left her paralyzed until she died a few days later. If that is the condition of the man on the gurney, he poses no threat.

As Durand's fear subsides somewhat, he is overcome with the feeling that this bizarre event is not about the old man and not about some doctor who might have screwed up, that it's about Durand and only Durand because he's special. Not just special—unique. He's heard the word *destiny*; with his IQ of 178, he understands it far better than would a seven-year-old of lesser intelligence. This strange encounter is a challenge, a test. There's something he is meant to do, something that will determine whether he'll become a superhero or a supervillain. He has known for a while that he is going to be a super something. He doesn't care which it is, just as long as it's a lot more exciting than growing up in a funeral home.

The paralyzed man's angry expression fades into puzzlement. He rolls his eyes, taking in as much of the cold-holding chamber as he can from his position.

"Give you what?" Durand asks.

Puzzlement sinks into bewilderment. "I . . . how . . . where?"

Taking a step toward the gurney, Durand says, "Give you what? Tell me. Tell me what you want."

The fluorescent light is a bleaching radiance. The respected guest is as white as the shroud had been when Durand first entered the room, and the shroud grows whiter by the minute. The walls are alabastrine, as though this frigid chamber is built of snow, an Inuit construct. The floor could be no whiter if it were paved with bone. Durand's remaining fear evaporates like a scrap of dry ice, and he is filled with the conviction that there's an action he can take to ensure he'll become the super something that he dreams of being. He must get it done before whiteness fills the chamber to such an extent that it is as blinding as pitch-blackness. The blue eyes are beacons in the ghastly face, the only color in the seamless eggshell that is forming around Durand, a blue that draws him toward the gurney and the burden on it.

"Give you what?" he asks again, and then repeats the question in a more demanding voice, "Give you what, old man?"

"Help," the old man says. "Help me. I can't move. I'm afraid." As pitiful as he sounds, there is nonetheless an air of deception about him. He looks sly, as if he's not the old man he once was, but only a body in which something demonic has clothed itself.

A wild assurance buoys Durand, a vicious courage, the belief that he can do anything he wishes here and be rewarded for it. The gurney has a hydraulic feature, and at the moment it is not lowered as far as it will go. He powers it down six or eight inches, until it will descend no farther.

"Help me," the old man repeats. The blue that was ferocious is now a weak, robin's-egg blue that inspires contempt. "Help me."

Looking down on the old man, feeling taller and stronger than he'd been just a minute earlier, Durand says, "Help you what? What do you want? Are you so stupid you don't know what you want?" He likes how he sounds when he says that in the tone of voice he often wants to use with his parents but dares not. "Stupid geezer can't even say what he wants."

"Call," the old fart says. "Call."

"Call who? You want to order a pizza?"

Amused by his joke, Durand laughs, but the geezer doesn't even smile. He says, "Don't."

This is a test, a challenge, and if Durand passes it, he will be something super, not right away but later, something amazing. He moves around to the head of the gurney.

The old fart rolls his head side to side, tries to tip it back to see what's happening, but he can't. He says, "No."

Durand says, "Oh, yes. I know what you really are," because he sees now what he's got to do to prove he's special, to show that nothing scares him. He must prove himself to the secret masters of the universe, who work in mysterious ways.

The overhead fluorescent panels bleach the elderly man still whiter, and Durand cups his right hand under the respected guest's stubbled chin, forcing the mouth shut. The man lacks the strength to resist. With his left hand, Durand pinches the nostrils tight. The quadriplegic can move nothing other than his head; he rolls it side to side, and for a minute he is vigorous in defense of his life, but he is not able to break his assailant's grip. The rightness of the boy's intention is confirmed for him when, as the light grows and the room blurs into a smooth sphere of whiteness, his pajamas seem to become a richer shade of yellow, shifting from saffron to lemon, and the hands that are instruments of suffocation flush with the color of life that a booming heart delivers. The man's resistance grows feeble. The boy's pajamas are now the yellow of an egg yolk, and his flesh is yet more darkly bronzed with urgent life, the blood vessels in his hands swollen to match his excitement, fingernails as pink as if they have been painted. When the geezer finishes dying, the blue of his eyes is a bleak frost, but Durand has become more vivid and colorful even than he has been in his most feverish night dreams of superpowers and violent adventures. His clamping hand relaxes, and his pinching fingers open. The blinding whiteness relents. Details of the cold-holding room return.

He has passed the test. The challenge has been met. He's afraid of nothing. Nothing. Not even of a man returned from the dead—or of some demon possessing a corpse.

Having proved he is special, he will eventually have the super future of which he dreams. He needs only to be patient and grow into his greatness. Patience is another test he must pass.

He arranges the shroud as it was when he came here.

After turning off the lights and stepping into the hall and closing the door, he switches on the penlight. He makes his way back to his room.

In bed, in the post-Halloween dark, as he flirts with sleep yet resists surrendering to it, the events in the basement rerun in his mind until he is trembling in remembered ecstasy. In time, he knows beyond doubt that the old man was not mistakenly declared dead and then sent here by an incompetent doctor. A dead man had returned to life, brought back among the living by the masters of the universe who search for those who are able to conquer fear and are worthy of being given superpowers. From the comic books that he reads and the cooler graphic novels that Gifford collects, Durand knows there *are* masters of the universe; they go by a variety of names in different series, and they work in mysterious ways. They are aware of him, have chosen him. The possibility that he has imagined all that happened occurs to him, but he dismisses it, allowing himself no doubt. And then he sleeps.

Thus the game had begun.

All these years later, it quickens toward an end. As at the beginning, the all-powerful masters of the universe require him to kill a dead man who returned to life. Thereafter, Durand Calaphas will win his way out of the game and into the next level, which his unshakable faith assures him is the highest and true reality, where he will become one of the masters. He has no doubts. Doubts are for losers.

His quarry is moving toward the coast.

And so he speeds south, in pursuit of the blinking signifier that is Michael Mace. He lives to kill and kills to live again, a product of the New Truth in which he does not believe any more than he believes in the old truth.

A MOMENT ON THE EARTH

As midnight fast approaches, robes of cloud slide northward down the sky, and in the clear high dark, stars map the universe beyond the silver moon.

While the solid and quiet Bentley floats through the dripping night, John sleeps in the back, upon a multimillion-dollar bed. With so much to process from this frantic day, he has material to inspire nightmares, but if dreams assault him, he keeps them to himself. He lies silently in the fetal position. Perhaps the purr of the sedan and the susurration of the tires on the highway approximate the sounds of life in the womb, the sustaining rush of umbilical blood, and bring him peace.

"He's so young," Nina says. "How can he cope with all this? What will it do to him?"

"Make him stronger," Michael says.

"I hope that's true."

"That's who he is. Most children are adaptable, survivors, if they're allowed to be, if adults don't layer their own neuroses on their kids. John's never going to need safe spaces like the infants in universities require these days. He won't waste his life being offended by 'microaggressions.' He knows the world is a hard place for everyone, that taking solace from—or finding virtue in—being a victim is a sure path to lifelong misery. He'll roll with whatever life throws at him, and he'll always find a way to be happy."

"I wish I could be sure of that," she says. "How can *you* be?"

"That's who he is because of you."

She sits taller, not in pride, but in humble resistance to what he has said. "Don't snow me. I've given him so little."

He almost smiles but doesn't want a smile to seem patronizing. "You've given him love, stability, proper guidance, and confidence. That's all any kid needs, and what too few receive."

"Because of me," Nina says, "John had a murderer—a monster—for a father."

"You took full responsibility for what you did. Because of you, John lives, and the world is better with him in it."

"You let me off the hook too easily."

"It only seems that way to you because you never let yourself off the hook to any extent at all."

She closes her eyes and rides in silence for a while. When he glances at her, he sees that she is biting her lower lip. Her cheeks are dry, but her eyelashes are jeweled.

Eventually she opens her eyes and says, "It feels so strange."

"What does?"

"Not being in control. Not knowing what's next or where."

"I'm just a bridge, remember?"

"Troubled water. But you're . . . more than a bridge."

"When we're across the flood, you'll soon be in control of your life, no less than you've always been."

"Their kind," she says, "they hate women. They think one dissed them, they'll never let it go. One day, I go out to the street to check the mailbox, they drive by shooting."

"Not if they can't find you. Not if you're someone other than Nina Dozier with a different past that public records will support through any intensity of investigation."

This is a different silence, and her hope is almost palpable. Reminded of his power, she says, "You could do that."

"Just think about what name you might like to be. And one for John. In a week or less, I'll have birth certificates, valid social security cards, a driver's license in your new name and on file with the DMV."

"I owe you so much."

"You owe me nothing. I had a deep debt to Shelby Shrewsberry, and what I've done is pay it back to him, through you."

About twenty miles north of San Diego, they turn inland from the ocean, toward Rancho Santa Fe, a residential community of mostly large homes and gated estates on significant acreage.

With darkness at its midpoint, the moon is high before them, reflecting its reflected sunlight across rolling hills that become less populated mile by mile, silvering the wild grass that is golden in daylight. Beyond the headlights, trees loom in dim silhouette, the stone pines standing motionless, the palm trees swaying with the dreamy flow of plants that grow in the bosom of the sea. Greater in number and height are eucalyptuses that stand sentinel across the slopes as well as in the vales.

Nina breaks their mutual silence. "What will you do?"

"I've already got three identities locked in the system."

"I don't mean who will you be. What will you do? What you've done for us, in Shelby's name, isn't all you can do. There's more you want to do, I think. Much more. Whatever it is, I can't even begin to imagine the . . . impact."

Their conversation has brought them closer to the personal issue that is most important to Michael. He won't press her further at this point. Until the Internal Security Agency and gangbangers have for certain been put behind them forever, the future is too fluid to be making plans.

He says, "I've thought about it a lot—the impact. How do you bring about major change without causing major destruction. Most of those who want to change the world also mean first to destroy it as it currently is and build back on the rubble. They're narcissists and lunatics. I like to think I'm not."

WITH SPIDERS I HAD FRIENDSHIP MADE

By the time Michael was nine years old, his mother seldom left their house, and when she did, it was always to make a spectacle of herself. She ranted at a helpless grocery-store clerk about the price of tomatoes, reaching such a peak of indignation that she threw the fruit on the floor and crushed it underfoot. She rose to her feet in a city council meeting and complained about the increase in parking-meter fees, which incensed her in spite of the fact that she had developed a fear of driving and had sold her car; refusing to adhere to a time limit for testimony, she raged at the council members, no epithets too crude for her use, until the sergeant at arms had to forcefully escort her from the chamber. A neighbor had to endure periodic tongue-lashings—as well as answer complaints to animal control—about a pit bull that did not exist.

In the summer before Michael entered fourth grade, his mother developed a terror of spiders. She had never been afraid of them before. Without apparent reason, she insisted that she'd become so allergic to arachnid bites that, if nipped, she would fall at once into anaphylactic shock, be unable to breathe, and die. It mattered not whether the species was poisonous. Years earlier, when Beth had secured their home against Lionel's animated corpse, which she said wanted to get into the house at night, the credulousness of extreme youth had left Michael vulnerable to her dark fantasies, and he had succumbed to that irrational fear. At nine, he better understood his mother, but initially he couldn't tell whether her dread of spiders was real or pretense. If she faked it, maybe she wanted to add drama to her life—for she loved drama—or maybe she was psychologically bent to such an extent that she took pleasure in tormenting a child. Eventually, he came to believe both things were true.

When she woke Michael in the night to hurry to her bedroom to kill a spider that had appeared while she was reading to overcome insomnia, or near dinnertime when she fled the kitchen in fear of a scurrying invader, the eight-legged threat would not always be where she'd seen it. An urgent spider hunt would ensue. *Find it, Mickey. Find it and kill it. Damn you, Mouse, you little shit, find it, kill it!* If the creature were found and squashed to her satisfaction, life could go on after a suitable period of lamentation regarding the death she would have suffered if she had been bitten. On those occasions when the spider couldn't be found—or never existed in the first place—the failed search was an excuse to attempt to settle her nerves with glass after glass of chardonnay or morbid talk about how suicide by pills would be a better way to go than by suffocating when her airway shut down from arachnid poison. *You'll miss me then. You'll miss me when you're alone, boything. Alone because you were too stupid to find it and kill it.*

He had done nothing to earn her animosity, with the possible exception of having been born. Even after he became convinced that she enjoyed manipulating him into conceding that her silly fears were legitimate, Michael was frequently exasperated with her, often impatient, indignant that she toyed with him—but he was never able to hate her. Whatever else Beth might be, she was his mother. He could no more love her than despise her, but pity came easily. He wondered if in *her* childhood she endured something that shaped her into what she was. If she could not strike back at whoever had been cruel to her, she might feel the need to pay her misery forward to her son, as wrong as that might be. Even if by nature Mother was a disturbed person, she was a pathetic rather than an evil figure. Watching her in near perpetual distress, some faked but much of it real, Michael was at times overcome by a tenderness toward her, and by a desire to fix whatever was broken in the woman, though he knew he hadn't the power to make her right. However, day by day, week by week, year by year, he came to see how he could console her with no risk of becoming like her; he could be amused by her, find sanctuary in his amusement, without disrespecting her. That was not an easy path to take, but he found a satisfaction in it that he could not name until he was much older—compassion, mercy, forgiveness.

The year of spider terror came to a quiet end. Having reason to be suspicious, Michael waited till his mother was across the street, berating neighbors for an offense they had not committed, whereupon he went into the attic. That place was forbidden to him, because his mother claimed it harbored hornet's nests and rats bearing numerous diseases. He found no hornets or rats, but he did find three quart-size mason jars with numerous pinholes in their lids. One was empty. The other two contained dead flies and pill bugs that Mother had provided as larder, a few drops of water, and a variety of spiders that she had somehow gathered and imprisoned, ten in all, clinging to life in ill-spun webs that sagged away from the glass walls. You can't depend on nature always to supply a spider when you most need one. Michael, Mickey, Mouse, Boything, Little Shit carried the jars downstairs. He took the occupied pair into the backyard and set the prisoners free. They scurried across his hands without biting him. In the kitchen, he washed the jars, dried them with paper towels, and stood them on the counter by the door to the pantry. He went to his room and was soon lost in a book. He heard his mother return home. She slammed the door and cursed the world on her way to the kitchen and the chardonnay. Her sudden silence lasted perhaps two hours, until she'd drunk enough to start softly singing Celtic songs to which she didn't know all the words. Later, she ordered in dinner from a restaurant on the corner, all his favorite dishes, allowed him to read his book at the table, and did not trouble him with conversation. Such were the limits of her grace and confession. Michael knew even this tacit recognition of the humanity of another was torment for her, and he asked nothing more.

A NAMELESS PLACE

Many of the larger estates in Rancho Santa Fe have names, but this sixteen-thousand-square-foot house on twelve acres currently lacks one. It changed hands a year earlier, and the new owners, having no interest in horses, removed the name from the entrance monument because it made reference to equine pursuits. They have three homes in other states and don't currently live here, but they are developing plans to extensively rebuild and expand the house, as well as to replace the stables with a museum to display an antique car collection. Meanwhile, they are exploiting the property as a vacation rental, for they have an aversion to holding assets that don't produce a return.

Even as he was leaving the dead orchard, Michael invaded the computer of a company that represents only luxury homes for vacation bookings by the most qualified renters. He has seldom earned enough in any four-month period to pay for two weeks in this residence, but on this occasion the cost is zero. A family from Boston will arrive here in five days. The property manager and three-person staff that will take care of the lodgers are on holiday but will return in three days to prepare the house.

By then, Nina and John will have rested, and Michael will have found a refuge, preferably out of California, where they can go to ground for a few weeks. In that next place, he will assist mother and son in acquiring new identities. There, too, he'll be able to think hard about what he wishes to achieve with his strange gift. Together, they can discuss how long and by what arrangement they might remain together, three against the world. He hopes they will want that as much as he does, but it isn't his place to assume what is best for them.

The property features white ranch fencing that extends from a pair of massive stacked-stone columns flanking a formidable bronze gate. A post beside the driveway offers a call button and intercom, as well as a lighted keypad. There's no one in the house to answer the call, or shouldn't be. As John wakes and sits up in the back, Michael powers down the driver's window and enters the guest code that's been assigned to the family that will be in residence here for two weeks. The halves of the ornate gate swing slowly inward.

The boy says, "Does a king live here?"

"A tech king owns it. He developed microchips that processed data five times faster than those that existed before him."

"Crazy. Imagine if they were ten times faster."

"He'd own the world," Michael says.

The long driveway is overhung by colonnades of live oaks. Low mushroom lamps pour pools of light onto the cobbled pavement, which ends in a large moon-washed motor court.

The two-story house is somewhat reminiscent of the work of Frank Lloyd Wright, with a low-pitched roof, broad overhanging eaves, and linear masonry. Michael parks near the front steps.

He retrieves the AR-15 and the two spare magazines he hasn't used. The boy brings the duffel bag, and when they climb the steps, Nina plays the beam of her Tac Light over the terrace-like front porch.

All the windows are dark, and no voice calls out to demand they explain their presence. Crickets and various night birds perform their timeless chorales.

The security package hasn't been modernized; no electronic lock exists for Michael to release. He uses the buttstock of the AR-15 to smash one of the panes in the door. Evidently, glass-break detection isn't part of the system, for no alarm sounds. He reaches inside, feels for the deadbolt, finds the thumb turn, and disengages the lock.

When he opens the door, the alarm begins to beep, counting down a grace period during which he can enter a disarming code. The one he has is that of the property manager, which earlier he fished from the security company's files. The beeping stops.

Nina turns on lights, revealing limestone floors. Dark wood walls with a glossy piano finish. A Persian rug in jewel tones. They move through the main rooms, which feature more of the same, the Wrightian furniture stands on rugs worth perhaps a couple hundred thousand each.

"I could live here," John says.

His mother advises, "We're just visiting, honey."

In the kitchen, they find that the two Sub-Zeros are stocked with items apparently ordered by the guests who will be forthcoming. John is especially taken with a freezer compartment full of premium gelatos.

Michael steps into the garage and switches on the lights. He finds six stalls and two vehicles, a Lincoln Continental and a Range Rover. The time has come to abandon the Bentley somewhere it won't be found for a while, before their luck runs out. If they take the Range Rover and get out of here as soon as early the day after tomorrow, they will have two days before the property manager and the house staff return. By then they can be in another state and find new wheels as well as a longer-term refuge than this one.

When Michael returns to the kitchen, Nina has found bowls and spoons, which she is setting on the kitchen island, at which John is already perched on a stool. "We're flat-out starving," she declares. "Cherry-chocolate-almond gelato is the agreed-upon first course."

Putting the AR-15 on a counter and opening the pantry door to search for trash bags, Michael says, "Count me in. I'm just going out to get the cash from the hidden compartment in the Bentley. We'll ditch the car tomorrow." He finds a box of eighteen-gallon bags and withdraws one. "Be right back."

WHO RIDES AT NIGHT,
WHO RIDES SO LATE?

Aware that he's losing his edge to weariness, Calaphas would like to stop somewhere for a large coffee, as black as it comes. However, the blinking signifier indicates he's less than fifteen minutes from the Bentley, ten if he puts the pedal down harder and relies on his training in high-speed pursuit.

The medical kit from the safe house is on the seat beside him. When he gets where he needs to be, he can pop the container open and find the bottle of caffeine tablets that will certainly be there. If the agency hasn't changed its list of standard amenities included in such kits, there will also be a four-pack of five-milligram bennies, Benzedrine tablets. One of those little cross tops, held under his tongue to dissolve, will quickly give him four hours of heightened alertness.

The hills roll, and the road swoops, and the hills roll, and the road falls and climbs through the midnight darkness of Rancho Santa Fe, which is relieved only by widely separated clusters of soft lights, none of which reveal anything significant. Beyond the small town center, the community has no streetlamps or sidewalks. Hard to believe this rural outpost is routinely listed among the wealthiest communities in America.

Belatedly, he realizes that the red dot on the screen of his iPhone is not moving. He isn't sure how long ago it stopped. Five minutes? Ten? He eases off the accelerator and snatches the phone from the cup holder. The Bentley is no more than half a mile ahead.

Letting his speed fall to thirty miles per hour, twenty, ten, Calaphas cruises over the brow of a hill and down a long slope, past white ranch fencing. The Bentley is somewhere to the left, off this road. On the small screen, it's difficult to judge how far the sedan has gone from the state highway. Calaphas's own vehicle is depicted as an unblinking blue dot, and when it draws even with the blinking red dot, he slows nearly to a stop. Immediately ahead, on the left, the white board fencing leads to pillars of stacked stone framing a tall pair of stately metal gates joined by an ornate medallion. A tree-lined driveway, subtly illuminated by low lamps, leads between palisades of what might be oak trees. Sixty or seventy yards away, darkness further relents to house lights. The Bentley is in the vicinity of that residence.

Not wanting to call attention to himself, Calaphas accelerates past the gate. Two to three hundred yards farther, he comes to the driveway of another residence. This place lacks a gate and sets half as far back from the road as the previous house. It is nonetheless a large home. Although most windows are dark, lights glow in rooms both on the first and second floor.

Until he has a better understanding of the situation, Calaphas isn't keen about approaching the estate where the transponder in the Bentley's cash hoard continues signaling. Michael Mace, the long-anticipated Singularity, is a formidable adversary on his own. With whom might he have joined forces? No better place exists to learn more than from a neighbor of whoever has given Mace shelter.

He drives ahead another hundred yards, until he arrives at a lay-by cupped in a semicircle of eucalyptuses. He parks off the pavement and kills the headlights.

Rummaging through the medical kit, he finds the bennies. He pops one out of the blister pack. If dissolved under the tongue, the Benzedrine will produce an effect slightly faster than if swallowed.

He doesn't mind the bitter taste.

From the glove compartment, he withdraws a custom-threaded sound suppressor for his Springfield Armory .45 and fits it to the pistol. His shoulder holster accommodates the weapon with silencer. He works his hands into the soft, gray, cotton-and-spandex gloves that he wore when wiping down the surfaces in Carter Woodbine's apartment, following the untimely death of the attorney and his associates.

He turns off the engine, gets out into the night, and locks the car. The air is redolent of eucalyptus oil. He inhales deeply a few times and stretches and rolls his head to work out a kink in his neck. Already, his weariness is sliding off him.

Without raincoat, dressed in his dark suit and white shirt and tie, he might be an itinerant Pentecostal messenger so indefatigable that he carries the truth of the Holy Gospel to doorstep after doorstep without regard to the weather or the hour.

AN ISSUE OF SOME IMPORTANCE

Nina and John sit side by side on stools at the kitchen island, bowls of gelato before them, working their spoons with pleasure. The cherry-chocolate-almond is delicious, perhaps the more so because little more than an hour earlier they escaped being murdered. The truth of that is almost impossible to process in any way that makes sense or that risks spoiling her appetite. She could eat an entire quart herself.

"Good," the boy says.

"Very good."

"What next?"

"Maybe there's cake."

"That would be good, too. But it's not what I meant."

"I know what you meant. Problem is, I have no idea what's next, honey."

"You always do."

"Well, in this case, all I know is that Michael will know."

"It's not just the Vigs after us. Somebody's after him, too."

"Government," she says. "They're after him hard."

"Because of what happened to him, what it made him into?"

"And because of what he can do."

"He told you this while I was sleeping?"

"No. He told me the first day he came to me and said he owed this to Shelby. He's been straight with me from the start."

"Are we always going to be on the run?"

"No. We'll be okay. I don't know how or when. But Michael will know."

Just then he enters the kitchen with a trash bag full of money, which he puts on the island. "Know what?"

"What's next," John says.

Nina says, "That's your spoon there. Your bowl is on a shelf in the nearer fridge, so it wouldn't melt too fast."

Michael takes his serving from the Sub-Zero, stands with bowl in hand, attends to the treat for a few spoonfuls, and then says, "From here, day after tomorrow, we should get out of state. Get lost in a city, maybe Phoenix, for ten days or two weeks, until we can acquire new ID for you and use some of this money to buy legitimate wheels."

"Can you make us invisible?" John asks.

"To an extent, yeah, but not like in the movies."

"Are they going to find us?"

"The next week is tricky. After that, once we settle you in a new life, you'll be safe."

"Will you stay with us? In our new life?"

With the tone of her voice, Nina advises the boy that his question is inappropriate. "Enough, John."

Glancing at Nina, Michael says, "I'll always be on call for you. Always. No less than that. Whether we go one way or our own ways . . . that's something we eventually have to work out together."

"Let's work it out right now," the boy says.

"In time," Nina says.

"Why not now?" John persists.

"At the moment, Mr. Mace has a lot on his mind."

"We all do."

"That's for sure," Michael agrees.

"If we work this out now," John says, "it's one *less* thing on our minds."

That observation inspires a smile from Michael and a sigh of embarrassment from Nina. She almost tells John the issue doesn't involve him; it's between her and Michael. In one sense that is true, but it's not the whole truth. In fact, whatever she and Michael decide they are—or could be—to each other, whether just friends or something more, will have an enormous, incalculable impact on the boy's life.

Into Nina's hesitation, Michael says, "I want whatever your mother wants, John. But you need to listen now and understand me. Given time, people as special as your mom always make the right decision. Guys like you and me, not so much. The best thing we can do, the only smart thing, is shut our traps and be patient. You keep pestering her about this, she might make a decision too quick, one she'll regret. We don't want her to live with regret. We want her to *know* she's taken the right path, don't we?"

"I guess so."

"You guess so? Want to clean that up?"

"Yeah. I mean, I want her to be happy."

"There you go."

Michael smiles almost shyly at Nina. She could adore him. But he's correct when he says she needs time. She feels as if she is on a tightrope, inching toward something so right and so precious that it's almost surely beyond her reach, given the missteps in her past. If she hurries, she will lose her balance.

Pushing the trash bag across the island to John, Michael says, "You finished your ice cream. I still have some of mine. Start the count, see how much we've got. Then we need to pack it in something that looks unimportant."

John gets off the stool and opens the bag. Across the granite countertop spill thick packets of cash, each individually secured with taped Saran Wrap or its equivalent.

"Looks like a double century in each packet," Michael says. "Twenty thousand per."

"More money than a bank," John says. "We're set for life."

Michael shakes his head. "Maybe. But the day's coming when they'll try to outlaw cash, force us into a digital dollar without blockchain privacy, total government control of everyone's accounts and finances. If that can't be stopped, it's important for us to scare up all the cash we can while it's still spendable and use it to insulate ourselves as much as possible."

Gripped by a cold disquiet, Nina says, "You know that for true? When you've been . . . swimming through the internet or whatever it is you do, you've seen proof they're scheming to do that?"

His deadpan expression isn't reassuring. "That and more. The worst people live for power. They work at it as industriously as bees in a hive. I've discovered so much in the past five days, I'm amazed my hair hasn't turned as white as snow."

Piling the parcels of cash five high—one hundred thousand dollars per stack—John pauses with a thicker bundle in hand. "Something's wrong with this one. It's twenties."

"It's still money," Nina says.

"Yeah, and there's been two others with twenties. Thicker like this. But this one is kinda funny. Loose. The plastic can't keep it straight."

"Let me see," Michael says.

Frowning, he takes the packet from John. The stack of bills is sufficiently unstable that the tape has peeled up. The plastic isn't as snug as it should be. He strips the tape off and folds back the Saran Wrap and lifts up a half-inch-thick quantity of whole bills, revealing that the center of the three-inch-high bundle has been hollowed out. Within lies an object Nina can't identify, nestled between two triple-A batteries.

Michael says, "A transponder with backup power sources."

THE NIGHT ISN'T DARK;
THE WORLD IS DARK

Active in the aftermath of the storm, crickets and night birds celebrate the freshly washed world.

Walking alongside the deserted highway toward his target residence, Durand Calaphas wonders if the higher reality above this game level will be afflicted with insects. If it's not home to bugs of any kind, it might also be birdless, as the primary purpose of many birds is to eat insects. Of course some birds dine on fish or, like owls, on rodents. If there are no insects on the level where the designers of the game reside, perhaps rodents also have no place there, which would leave only fish-eating birds. Bats eat insects, so they would have no reason to exist in the world above. Calaphas doesn't care whether or not there will be bugs, birds, and bats in his next life; he's just curious. All that matters to him is that there will be people to use and kill, that he will have earned an unqualified license to use and kill them, and that he won't have to answer to moronic bureaucrats like Julian Grantworth and Katherine Ormond-Wattley.

As he turns into the driveway, no rag of cloud remains to wrap the moon. In that cold radiance, the white roses and calla lilies, plentiful in the front garden, are not lost in gloom like the other plants, but swell out of the darkness on thorny brambles and meaty stalks. They aren't lovely but ghastly, although he can't say why.

He is halfway to the house when he becomes aware of an eerie quietude. The crickets and night birds have fallen silent, like they do when something that fills them with dread enters their domain. Alerted by this sudden disturbing hush, Calaphas stands statue-like, listening intently. Whatever threat has muted the night song might be a danger to him. He fears nothing; however, in moments like this, a wise player must be cautious in the game. The light-filled windows on the main level are hazed by sheer curtains, but those at an upstairs room are not. No face or shadow appears at the glass either on the ground floor or above. After a minute passes, when no menace appears out of the broad yard or the garden or from among the trees, he continues to the back of the residence.

Fragmented reflections of the moon ripple across the black water in a large swimming pool. A flagpole stands flagless. White chairs, lounges, and tables furnish a patio. All the windows at the back of the house are dark.

Through the four panes in the upper half of the kitchen door, he can see the green numbers on the digital clocks of the ovens. He tries the lever handle, but it doesn't move. He slides the thin pick of the lock-release device into the keyway, pulls the trigger three times, tries the handle again, squeezes the trigger a fourth time, and the lock is disengaged. He draws his pistol.

He steps inside, eases the door shut, and stands with his back to it, listening. The refrigerator hums. Warm air sighs through the vanes of a heating vent high in one wall. If the family had a dog, Calaphas would already hear it coming.

Except for the influence of the moon, his eyes became mostly dark-adapted on his way here. He waits until details of the kitchen resolve further out of the gloom. Then he moves cautiously toward an open doorway that is vaguely defined by light issuing from another room farther along the main hall. The hallway itself is not lighted, and a plush runner that carpets the center of the wood floor ensures his silent progress.

The light issues from a book-lined study, a masculine space. Handsome mahogany desk. Button-tufted burgundy-red leather sofa. Seascape paintings with sailing ships.

A fiftysomething man, white-haired, sizable and fit, in pajamas and robe, sits in a leather armchair, slippered feet propped on a footstool, a hardcover book in his hands, reading glasses partway down his prominent nose. He looks up, without apparent surprise, certainly not with alarm, but with interest and calculation. He has the self-possession of a military man who has had to remain calm through times of crisis and chaos.

Stepping into the room, easing the door shut behind him, pistol ready, Calaphas says, "You should have a dog."

"We did. She was a good old girl, passed a month ago."

"Bad timing," says Calaphas.

"She was a golden retriever. She would've let me know you were coming, but she still would've loved you up if you'd let her."

"Who else is in the house?"

"Just Colleen, my wife. Whatever this is, it's nothing to do with her."

"That's why I'm keeping my voice low," Calaphas says. Instinct warns him that this is one of those characters in the game on whom the fate of the player can suddenly take an unexpected turn. "I'm not here to hurt anyone. I just need some help, information. You have a name?"

"Why ask when you must know it? Vincent."

"So, Vince, what branch was it—navy?"

"Hard to believe you'd come here without knowing my history. Marine intelligence."

"This isn't about your service. Fact is, this isn't any more about you than it is about Colleen."

Vincent marks his place in the book with a dust-jacket flap, closes the volume. Rather than put it on the side table, under the lamp, he places it on his lap, still cupped in his right hand. If he has the opportunity, he means to throw it—as feeble a weapon as it is, it's all that he has—and come out of the chair fast after it. "You're no common burglar."

"It's about your neighbor, the property with the big gate."

"You're an agency man, though I can't figure which agency."

With his left hand, Calaphas produces his ID wallet, flips it open, displays the badge card. "ISA. National security matter."

"All right. Then you don't need a gun with me."

"You're wondering if the ID is fake. It's not."

"I'll take you at your word."

Putting the wallet away, Calaphas says, "You've spent a career taking no one at his word. It's how you were trained. As I was."

"I'm retired now."

"But still the same man," Calaphas says. "With all due respect, this situation is too pressing to risk you taking the gun away from me and throwing a wrench into the operation. Minutes matter."

"Call in your partner. I'm an old guy, can't take two of you."

Instead of answering, Calaphas says, "Who lives next door?"

"You must have access to anything you want to know. Agencies do. You don't need me."

"Unfortunately, I do. Urgently. It's a very special situation. National security still matters to you, doesn't it?"

"Of course."

"So who lives over there?"

"Sanjay Chandra and his wife own the property, but they don't live there yet. It's a short-term, luxury vacation rental until they're ready to renovate it."

"Somebody's renting it now?"

"I don't think so. But I wouldn't know for sure."

"Household staff?"

"Yes, staff takes care of renters when anyone's in residence."

"He wouldn't want staff, people knowing he was there."

"Who wouldn't?"

"Just thinking out loud."

As if it is the most natural thing to do, Vincent takes his legs off the footstool.

"Put them back," Calaphas says, gesturing with the pistol.

Vincent obeys, but there's a new tension in his body.

"You're thinking too much," Calaphas says. "Help me, and you might even get a commendation from the president."

Vincent says nothing.

"They have dogs over there? Guard dogs?"

"I never hear any barking."

"That's a politician's answer."

"I'm not trying to mislead you. As far as I know, there aren't any dogs, guard dogs or pets."

The tension is in Vincent's eyes now, too, a dire conviction.

"I'm curious," Calaphas says. "What just changed?"

"You're after a fugitive."

"So?"

"If it's a national security matter, you'd have a team here. Not just a partner. A team."

"I do. They're watching the place next door."

"I'd love that to be true. You're agency, but you've gone rogue. You're on a personal vendetta. Or you've sold out." He carefully sets the book on the table beside his chair, resigned to his own fate. "When you're done with me, you don't need Colleen."

"She could come down and find you, call the police, suddenly the night is full of sirens. I lose the element of surprise with my target."

"She's gone to bed. Reading until she can sleep. She never comes down after she's gone to bed."

Calaphas studies him. "I think you're telling the truth."

"I am. She won't be down until morning, hours from now."

"You're a man of honor."

"The house is well insulated. Sound doesn't travel well room to room, floor to floor. If that's an effective sound suppressor on your piece, she won't hear anything."

"It's the best. One question. A career in service, how did you afford a house like this?"

"I married well, in every sense of the word."

"Married into money."

"We were both twenty-three. She gave up a lot to be a Navy wife. She's a wonderful woman, a fine person."

"Then I'll take a chance with her."

"Will you?"

"I don't enjoy this."

"Who would?" Vincent says.

"She'll live to mourn you. I'm not a man of honor," Calaphas says, "but I'll keep this promise."

"You could trust me, too."

"The problem with that is, I wasn't blowing smoke. Seems clear to me you *are* a man of honor."

"Life matters more than honor."

"To most people. Not to you. It's not everything to you, but it's something. Is that true or is it true?"

With a small sound that's almost an ironic laugh, Vincent says, "True."

Raising the pistol, Calaphas steps farther into the room. He squeezes the trigger twice. One round point-blank in the chest. The other in the head. The reports are like two coughs by an end-stage tuberculosis patient who lacks sufficient breath to make more than the smallest, most discreet of sounds.

Calaphas turns off the table lamp. Before leaving the room, he extinguishes the overhead light. He steps into the hall and quietly closes the door behind him.

He stands listening. The house is as deeply quiet as the rooms in the funeral home where he grew up, the only differences being the lack of a floral fragrance on the air and the fact that no viewing has been scheduled. Apparently, Colleen has heard nothing.

Because this is a familiar situation in video games, because a player cannot move on to the next scripted encounter with a target left behind and still expect to be a winner, he heads to the second floor to kill Colleen.

The stairs are soundly built, and if there are a few subtle creaks, the carpet runner muffles them effectively.

The master bedroom is at the front of the residence, the only upstairs room with light.

When he steps through the open door, he finds a vestibule and beyond it the larger chamber, everything in shades of peach with pale-green accents. In matching green pajamas, perfectly coordinated with her elegant surroundings, Colleen is propped against a pile of pillows, her book having slipped from her hands into her lap when she fell asleep. She is a beautiful woman who is aging well and will no doubt be still quite lovely in her eighties. Or would have been.

He's tempted to wake her to see what their conversation might be like. He suspects that she'll be as cool a customer as her husband, and amusing. Time is not running out, but it is of the essence, so he shoots her twice in the chest, leaving her face untouched. As she makes an instantaneous transition from mere sleep to eternity, her expression becomes grievous, but only briefly, and then once more she looks as if she is only dreaming.

Maybe they're safe and no one knows where they are, but they feel as watched as if they're in a fishbowl. The windows feature motorized shades, with a hand control in every room. "I'll shut them throughout the ground floor," Nina declares as she powers down the shades in the large kitchen. The front door can be locked, though anyone can disengage the deadbolt by reaching through the pane that Michael shattered. "We'll use a chair as a brace, pile lots of noisy things on it," she says, and hurries off with the boy in tow.

Michael stares at the transponder packed into the hollowed-out stack of twenties. Woodbine put it here, of course, to find his cash in the unlikely event that someone took it out of the Bentley. The sedan's GPS navigation was turned off, so the vehicle hasn't been trackable that way, but this transponder has been painting a target on Michael for twenty-one hours, since he took the sedan. In all that time, a man with the attorney's resources—including a small army of murderous drug dealers and his cozy relationship with the ISA—should have found him, killed him, and retrieved the Bentley. He isn't fool enough to believe that luck has spared him, that the transponder has gone dead. For some other reason, the attorney has been unable to find him.

He recalls the conversation that he'd heard between Durand and Julian Grantworth, which the deputy director of the ISA had recorded in a restaurant while the agent was at dinner. If Durand went to the offices of Woodbine, Kravitz, Benedetto, and Spackman as scheduled—more than four hours ago—the frustrated attorney would surely have told him about the hidden transponder. Otherwise, Woodbine would seem to have no reason to turn to the ISA and call in a favor they owed him. If the transponder problem was something like a range-of-transmission issue related to the app that linked it to Woodbine's phone, whatever, the ISA possessed search resources immeasurably greater than any the attorney could muster. The agency would have located the signal in short order. The ISA is like an ineradicable fungus that has spoored across the country over fifteen years. Their desire to snatch Michael and imprison or kill him is more powerful and urgent than Woodbine's petty desire to recover his three million dollars and exact revenge. Michael is the most wanted man in the country. At any moment in the past two hours, having pinpointed the transponder, the ISA should have sent a tsunami of agents crashing down on him. Instead, nothing. Nothing *yet*.

Calaphas. He's the assigned agent, the main man on the scene at Beautification Research five days earlier. He is Javert to Michael's Jean Valjean.

While at the house in Corona del Mar, Michael planted triggers in the ISA system to inform him any time that his name and that of Calaphas appeared within two hundred characters of each other in written reports or within thirty seconds of each other in recorded statements or conversations. Having received no alerts since coming south from there, he's assumed that the agent has made no progress.

He possesses the GPS identifier of Calaphas's smartphone and has previously intruded into that device to explore the agent's contacts. Now he goes online, enters Verizon's system, where he has been before, and finds that phone's locating signal. Calaphas seems to be nowhere near Rancho Santa Fe, at an address near the southern end of Los Angeles County, perhaps two and a half hours from here.

Seems to be. The phone is not the person. If Calaphas has been accurately speculating on Michael's extraordinary abilities, he is likely to have concluded that he shouldn't be carrying a phone that can establish his location and allow his quarry to follow his every move. If he is now carrying a phone that is not linked to his name, Michael has no way of finding him—but Calaphas may well be able to track the transponder in this brick of twenty-dollar bills. In fact, even Pollyanna wouldn't be so illogically optimistic as to think that Calaphas could not do so.

Michael reaches for the transponder, intending to hammer it into ruin—but hesitates. He looks at the shades that cover all the kitchen windows, and he wonders if Calaphas could be out there now, watching the house, waiting for backup. Or perhaps backup has already arrived, and a score of ISA agents are currently taking up positions. The moment the transponder ceases transmitting, they will conclude it's been found, and they might accelerate whatever assault they have planned.

In a fraction of a minute, Michael reviews the extensive ISA file on Calaphas, which was earlier downloaded into the vast data-storage capacity of Shadow Michael and is his to pore through at high speed. Calaphas the manageable sociopath. His utter lack of conscience. His great pleasure in the application of extreme force. The murder of his brother. His numerous sanctioned killings. The atrocities he's committed and for which he has been granted clemency in the course of his career include the brutal execution not only of his targets but on some occasions also of the spouses and children.

In most assignments, Calaphas has acted alone. It's apparent why. In the company of sane agents, he is to some degree restrained, less able to indulge in his taste for barbarous cruelty. His history suggests why a platoon hasn't descended on Michael. Calaphas intends to come after him alone. And the monster is most likely en route to Rancho Santa Fe and closing fast. Or already here.

DEEP INTO THE DARKNESS PEERING

Returning to his agency sedan, where the arc of eucalyptus trees faintly rustles even in the post-storm stillness, Calaphas retrieves the loaded AR-15 and three spare magazines. He doubts he will expend so many rounds, but when he goes hunting, he likes to know that he possesses far more firepower than his prey. He takes the ATN PVS7-3 night-vision goggles—Mil-Spec, Generation 4 gear—and hangs them around his neck in case he needs them later.

He pops another bennie from the blister pack. The first bennie is still cranking his engine. He doesn't really need a second, but he's very excited about this kill, this game-winning kill. He wants to be wired when he takes out Michael Mace. He feels everything more intensely when he's wired. He doesn't often take drugs, certainly not every time that he kills someone; such frequency would lead to addiction. He isn't a recreational user. It's about increasing the pleasure he takes *from his work* and therefore doing a better job. Doing a perfect job is how he's going to get out of the game and into a higher level of life. He can tolerate a second five-milligram dose. He's done it before. He never suffers tremors or confusion, and the stuff doesn't make him talkative like it does most people. It just makes him hyper alert and eager for action. Yes, it can make him irritable, and it always heightens his aggression, but those aren't necessarily bad effects. He puts the tablet under his tongue.

After locking the car, he sets out briskly for the Chandra house, ready to dodge off the road at the first sign of headlights in the distance. Although the moon is higher than before and should seem smaller than when it's nearer the horizon, it looks enormous, the biggest moon he's ever seen. The strange enormity of the moon must be a sign, and if it's a sign, then it is the gamemakers' way of signifying that Calaphas is one kill away from being the next champion to earn a life in the higher reality for which he has yearned since childhood. He feels like breaking into song. He's not one who sings along with music on the radio. In fact, he doesn't have a good voice for singing and never indulges in it. He feels so good, however, that he wants to sing, and he might do so if it would not draw attention to him at a moment when he needs to be stealthy. Even if breaking into song weren't likely to jeopardize his mission, he couldn't do so because he's so disinterested in music that he doesn't know the lyrics to any songs. He is hyper alert and feeling more wonderfully aggressive even than he was at Vince and Colleen's house; he is exhilarated.

Before he comes to the imposing gate, he climbs the white board fence and drops into the yard at the Chandra place. He isn't going to make a bold approach on the lighted driveway, but he likes the cover of the California oaks marshalled along its length. Because the trees are year-around shedders, the ground is mantled with small, dry, oval leaves like beetle shells that crunch underfoot. The sound isn't loud enough to draw the attention of anyone in the house, and Calaphas likes it so much that he takes shorter and more steps than necessary; the sound makes him feel powerful, like a giant scoring points by stomping through the puny structures of elves, like a massive dragon under whose taloned feet the bones of vanquished knights are crushed to splinters and dust.

Killing is always satisfying work. The pathetic plea for mercy, whether spoken or unvoiced. The desolate last cry of pain and fear. The pale clouding or else the sudden bloody brightness of the eyes. The rattle in the throat, the stuttering of a last word that can't quite be pronounced. The final flexing of the hands as they grasp at what they may no longer have. The terminal cascade of fluids. The spasms and shudders before the long stillness. As rewarding as it is to execute and witness any murder, by far the best experiences are those in which the labor is as hands-on as possible. Recently, with events moving at roller-coaster speed, Calaphas has been required by circumstances to use only a gun and finish the task expeditiously. He theorizes that advancement through the game occurs more rapidly when the killings are intimate and the thrill is therefore greatest: strangulation with bare hands, bludgeoning either with fists or a hammer, stabbing and slashing, a good long smothering with a pillow, a wire garrote applied with such measured force that the victim is able to hold on to false hope for an agonizing minute. If Michael Mace is the game-winning kill toward which Calaphas's life has been directed, perhaps a disabling gunshot wound can be only preliminary to a more protracted and entertaining little circus of pain and blood.

Amped on bennies, having become a dragon if only in his mind, with a priapism that can be relieved only by orgasmic violence, Calaphas arrives at the motor court in front of the grand residence. Near the steps to the terrace stands Carter Woodbine's Bentley—the treasure that symbolizes absolute power and that every game worth playing comes to in the end—enveloped in a supernatural glow, the moon favoring it above all things.

At the house, the second-floor windows are dark, but light is universal downstairs. As Calaphas approaches the Bentley, intending to pause there to reconnoiter further, he sees a woman at a window. He has come this far under the presumption that Michael Mace is on the run alone, as he was when he escaped Beautification Research and as he still seemed to be, less than

307

twenty-four hours earlier, when he took half a million dollars from Woodbine. Calaphas doesn't know this woman, can't imagine who she might be or why she might have cast her lot with Mace. Then his astonishment swells into perplexity when a young boy appears next to her. They seem to be examining some small device that she is holding. Then the window shades power down, and they are gone from view.

He crouches beside the sedan, in a fever of speculation. He soon comes to the conclusion that it doesn't matter who the woman and the boy might be. This is nothing more than one of those sudden twists that the designers of the game include to thwart players less astute and adaptable than Calaphas. She and the child have no more purpose or meaning than the bumpers, gates, and trap holes on the field of a pinball machine. If here, in the penultimate chapter of the narrative, he must kill three to claim the prize, that is not a job that exceeds his talents.

As his priapism stiffens almost to the point of pain, he sees this development as less a challenge than a reward. Even as he'd walked here from his car in the eucalyptus grove, he bemoaned the lack of intimacy in recent killings. Now before him waits a sweet opportunity to go out of the game not merely in triumph but in a condition of prolonged ecstasy. If *he* were designing the script for this lower reality, that is precisely how this existence would end and one more exciting would begin. His heart is racing. He is into this. He is cranked.

With his combat knife, he punctures the sidewall on the front passenger-side tire. He repeats this bit of sabotage on the rear tire.

SIX: NO WAY OUT

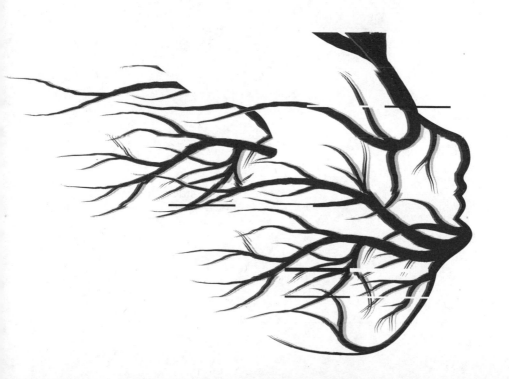

FIREPOWER

After shutting all the shades on the ground floor, Nina and John had ventured into the garage in search of something in which to pack the three million dollars and disguise the treasure. When it's in the back of the Range Rover, it will be visible to anyone who looks through a window. The solution is two large, insulated picnic coolers, which they have brought to the kitchen. The money, already sealed in plastic, can be packed in the bottom of each cooler and then covered with aluminum foil. Take ice from the kitchen icemaker, pile it on the foil, add beer and soda from the pantry, and no one knows there's a fortune under the beverages.

"Fast as you can," Michael urges.

He leaves them to it. With the AR-15, he patrols the ground floor, thinking furiously, wishing the Singularity had sharpened his mind like the tech visionaries promised. He has three options, none good.

Make a break for it in the Range Rover. If Calaphas arrives after they leave, he won't know what vehicle they took, at least for an hour or two. However, if the agent is in place, watching them now, waiting for the right moment to make his move, he'll cut them down before they reach the gate at the end of the driveway. Calaphas isn't walking into this with just a sidearm. He's sure to have the equivalent of an AR-15, perhaps one that's been modified for fully automatic fire.

Alternately, Michael can go to the second-floor deck at the front of the house. Nina drives the Rover, with John lying on the back floor. She exits the garage at high speed. The instant Calaphas reveals himself, Michael takes him out. The obvious problem is that the agent will reveal himself *by opening fire*, perhaps killing

Nina before he can be killed. Or say that Nina gets away. Then she waits somewhere safe. Michael has to find and kill Calaphas before being able to call her back to pick him up. He figures he's got at least a 50 percent chance of dying. In that case, Nina and John are on their own. And even though they have all that money, they don't possess the ability to invade official computers and create new identities for themselves.

The third option is hunker down and wait for Calaphas to come into the house after them. Nina goes upstairs with John and hides somewhere. She has a handgun if the situation goes hard south. Calaphas comes inside. There's either an immediate confrontation between him and Michael, or they end up stalking each other. But maybe Calaphas gets tired of waiting, for whatever reason decides not to be a loner this time, and calls in backup. Plus there are maybe twenty other ways that scenario could go wrong.

The issue is firepower. Michael needs more of it. He needs the kind of backup that Calaphas could have with a phone call. But he has no one to call, no authorities who wouldn't, in the end, turn him over to those SOBs at the Internal Security Agency.

"What's our S-O-B doing here?" Shelby Shrewsberry's voice echoes in memory. Referring to Dr. Simon O. Bistoury. About two weeks before the catastrophe.

Michael halts. He's in the living room, but in the eye of memory, he sees the cafeteria at Beautification Research.

"Damn, he got coffee . . . coming this way."

Looming over them, Simon had said, *"The bastards down at Encinitas . . . knocked it out of the park."*

"I don't follow baseball."

". . . dog-form bots . . . AI autonomy or remote-controlled . . . integrated action in the autonomous mode."

BACKUP

San Diego County is home to several military installations, among them Miramar Marine Corps Air Station, the 125,000-acre Camp Pendleton Marine Base, Point Loma Naval Base, North Island Naval Air Station, and the Coronado Naval Amphibious Base. Numerous defense contractors and defense research companies maintain facilities throughout the county. Protean Cybernetics, located on the outskirts of Encinitas, is housed in sixty thousand square feet of buildings on ninety acres. The property is encircled by a ten-foot chain-link fence constructed on a four-foot-deep reinforced-concrete footing, topped by a forty-five-degree out-ward-angled scaling-spoiler panel wrapped in razor wire. The east gate and the west gate are manned twenty-four hours a day, seven days a week, by armed guards.

Protean Cybernetics has two discrete computer systems, which the company's IT mavens informally refer to as Homer and Lisa. The first enables employees to engage in emails with suppliers and others outside of the company; it has no links whatsoever to the other system, so that even someone as stupid and careless as Homer Simpson, of TV fame, could use it with no risk of the company's most important and privileged information being compromised. The second system is for online research, lab computation, strictly internal communications, and project data storage. It is protected by a series of firewalls, and the employees authorized to use it must access the system with both a pass code and a retinal scan; it's the kind of failsafe network that a grownup Lisa, arguably by far the smartest member of the Simpson family, might design.

Michael enters as easily as opening a door. Several projects are underway here, but it is only the robot dogs that interest him. In four seconds, he learns they're housed in Building Four, adjacent to a thirty-acre testing ground at the north end of the property. Protean Cybernetics does not have a graveyard shift, so the building is quiet and dark. The security system is monitored and operated through the computer. Cameras are pretty much everywhere, and they have infrared capability, providing him with sufficient detail for his purpose and access everywhere except the lavatories. Because he's not here in a corporeal sense, he has no need of a bathroom; besides, his visit isn't likely to last longer than two minutes. He's been on site fourteen seconds when he finds the robot canines in a windowless room, standing in their charging stations.

They are thirty-six inches high, approximately the size of a Great Dane, but they are like dogs only in a skeletal sense. They have cameras in the front and the back of the head, with both day and night vision. With current-best AI, they are able to act in an autonomous manner and coordinate one with the other to an impressive extent, or they can be operated by remote control in the manner of drones. Having been given auditory receptors and provided with a vocabulary of commands, they can also respond to a human companion whose voice pattern they have been pro-grammed to recognize and obey. Eight lithium batteries provide power that lasts between six and ten hours of continuous oper-ation, depending on the level of activity. They are able to climb steep hills, wade shallow water, and run at a top speed of eighteen miles per hour. Incorporated in each unit is a rifle that fires a 7.62 mm round with a muzzle velocity of seven hundred meters per second. A curved-box magazine contains fifty cartridges. They are capable of either semiautomatic or automatic fire. The mag-azines have been fully loaded in preparation for a field test in the morning. The long-term intention is for robots to one day accompany infantrymen into battle both to increase firepower and reduce the number of flesh-and-blood soldiers who must put their lives at risk.

Seen through cameras registering in the infrared spectrum, these steel-alloy canines appear ominous. When Michael extends himself into the Lutron lighting controls and brings up the room lights, the four-legged terminators are no less menacing; in fact, they're demonic. The executive at Protean who officially named them Gog and Magog either doesn't know what those names refer to in the Book of Revelation or he's a closet reactionary among the ranks of the technology-besotted with whom he works. Most people in the company call them Rover and Spot.

Reviewing the protocols of the remote-control mode until he fully understands operational methods and limitations, Michael then takes Gog and Magog under his authority. He orders them to come off their storage platform. They disconnect from their charging stations and, with a scissoring-stilting of their three-jointed legs, they move quickly to the center of the room and stand to attention, heads up like alert Dobermans. Even though they have only four legs, when in motion they remind Michael more of insects than of dogs. Perhaps that comparison is too disturbing for those who are developing these weapons; instead, thinking of them as dog-form companions evokes memories of Lassie and Scooby-Doo.

Having been at Protean Cybernetics just forty-one seconds, he next transmits the address of the Chandra house into the mission-program center of Gog's and Magog's brains, designating that property as the sole battlefield in order to insure against collateral damage between here and there. He invades Durand Calaphas's employee file at the ISA and transmits the agent's photograph to Gog and Magog, designating the man as the sole target until Michael tells them otherwise.

While overriding the security system, Michael opens all the electronic locks in the building. Under his control, the robots proceed quickly into the moonlit night.

Fifty-six seconds and counting.

MAN OF ACTION

Yancy Norbert is working the graveyard shift at the east gate of Protean Cybernetics. He is twenty-five and believes that he looks like a young Brad Pitt. He styles his blond hair as Brad wore it in *World War Z.* Periodically, before a mirror, he practices Bradian smiles and other expressions he believes are unique to the actor, in the interest of having greater success with women. He has memorized numerous lines of dialogue from movies in which Brad is a romantic figure, but thus far he hasn't gone on many dates where he's had an opportunity to insert those words into a conversation in such a way that they are natural and effective. In truth, he's not had nearly as many dates as he feels he ought to have had. The reason for his poor record with the ladies has mystified him, and recently he has begun to wonder if women of his approximate age do not find Brad to be the irresistible hunk that previous generations did.

In addition, Yancy is a man of action in waiting. Initially, he intended to be a police officer. He opted instead to take this job as an armed security guard, because he could still have a gun, with much less risk of people shooting at him. He knows in his bones that the day will come when he'll be caught up in action and adventure to match that of any Brad film; he just needs to be patient. Meanwhile, working the midnight-to-eight shift, when no one is coming to or going from Protean, he has a lot of time to read novels of action, everything from Westerns to contemporary novels with heroes who are halfway to seven feet tall and so hard bodied that the density of their chest muscles can stop a bullet.

On this occasion, he's sitting in his guardhouse chair, sipping Classic Cinnamon Roll coffee brewed with the Keurig machine that the company provided. He's reading a thriller in which the hero is going to take down six thugs in three minutes. The guy has already wiped out three in a minute and a half—five pages of ferocious action—when Yancy's iPhone pings with a text message. It's from Buck Duncan, the guard at the west gate: Got 2 take a dump. Watch my gate?

Yancy can watch the east gate through the guardhouse window. The video console in front of him allows access to any exterior camera at Protean that is in the vicinity of a motion detector and sends an alert, which almost never happens. When it does occur, the alert is always triggered by a night bird. Now he selects the four cameras related to the west gate, and the screen divides into equal quadrants to display them. He sends a text to Buck: Got it.

In the novel, where the alleyway is poorly lighted and mean, the hero hears the distinct sound of a handgun being drawn from a belt scabbard, followed by the reverberant toll of metal knocking the side of a nearby dumpster. He intuits that the fourth assassin is about to step out from behind the trash container, against which the creep accidentally rapped his weapon when drawing it. The hero drops and rolls—

The phone pings with a text message from Buck: Got what?

Yancy is *not* going to put down the book in the middle of this exciting paragraph. The hero has extraordinarily sharp reflexes; a full description of the moves he makes to evade the assassin's first shot and then roll into a shooter's crouch and then drill a round through his assailant's left eye takes almost an entire page. There are still two more assassins to be taken down, but that's another three pages, so Yancy puts the book aside and responds to Buck Duncan: Got your gate. So go take a dump.

The hero is out of ammo when the fifth assassin explodes into the alley through the kitchen door of a restaurant, squeezing off rounds as he comes, before he even knows his target's position, counting on sheer volume of shots to get the job done. That is the kind of undisciplined action the hero would never take and of which he's highly disdainful. So it's no surprise—but exhilarating—when one of the hatchet man's rounds ricochets back on him, wounding him in the shoulder and staggering him, so that the hero is able to draw his knife and go in for—

The phone pings.

"Damn it all, Buck," Yancy mutters, but he sets aside the book again and checks the text message. Y r u telling me 2 take a dump? U off coffee, on booze?

Frowning, Yancy glances at the four video-display views of the west entrance to Protean. Then he looks at the guardhouse window in front of him. The big motorized gate is twenty feet away. For an instant, he has the impression that it's moving, that it just rolled shut along the last few inches of its track, but that can't be the case because only he can operate it.

NOTHING AT ALL AROUND ME
BUT THE BEAST

Much of the land lies undeveloped, either publicly held or preserved in ranches, undulating so gracefully that the poetry of nature is evident even to those who care not for poetry and are indifferent to nature. Live oaks, California peppers, olive trees, and plentiful eucalyptuses stand testament to the tireless efforts of wind, sun, rain, seismic pressures, and humanity.

In swift and shrieking pursuit of a rabbit, excited by the scent of warm flesh and their knowledge of the blood therein, the coyotes abruptly give up the chase and scatter at the sight of the two moon-bright forms that lope in wolflike fashion through the wild grass. Hissing bobcats abandon the ground for trees. The interlopers pass under the limbs on which the big cats perch, and they sprint away like predators on the trail of prey, though they exude only a lifeless odor of their own.

Gog and Magog are guided by GPS and internal maps, by night vision and by the address Michael inserted in them. They don't need his continuous guidance. For a moment, however, as he stands in the living room of the Chandra house, he is transfixed by the land as seen through the robots' eyes. The Mil-Spec Generation 4 night-vision apparatus gathers available light, even infrared that isn't visible to the human eye, and amplifies it eighty thousand times. The 120-degree field of view is presented in eerie green hues, the wavelength of light nearest 550 nanometers on the spectrum, which allows clarity at a lower power draw, conserving the batteries. The scene presented is so strange that it stirs in Michael a disquieting sense of looking *through* the apparent world at another and yet more ominous existence that lies beyond it.

Even as that thought occurs to him, an extraordinary thing happens. A quarter of a mile earlier, leaving Protean Cybernetics, Gog and Magog crossed the nearest highway; they are a mile and a half from the next two-lane back road, between towns and in rough terrain. They top a rise, and at the bottom of the hill stands an SUV, recently arrived and warm enough to project a strong heat signature. As the dog-form robots pass the vehicle, an eerie figure materializes beyond it, a tall man, all but faceless in this green light that favors shape over detail. He isn't as bright as the SUV, though brighter than everything else in the night. In his arms, he's carrying what seems to be the limp body of a woman. Michael takes control of Gog and Magog, halting them, turning them toward this apparition. Man and machines face off at a distance of fifteen feet. By its fabricated shape, which contrasts with the rambled wildness of grass and brush, one other object declares its significance—what appears to be a spade that has been spiked in the earth by its blade and stands erect.

After a frozen moment, the green figure, like a specter that might have risen out of dark waters deep in the hollows of the Earth and might now wither back into that sea of damnation, instead drops the body in its arms and pivots toward the SUV. The dead woman doesn't strike the ground and lie in a pale greenness of tangled limbs, but disappears entirely into the grave that has been dug for her. The license plate of the SUV is fuzzy, the numbers and letters like smeared ink on the green background, but readable. Gog and Magog record it, and Michael burns it in his memory. Although no trial seems necessary to determine guilt, he doesn't command the robots to shoot down the killer, and they return to the journey on which they were embarked as the engine of the SUV fires up and it wheels away from the open grave.

Before his death—or something like death—Michael lamented the evil that humanity condoned. Since his return to life, he's come to see that the evil he previously recognized was like an ultrasound image of a suspicious mass; with his new gift, he has surgically opened the patient and has found that the cancer is more widespread than he ever imagined. If it is true, as some say, that a beast of supernatural nature is the prince of this world, then no task of greater importance exists than to bring hard justice to him and his legion of princelings in the name of the innocent and generations yet unborn. Since coming to life in a makeshift morgue, Michael has not been able quite to see the shape of his future, to understand how he can best use his power. The encounter at the lonely grave has clarified his intentions for him. If he survives this night, he has a good idea how to be the agent of truth that events have made him.

Already he has slid into the DMV records and learned the name of the owner of that SUV. He has obtained the GPS code from the manufacturer of the vehicle and will know where it stops when the fleeing murderer garages it. He has also found a smartphone GPS locater issuing from the identical position of the SUV and moving with it now. It surely belongs to the killer.

Rifle in hand, he hurries into the kitchen. Nina and John have packed one cooler and closed it. The boy is almost done layering the last of the money in the second cooler, and Nina is shaping a length of aluminum foil to lay over it. Michael puts the AR-15 down and helps with the ice, then with the cans of soda and beer. They're finished with the task in two minutes.

Nina expects to load the containers in the back of the Range Rover, but Michael says, "No time. Leave them here and come with me. Bring your Tac Light."

"Come where?"

"Upstairs. An attic if there is one. As far off the battlefield as we can get."

John is confused. "We're hiding?"

"I'll explain when we're safe." He snatches the rifle off the counter. "They're less than three miles away, maybe eight minutes out."

Mother and son are equally baffled and speak simultaneously: "Who? Who is?"

"The cavalry," he says and further startles them by unlocking the back door.

He brooks no further delay, herding them through the ground floor to the front stairs.

Throughout the kitchen work, Michael has been both there and elsewhere, scooping ice but also swimming through the shared data networks of the nation's telecom providers, seeking a name to match with the GPS signal issuing from the SUV that had been parked near the grave. By the time that he follows Nina and John as far as the landing between floors, he has the identity of the man who possesses the phone; it's the same name the DMV lists as the owner of that vehicle. The murderer.

Like a falcon on its hunting gyre, Calaphas circles the house. The stillness of the night's creatures is reminiscent of the hush of the funeral home in which he was raised. Soon he will silence three more voices, bringing an even deeper quiet to this isolate, fateful property. His rifle comes with a sound suppressor attached, but even if the crack of a shot carries some distance through these hills of sleepers dreaming, and if a few awake, they will not know from what direction the sound came and will think it's merely part of whatever stories they were telling themselves in sleep.

The hugeness of the moon, as he perceives it, and its icy appearance remind him of the terrible eyes of a woman named Britta Holdstrom, who was brought to Calaphas's father on a December night, almost two months after the Halloween when Durand pinched off the breath of the old man on the gurney in the basement holding room. Britta was a twenty-nine-year-old schoolteacher, a beauty, who came home from Christmas shopping one night when a student, seventeen-year-old Gerry Grady, was lying in wait for her in the furnace closet off the garage. He rushed her after she unlocked the door between the garage and the laundry room, and a struggle occurred from there into the kitchen, where Britta fell and struck her head on the refrigerator and again when she collapsed to the floor. Not the brightest of lads, Grady intended to kill her after raping her, but somehow make murder pass for a suicide. Now she appeared to be dead. Coupling with a corpse didn't excite him. Panicked, he decided to drag her into the garage, load her in her car, drive her to the old quarry road, and push her sedan into the depths of the abandoned stone mine with her behind the wheel, which he imagined would be taken for an accident. He conveyed her as far as the garage before his panic overwhelmed him, whereupon he fled the house. Britta was found two days later, after lying on a concrete floor beside her car, where the temperature had fallen to twenty-five degrees. The coroner concluded she didn't die of head injuries. Still alive when Gerry Grady dragged her into the garage, she perished of exposure—essentially froze to death—while lying there unconscious.

Past midnight, the first hour of December twenty-sixth, back in the day. Having been emboldened by his Halloween adventure, young Calaphas waits until his family is asleep, and then he goes to the basement. There he will complete the transition from a mere boy to a boy with a great destiny that began two months earlier, though completing the transition isn't his conscious intention. He visits the cold-holding room for two purposes: first, to see what Britta Holdstrom looks like naked; second, to determine what damage, if any, the limited autopsy did to her.

When he pulls out the morgue drawer and turns back the shroud from her head, he is looking into eyes as white as snow. Whether they crystalized as she lay dying in the frigid garage or some other cause explains them, Calaphas doesn't know. Meeting that icy-white gaze, he remembers an animated film about a beautiful princess who is bewitched into eternal sleep—until she is awakened by the kiss of a prince. If he, a seven-year-old boy, can take the life from an old man and get away with it, perhaps he can restore life to this woman, which will mean that he must be a prince or will become one. He has no fear. His experience with the old man has cured him of fear. He presses his mouth to Britta's cold lips, but she fails to wake. Although somewhat disappointed, he doesn't close the drawer and leave. He remains curious about the size and shape of Britta's breasts. When Durand draws the shroud farther down, revealing the objects of his curiosity, between those mounds lies a Hershey's Kiss.

His humiliation is immediate and intense, his face burning with shame. Gifford has foreseen this moment, and by this bit of mockery has tarnished the triumph of his little brother's Halloween visit to this chamber, when the hiding of a Hershey's Kiss in a cabinet was proof of courage. Mortification shakes him as if it's a wind risen out of his bones, storming through him. Leaving the chocolate drop where Gifford placed it, he draws the shroud over Britta—but then realizes the genius of the trap that has been laid. In the morning, when his father tends to the embalming, he will find the morsel of candy. Gifford has surely schemed a way to be sure that his brother will be blamed, though Durand can't figure out how. If he takes the Kiss, there will be no outraged father in the morning, and Gifford will know what has happened. Then the endless jokes and torments will begin. Bitter resentment washes through Durand as he pulls back the shroud, retrieves the candy, covers Britta again, and closes the drawer. Making his way to his room by the thin beam of his penlight, he is blinded more by anger than by darkness, stumbling twice on the stairs, narrowly avoiding a collision with a console in the upper hallway.

When he reaches his bed, on his pillow is another piece of Hershey's finest and a note: HOW DID HER NIPPLES TASTE, PERV? Anger has always been Durand's weakness, anger and pride. Not covetousness or lust. Neither envy nor gluttony. Not sloth. Now his pride bleeds and his anger swells into rage, into fury, such a blazing wrath that he feels as if he might melt. And here the transition becomes complete. The incident on Halloween cured him of fear; ferocious anger burned it out of him forever. Now even hotter anger purges from him any capacity for guilt or shame. No fear, shame, or guilt ever again. He warns himself not to acknowledge finding either of the two Hershey's Kisses or this note, never to respond to Gifford's taunts, which will be coming by the hundreds. He must never give his brother the satisfaction of seeing him angered. If Durand keeps his fury unrevealed, the day will come, perhaps many years from now, when Gifford no longer expects revenge for this mockery. Then revenge can be taken.

All these years later, Gifford is long dead, having gotten what was coming to him, that rich moment on his fancy boat when Durand's score in the game soared. Now, here in Rancho Santa Fe, the game clock counts down to a glorious end.

The memory of Britta in the morgue drawer and the vicious note on his pillow has amped Calaphas's anger no less than have the two bennies. No beast on Earth is as strong and dangerous and determined as he is now.

In addition to its three double-wide roll-up doors, the garage features a man-size door at the back. Calaphas lifts the night-vision goggles from around his neck and fits the unit to his eyes. The world goes from death-black and moon-silver to green. He employs his lock-release device, used earlier at the home of Vincent and Colleen, to defeat the deadbolt. He puts the device away and eases the door open. He enters.

As he hoped, he quickly finds two electric-service panels. He opens the metal door of the first, rapidly flips off the breakers one by one, then repeats the process with those in the second panel. Michael Mace and his two nameless companions have been plunged into darkness. Triumph awaits in several eerie shades of green.

Ascending the second run of stairs, Nina nervously turns the Tac Light in her hand, and vertiginous patterns of shadow and light wheel up the wall. As John follows her and as Michael steps onto the landing, darkness cascades through the rooms below. The mechanical systems of the house shut down; the faint humming-ticking-buzzing-sighing of motors and pumps and fans and air in circulation, all the muffled sounds of a living home that are monotonous enough to seem like silence, suddenly become true silence so deep that it summons dread.

Calaphas is here. He has cut the power to the residence, which means he's in the garage where earlier Michael had noticed electric-service panels. He'll be inside the house proper in a minute or two. Thereafter, any sound they make will approximately locate them, diminishing the need for the agent to stalk them cautiously room by room.

Evidently, this same realization occurs to Nina, for she takes the remaining stairs two at a time, heedless of the noise she makes while the enemy is still in the garage.

When Michael joins her and the boy at the stairhead, a raveling of luck is offered to them when the beam of the Tac Light silvers the fibers of a dangling cord at the far end of the upstairs hall—the pull rope for the attic trapdoor. If they had to search all the rooms and walk-in closets to find the way higher, they would never reach the wanted refuge in time.

The end of the rope passes through a hole in a red rubber ball and ends in a knot. He pulls the trapdoor down, and an automatic ladder unfolds in three sections. With the light, Nina leads John into the high redoubt. Left in near darkness,

Michael follows, sure that Calaphas is entering the house or already inside.

In the high room, Michael puts down his rifle. He turns and drops to his knees and reaches through the open trap and pulls hard on the uppermost rails of the spring-loaded ladder, reversing its action, muscling it back into position. The sections fold upward with somewhat more clatter than they unfolded, but he is able to prevent the loaded trap from thumping noisily when it seats once more in its frame.

This last-ditch bastion, where nothing is currently stored, extends over the entire top floor of the house, offering in excess of seven feet of clearance. It is fully floored with particleboard attached to the second-floor ceiling studs with recessed screws that shine in Nina's light. The chief advantage of this refuge is that there's only one way into it, so that if Calaphas pulls down the ladder, they'll know he's coming; he won't be able to climb at a run, and he'll be leading with his head, the preferred target. The primary disadvantage is that there's also only one way out of here.

Nevertheless, Michael prefers it over all other options because he cannot be absolutely certain Calaphas has come alone. If other agents have joined the hunt, then the battleground won't be just the house but also the twelve acres on which it stands, with nowhere below to safely shelter from the barrages of gunfire that might be exchanged when the robots arrive. Because the caliber and high velocity of the ammunition of all parties is capable of penetrating walls, it makes sense to put as much distance and as many partitions as possible between the three of them and the combatants.

Michael will direct Gog and Magog to enter the house through the back door he unlocked for them, which is toward the north end of the house. With that in mind, he shepherds Nina and John to the southeast corner of the attic, where they sit with their backs to an outer wall that, on the exterior, is of stacked stone and thus impervious to gunfire.

Nina sweeps the spacious garret with the beam. Perhaps she wants to be sure that she has the details of the place firmly in mind when she shuts off the Tac Light and must wait in a darkness pulsating with threats. Under these circumstances, even those who are well grounded and stouthearted can imagine things that bring a thin sweat to the brow and the nape of the neck.

Along the ridgepole, among the rafters and the collar beams, spiders have added their architecture to that of the house. Michael remembers a day when he was nine, carrying two mason jars into the backyard, setting the eight-legged prisoners free in the garden. He smiles at these residents of the attic as the light fixes on one and then another, their exaggerated shadows crawling the time-paled wood behind them. He takes their presence to be a good omen, and he says, "Old friends."

The light goes out, and with nothing here to see, he reenters the Protean Cybernetics computer system and possesses Gog and Magog. They are running through darkness relieved only by the light of the moon and stars that reflects off different objects in a myriad of ways and is amplified in shades of green seldom seen in nature—acid fuchsine, glauconite, chrome oxide—moving parallel to a two-lane blacktop, less than five minutes from the Chandra house. Suddenly a shaft of intense light finds and blinds them, so that they switch from night vision to standard perception in order to keep advancing, but the light moves with them.

PRIDE AND ANGER, ALWAYS AND ONLY

At the door between the garage and the house, Calaphas uses his lock-release device to throw the deadbolt pins to the shear line and gain entrance. A hallway offers no light to be amplified except that infrared produced by the friction of molecules that are in motion in all things, which is enough to reveal closed doors on either side, as he comes to them. Sources in a room at the far end produce a dim spectral radiance that in some cheesy movie might represent spirits encouraging the soul of a dead man to follow a long passageway between life and the afterlife.

He opens doors without hesitation. He clears thresholds as he was trained to clear them, sweeping the rifle left to right, right to left. He explores without trepidation, having conquered all fear long ago, when he pinched the breath from a dead man, discovered the ecstasy of murder, realized that the world is a simulation and a game, and understood that he is destined to win his way through all challenges to some higher existence. Which is now within his reach. To the right, a door and a shallow closet beyond. To the left, a maid's suite is revealed by the soft influx of green moonlight from a window left unshaded. On the right, a day room with kitchenette, where the household staff takes lunch. On the left, a laundry room illuminated by a lighted wall clock that his gear amplifies.

At the end of the hall, he pushes open a half-closed door and moves into the spectral radiance that reveals not an afterlife, but instead a kitchen with appliances that feature digital clocks and readouts. The window shades glow softly with lunar backlight.

On the center island are three bowls with spoons. He feels one bowl and finds it cold to the touch. He wipes a finger through a puddle of coolness in the bottom and brings it to his mouth for a taste. Perhaps melted ice cream. Chocolate. Cherry. A third flavor he can't name.

On arrival, the fugitives felt safe enough to indulge in this treat, which deeply displeases Calaphas. He believes he understands enough about Michael Mace's powers to be certain that the former security specialist has invaded the ISA's computer system and knows exactly who is on his trail. At the safe house, Calaphas changed phones and cars without signing for either, leaving his quarry with no way to track him by GPS. That his pursuer has dropped off the map should alarm Mace and encourage him to keep moving. Instead, he and his two mysterious companions enter this house, somehow aware that it's untenanted, and they sit down for ice cream.

Calaphas's displeasure swells into indignation that these people seem not to take seriously the threat that he poses. Being underestimated particularly offends him. Being underestimated is equivalent to a slap in the face, an unforgivable act of contempt and belittlement, an affront not to be tolerated. Indignation flames into exasperation as he moves through an open door, along the main downstairs hall. He has conducted himself according to the rules of the game, achieving such an impressive kill total over twenty-six years, since the old man on the gurney, that he has come now to the last kill in this simulation, to the final gate and the ultimate reward beyond, but suddenly two new characters are introduced, two more whom he must eliminate, which is aggravating. Calaphas enjoys it, yes, and he will take pleasure in their fear and pain, but he wonders—as he has on a few occasions in the past—if the game is rigged so that it can never be won, additional new challenges added just when he is reaching for the well-earned gold ring, a new life of greater power and prestige. *Rigged!* The possibility enrages him, suggests that the game isn't a game at all, but some kind of never-ending frat-boy hazing, as if the designers of this simulation take delight in mocking his expectation of being elevated to their level. It isn't true, can't be true, *must not be true* that his efforts have been a fool's quest. The simulation is not, is not, is not, damn it, a sophisticated, cruel carnival of humiliations. *How did her nipples taste, perv?* It hasn't been crafted for his endless mortification, but for his transcendence. The hateful memory of the candy between Britta Holdstrom's breasts compounds exasperation into rage, even as his priapism is as painful as a grossly swollen boil. When he killed Gifford, his brother's widow had given him the dead man's solid-gold Rolex, which was an omen—a sign, a promise that his time was coming, his glorious future. The gamemakers need to be reminded of that promise. Gifford can't be killed twice, though it would be *such a relief* if he could be killed again and again. Here, now, Calaphas can find *no one* to kill, no one at all, by the time that he reaches the foyer. Then comes a clattering noise. Like wood knocking wood. Elsewhere in the house. His attention is drawn to the stairs, to the second floor, to the revived prospect of triumph and relief.

NEIGHBORHOOD WATCH

Juan is seventy-four, and Walter is seventy-five. They are retired, and a life without work doesn't sit well with them. Once successful entrepreneurs, they can spend only so much time on the golf course, on the bocce ball court, competing in pickleball tournaments, and playing cards with their wives and friends before they start adding double shots of vodka even to their nightly beakers of Metamucil. Consequently, they are always seeking new pursuits and projects, what Juan calls "reasons not to go crazy while we're waiting for Alzheimer's." During the past six months, they have been acting as an unofficial neighborhood watch one or two nights every week, mostly between eleven o'clock in the evening and three o'clock in the morning, cruising the community in Juan's F-150 pickup.

Back in the day, two burglaries a year was a crime wave. Now that Central American gangs have flooded across the open border, life here has gotten to be more of an adventure than it once was, with two burglaries a month. And the perpetrators aren't lone wolves anymore. They come in crews of four or more, in paneled trucks well disguised as vehicles belonging to one public utility or another, or to a federal bureau like the ATF or the EPA, and they have several methods of defeating alarm systems. Unlike burglars in the past, these new boys aren't after a few pieces of good jewelry, a little cash, and maybe a hockable sterling-silver tea service. In addition, they take antiques, art, audio-video equipment, major appliances, and a luxury automobile or two. Because people foolishly share their lives on social media, the bad guys are now expert at discovering who is on vacation. If people happen to be at home, they are beaten or threatened at gunpoint, tied up, and tucked away in a closet for the duration of the operation, which can take a few hours.

Juan and Walter have no patience for crap like that. They call themselves "geezers with attitude." As is the case with most law-enforcement agencies in recent years, the sheriff's department's budget isn't what it once was. The number of patrols have been cut back especially from ten o'clock at night until six in the morning. Neither Juan nor Walter is either deputized or armed with anything more than pepper spray, but their efforts are appreciated by the beleaguered local authorities. They cruise, looking for suspicious activity. When they see it, they alert the sheriff's dispatcher by phone, and he sends a deputy to investigate. So far, they have helped prevent three burglaries, two carjackings, and an attempted arson.

On this occasion, when Walter spots something unusual moving through the grass and scrub, Juan switches on the two motorized spotlights fixed to the vehicle's roof rack, and he directs one toward the bogey.

"You see this?" Juan asks.

"Alien robots," Walter says.

Juan says, "Might be Earthmade."

"You see them sold at Costco?"

"So then . . . do what?"

Walter says, "Burglars are burglars."

"This planet's our home, not theirs," Juan agrees.

The robots veer away from the road.

"Hold on," Juan says, and he wheels off the pavement in pursuit of the invaders.

EVERYTHING THAT RISES
MUST CONVERGE

Through the cameras of Gog and Magog, Michael Mace sees the license-plate number of the Ford F-150. He knows where to find what he requires, and he is so familiar with the California DMV system that he doesn't need to imagine himself in a Bentley, driving the infinitely layered highways of the internet until he arrives at his destination. He slips into the DMV data pool and, in seven seconds, has the names of the owners of the pickup truck—Juan and Angela Gainza. He expects that the manufacturer's records—where he has been before and to which he now returns—will yield the signifying number of the transponder in the pickup. But the vehicle doesn't have a navigation system, a feature that the buyer didn't want. Consequently, Michael can't slide down a microwave signal that doesn't exist, can't enter the F-150 and affect its operation.

◆ ◆ ◆

Bennies. Bennies from Heaven. His heart is racing, his muscles taut with power, such power, reflexes quick and quicker, a rampant beast that will not be denied. Excited, eager, enraged, leading with the rifle. The clatter that attracts him lasts only a few seconds, but Calaphas surges up the stairs, across vaguely defined green treads and black risers, into the second-floor hallway, just as the noise ends. Even here aboveground, every room is a cold-holding room or an embalming chamber. The not-yet dead are the soon-to-be dead. His prey are armed, but also blind. He blinded them. Three blind mice. The windows up here admit murky moonlight, a considerable assistance to Calaphas as his night-vision gear greatly amplifies every lumen, but the moon is of no help to the mice, the soon-to-be dead. They can shoot toward whatever noise he makes, but he will see them before they can accurately fix the location of the sound, and he'll cut the legs out from under them with an extended burst of fire. When they're down, screaming, their flesh torn and bones shattered, in too much pain to hold fast to their guns, he'll be all over them, hammering them with the buttstock of his weapon, finally making the encounter intensely personal by ripping with his knife. When the screaming stops and a hush returns, Durand will be alone here with the quiet and respected guests, as so often he has been in the past. Alone with them even before the embalming occurs. Before they're groomed for burial. Before the cosmetician arrives to restore to their faces the illusion of mere sleep. Then he will kiss them, one by one, and like Britta Holdstrom, each will fail to wake. Because Gifford no longer exists to mock his younger brother, the game will end at last, end in Durand's triumph. He will be elevated out of this simulation into the higher realm of the gamemakers.

All that remains to be done is find the room to which they have retreated. That will involve little risk if he plays this by his own rules rather than by those the ISA trainers teach. With his spare magazines, he has more than enough ammunition to pump a few rounds through each door and dodge aside to see whether the response is a scream or return fire, or silence.

Even as he is about to begin, however, his attention is drawn to a mysterious, oscillating object in the stillness of the hall. A slender green something terminating in a larger green form. Swinging side to side like a clock pendulum. Counting down to the end of the game. As he approaches the article, the width of its arc diminishes. There is not even the faintest draft. Some past action has set this thing in motion. The clattering noise that occurred a few seconds ago and drew him here. The object is a rope that's threaded through and knotted to a ball. Like a locket dangling on a chain from the hand of a hypnotist, it invites a mesmerizing fascination. He takes the ball in hand and squeezes it. Rubber. He can barely make out the lines in the ceiling drywall that describe the size and shape of the attic trapdoor.

◆　◆　◆

Sometimes, for a part of their community-watch tour, Juan and Walter switch on the radio and listen to a popular talk show that features discussions of out-of-body experiences, visitors from other dimensions, shadow people, spontaneous human combustion, incredible disappearances in the Bermuda Triangle and elsewhere, ghosts, time travelers, predictions of psychics and prophets, end-of-the-world scenarios, and space aliens. With one exception, they don't believe in any of those things. They listen to the program mainly for the amusement value. The one exception is space aliens.

Neither Juan nor Walter has been abducted by ETs and taken aboard a mother ship. They have never seen one of those hairless huge-eyed spatula-fingered Grays described by so many abductees. They have witnessed no strange, unexplainable objects in the sky. Throughout their childhood and adolescence, TV series such as *The Twilight Zone* and *The Outer Limits*, as well as scores of movies like *Invaders from Mars* and *Invasion of the Body Snatchers*, pretty much programmed them to believe wholeheartedly in extraterrestrials. This vaguely embarrasses them, for they had been clear-eyed businessmen during their long careers. However, they are agreed that it's better to be UFO believers than to have been indoctrinated instead with any of the venomous ideas with which various politicians have poisoned the minds of once happy people that previously had been capable of reason. Here, now, suddenly, in the presence of alien machines, all embarrassment is burned away by the thrill of first contact, wonder, mystery, and a measured fear of the unknown.

The robots are quick and nimble, all but gliding across the open land at between fourteen and sixteen miles per hour. In the moonlight, their exquisitely engineered bodies are as silvery and seem almost as liquid as if they are shapes of coherent mercury.

Although the F-150 is capable of far greater speed than their quarry currently exhibit, Walter says, "Don't lose them."

"I won't lose them," Juan declares.

"They're probably scouts."

"Yeah. I'm hoping they'll lead us to the ship."

"Is that a good thing?" Walter wonders.

"Why wouldn't it be a good thing?"

"What if the aliens are evil?"

"They aren't evil."

Walter says, "You would know—how?"

"I'm more with Spielberg than Ridley Scott."

"So it's an issue of faith with you."

"No. Logic. The ETs in *Alien* were just bugs. They weren't able to build robots, spaceships. ETs with spaceships are advanced beyond violence."

At the top of a hill, the robots halt and turn and rear up on their hind legs, mantis-like in the headlights, and something about their posture suggests they might be equipped with weapons.

◆　◆　◆

In the lightless attic with Nina and John to his left, sitting with his back to the wall, Michael Mace takes over control of Gog and Magog out there in the night, while he also enters the universal service network that all telecom companies share. He locates the provider of service to Juan Louis Gainza, who was earlier identified in the DMV files as the owner of the F-150.

Perhaps because she is sitting shoulder to shoulder against Michael, Nina senses him reacting to the crisis. "What's wrong?" she whispers.

He murmurs, "Stay calm. I've got to make a call. I'll explain later."

Once he has Juan Gainza's number, he is able to identify the maker of the phone in six seconds. Apple. He's been there before. Easy to enter their system. From Apple's ocean of data, he siphons the transponder code built into that particular iPhone. He departs Apple and trampolines from the internet to an orbiting navigation-service satellite from which he seeks the current location of the signal being emitted by Gainza's phone. He finds it, funnels down the microwave linkage into that device, and switches it on. Mindful that Calaphas is searching the house below them, he keeps his voice as low as he can without whispering, while nonetheless sounding authoritative. "Juan Gainza, stop."

◆　◆　◆

Evidently, the trap ladder was retracted from above. Calaphas isn't so foolish as to pull it down and use it. The noise will alert them. Mace will be in the most advantageous position he could find. Calaphas can't climb a steep ladder quickly, with a rifle in both hands. No one can. Impossible. That's Hollywood action. He isn't John Wick or Jason Bourne or Harry Callahan. Neither were Keanu Reeves nor Matt Damon nor Clint Eastwood, not for real. The bennies have pumped him up. He's wound so tight with rage that his ears are ringing. He feels the arteries throbbing in his neck. The taste of blood is in his mouth because he's bitten his lip in frustration, such is his need for action. But when those in the attic sense that he's nearing the top of the ladder, they'll pin him with at least one beam of light. Probably two. Directed by the woman and the boy, maybe neither of them anywhere near Mace. If Calaphas is wearing the night-vision gear, he'll be blinded by the amplified light. If he *isn't* wearing the unit, he might not see where his primary target waits in the shadows. In either case, Mace won't hesitate; he'll go for a head shot.

Calaphas stands gazing up at the trapdoor. His mind races, chemically enhanced. Thanks to the bennies, he doesn't feel tired. He is clearheaded, and every thought is as sharp as a blade flashing off a stropping stone. He knows exactly what to do.

The robots halt and pivot and rear up on their hind legs.

Juan brakes to a full stop about ten yards from them, halfway up the hill, and Walter says, "You still all Spielberg about this?"

"We've got to be careful here," Juan says. "We do the wrong thing, and it's misunderstood, could seal the fate of humanity."

"Like in *The Day the Earth Stood Still*."

"Maybe. Though that was a lame movie."

"It was lame," Walter agrees.

Juan's phone is fixed in a WeatherTech device that fits in a cup holder. The screen brightens, displaying the familiar photo of Juan's much loved—and recently deceased—golden retriever, Jasper. The phone doesn't ring or vibrate, but a male voice issues from it: *"Juan Gainza, stop. Shut off your engine. You've accidently strayed into a Department of Defense field test."*

"Shit," Walter says.

"Stop where you are. We'll be coming to take your statement."

"Are we going to be arrested?" Juan asks. When the screen goes dark, he says to Walter, "Angelina will kill me if I'm arrested."

"They won't arrest us," Walter assures him.

Killing the engine, Juan says, "Why wouldn't they?"

"Like he said, it was accidental."

In the headlights, the robots stand watching them for a moment. Then the machines drop to all fours, prowl across the crest of the hill, and vanish into the night.

A sense of proper architectural proportions, such as Calaphas has long possessed, has great value.

For example, the dimensions of the interior of a coffin must be adjusted with various materials and techniques to display the quiet and respected guest to the best advantage. A short, slender person should not appear elfin and comical because she or he lies with a lot of empty space to all sides. Shaped blankets can fill the voids and be concealed with lengths of soft-sheen satin that suggest the beauty and peacefulness of the next life to which the deader has departed. Likewise, a fat person should never appear to have been stuffed into a too-small box as though he or she is a sausage in a casing.

In a funeral home with chambers of ideal proportions, a viewing room is rectangular, so that the casket stands elevated against the shorter wall that is farther from the door. Sufficient space exists to both sides of the catafalque to accommodate floral arrangements displayed in tiers. The approach to the deceased should allow for a generous open area where family and friends gather to express their sorrow and sympathy, with folding chairs against both long walls.

If such a room is correctly proportioned, a curious child as young as five or six can descend from the living quarters upstairs, enter in absolute darkness, close the door, and approach the deader with confidence that he won't collide with anything and that he'll know precisely how many steps will bring him to the casket, where it rests on a platform. A hidden pull-out step on that low catafalque is there to assist a short member of the staff who needs to reach across the deceased to make final adjustments to the overlay or other bedding, and a boy who knows about that feature can, even in the blinding dark, get close to the quiet and respected guest who will be center stage at the forthcoming morning's events. In fact, the boy can get so close that he is able to whisper in the nearer ear of the deceased and share confidences. If the occupant of the casket is a pretty woman, the boy can kiss two of his fingers and, even in the deep dark, accurately press them to her lips, and then press them to his own, lest she be a princess who can be revived. He visits only those who died in youth or middle age. He has learned that very old dead people are frightening; they seem so . . . *knowing*.

Here in the Chandra house, in a state of amphetamine euphoria, an exhilarating rage, Calaphas stands under the trapdoor, grinning and shifting his weight from foot to foot, reviewing what he knows of the architecture of the residence from having approached the house and having circled it to find the back entrance to the garage. The ground floor is substantially larger than the second floor. The pitch of the roof suggests that the attic extends over the entire upstairs. The trapdoor is not centered on the space above, but is near the eastern end of the structure. Because Mace will want to defend the only entrance to that high refuge, he is likely to remain as near the trap as seems safe, though he might send the woman and boy to a far end of the attic. Whether they are together or separate, they will shelter in corners, because instinct tells them to protect their backs and because Mace is smart enough to know that the corner posts—with the associated framing and masonry in those locations—provide greater protection from gunfire.

Moving toward a door on the right side of the hall, he murmurs so softly that he can barely hear his voice. "You're dead, and I'm not. You're dead, and I'm not." As a young child, he had whispered those words in the ears of the quiet and respected guests in their caskets. That taunt reassured him then, and it excites him now, a mantra for anyone who—in Calaphas's opinion, wisely—believes in nothing but himself.

As he enters the room at the southwest corner of the house, where the moon-bathed windows green the space, he hears a voice that seems to come from overhead. Most of the words are muffled, and the others make a strange assertion: ". . . you are . . . becoming . . . your statement."

◆　◆　◆

Little relieved by moonlight, darkness has gathered around the quieted pickup.

"They should be field-testing on a military base," Juan says the moment the robots are gone from sight.

Walter says, "This isn't military land."

Juan says, "And that phone call wasn't a phone call."

"Never rang," Walter says. "Like the message was beamed at us."

"Beamed," Juan agrees.

Walter concludes, "Alien technology."

"Damn, we've been gaslighted," Juan says, as he starts the engine and switches on the headlights. "They're aliens, all right."

"Those sons of bitches," Walter declares.

"One thing I can't stand," Juan says.

Walter knows what he means. "Liars."

Accelerating toward the crest of the hill, where the robots vanished, Juan says, "Damn all liars, no matter where they're from."

"Pedal to the metal."

"I'm doin' it."

"They don't have much of a lead on us."

"This is history," Juan says.

The truck cannons off the top of the hill and down the next slope at more than fifty miles per hour, rocking and bouncing across the rough terrain, spewing up chunks of earth and tangles of wild grass, the fuel tank and drivetrain spared because the Ford is jacked up on oversize tires. At the bottom of the hill, their sleek limbs rippled with moonlight, the spawn of another planet turn left into the narrow valley and head east. Juan angles across the slope as he descends it, closing fast on the alien machines.

"You ramming them?" Walter asks.

Juan says, "Just gonna cut them off."

Walter agrees. "Keep them from the mother ship."

"Better call the sheriff's dispatcher," Juan says.

Walter plucks the phone from its holder—"Holy shit!"—and drops it on the floor. "Hot like it came from an oven."

"Bastards," Juan says. "Use *your* phone."

"Didn't bring it."

They are in the narrow vale, parallel to the sprinting robots.

"Maybe they have weapons," Walter says.

Juan declares, "I'm not backing off."

"Me neither. Just sayin'."

They quickly pull ahead of the off-worlders. Walter can see them in the side mirror as they fall farther behind. "They're not changing course."

"I see the bastards," Juan says, shifting his attention back and forth between the way ahead and the rearview mirror.

They are ten years beyond retirement and wishing they never signed on for rest and relaxation, long resigned to the fact that life will never again present them with fresh excitement of the best kind, that henceforth it's rocking chairs on the porch and walks in the park and did-you-see-this-or-that crap on one streaming service or another until they're slammed dead by a heart attack or a stroke, or wind up in hospice for a final month. This close encounter is a gift, a miracle, maybe a chance to warn the world of—and thwart—an impending invasion. They're young men again—hell, they're *boys* again—full of wonder and reckless courage.

When he has opened a sufficient lead, Juan hangs a U-turn as sharply and adroitly as any stunt driver might have executed in the movies, and he jams on the brake. The oncoming robots flare in the headlights, come to a halt, and once more rear up on their back legs.

Showdown.

◆ ◆ ◆

The night has been a journey from one darkness to another, each seeming to be absolute until the next proves darker yet, inspiring a superstitious dread that their inevitable destination is an eternal lightlessness, mere minutes away.

Nina isn't convinced that the attic is the safest place to be. They have abandoned whatever other options they might have had—unless there's a way from here onto the roof. And from the roof?

In spite of her concern, she's followed Michael's instructions without hesitation, fully trusting him. She had learned to trust her parents without reservation in the years before they died. However, as is the case with John, her confidence in Michael is more than implicit trust. It is *belief*, and not just belief based on personal observation, but belief of the heart; her reliance on this man is a matter of *faith*. That this should be the case, after she has known him such a short time, amazes but doesn't trouble her. In spite of the strange power that has been bestowed on Michael, he is humble. He has about him the air of one who, for many years, has suffered much and lost much. But if his losses have resulted in a settled sorrow, his melancholy is a shoal rather than an abyss. He isn't a sad or bitter person; he's quite the opposite of that. In Nina's experience, except between mother and child, genuine love doesn't bloom as quickly as a rose from bud to full flower, but requires years instead. Yet her faith in Michael is such a yearning of the soul that she has been brought to love. She doesn't understand why they are here in the attic, doesn't know what he means when he insists that the cavalry is on its way, but there will be time for explanations when the threat has passed and their safety assured. Faith and love are the source of a hope that inspires courage and leaves no room for doubt.

One, two, three, four, five: Gunfire tears through the attic flooring, and the air is filled with bits of flung debris.

◆ ◆ ◆

"Light!" Michael says, and Nina switches it on even as gunfire echoes off the rafters, where alarmed spiders shiver across their gossamer constructions.

They are in the southeast corner of the attic. If they had been in the south*west* corner, one or more of them might be bleeding out on the pocked and splintered flooring.

Gog and Magog should be here, but Juan Gainza and his unknown companion are delaying them. The upper-right quadrant of Michael's vision displays the view from a robot's forward cameras: the blazing headlights of the pickup, moths dancing in the washed air of the post-storm night.

Assuming that Calaphas intends to quarter the attic with gunfire from below, Michael whispers, "Far end. Quick."

They can't cross that long space quietly, but noise no longer matters. Calaphas already knows where they are. What noise they make will translate across the width and length of the floor, so their would-be executioner won't be able to pinpoint them while they're on the move.

As he follows John and Nina to the north end of the attic, Michael is also active in the fields of the night, bringing both robots erect. In their most menacing posture, they are harbingers of a future in which humankind has been unmade by what it made. He can instruct them to evade the F-150, but the pickup has the advantage of greater speed. Gainza will only further delay them—or pursue them to this house. Michael can't afford to have witnesses either to his presence or to what Gog and Magog will do to Calaphas.

He settles into the northeast corner of the attic with Nina and John. There's no need to switch off her light. They can't any longer hope to lure Calaphas to his well-deserved end. The agent won't be pulling the ladder and ascending until he believes they're all dead. Evidently, he has a lot of ammo, enough to quarter the attic until luck is with him and no longer with them. Their best hope now is that the dogs of Protean Cybernetics arrive in time to save them.

◆　◆　◆

They scurry like frightened attic rats. Unlike rats, which are able to squeeze their spongy skulls and flexible bodies through any chink that's half an inch or wider, Mace and his companions can't escape from the refuge that has become their prison. The promise of human evolution accelerated by technology, the vaunted Singularity, has produced nothing more than a desperate outsider, a man-machine who is less than either a man or a machine, who has become nothing more than an animal on the run.

In high spirits, Calaphas leaves the bedroom at the southwest corner of the house, crosses the hallway, and enters the room at the southeast corner. He is the Pied Piper, and this house is Hamelin, soon to be rid of all rats. He's brother to the farmer's wife with her carving knife and bloody collection of rodent tails. He's the exterminator, annihilator, eradicator, obliterator, and his moment of ultimate triumph is at hand. No one can stand against him. In a flash of profound insight, he realizes that he is Death; either he always has been Death but unaware, or he's an apprentice to Death and has by his dedication earned the hooded robe and scythe. The kingdom of Death is everywhere and always, not just in this present simulation but also in the higher realm to which he'll soon ascend. Everyone is born to die, but he is not of their kind. He is Death, and therefore deathless, harvesting lesser beings throughout all of time. When this night's work is done, he must think about this new understanding, the ramifications, the power. The revelation is so exhilarating that he wonders what even greater satori might be visited on him if he took *another* ten milligrams of Benzedrine.

In the southeast corner of the southeast room, Durand Calaphas aims the rifle at the ceiling and squeezes off five rounds in rapid succession. No one screams, but he isn't disappointed. They will be screaming soon enough. When eventually he goes into the attic, he will thrust his priapism into the woman, whether she is alive or dead, and he will kiss her on the lips. He will kiss the dead boy, and he will kiss the dead Singularity, and this virtual world will dissolve around him, and he will rise into his kingdom.

◆ ◆ ◆

Showdown.

Juan and Walter share the same fear, and it's not a fear of death, a prospect to which they've adapted during their long lives. They are afraid that these alien machines will escape, that they will have no evidence that this encounter occurred, that they will therefore not be able to tell anyone about this most astonishing event in their lives, for fear of being dismissed as liars or as dupes who fell for an absurd hoax. Walter says, "Marty Bellock," whereupon Juan says, "Exactly what I was thinking." Marty had been an acquaintance of theirs long ago, a successful businessman who claimed to have bedded the sexiest actress of that decade, a star for whom millions lusted. The details of his story were verifiable to the extent that he and the actress had been in the same city at the same event and had booked rooms in the same hotel. He even had a photo of him and her, which was signed by her and inscribed "What a night!" However, she hadn't given him her phone number or address, and he preserved none of her DNA that might have lent a measure of credibility to his story. Besides, he was round faced and stocky, not a Greek god to whom women were irresistibly drawn. Although everyone previously thought Marty was a man of principles, reliable and trustworthy in all matters, his insistence on the truth of this unlikely one-night stand damaged his reputation beyond repair, and no one ever again quite believed anything he said.

Consequently, when the alien machines rush forward, each on two legs, when one of them proves to have a weapon incorporated into it, when a muzzle flashes twice, and when the shots strike with laser-guided accuracy, blowing out both front tires on the F-150, Juan is motivated to stand on the accelerator. The shrieking truck surges forward on shredding tires. The robots fall onto all fours and peel off in opposite directions. One escapes. The other is clipped hard and tumbles away, casting off showers of multicolored sparks, as if it is a Fourth of July rocket that, having failed to launch, wastes its wonders in the tall, wet grass.

◆　◆　◆

With no cupped hand limiting it, the powerful LED beam spreads its bright cone the length of the attic. When the second barrage of gunfire rips through the floor, crickets of pressed wood leap into the air; swallowtails of pink fiberglass insulation flutter up and then float in the silence of the aftershock.

Gog is down, but Magog is less than a mile away and coming, guided by the coordinates of the Chandra house that had been installed earlier.

Michael's mind is processing data slower than a supercomputer would process it, but he's coming to a wet-brain conclusion no different from that arrived at by dry-circuit silicon. The first volley of shots had shattered into the southwest corner, and the second had riddled the southeast corner, with no salvos between those two widespread points. Below the attic, the second floor of the house provides rooms on each side of a hallway. After the first fusillade, Calaphas had left one room and directly entered the room across the hall before opening fire again. Seconds are racing away. He's on the move, seconds are racing away, and he isn't shooting. Because he isn't quartering the attic. He is going from corner to corner. Calaphas assumes that both instinct and some knowledge of construction will draw them into the greater safety of a corner, the *presumed* safety. First southwest, then southeast. Now he's coming the length of the second floor, toward the northeast corner. They are in the northeast corner.

John in a watchful crouch. Nina still on her feet. A warped and loose and perhaps mold-eaten sheet of particleboard creaks as she shifts her weight from one foot to the other.

Michael says, *"He's right under us!"* As he speaks, he grabs a fistful of the boy's jacket and lifts him out of the crouch, almost off his feet, thrusting him away from the corner.

A rattle of wood on wood, a cracking sound: Foiled by loose flooring, Nina stumbles and cries out involuntarily.

Pivoting toward her, seeing her fall with the Tac Light firmly in hand, the sheet of particleboard now angled and overlapping the sheet adjacent, Michael is nowhere else but here, neither with Magog crossing a length of ranch fence nor drawn by horrified speculation as to what the next few seconds will bring, but only here, where the past matters not and there is no expectation of a future. There is never other time than the current moment; the suspension bridge beneath your feet is a fragile construct, as if fabricated from ropes and wooden slats, each slat a moment, your crossing begun at birth, the time of death at a point en route when a slat fails to support your weight and falls into the gorge, you with it. And the time of death is always. Now time doesn't stop for Michael Mace, and neither does he step outside of time. Instead, he ceases thinking, commits himself to action by the guidance of another—he can't say who—but it isn't mere instinct. Afterward, he is unable to remember what he did, how he snatched Nina off the floor and into his arms as if she were weightless, how he strode twenty feet from the corner—in a seeming instant. Calaphas is so certain of his intuitive targeting that the crack of rifle fire comes four times, three more, three again. As the floor shakes, as debris is flung up but also spills from the bullet-pocked ceiling, Michael stands before the boy, whose eyes are shocked wide, though no wider than his own.

As the overlapping echoes of the barrage fade into an expectant and fearsome quiet, he sets Nina on her feet. He looks toward the fourth corner, as yet not assaulted, then at the floor under them, and he knows one place is no safer than another. He knows, as well, that it wasn't the nanotech in his cells, not Shadow Michael, that gave him the extraordinary strength and reflexes to do what he just did. The inspiration for the action he took, the source of his power and adroitness, was as basic and human as it gets—love.

He has led his life without committing to any woman, for fear the consequences will be deceit, betrayal, torment, and loss, of which he knew too much in childhood. But here he is. Here he is because of Shelby Shrewsberry, because their lifelong friendship required him to care about a stranger for whom Shelby had deep but unexpressed affection, and that caring has become a love Shelby didn't live to experience. There is sadness in that, as well as guilt unearned but felt, yet there is also a new hope. Here he is, and Nina knows it, and he knows that what he feels for her is alike to what she feels for him. Now all they need to do is survive.

Before he opens fire, Calaphas hears a woman's cry, the source immediately above him, in the northeast corner of the attic, a cry of surprise rather than pain, followed by something being dropped or someone falling. Whoever she might be, her exclamation thrills him, as though it's the annunciation of his rebirth as the dark angel of Death, his sacred identity confirmed. He squeezes off four rounds at the ceiling, pauses but a second to enjoy the screams, which do not come, and fires six more times. Even if three bullets found three brains, they couldn't all have died in the same instant. Ten rounds have raised not a shout or shriek of pain, not one plaint of horror. The only sounds are quick footfalls as they react to a new awareness of his strategy, avoiding corners, hoping that he lacks enough ammunition to keep harassing them back and forth through that high space until their luck runs out.

He is impatient to transcend. Perhaps his rage abated with the realization of his true immortal nature, but now it swells hot once more. If this game has one rule, it is that in all situations and circumstances, violence is the only winning course of action. *The violent bear it away.* The future belongs to the violent. They bear away those who choose not to kill. They bear away everything of which they disapprove, all art and music and writing and philosophy that they find displeasing, all *thought* that offends them. They bear away all traditions, institutions, and ultimately all civilization as it was once constituted. He *knows* this game. He is the *master* of this game, and he is infuriated that at this late hour, with one move left to clear the board, he is being frustrated.

He ejects the depleted magazine. Slaps in a fresh one. He has twenty additional rounds available in yet a third magazine.

Stepping into the hall, he surveys the ceiling, which is a darker shade of green than the walls. He cocks his head left and right, trying to gauge the trio's location by the telltale sounds they're making. He enters the next room on the right, wishing that their body heat could reveal them by translating through the attic floor and manifesting as green glowing footprints on this ceiling, an irrational desire perhaps related to the Benzedrine. He squeezes off three rounds to no effect and returns to the hallway, attention focused overhead.

A scissoring sound, blade against blade, and a series of soft clicks puzzle him. He can't figure out what Mace and his companions are doing up there, and then he realizes the source of the noise is not in the attic. When he looks south, a daunting apparition comes off the stairs and into the hallway, an entity so bizarre that it evokes in him the closest thing to fear that he has felt since he was seven years old and purged himself of that hampering emotion. Never before have mere bennies troubled him with hallucinations. At first, in the strange light that his goggles conjure from the dark, the intruder seems spiderlike, the number of its legs difficult to discern. Then it goes erect on its two back limbs, revealing that it has only four legs, and its body appears to reconfigure in some way, with a soft whir and a softer *chunk-chunk-chunk*. As Calaphas begins to realize that this is neither a hallucination nor some monstrous insect, that it's a *machine*, and as alarm rises in him, the intruder projects a broad beam of light—

—*LIGHT* so bright that the night-vision unit is overwhelmed. Calaphas can see nothing. He yanks off the headset and throws it aside and begins to bring up his rifle, but he is slower than he needs to be. The roar of gunfire—none of it his—floods the hall, and Calaphas seems to be lifted, seems to be swept backward and up in the ascension he has expected. The world, which was green and then white, becomes all red and then black. What seems to be an ascension is not.

◆ ◆ ◆

When they descend the ladder, John marvels at the robot, and Nina marvels at Michael.

He says, "I'll explain in the car. Let's hurry."

The machine drops to all fours as if to follow, but Michael instructs it to power down to minimal awareness and wait here. The scene must be left as is, so that the killing of Calaphas can't be pinned on anyone other than Magog.

Michael pats its head and says, "Good dog."

The shots were all fired inside, and the walls muffled much of the clamor. The acreage around the residence also provides a buffer. However, the sound has surely traveled, and someone is even now trying to determine from where it came.

They load the ice chests in the Range Rover, each selecting a beverage before closing the liftgate. Calaphas has been dead less than three minutes when they set out for Arizona.

HOME IS THE HUNTER

Royce Kinnel is so shaken by events that the moment he arrives home, he washes his hands until they are red, selects an album of nerve-soothing easy-listening piano for the through-house music system, takes a tablet of Prozac, brews a pot of tea, and opens a tin of butter cookies that have been finished with a cinnamon glaze and sprinkled with sea salt.

Before indulging in this predawn repast, he descends to the windowless room in the finished basement, where he opens a secret panel with a touch latch and then opens the heavily insulated steel door that is thus revealed. In the love nest, he strips the sheets off the bed and loads them in the washing machine that he uses only for this task. He's finicky about consigning his own garments to the same machine that he uses to launder the bedclothes in which have lain the women he keeps here.

Upstairs once more, seated at the kitchen table with tea and cookies, he laments the passing of Lenore, whom he had kept in the basement for seven delightful months. She was especially lovely and, once properly trained, precisely as submissive as he requires. All things must come to an end, however, for he is a man who needs a certain degree of variety.

Royce is thirty, heir to a trust fund that spares him from the need to work. However, with financial independence comes the worry that those who seem to like you actually have contempt for you and are nice to you only because you have money. Dating is a dangerous enterprise for a young man of his position. Fortunately, he has the skills and courage to resolve the problem with such as Lenore. He adopted this style of courtship when he was twenty-one, and in the past nine years has had the pleasure of twelve beauties.

He terminates these relationships by strangulation, which is less messy than most alternatives but also invigorating for reasons that he finds difficult to explain. He dislikes messiness, and when he's not in his current girlfriend's room, engaged in six- or eight-hour sessions of amorous pursuits, he spends a lot of time cleaning the house. Fortunately, he enjoys housekeeping, which eliminates the need to have a domestic employee. His residence is spotless. Royce believes in doing things the right way, with diligence and care.

In the case of his previous eleven girlfriends, after breaking up with them, he removed them from his life with such forethought and care that only one was ever found. To this day, he can't imagine how Jennifer—the second Jennifer, not the first—floated into Dana Point Harbor on a Sunday morning, after he had, on Friday, packed her in a metal steamer trunk and buried her at sea, ten miles south of there and nine miles from land. The trunk was bound in chains to which were attached six twenty-pound barbells; a hydraulic hand truck with a five-hundred-pound capacity was needed to get that package onto his boat and later raise it over the gunwale to slide it into the sea. If Royce believed in ghosts, he might wonder if the spirit of Harry Houdini freed Jennifer's corpse for some macabre reason.

After strangling a girlfriend, he never deposits her in a place where he has left another one. Indeed, he has conveyed two of them to New Mexico, wrapped in plastic drop cloths that he sprayed with lubricant before dropping them into ancient lava pipes, long tubes about three or four feet in width, leading down through solid stone, up which lava had gushed in an epoch long before the creation of humanity. Those lovelies lie hundreds—perhaps thousands—of feet below the possibility of discovery. Another he cremated in Arizona, by leaving her in an abandoned church to which he set fire.

He had chosen to bury Lenore on public land, in a lonely vale more than thirty miles from his home. He had found the site before he strangled her and had tested the texture of the soil to be sure he could dig a grave easily enough with pick and spade. He almost had her in the ground when the robots appeared.

After enough time has passed, many episodes in Royce Kinnel's life seem surrealistic, phantasmagorical, too colorful and quirky to have played out as they did, more like vivid dreams than real-life experiences; reliving them in memory is far more entertaining than anything on television. Thinking back, Royce is often amazed at what he's done and that he's gotten away with it, although at the time his actions seemed as mundane as taking out the trash. A few hours earlier, however, the incident near Rancho Santa Fe struck him as surrealistic even as it occurred. Robots. As big as Great Danes. Appearing out of nowhere.

Royce isn't interested in either science fiction or science. He's not interested in much of anything other than his girlfriends and housekeeping; he doesn't care what's cool in movies or music or art or fashion, and he has no politics. People say there will be robots everywhere one day, but he's sure that is at least a decade from now. So, aliens. A lot of people seem to be fascinated with UFOs, but Royce isn't. He couldn't care less about aliens. Whatever extraterrestrial females are like, they won't be hot in any way that's likely to get his sap rising. Earth girls are enough for him.

He wishes the robots hadn't so unnerved him. He can't go back and fill the grave now. That's like asking to be caught.

Although he panicked and although Lenore will now be found sooner than later, he is confident that no one can connect her to him. One of the benefits of his style of romance is that no one ever sees him in public with any of his ladies. He abandoned the shovel and pick, but he bought them for cash at a yard sale years earlier. The tools can't be traced to him, and he always wears gloves when handling them. As for Lenore, subsequent to breaking up with her, he submerged her lovely body in a special chemical bath and took other steps to ensure that no trace of his DNA can be found on or in her. Proper handling of an ex-girlfriend is a housekeeping chore more crucial than any other. After fleeing the robots—how crazy that sounds!—he drove several miles to another lonely place, where he used a powerful handheld vacuum to go over the interior of his Lexus SUV. He purchased the vehicle months after he'd abducted Lenore, and she'd been in it only once, after her body was sealed in plastic sheeting; however, just in case one hair of hers somehow found its way into the vehicle, an hour of vacuuming was the right thing to do. He stopped at a public park to throw the hand vac in a trash can. He drove the SUV through an automatic car wash that was open around the clock—and then drove it through again.

The Prozac, the tea, the cookies, and his singular housekeeping habits give him confidence that all will be well. After a few days of rest, he will start scouting for his next girlfriend. He needs between two and four months, on average, to find a new companion, research her routines, plan the acquisition of her, bring her home unseen, and teach her how to be happy and fulfilled by making *him* happy. It is an arduous process—but fun!—and rewarding when she's at last in place and trained.

Dawn paints reefs of gold and coral pink across the sky as Royce finishes washing and drying the teapot. No longer shaken by the surreal events of the night, pleased to be moving into a new phase of his life, with the robots merely a curiosity to be wondered about in years to come, he makes his way along the downstairs hall to the foyer, exhausted and ready to go upstairs to bed, when the chimes announce a visitor.

At one of the sidelights flanking the front door, a man in a uniform peers into the foyer. A policeman. For a moment, Royce can't draw a breath. The policeman smiles and nods and raises one hand as if to say, *Hi, there.* Because it is impossible that a link exists between Royce and Lenore in the open grave, the policeman's warm smile is surely genuine, his purpose benign. Royce opens the door.

Two officers, not just one, step inside, and the second isn't smiling. He says, "Royce Kinnel?" Royce moves to quell any suspicion they have by being respectful, polite, relaxed, and puzzled rather than either fearful or angry. Nevertheless, the smiling policeman presents him with a search warrant, announces that they will be impounding the Lexus, and informs Royce that he is under arrest.

Royce cheated his way through private schools and college, and not one teacher ever tumbled to his scams and plagiarisms because he manipulated them into seeing him as an earnest and dedicated—though not exceptional—student. In much the same way, he has manipulated his girls to believe that he is a deeply troubled but not violent man who will eventually free them if they do all that he desires, even if some of it is disgusting or even painful. He is tall and handsome, has a firm handshake and always makes eye contact and has white teeth and is well-mannered, and he comes from a family of some prominence. That is all he has needed to skate in the past, and he believes it is all he needs now, if he just remains calm.

The unsmiling officer produces an unusual eight-by-ten photo. Everything captured by the camera is in eerie shades of green and gradations of black. The perspective is from a low angle. A spade stands with its point buried in the earth. A man looms. Cradled in his arms is a woman. The night was too dark for anyone to have seen his face. But in this green version of events, Royce Kinnel has no difficulty recognizing himself.

As the smiling officer says something about an attorney and a right to remain silent, Royce hears footsteps behind him and turns to see that two more policemen have entered the hallway from the back of the house.

The insistently glum officer returns the photograph to a manila envelope and refers to an anonymous informant in the company that provides navigation service to the Lexus. Royce has long enjoyed the convenience of GPS navigation, but he hasn't realized that a record exists of everywhere he has gone. He's not into all this tech stuff. It's boring. He doesn't have time for it, what with his domestic chores and his uniquely vigorous love life. Even if he'd known about such a record, he'd have done nothing different. He's been careful, so very careful, to make sure no one ever sees him with one of his girlfriends, because if no one sees them with him, it doesn't matter where he goes in his vehicle; there's nothing to connect him to the poor dears. Until the alien robots. And how surreal is that? Now Officer Always Scowling informs him that GPS records of his previous vehicles are archived and will be subpoenaed.

They seem to expect Royce to confess, but of course he has no such intention. He is still tall and handsome, has a firm handshake and always makes eye contact and has white teeth and is still well-mannered, and his family is as prominent as ever.

In addition, there is the Constitution of the United States and the rights guaranteed in it. Royce has no interest in history and knows not much more about the Constitution than that it exists, but he's pretty damn sure no court will allow them to introduce photographic evidence provided by invading space aliens whose advanced technology allows them to fake the image beyond anyone's ability to detect the fakery, just as they can hack and fiddle with archived navigation-system records. He will surely skate.

OF WHAT IS PAST, OR PASSING,
OR TO COME

In the Caribbean Sea, the jewel-tone waters are warm and clear. Of the many islands, the Caymans are among the smallest.

On Grand Cayman is a bank. In the bank is an account held in the name of Only Truth, Inc.

In Idaho lies a hundred-acre ranch of grassy fields and forests that is owned by Only Truth, Inc. It isn't a working ranch, at least not in the traditional sense.

On the ranch is a modest but beautifully finished house in the Craftsman style.

Residing in the house are Peter and Susan Pevensie, husband and wife, who are financially independent and who say they retired early to write novels. Their only child, Edward, is homeschooled, and they have a dog named Lucy. More than two years have passed since any of them has mistakenly spoken the names Michael or Nina or John even in the privacy of their home.

Also on the property is a stable for eight horses, though only three are currently in residence: Bree, Hwin, and Puzzle—one mare and two stallions.

The family rides together, canoes together, skis together, attends church together, and participates in the life of the small town of Baskin Springs to such an extent that none of the locals ever thinks of them as in any way mysterious.

As peaceful and idyllic as life can be in rural Idaho, this is the worst of times and the best of times in the wider world, an age of great turmoil, though the changes underway are mostly nonviolent. Someone whom the media calls "Superhacker" controls the internet and maintains access to all data in every computer, cell phone, device, and system that's internet dependent. Telecom, banking, and social media entities; the power grid; private enterprises; all government bureaus and agencies: He enjoys unrestricted access to pretty much everything. Worldwide. Superhacker isn't really anything as ordinary as a hacker, but something stranger and more powerful for which no one has yet come up with a better name. Many billions of dollars and countless man-hours have been spent trying to locate Superhacker or wrest control from him or her, all to no avail. In some ineffable way, this villain has reconfigured the internet so that those who thrive on anonymity and illegal enterprise can opt out only at the unbearable cost of collapsing their company or agency and being denied all forms of electronic communication ever after.

Much has been said and written about the totalitarian threat posed by Superhacker, but it has not materialized. The first change imposed by this individual was to make it impossible to be anonymous in social media or elsewhere. In one day, every concocted handle was translated into the user's real name; now every attempt to go online incognito fails. The abrupt collapse of the ability to deceive and harass by such means has been a societal shockwave. But fascism grows in the dark, not in the light, and so it doesn't grow.

Just a week later, everyone with an email account—*everyone*—received in his or her mailbox reams of incontrovertible evidence of the massive corruption of fifteen members of Congress, paired with the emails and recorded phone conversations of justice department officials and law-enforcement personnel and media figures who had secretly conspired with those politicians to assist them in escaping prosecution and preserving their power, their reputations. That was only the *first* fifteen.

During the past three years, politicians at federal, state, and local levels, as well as bureaucrats, journalists, media executives, businesspeople, judges, clergy, teachers, university presidents, and citizens in all walks of life have been outed for testifying falsely before a grand jury, for lining their pockets with millions in graft and bribery and embezzled funds, for bold tax evasion, for selling national defense secrets to the government of China, for rape or murder or, in two cases, treason. Indicted by their own emails and recorded phone calls and bank records, they face such mountains of evidence that only a few escape prison; none has held on to his or her previous office or position.

These developments have resulted in much outrage and threats and limited violence. The most egregious criminals are those who issue the loudest, most bitterly insistent denials of their guilt. Because the wicked often have a charisma that the naive view as godliness, rather than demonic suasion, some miscreants for a time raise mass movements in their defense. In those cases, Superhacker exposes them again—and as before—with their own voices and with video of them engaged in conspiracies to deceive. Of the naive who join those crusades, most fall away when they see they have been duped, and only the most self-blinded cling to their faith in their faithless manipulators.

If, for a while, the social cohesion of the nation seemed sure to break from the strain of these changes, a new and better order asserted itself sooner than Superhacker hoped. Once depressed or cynical judges of an honest bent were heartened by the impeachment and conviction of their colleagues whom they knew to be corrupted by money or ideological passion. They found the courage to take over their state bar associations, state attorneys general offices, and even the justice department of the United States to strive for a fairer system swept clean of spoils and wild unreason. Institution after institution is evolving, not always with enthusiasm, because it has lost the power to define truth. The power of the state to rule by fear and moral exhortation based on lies is fading in a society where raw truth is available for everyone to see and where lies are quickly revealed by the liars' own indiscretions and a narcissistic certainty of their cleverness.

Superhacker is expanding operations to other nations, where changes have already been occurring in dreaded anticipation of his or her intention to broaden the mission. What will be will be, but what was before had become intolerable.

There are those who say that the human heart is deceitful above all things (which is true) and that lying is essential to grease the often grinding wheels of human relationships (which might be true as concerns relatively harmless falsehoods like insincere compliments, even flattery). But when Superhacker began to press the case that truth and the derivative of truth called "common sense" were in such short supply as to threaten the world, civilization had been fast sliding toward an abyss from which there might have been no return, a future of lawlessness, ginned-up hatred, irrational ideologies, and war. Perhaps this experiment in veracity will ultimately fail, but all polls show that a large majority of the populace finds that life is better these days, and polls can't be fudged in this new world.

Winter has arrived in Idaho. Yesterday, the sky was clear, and birds glided across like figure skaters on wind-polished ice. This morning, the clouds are thick and gray and lowering with a warning that autumn will soon seem to have been a dream. The big thermometer fastened to the wall of the back porch indicates the temperature is thirty-eight degrees and falling.

After a breakfast of bacon, eggs, fried potatoes, thick cuts of toasted and lavishly buttered raisin bread, washed down with orange juice or coffee, Peter and Susan and Edward mount their horses. They ride the meadows high and higher, their breath smoking from them in lesser plumes than it smokes from Bree and Hwin and Puzzle.

They rarely speak, for the evergreen forests and the golden meadows and the great mountains rising to bare-rock summits are nature's version of a cathedral. No matter how familiar the scene, their hearts are taken by awe. The vistas are supremely grand, so that the world seems newly created, full of promise and free from iniquity across its hemispheres, which is but a lovely illusion. Peter knows that the Earth will never be as innocent as it appears here and now. A reckoning can't be avoided, only delayed—but it has always been thus.

Lucy, a golden retriever, accompanies them, often straying toward one scent or another that intrigues her, never venturing too far. She races ahead to roll and wriggle in the grass. Come spring, such frolicking will bejewel her coat with the bright petals of torn wildflowers, and soon there will be snow to drape her in ermine.

A rifle is sleeved on Peter's saddle. After a long absence, gray wolves make their home in this territory once more, but he's watching primarily for a mountain lion, which is the greater threat to Lucy. He hasn't used the rifle for any purpose other than to fire a shot that scares a predator away. He hopes to get through life without killing another human being, and he prefers to pass his remaining years without killing any creature at all.

The vision of an eventual Singularity, a decades-long dream of transcendence, that is in fact a yearning for absolute power, has come to pass in him. And here is the irony always present in human affairs: He wants no power over others. He is trying to use his gift to thwart those who want control over their fellow men and women, to use truth to disperse power more widely than it's ever been before, so each person is free from the lies that have previously trammeled them. Succeed or fail, it will be a fine adventure.

Toward the end of the second hour of their ride, as they are heading home, the first snow falls. With no wind to hurry them, the huge flakes wheel down in graceful spirals. Lucy halts, looks up in wonderment, and then gambols across the meadow, leaping to bite the flakes from the air as if they must be manna.

Words come to Peter from a poem by William Butler Yeats that Shelby Shrewsberry loved: *We must laugh and we must sing / We are blest by everything / Everything we look upon is blest.*

NOTE

Some of the chapter titles in this novel are taken from poetry that I admire. A list is provided here for the curious reader.

A Bridge over Troubled Water. "Bridge over Troubled Water" by Paul Simon.

Leaning Together, Headpieces Filled with Straw. "The Hollow Men" by T. S. Eliot.

Voices as Meaningless as Wind in Dry Grass. "The Hollow Men" by T. S. Eliot.

In the Twilight Kingdom. "The Hollow Men" by T. S. Eliot.

The Pain of Living and the Drug of Dreams. "Animula" by T. S. Eliot.

The Red-Eyed Scavengers Are Creeping. "A Cooking Egg" by T. S. Eliot.

We Are Encompassed with Snakes. "Choruses from 'The Rock.'" by T. S. Eliot.

What Life Have You If You Have Not Life Together? "Choruses from 'The Rock'" by T. S. Eliot.

The Only Wisdom We Can Hope to Acquire. "East Coker" by T. S. Eliot.

Here in Death's Dream Kingdom. "Eyes That I Last Saw in Tears" by T. S. Eliot.

Life You May Evade, but Death You Shall Not. "Choruses from 'The Rock'" by T. S. Eliot.

A Troubled Guest on the Dark Earth. "The Holy Longing" by Johann Wolfgang von Goethe.

There Comes a Moment When Everything Is Still and Ripens. "Grappa in September" by Cesare Pavese.

With Spiders I Had Friendship Made. "The Prisoner of Chillon" by Lord Byron.

Who Rides at Night, Who Rides So Late? "The Invisible King" by Johann Wolfgang von Goethe.

The Night Isn't Dark; the World Is Dark. "Departure" by Louise Glück.

Deep into the Darkness Peering. "The Raven" by Edgar Allan Poe.

Nothing at All around Me but the Beast. "The Inferno" by Dante Alighieri.

Everything That Rises Must Converge. The title of a short story by Flannery O'Connor.

Of What Is Past, or Passing, or to Come. "Sailing to Byzantium" by William Butler Yeats.

ABOUT THE AUTHOR

International bestselling author Dean Koontz was only a senior in college when he won an *Atlantic Monthly* fiction competition. He has never stopped writing since. Koontz is the author of *The House at the End of the World*, *The Big Dark Sky*, *Quicksilver*, *The Other Emily*, *Elsewhere*, *Devoted*, and seventy-nine *New York Times* best-sellers, fourteen of which were #1, including *One Door Away from Heaven*, *From the Corner of His Eye*, *Midnight*, *Cold Fire*, *The Bad Place*, *Hideaway*, *Dragon Tears*, *Intensity*, *Sole Survivor*, *The Husband*, *Odd Hours*, *Relentless*, *What the Night Knows*, and *77 Shadow Street*. He's been hailed by *Rolling Stone* as "America's most popular sus-pense novelist," and his books have been published in thirty-eight languages and have sold over five hundred million copies worldwide. Born and raised in Pennsylvania, he now lives in Southern California with his wife, Gerda, their golden retriever, Elsa, and the enduring spirits of their goldens Trixie and Anna. For more information, visit his website at www.deankoontz.com.